Singers of Strange Songs

A Celebration of
Brian Lumley

More Titles from Chaosium

Call of Cthulhu® Fiction

Pendragon™ Fiction

Call of Cthulhu® Fiction

Singers of Strange Songs
A Celebration of Brian Lumley

BRIAN LUMLEY

BENJAMIN ADAMS

DONALD R. BURLESON

DON D'AMMASSA

LOIS H. GRESH

C. J. HENDERSON

TINA L. JENS

GREGORY NICOLL

STEPHEN MARK RAINEY

JAMES ROBERT SMITH

JOHN TYNES

SELECTED BY SCOTT DAVID ANIOLOWSKI
COVER ART BY H. E. FASSL
INTERIOR ART BY ALLEN KOSZOWSKI

A Chaosium Book
1997

Singers of Strange Songs is published by Chaosium, Inc.

This book is copyrighted as a whole by Scott David Aniolowski, ©1997; all rights reserved. This edition published by arrangement with Chaosium, Inc.

"City Out of Time" ©1995, "Cement Surroundings" ©1969, and "Spaghetti" ©1985 by Brian Lumley; all appear by permission of the author. All other stories are ©1997 by their respective authors. All rights reserved.

Cover art by H. E. Fassl. Interior art by Allen Koszowski. Chthonian by Earl Geier. Cover layout by Charlie Krank. Editing and interior layout by Janice Sellers. Editor-in-chief Lynn Willis. Proofreading by Tod Briggs and James Naureckas.

Please address questions and comments concerning this book, as well as requests for free notices of Chaosium publications, by mail to Chaosium, Inc., 950 56th St., Oakland, CA 94608-3136, U.S.A. Also visit our web page at:

http://www.sirius.com/~chaosium/chaosium/html

FIRST EDITION

1 2 3 4 5 6 7 8 9 10

Chaosium Publication 6014. Published in August 1997.

ISBN 1-56882-104-2

Printed in Canada.

Contents

Introduction:

The Caller of the Black and the Lord of the Worms

Yes, they had been the same sort of nightmares, those dreams of Hamilton's; hadn't he admitted that 'Cthulhu comes to me in dreams'? And had the dreams themselves not heralded the greater horrors?

—Brian Lumley, "The Fairground Horror"

Welcome to *Singers of Strange Songs*, and to the weird, dreamy, nightmarish realms of Brian Lumley.

I first discovered Brian Lumley many full moons ago. I had not long before unearthed the writings of Howard Phillips Lovecraft when a good friend lent me his copy of Edward P. Berglund's landmark Daw Books anthology *The Disciples of Cthulhu*. Brian Lumley's "The Fairground Horror" was the first story in that brilliant anthology that I read, and it also just happened to be the first non-Lovecraft Cthulhu Mythos tale I'd read. I loved "The Fairground Horror" and soon after purchased copies of Lumley's Arkham House collections *The Horror at Oakdeene* and *The Caller of the Black* (among many others), and began my long search for my own copy of the Berglund anthology.

Brian Lumley, a career man in the British military, made his first Arkham House appearance in a 1968 issue of *The Arkham Collector* with "The Cypress Shell." The following year "The Sister City" and "Cement Surroundings"—one of Lumley's finest Cthulhu Mythos tales, and the one to introduce Shudde-M'ell and its chthonian minions—appeared in *Tales of the Cthulhu Mythos*. (Incidentally, the 1990 edition of *Tales of the Cthulhu Mythos* dropped both tales, and replaced them with "Rising with Surtsey.") In 1971 Arkham House produced its 124th title, Brian Lumley's first collection, *The Caller of the Black*. Lumley became one of the most prolific authors of Lovecraftian stories, with numerous Cthulhu Mythos short stories and novels to his credit. His additions to the Mythos include the Old Ones Shudde-M'ell (and the chthonians), Yibb-Tstll (and the Black), Kthanid, Summanus, and Cthylla; occult investigators Titus Crow and Henri-Laurent de Marigny (son of Lovecraft's Étienne-Laurent de Marigny) and their Clock of Dreams; Dreamlands adventurers David Hero and Eldin the Wanderer; the dreaded tomes *Cthaat Aquadingen, Tuscan Rituals*, and *G'harne Fragments*; the haunted fabled cities of G'harne and Lh-yib; the infamous Oakdeene Sanatorium; the Wilmarth Foundation; and others. In recent years, Lumley has gotten away from the Cthulhu Mythos (although has not abandoned it altogether—he still pens a new Lovecraftian tale now and again), and has found incredible worldwide success most recently with his *Necroscope* series.

Unfortunately, Mr. Lumley's busy schedule did not allow him to write anything new for this collection in time for my publication deadline (released to coincide with his appearance at NecronomiCon '97). He did, however, generously offer to allow me to reprint some of his rarer tales. He suggested a few stories, and I had a list of my own. "Cement Surroundings", "In the Vaults Beneath", and "Spaghetti" were his suggestions. I wanted to include my own personal favorites "The Fairground Horror", "What Dark God?", "The Horror at Oakdeene", and others. Of course, the constraints of space made my growing wish list impossible, and I settled on "Cement Surroundings", "Spaghetti", and the poem "City Out of Time." "Cement Surroundings" was a given since it introduces Lumley's most famous Mythos creations—those dreaded Burrowers Beneath—the chthonians. "Spaghetti" is a rather obscure tale that probably has not been seen by most readers, and as such it is a pleasure to be able to reprint it here. I truly wish there'd been space to permit me also to use the corrected text of "In the Vaults Beneath."

That leaves the rest of the contents of *Singers of Strange Songs*. I resisted individual story introductions in each of my three previous books, and I do so again here. I'm not terribly keen on the idea of the editor giving away something about a story the reader is about to dive into, nor do I feel it the place or responsibility of the editor to foist his own interpretations and opinions on the reader by explaining an impending read. Also, each page used to babble on about the book's contents is one less page dedicated to the fiction—the *point* of the whole endeavor! With that said, I'll just add that I have selected the works herein because each made good use of some part of Brian Lumley's Cthulhu Mythos material and creations. So you will find tales on the following pages about Yibb-Tstll, the Oakdeene Sanatorium, Ithaqua (not a Lumley creation, but one which he enjoyed using), Bugg-Shash, Cthylla, Hodgson's Funfair, and chthonians—oh, yes, chthonians!—among other dark things. There are elements of adventure and science fiction—of fantasy and, of course, *horror*! Something, I hope, for every taste and every reader. Unpleasant dreams ....

I would like to offer my thanks to everyone involved in this project: to Lynn Willis of Chaosium, for taking on the book and putting up with me throughout the completion of the project; to Robert M. Price, for suggesting the idea to me in the first place; to artists Harry Fassl and Allen Koszowski; and to all the very talented authors who took the time to contribute. I especially thank Brian Lumley and his agent for being a part of this project, and I thank Mr. Lumley for all the dark delight and insane inspiration his fiction has brought me over the years.

—Scott David Aniolowski
Lockport, NY
April 25, 1997

One of those places King Randolph Carter told us about—where Cthulhu's engines of nightmare pound away down in the black, reeking underworld, manufacturing madness with which to disease the subconscious minds of men and subvert them to his cause.
—Brian Lumley, *The Clock of Dreams*

Dedication

Robert Bloch was hailed as a master of the horror genre by everyone from Brian Lumley to Stephen King, from Ray Bradbury to Arthur C. Clarke, from Harlan Ellison to Ramsey Campbell. Not only was he a brilliant author, but Bloch was foremost a truly great man. I had the great pleasure of meeting Bloch once, and we later exchanged a few letters. He had expressed some interest in an anthology I was assembling, but by then was too ill to participate. Sadly, we lost Bob on September 23, 1994. This book is dedicated to him with admiration and appreciation. Bob Bloch—the Master—is sadly missed.

City Out of Time

by Brian Lumley

Betrayed by dreams I wander weirdling ways,
Beneath the fronds of palms in jungles old
When Earth herself was young and brave and bold.
Where hybrid blooms sway serpentine I gaze
On ruins which no other eyes have seen,
Whose black foundations sink in primal green,
A-crawl with efts of prehistoric days.

Beyond odd-angled ruins ceaseless pound
The waves of frenzied ocean freshly borned
Which never met Man's ancestor have spawned.
And here I find strange mysteries profound:
These monoliths of which I stand in awe—
Who builded them upon this primal shore?
And what wild secrets have the ages drowned?

From books in waking worlds I know the name
Of such a city lost in oceans deep,
Where Ancient Ones in unquiet slumbers keep
The lore of dark dimensions and the flame
of elder magicks burning, 'til a time
When upward from aeon-silted slime
Vast shapes will come as once before they came.

Aye, and that fane of evil was R'lyeh,
Where dreaming Cthulhu lies in chains that bind,
Sending his nightmares out to humankind,
Drowning their noble dreams in nameless mire,
And dreaming still I start as from the pile
Snake tentacular arms and in a while
A *face* that crowns the bulk of Evil's sire!

Cement Surroundings

by Brian Lumley

1

It will never fail to amaze me how certain allegedly Christian people take a perverse delight in the misfortunes of others. Just how true this is was brought forcibly home to me by the totally unnecessary whispers and rumours which were put about following the disastrous decline of my closest living relative.

There were those who concluded that just as the moon is responsible for the tides, and in part the slow movement of the Earth's upper crust, so was it also responsible for Sir Amery Wendy-Smith's *behaviour* on his return from Africa. As proof they pointed out my uncle's sudden fascination with seismography—the study of earthquakes—a subject which so took his fancy that he built his own instrument, a model which does not incorporate the conventional concrete base, to such an exactitude that it measures even the most minute of the deep tremors which are constantly shaking this world. It is that same instrument which sits before me now, rescued from the ruins of the cottage, at which I am given to casting, with increasing frequency, sharp and fearful glances. Before his disappearance my uncle spent hours, seemingly without purpose, studying the fractional movements of the stylus over the graph.

For my own part I found it more than odd the way in which, while Sir Amery was staying in London after his return, he shunned the underground and would pay abortive taxi fares rather than go down into what he termed "those black tunnels". Odd, certainly—but I never considered it a sign of insanity.

Yet even his few really close friends seemed convinced of his madness, blaming it upon his living too close to those dead and nigh-forgotten civilisations which so fascinated him. But how could it have been otherwise? My uncle was both antiquarian and archaeologist. His strange wanderings to foreign lands were not the result of any longing for personal gain or acclaim. Rather were they undertaken out of a love of the life, for any fame which resulted—as frequently occurred—was more often than not shrugged off onto the ever-willing personages of his colleagues. They envied him, those so-called contemporaries of his, and would have emulated his successes had they possessed the foresight and inquisitiveness with which he was so singularly gifted—or, as I have now come to believe, with which he was cursed. My bitterness towards them is directed by the way in which they cut him after the dreadful culmination of that last, fatal expedition. In earlier years many of them had been "made" by his discoveries but on that last trip those "hangers-on" had been the uninvited, the ones out of favour, to whom he would not offer the opportunity of fresh, stolen glory. I believe that for the greater part their assurances of his insanity were nothing more than a spiteful means of belittling his genius.

Certainly that last safari was his *physical* end. He who before had been straight and strong, for a man his age, with jet hair and a constant smile, was seen to walk with a pronounced stoop and had lost a lot of weight. His hair had greyed and his smile had become rare and nervous, while a distinct tic jerked the flesh at the corner of his mouth.

Before these awful deteriorations made it possible for his erstwhile "friends" to ridicule him, before the expedition, Sir Amery had deciphered or translated—I know little of these things—a handful of decaying, centuried shards known in archaeological circles as the *G'harne Fragments*. Though he would never fully discuss his findings I know it was that which he learned which sent him, ill-fated, into Africa. He and a handful of personal friends, all equally learned gentlemen, ventured into the interior seeking a legendary city which Sir Amery believed had existed centuries before the foundations were cut for the pyramids. Indeed, according to his calculations, Man's primal ancestors were not yet conceived when G'harne's towering ramparts first reared their monolithic sculptings to pre-dawn skies. Nor with regard to the age of the place, if it existed at all, could my uncle's claims be disproved. New scientific tests on the *G'harne Fragments* had shown them to be pre-Triassic and their very existence, in any form other than centuried dust, was impossible to explain.

It was Sir Amery, alone and in a terrible condition, who staggered upon an encampment of savages five weeks after setting out from the native village where the expedition had last had contact with civilisation. No doubt the ferocious men who found him would have done away with him there and then but for their superstitions. His wild appearance and the strange tongue in which he screamed, plus the fact that he had emerged from an area which was "taboo" in their tribal legends, stayed their hands. Eventually they nursed him back to a semblance of health and conveyed him to a more civilised region from where he was slowly able to make his way back to the outside world. Of the expedition's other members nothing has since been seen or heard and only I know the story, having read it in the letter my uncle left me. But more of that later.

Following his lone return to England, Sir Amery developed those eccentricities already mentioned and the merest hint or speculation on the part of outsiders with reference to the disappearance of his colleagues was sufficient to start him raving horribly of such inexplicable things as 'a buried land where Shudde-M'ell broods and bubbles, plotting the destruction of the human race and the release from his watery prison of Great Cthulhu ....' When he was asked *officially* to account for his missing companions he said that they had died in an earthquake and though, reputedly, he was asked to clarify his answer, he would say no more ....

Thus, being uncertain as to how he would *react* to questions about his expedition, I was loath to ask him of it. However, on those rare occasions when he saw fit to talk of it without prompting, I listened avidly for I, as much as if not more so than others, was eager to have the mystery cleared up.

He had been back only a few months when he suddenly left London and invited me up to his cottage, isolated here on the Yorkshire moors, to keep him company. This invitation was a thing strange in itself as he was one who had spent months in absolute solitude in various far-flung desolate places and liked to think of himself as something of a hermit. I accepted, for I saw the perfect chance to get a little of that solitude which I find particularly helpful to my writing.

2

One day, shortly after I had settled in, Sir Amery showed me a pair of strangely beautiful pearly spheres. They measured about four inches in diameter and though he had been unable to identify positively the material from which they were made, he was able to tell me that it appeared to be some unknown combination of calcium, chrysolite, and diamond-dust. How the things had been made was, as he put it, 'anybody's guess'. The spheres, he told me, had been found at the site of dead G'harne—the first intimation he had offered that he had actually *found* the place—buried beneath the earth in a lidless, stone box which had borne upon its queerly angled sides certain utterly alien engravings. Sir Amery was anything but explicit with regards to those *designs*, merely stating that they were so loathsome in what they suggested that it would not do to describe them too closely. Finally, in answer to my probing questions, he told me they depicted monstrous sacrifices to some unnameable, chthonian deity. More he refused to say but directed me, as I seemed so 'damnably eager', to the works of Commodus and the hag-hidden Caracalla. He mentioned that also upon the box, along with the pictures, were many lines of sharply cut characters much similar to the cuneiform etchings of the *G'harne Fragments* and, in certain aspects, having a disturbing likeness to the almost unfathomable *Pnakotic Manuscripts*. Quite possibly, he went on, the container had been a toy-box of sorts and the spheres, in all probability, were once the baubles of a child of the ancient city; certainly children or young ones were mentioned in what he had managed to decipher of the odd writing on the box.

It was during this stage of his narrative that I noticed Sir Amery's eyes were beginning to glaze over and his speech was starting to falter—almost as though some strange, psychic block were affecting his memory. Without warning, like a man suddenly gone into a hypnotic trance, he began muttering of Shudde-M'ell and Cthulhu, Yog-Sothoth and Yibb-Tstll—'alien Gods defying description'—and of mythological places with equally fantastic names: Sarnath and Hyperborea, R'lyeh and Ephiroth and many more ....

Eager though I was to learn more of that tragic expedition I fear it was I who stopped Sir Amery from saying on. Try as I might, on hearing him babbling so, I could not keep a look of pity and concern from showing on my face which, when he saw it, caused him to excuse himself hurriedly and flee to the privacy of his room. Later, when I looked in at his door, he was engrossed with his seismograph and appeared to be relating the markings on its graph to an atlas of the world which he had taken from his library. I was concerned to note that he was quietly arguing with himself.

Naturally, being what he was and having such a great interest in peculiar, ethnic problems, my uncle had always possessed—along with his historical and archaeological source books—a smattering of works concerning elder-lore and primitive and doubtful religions. I mean such works as the *Golden Bough* and Miss Murray's *Witch Cult*. But what was I to make of those other books which I found in his library within a few days of my arrival? On his shelves were at least nine works which I know are so outrageous in what they suggest that they have been mentioned by widely differing authorities over a period of many years as being damnable, blasphemous, abhorrent, unspeakable, and literary lunacy. These included the *Cthaat Aquadingen* by an unknown author, Feery's *Notes on the* Necronomicon, the *Liber Miraculorem*, Eliphas Lévi's *History of Magic*, and a faded, leather-bound copy of the hideous *Cultes des Goules*. Perhaps the worst thing I saw was a slim volume by Commodus which that "Blood Maniac" had written in A.D. 183 and which was protected from further fragmentation by lamination.

And moreover, as if these books were not puzzling enough, there was that other thing!! What of the indescribable, droning *chant* which I often heard issuing from Sir Amery's room in the dead of night? This first occurred on the sixth night I spent with him and I was roused from my own uneasy slumbers by the morbid accents of a language it seemed impossible for the vocal cords of Man to emulate. Yet my uncle was weirdly fluent with it and I scribbled down an oft-repeated sentence-sequence in what I considered the nearest written approximation of the spoken words I could find. These words—or *sounds*—were:

> Ce'haiie ep-ngh fl'hur G'harne fhtagn,
> Ce'haiie fhtagn ngh Shudde-M'ell.
> Hai G'harne orr'e ep fl'hur,
> Shudde-M'ell ican-icanicas fl'ur orr'e G'harne ....

Though at the time I found the thing impossible to pronounce as I heard it, I have since found that with each passing day, oddly, the pronunciation of those lines becomes easier—as if with the approach of some obscene horror I grow more capable of expressing myself in the horror's terms. Perhaps it is just that lately in my dreams, I have found occasion to speak those very words and, as all things are far simpler in dreams, my fluency has passed over into my waking hours. But that does not explain the tremors—the same inexplicable tremors which so terrorised my uncle. Are the shocks which cause the ever-present quiverings of the seismograph stylus merely the traces of some vast, subterrene cataclysm a thousand miles deep and five thousand miles away—*or are they caused by something else?* Something so outré and fearsome that my mind freezes when I am tempted to study the problem too closely ....

3

There came a time, after I had been with him for a number of weeks, when it seemed plain that Sir Amery was rapidly recovering. True, he still retained his stoop—though to me it seemed no longer so pronounced—and his so-called eccentricities, but he was more his old self in other ways. The nervous tic had left his face completely and his cheeks had regained something of their former colour. His improvement, I conjectured, had much to do with his never-ending studies of the seismograph: for I had established by that time that there was a definite connection between the measurements of that machine and my uncle's illness. Nevertheless, I was at a loss to understand why the internal movements of the Earth should so determine the state of his nerves. It was after a trip to his room, to look at that instrument, that he told me more of dead G'harne. It was a subject I should have attempted to steer him away from ....

'The fragments,' he said, 'told the location of a city the name of which, G'harne, is only known in legend and which has in the past been spoken of on a par with Atlantis, Mu, and R'lyeh. A myth and nothing more. But if you give a legend a location you strengthen it somewhat— and if that location yields up relics of the past, of a civilisation lost for aeons, then the legend becomes history. You'd be surprised how much of the world's history has in fact been built up that way.

'It was my hope, a hunch you might call it, that G'harne had been real—and with the deciphering of the fragments I found it within my power to prove, one way or the other, G'harne's elder existence. I have been in some strange places, Paul, and have listened to even stranger stories. I once lived with an African tribe who declared they knew the secrets of the lost city and their story-tellers told me of a land where the sun never shines; where Shudde-M'ell, hiding deep in the honeycombed ground, plots the dissemination of evil and madness throughout the world and plans the resurrection of other, even worse abominations!

'He hides there in the earth and awaits the time when the stars will be *right*, when his horrible hordes will be *sufficient* in number, and when he can infest the entire world with his loathsomeness, and cause the return of others more loathsome yet! I was told stories of fabulous star-born creatures who inhabited the Earth millions of years before Man appeared and who were still here, in certain dark places, when he eventually evolved. I tell you, Paul,' his voice rose, '*that they are here even now—in places undreamed of!* I was told of sacrifices to Yog-Sothoth and

Yibb-Tstll that would make your blood run cold and of weird rites practised beneath prehistoric skies before the old Egypt was born. These things I've heard make the works of Albertus Magnus and Grobert seem tame and de Sade himself would have paled at the hearing.'

My uncle's voice had been speeding up progressively with each sentence, but now he paused for breath and in a more normal tone and at a reduced rate he continued:

'My first thought on deciphering the fragments was of an expedition. I may tell you I had learned of certain things I could have dug for here in England—you'd be surprised what lurks beneath the surface of some of those peaceful Cotswold hills—but that would have alerted a host of so-called "experts" and amateurs alike so I decided on G'harne. When I first mentioned an expedition to Kyle and Gordon and the others I must have produced quite a convincing argument for they all insisted on coming along. Some of them though, I'm sure, must have considered themselves upon a wild goose chase for, as I've explained, G'harne lies in the same realm as Mu or Ephiroth—or at least it did—and they must have seen themselves as questing after a veritable Lamp of Aladdin; but despite all that they came. They could hardly afford *not* to come, for if G'harne *was* real .... Why! Think of the lost glory .... They would never have forgiven themselves. And that's why I can't forgive *myself*, but for my meddling with the fragments they'd all be here now, God help them ....'

Again Sir Amery's voice had become full of some dread excitement and feverishly he continued.

'Heavens, but this place sickens me! I can't stand it much longer. It's all this grass and soil. Makes me shudder! Cement surroundings are what I need—and the thicker the cement the better. ... Yet even the cities have their drawbacks ... undergrounds and things .... Did you ever see Pickman's *Subway Accident*, Paul? By God, what a picture .... And the night ... that *night*! If you could have *seen* them—coming up out of the diggings! If you could have felt the tremors .... Why! The very ground rocked and danced as they rose. ... We'd disturbed them, d'you see? They may have even thought they were under attack and up they came .... My God! What could have been the reason for such *ferocity*? Only a few hours before I had been congratulating myself on finding the spheres, and then ... and then ....'

Now he was panting and his eyes, as before, had partly glazed over. His voice had undergone a strange change of timbre and his accents were slurred and alien.

'*Ce'haiie, Ce'haiie*. ... The city may be buried but whoever named the place *dead* G'harne didn't know the half of it. *They were alive!* They've been alive for millions of years; perhaps they can't die .... And why shouldn't that be? They're Gods aren't they, of a sort ...? Up they come in the night ....'

'Uncle, please!' I said.

'You needn't look at me so, Paul, or think what you're thinking either. ... There's stranger things happened, believe me. Wilmarth of Miskatonic could crack a few yarns, I'll be bound! You haven't read what Johansen wrote! Dear Lord, *read the Johansen narrative! Hai ep fl'hur* ... Wilmarth ... the old babbler .... What is it he knows which he won't tell? Why was that which was found at those Mountains of Madness so hushed up, eh? What did Pabodie's equipment draw up out of the earth? *Tell me those things, if you can?* Ha, ha, ha! *Ce'haiie, Ce'haiie—G'harne icanica* ....'

Shrieking now, and glassy-eyed, he stood, with his hands gesticulating wildly in the air. I do not think he saw me at all, or anything, except—in his mind's eye—a horrible recurrence of what he imagined had been. I took hold of his arm to calm him but he brushed my hand away, seemingly without knowing what he was doing.

'Up they come, the rubbery things .... Goodbye Gordon .... Don't scream so—the shrieking turns my mind .... Thank heavens it's only a dream ...! A nightmare just like all the others I've been having lately .... It is a dream, isn't it? Goodbye Scott, Kyle, Leslie ....'

Suddenly, eyes bulging, he spun wildly round.

'*The ground is breaking up! So many of them .... I'm falling ....* It's not a dream! Dear God! IT'S NOT A DREAM! No! Keep off, d'you hear! Aghhh! *The slime* .... Got to run ...! Run ...! Away from those—voices?—away from the sucking rounds and the chanting ....'

Without warning he broke into a chant himself and the awful sound of it, no longer distorted by distance or the thickness of a stout door, would have sent a more timid listener into a faint. It was similar to what I had heard before in the night and the words do not seem so evil on paper, almost ludicrous in fact, but to hear them issuing from the mouth of my own flesh and blood—and with such unnatural fluency:

'*Ep ep fl'hur G'harne, G'harne fhtagn Shudde-M'ell hyas Negg'h.*'

While chanting these incredible mouthings Sir Amery's feet had started to pump up and down in a grotesque parody of running. Suddenly he screamed anew and with startling abruptness leapt past me and ran full tilt into the wall. The shock knocked him off his feet and he collapsed in a heap on the floor.

I was worried that my meagre ministrations might not be adequate, but to my immense relief he regained consciousness a few minutes later. Shakily he assured me that he was 'all right, just shook up a bit' and, supported by my arm, he retired to his room.

That night I found it impossible to close my eyes so I wrapped myself in a blanket and sat outside my uncle's room to be on hand if he were disturbed in his sleep. He passed a quiet night, however, and paradoxically enough, in the morning, he seemed to have got the thing out of his system and was positively improved.

Modern doctors have known for a long time that in certain mental conditions a cure may be obtained by inciting the patient to *re-live* the events which caused his illness. Perhaps my uncle's outburst of the previous night had served the same purpose, or at least, so I thought, for by that time I had worked out new ideas on his abnormal behaviour. I reasoned that if he had been having recurrent nightmares and had been in the middle of one on that fateful night of the earthquake, when his friends and colleagues were killed, it was only natural that his mind should temporarily become somewhat unhinged upon waking and discovering the carnage. And if my theory were correct, it also explained his seismic obsessions ....

4

A week later came another grim reminder of Sir Amery's condition. He had seemed so much improved, though he still occasionally rambled in his sleep, and had gone out into the garden 'to do a bit of trimming'. It was well into September and quite chill, but the sun was shining and he spent the entire morning working with a rake and hedge clippers. We were doing for ourselves and I was thinking about preparing the midday meal when a singular thing happened. I distinctly felt the ground move fractionally under my feet and heard a low rumble. I was sitting in the living room when it happened and the next moment the door to the garden burst open and my uncle rushed in. His face was deathly white and his eyes bulged horribly as he fled past me to his room. I was so stunned by his wild appearance that I had barely moved from my chair by the time he shakily came back into the room. His hands trembled as he lowered himself into an easy chair.

'It was the ground …. I thought for a minute that the ground ….'
He was mumbling, more to himself than to me, and visibly trembling
from head to toe as the after-effect of the shock hit him. Then he saw
the concern on my face and tried to calm himself. 'The ground. I was
sure I felt a tremor—but I was mistaken. It must be this place. All that
open space …. I fear I'll really have to make an effort and get away from
here. There's altogether too much soil and not enough cement! Cement
surroundings are the thing ….'

I had had it on the tip of my tongue to say that I too had felt the
shock but upon learning that he believed himself mistaken I kept quiet.
I did not wish to add needlessly to his already considerable disorders.

That night, after Sir Amery had retired, I went through into his
study—a room which, though he had never said so, I knew he considered inviolate—to have a look at the seismograph. Before I looked at the
machine, however, I saw the notes spread out on the table beside it. A
glance was sufficient to tell me that the sheets of white foolscap were
covered by fragmentary jottings in my uncle's heavy handwriting and
when I looked closer I was sickened to discover that they were a ram-
bling jumble of seemingly disassociated—yet apparently *linked*—occurrences connected in some way with his weird delusions. These notes have
since been delivered permanently into my possession and are as repro-
duced here:

HADRIAN'S WALL
A.D. 122-128. Limestone Bank. (Gn'yah of the *Fragments*)??? *Earth
tremors* interrupted the diggings and that is why cut, basalt blocks were
left in the uncompleted ditch with wedge holes ready for splitting.

W'nyal-Shash (MITHRAS)
Romans had their own deities *but it wasn't Mithras* that the disciples of
Commodus, the Blood Maniac, sacrificed to at Limestone Bank! And
that was the same area where, fifty years earlier, a great block of stone
was unearthed and discovered to be covered with *inscriptions and engraven
pictures!* Silvanus the centurion defaced it and buried it again. A skeleton, positively identified as Silvanus's by the signet ring on one of its
fingers, has been lately found *beneath the ground (deep)* where once stood a
Vicus Tavern at Housesteads Fort—but we don't know *how* he vanished!
Nor were Commodus's followers any too careful. According to Caracalla
they also vanished overnight—*during an earthquake!*

AVEBURY
(Neolithic *A'byy* of the *Fragments* and *Pnakotic Ms*???) Reference
Stukeley's book, *A Temple to the British Druids*, incredible …. Druids,
indeed …. But Stukeley nearly had it when he said Snake Worship!
Worms, more like it!

COUNCIL OF NANTES
(9th century) The council didn't know what they were doing when they said: 'Let the *stones* also which, deceived by the derision of the *demons*, they worship amid ruins and in wooded places, where they both make their vows and bestow their *offerings*, be *dug up* from the very foundations, and let them be cast into such places as never will their devotees be able to find them again ....' I've read that paragraph so many times that it's become imprinted upon my mind! *God only knows what happened to the poor devils who tried to carry out the Council's orders ....*

DESTRUCTION OF GREAT STONES
In the 13th and 14th centuries the Church also attempted the removal of certain stones from Avebury because of *local superstitions* which caused the country folk to take part in *heathen worship* and *witchcraft* around them! In fact some of the stones were destroyed—by fire and douching—'because of the *devices* upon them'.

INCIDENT
1920-5. Why was a big effort made to bury one of the great stones? An *earth-tremor* caused the stone to slip, trapping a workman. *No effort appears to have been made to free him.* ... The "accident" happened at dusk and two other men *died of fright!* Why did other diggers flee the scene? And what was the titanic *thing* which one of them saw wriggling away into *the ground?* Allegedly thing left monstrous *smell* behind it. ... *By their SMELL shall ye know them.* ... Was it a member of another nest of the timeless ghouls?

THE OBELISK
Why was Stukeley's huge obelisk broken up? The pieces were buried in the early 18th century but in 1833 Henry Browne found burnt *sacrifices* at the site. ... And nearby, at Silbury Hill .... *My God! That devil-mound!* There are some things, even amidst these horrors, which don't bear thinking of—and while I've still got my sanity Silbury Hill better remain one of them!

AMERICA: INNSMOUTH
1928. What actually happened and why did the Federal government drop depth charges off Devil Reef in the Atlantic coast just out of Innsmouth? Why were half Innsmouth's citizen's banished? What was their connection with Polynesia and what also lies buried in the lands *beneath the sea?*

WIND WALKER
(Death-Walker, Ithaqua, Wendigo, etc. ...) Yet another *horror*—though of a different *type*! And such *evidence*! Alleged *human sacrifices* in Manitoba. Unbelievable circumstances surrounding *Norris Case*! Spencer of Quebec University literally affirmed the validity of the case. ... And at

But that is as far as the notes go and when I first read them I was glad such was the case. It was quickly becoming all too apparent that my uncle was far from well and still not quite right in his mind. Of course, there was always the chance that he had written those notes *before* his seeming improvement, in which case his plight was not necessarily as bad as it appeared.

Having put the notes back exactly as I found them I turned my attention to the seismograph. The line on the graph was straight and true and when I dismantled the spool and checked the chart I saw that it had followed that almost unnaturally unbroken smoothness for the last twelve days. As I have said, that machine and my uncle's condition were directly related and this proof of the quietness of the earth was undoubtedly the reason for his comparative well-being of late. But here was yet another oddity .... Frankly I was astonished at my findings, for I was certain I had felt a tremor indeed I had *heard* a low rumble—and it seemed impossible that both Sir Amery and myself should suffer the same, simultaneous sensory illusion. I rewound the spool and then, as I turned to leave the room, I noticed that which my uncle had missed. It was a small brass screw lying on the floor. Once more I unwound the spool and saw the countersunk hole which I *had* noticed before but which had not made an impression of any importance upon my mind. Now I guessed that it was meant to house that screw. I am nothing where mechanics are concerned and could not tell what that small integer played in the workings of the machine; nevertheless I replaced it and again set the instrument in order. I stood then, for a moment, to ensure that everything was working correctly and for a few seconds noticed nothing abnormal. It was my ears which first warned of the change. There had been a low, clockwork hum and a steady, sharp scraping noise before. The hum was still attendant but in place of the scraping sound was a jerky scratching which drew my fascinated eyes to the stylus.

That small screw had evidently made all the difference in the world. No wonder the shock we had felt in the afternoon, which had so disturbed my uncle, had gone unrecorded. The instrument had not been working correctly then—*but now it was ... now it could be plainly seen that every few minutes the ground was being shaken by tremors which, though they were not so severe as to be felt, were certainly strong enough to cause the stylus to wildly zigzag over the surface of the revolving graph paper....*

I felt in a far more shaken state than the ground when I finally retired that night. Yet I could not really decide the cause of my nervousness. Just why should I feel so apprehensive about my discovery?

True, I knew the effect of the now—correctly?—working machine upon my uncle would probably be unpleasant and might even cause another of his "outbursts", but was that knowledge all that unsettled me? On reflection I could see no reason whatever why any particular area of the country should receive more than its usual quota of earth-tremors. Eventually I concluded that the machine was either faulty or far too sensitive and went to sleep assuring myself that the strong shock we had felt had been merely coincidental to my uncle's condition. Still, I noticed before I dozed off that the very air itself seemed charged with a strange tension and the slight breeze which had wafted the late leaves during the day had gone completely, leaving in its passing an absolute quiet in which, during my slumbers, I fancied all night that the ground trembled beneath my bed ....

5

The next morning I was up early. I was short of writing materials and had decided to catch the lone morning bus into Radcar. I left before Sir Amery was awake and during the journey I thought back on the events of the previous day and decided to do a little research while I was in the town. In Radcar I had a bite to eat and then I called at the offices of the *Radcar Recorder* where a Mr McKinnen, a sub-editor, was particularly helpful. He spent some time on the office telephones making extensive inquiries on my behalf. Eventually I was told that for the better part of a year there had been no tremors of any importance in England, a point I would obviously have argued had not further information been forthcoming. I learned that there *had* been some *minor shocks* and that these had occurred at places as far away as Goole, a few miles away (that one within the last twenty-four hours) and at Tenterden near Dover. There had also been a very minor tremor at Ramsey in Huntingdonshire. I thanked Mr McKinnen profusely for his help and would have left then—but, as an afterthought, he asked me if I would be interested in checking through the paper's international files. I gratefully accepted and was left on my own to study a great pile of interesting translations. Of course, most of it was useless to me but it did not take me long to sort out what I was after. At first I had difficulty believing the evidence of my own eyes. I read that in August there had been 'quakes in Aisne of such severity that one or two houses had collapsed and a number of people had been injured. These shocks had been likened to those of a few weeks earlier at Agen in that they seemed to be caused more by some *settling of the ground* than by an actual tremor. In early July there had also been shocks in Calahorra, Chinchon, and Ronda in Spain. The trail went as straight as the flight of an arrow and lay across—*or rather under*—the Straits of Gibraltar to Xauen in Spanish Morocco, where an entire street of houses had collapsed. Farther yet, to .... But I had had enough. I dared look no more; I did not wish to know—not even remotely—the whereabouts of dead G'harne ....

Oh! I had seen more than sufficient to make me forget about my original errand. My book could wait, for now there were more important things to do. My next port of call was the town library where I took down Nicheljohn's *World Atlas* and turned to that page with a large, folding map of the British Isles. My geography and knowledge of England's counties are passable and I had noticed what I considered to be an oddity in the seemingly unconnected places where England had suffered those *minor 'quakes*. I was not mistaken. Using a second book as a straight edge I lined up Goole in Yorkshire and Tenterden on the south coast and saw, with a tingle of monstrous foreboding, that the line passed very close to, if not directly through, Ramsey in Huntingdonshire. With dread curiosity I followed the line north and, through suddenly fevered eyes, saw that it passed *within only a mile or so of the cottage on the moors!* I turned more pages with unfeeling, rubbery fingers until I found the leaf showing France. For a moment I paused— then I fumblingly found Spain and finally Africa. For a long while I just sat there in numbed silence, occasionally turning the pages, automatically checking names and locations .... My thoughts were in a terrible turmoil when I eventually left the library and I could feel upon my spine the chill, hopping feet of some abysmal dread from the beginning of time. My previously wholesome nervous system had already started to crumble ....

During the journey back across the moors in the evening bus, the drone of the engine lulled me into a kind of half-sleep in which I heard again something Sir Amery had mentioned—something he had murmured aloud while sleeping and presumably dreaming. He had said:

'They don't like water. ... England's safe. ... Have to go too deep ....' The memory of those words shocked me back to wakefulness and filled me with a further icy chill which got into the very marrow of my bones. Nor were these feelings of horrid foreboding misleading, for awaiting me at the cottage was that which went far to completing the destruction of my entire nervous system ....

As the bus came round the final wooded bend which hid the cottage from sight *I saw it!* The place had collapsed. I simply could not take it in! Even knowing all I knew—with all my slowly accumulating evidence—it was too much for my tortured mind to comprehend. I left the bus and waited until it had threaded its way through the parked police cars before crossing the road. The fence to the cottage had been knocked down to allow an ambulance to park in the queerly *tilted* garden. Spotlights had been set up, for it was almost dark, and a team of rescuers were toiling frantically at the incredible ruins. As I stood there, aghast, I was approached by a police officer and having stumblingly identified myself was told the following story.

A passing motorist had actually seen the collapse and the tremors attendant to it had been felt in nearby Marske. The motorist had realised there was little he could do on his own and had speeded into Marske to report the thing. Allegedly the house had gone down like a pack of cards. The police and an ambulance had been on the scene within minutes and rescue operations had begun immediately. Up to now it appeared that my uncle had been out when the collapse occurred for as yet there had been no trace of him. There had been a strange, poisonous *odour* about the place but this had vanished soon after the work had started. The rescuers had cleared the floors of all the rooms except the study and during the time it took the officer to bring me up to date even more debris was being frantically hauled away.

Suddenly there was a lull in the excited babble of voices. I saw that the gang of rescue workers were standing looking down at something. My heart gave a wild leap and I scrambled over the debris to see what they had found.

There, where the floor of the study had been, was that which I had feared and more than half expected. It was simply a hole. A gaping *hole* in the floor—*but from the angles at which the floorboards lay, and the manner in which they were scattered about, it looked as though the ground, rather than sinking, had been pushed up from below ....*

6

Nothing has since been seen or heard of Sir Amery Wendy-Smith and though he is listed as being *missing* I know in fact that he is dead. He is gone to worlds of ancient wonder and my only prayer is that his soul wanders on *our* side of the threshold. For in our ignorance we did Sir

Amery a great injustice—I and all the others who thought he was out of his mind. All his queer ways—I understand them all now, but the understanding has come hard and will cost me dearly. No, he was not mad. He did the things he did out of self-preservation and though his precautions came to nothing in the end, it was fear of a nameless evil and not madness which prompted them.

But the worst is still to come. I myself have yet to face a similar end. I know it, for no matter what I do the tremors haunt me. Or is it only in my mind? No! There is little wrong with my mind. My nerves are gone but my mind is intact. I *know* too much! *They* have visited me in dreams, as I believe *they* must have visited my uncle, and what *they* have read in my mind has warned *them* of *their* danger. *They* dare not allow me to investigate, for it is such meddling which may one day fully reveal *them* to men—*before they are ready* .... God! Why has that ancient fool Wilmarth at Miskatonic not answered my telegrams? There must be a way out! Even now *they* dig—those dwellers in darkness ....

But no! This is no good. I must get a grip of myself and finish this narrative. I have not had time to try to tell the authorities the truth but even if I had I know what the result would have been. 'There's something wrong with all the Wendy-Smith blood' they would say. But this manuscript will tell the story for me and will also stand as a warning to others. Perhaps when it is seen how my—*passing*—so closely parallels that of Sir Amery, people will be curious; with this manuscript to guide them perhaps men will seek out and destroy Earth's elder madness before it destroys them ....

A few days after the collapse of the cottage on the moors, I settled here in this house on the outskirts of Marske to be close at hand if—though I could see little hope of it—my uncle should turn up again. But now some dread power keeps me here. I *cannot* flee .... At first *their* power was not so strong, but now .... I am no longer able even to leave this desk and I know the end must be coming fast. I am rooted to this chair as if grown here and it is as much as I can do to type! But I must ... I must .... And the ground movements are much stronger now. That hellish, damnable, mocking stylus—leaping so crazily over the paper.

I had been here only two days when the police delivered to me a dirty, soil-stained envelope. It had been found in the ruins of the cottage—near the lip of that curious hole—and was addressed to me. It contained those notes I have already copied and a letter from Sir Amery which, if its awful ending is anything to go on, he must have still been writing when the horror came for him .... When I consider, it is not surprising that the envelope survived the collapse. *They* would not have known what it was, and so would have had no interest in it. *Nothing* in the cottage was purposely damaged—nothing *inanimate*, that is—and so far as I have been able to discover the only missing items are those terrible spheres, *or what remained of them.* ... But I must hurry ... I cannot escape and all the time the tremors are increasing in strength and frequency .... No! I will not have time. No time to write all I wanted to say .... The shocks are too heavy ... to o hea vy.... Int erfer in g with m y t yping .... I will finis h this i n th e only way rem ain ing to me and staple S ir Amer y's lette r to this man usc ript ... now

* * *

Dear Paul.

In the event of this letter ever getting to you, there are certain things I must ask you to do for the safety and sanity of the world. It is absolutely necessary that these things be explored and *dealt with*—though how that may be done I am at a loss to say. It was my intention, for the sake of my own sanity, to forget what happened at G'harne. I was wrong to try and hide it. At this very moment there are men digging in strange, forbidden places and who knows what they may unearth? Certainly all these horrors must be tracked down and rooted out—but not by humbling amateurs. It must be done by men who are ready for the ultimate in hideous, cosmic horror. Men with weapons. Perhaps flame-throwers would do the trick ... certainly a scientific knowledge of war would be a necessity ... devices could be made to track the enemy .... I mean specialised seismological instruments .... If I had the time I would prepare a dossier, detailed and explicit, but it appears that this letter will have to suffice as a guide to tomorrow's horror-hunters. You see, *I now know for sure that they are after me!* And there's nothing I can do about it. It's too late! At first even I, just like so many others, believed myself to be just a little bit mad. I refused to admit to myself that what I had seen happen had ever happened at all! To admit that was to admit lunacy! But it's real all right .... It *did* happen—and *will again!*

Heaven only knows what's been wrong with my seismograph but the damn thing's let me down in the worst possible way! Oh, *they* would have got me eventually, but I might at least have had time to prepare a proper warning. ... I ask you to think, Paul ... think of what has happened at the cottage. ... I can write of it as though it had *already hap-*

pened; because I know *it must! It will!* It is Shudde-M'ell, come for his spheres. … Paul, look at the manner of my death, for if you are reading this then I am either dead or disappeared—which means the same thing. Read the enclosed notes carefully, I beg you. I haven't the time to be more explicit but these old notes of mine should be of some help. … If you are only half so inquiring as I believe you to be, you will surely soon come to recognise a fantastic horror, which, I repeat, the whole world must be *made* to believe in. … The ground is really shaking now but, knowing it is the end, I am steady in my horror … not that I expect my present calm state of mind to last … I think that by the time *they* actually come for me my mind will have snapped completely. I can imagine it now … the floor splintering, erupting, to admit *them*. Why! Even *thinking* of it my senses recoil at the terror of the thought. … There will be a hideous *smell*, a *slime*, a *chanting* and gigantic *writhing* and … and then ….

Unable to escape, I await the thing. I am trapped by the same hypnotic power that claimed the others at G'harne. What monstrous memories! How I awoke to see my friends and companions sucked dry of their life's blood by wormy, vampirish *things* from the cesspools of time! Gods of alien dimensions …. I was hypnotised then by this same terrible force, unable to move to the aid of my friends or even to save myself! Miraculously, with the passing of the moon behind the wisps of cloud, the hypnotic effect was broken. Then, screaming and sobbing, temporarily out of my mind, I fled; hearing behind me the vile and slobbering *sucking* sounds and the droning, demoniac chanting of Shudde-M'ell and his hordes.

Not knowing that I did it, in my mindlessness I carried with me those hell-spheres …. Last night I dreamed of them. And in my dreams I saw again the inscriptions on that stone box. Moreover, *I could read them!* All the fears and *ambitions* of those hellish things were there to be read as clearly as the headlines in a daily newspaper! "Gods" they may or may not be but one thing is sure; the greatest setback to their plans for conquest of the Earth is their *terribly long and complicated reproductory cycle!* Only a handful of young are born every thousand years; but, considering how *long* they have been here, the time must be drawing ever nearer when their numbers will be *sufficient!* Naturally, this tedious build-up of their numbers makes them loath to lose even a single member of their hideous spawn. *And that is why they have tunnelled these many thousands of miles, even under deep oceans, to retrieve the spheres!* I had wondered why they could be following me—and now I know. I also know how. Can you not guess how they know where I am, Paul, or why they are coming? Those spheres are like a beacon to them; a siren voice calling. *And just as any other parent—though more out of awful ambition, I fear, than any type of emotion we could understand—they are merely answering the call of their young!*

But they are too late! A few minutes ago, just before I began this letter, the things hatched. ... Who would have guessed that they were *eggs*—or that the container they were in *was an incubator*? I can't blame myself for not knowing it. I even tried to have the spheres X-rayed once, damn them, but they reflected the rays! And the shells were so *thick*! Yet at the time of hatching they just splintered into tiny fragments. The creatures inside were no bigger than walnuts. ... Taking into account the *size* of an adult they must have a fantastic growth rate. Not that those two will ever grow! I shrivelled them with a cigar ... *and you should have heard the mental screams from those beneath!*

If only I could have known earlier, *definitely*, that it was not madness, there might have been a way to escape this horror .... But no use now .... My notes—look into them, Paul, and do what I should have done. Complete a detailed dossier and present it to the authorities. Wilmarth may help and perhaps Spencer of Quebec University .... Haven't much time now ... cracks in ceiling ....

That last shock ... ceiling coming away in chunks ... coming up. Heaven help me, they're coming up ... I can feel them groping inside my mind as they come

* * *

Sir,

Reference this manuscript found in the ruins of number 17 Anwick Street, Marske, Yorkshire, following the earth-tremors of September this year and believed to be a "fantasy" which the writer, Paul Wendy-Smith, had completed for publication. It is more than possible that the so-called disappearances of both Sir Amery Wendy-Smith and his nephew, the writer, were nothing more than promotion stunts for this story. ... It is well known that Sir Amery is/was interested in seismography and perhaps some prior intimation of the two 'quakes supplied the inspiration for his nephew's tale. Investigations continuing ....

Sgt J. Williams.

Yorks. County Constabulary. October 2, 1933.

Bad Soil

by Don D'Ammassa

The effect was first noticeable in the high school tennis court but within days it had replicated itself in one fashion or another all through the area.

I had the luck, if that's the appropriate term, to be present at the very first. Not that I play tennis myself. I've neither the reach nor the stamina to excel, and I've never been happy committing myself to any activity I could not perform well. But at fourteen my niece Rianne was firmly committed to the sport and I occasionally consented to be her escort to the courts. The handful of young boys who regularly convened in the area had never offered her any harm, but they were rowdy and disrespectful and I know Rianne and her friend Julie felt better for my presence.

They'd been volleying for an hour or so and I was getting restless. I had vowed to finish the ninth chapter of my book by the weekend and I was already two full days behind my self-imposed schedule.

Just as I was about to suggest that we leave, Julie managed a quite nice backhand that almost caught Rianne flatfooted. She recovered quickly, driving across the court and toward the net. The ball dropped to the ground at a sharp angle, but Rianne was already anticipating its trajectory. Her arm cut the air gracefully as she extended her body in a perfect maneuver.

But her racket swished through empty air, for the ball had stopped dead the moment it struck the ground. In one of her less graceful moments, Rianne staggered and fell to one knee.

This seemed a perfect moment to call it a day, so I arose and approached. Julie seemed to sense the same thing, and had already come cross court. Rianne remained where she was, staring at the motionless ball a few feet away.

"What happened?" I asked unnecessarily. "Bad ball?"

Julie scooped it up, tossed it lightly into the air and caught it on her racket. "Feels okay to me. Must've been a soft spot in the ground."

Rianne stood up awkwardly and I could see she'd skinned her knee. "I never had that happen before. Let me see."

Julie tossed her the ball. Rianne bounced it off the ground, caught it, bounced it again. Thoughtfully she walked past her friend toward the net, paused, bounced it a third time.

The ball hit the ground and remained there.

I joined her as she knelt, running her fingers across the clay. "There must be a bad spot," I suggested.

Rianne looked puzzled. "We play here all the time. I've never noticed this before."

We could feel the difference. Although the surface looked the same, it felt soft, moist, vaguely repulsive. It was exactly the sensation one gets picking up a piece of bad fruit.

* * *

Mrs. Parkhurst's garden went bad that same day. I heard her complaining in Del's Hardware when I stopped by for light bulbs just before supper.

"There must've been something bad in that fertilizer you sold me, Delbert Scott. Everything was fine until I used it. Now all the plants are dying."

"It's not the fertilizer, Minnie. I told you, I use it all the time at home."

"Well you just come over then and tell me what's wrong with my flowers. This morning they were all bright and healthy, and this afternoon they're flat on the ground. My prize roses are already mush."

"If it's not insects, it must be something in the soil. You're downhill from the print shop, aren't you? Maybe they dumped something into the ground and it's washed down to your property."

They were still arguing when I paid for my purchases and left.

* * *

The Crawley Street bridge collapsed some time during the night. Eve Goddard discovered it on her way to work. Unfortunately, she discovered it by driving off the edge. Fortunately, her little Fiat bottomed out and got hung up on the edge rather than falling into Murly Chasm.

"Damnedest thing I've ever seen." Marty Carlisle was milking the incident for all it was worth, talking so loud at Kat's Kafe that we could hear him all the way over on the opposite side of the diner. "The bridge supports all look fine. But the ground went soft under the north abutment and the bridge just let go. Soil's so bad, you stab a knife into it, the blade just falls right over. Nothing there to hold it up. But it's not like beach sand either. It's more like wood punk. You know, no body to it."

I was thinking about the tennis court, but just about then Kat put a bowl of stew in front of me and I never made the connection. Not till later.

Not till Rianne came to see me.

* * *

It was three days after the bridge incident and I was finally back on schedule with my book. Months of research at the Arkham and Sheffield Libraries had convinced me that there was a link between the strange madness that had infected the town of Dunwich and the so-called "quiet riot" in Managansett in the late 19th century, and I had enough material to produce a book on the subject, if I could just enforce the self discipline necessary to bring it to fruition.

The front door opened. "Hello, Rianne." I never kept it locked, but I knew she was the only one who would enter without knocking first.

"Hi, Uncle Bob. Can I come in?"

"A little late to be asking, isn't it?" The exchange was our regular greeting. "What's up?"

Rianne settled into the sofa and curled up with her legs underneath. She was a pretty child, spoiled rotten by her parents, not so much innocent as oblivious. Frankly, I thought her parents sheltered her a bit too much. At times, she acted well below her age, petulant, self-centered, prone to fits of giggling that were decidedly unattractive. But in her better moments she could be charming, honestly affectionate, and clever. She often made me regret that Elaine and I had deferred a family until too late, and then the cancer made it all impossible.

"Do you remember that day on the tennis court?"

I raised my eyebrows. "Which day was that, might I ask? We were last there Tuesday, but also Saturday, Friday, and the previous Wednesday. I remember distinctly because I've been up past midnight these past three days trying to make up all the time I've lost escorting you here and there."

"It was only a few hours, Uncle Bob, and you told me there's no real deadline for your book anyway."

"Just my own," I admitted. "But standards are important, Rianne, even if they're artificial ones."

"Yes, sir," she answered with mock gravity.

"So what brings you here today?" I glanced out the window. A steady drizzle had started during the night and showed no sign of abating. "Not tennis, obviously."

"Not exactly. You remember when Julie made that shot and we found the bad spot in the clay?"

"Yes, of course I do. How's the knee, incidentally?"

"Fine," she said dismissively. "The thing of it is, I found a couple of other places like that out near our house. Places where the grass died and the dirt is mushy."

Rianne's family lived a block from Mrs. Parkhurst, I recalled. "I wonder if there's something seeping into the soil. One of your neighbors mentioned the same thing the other day." I massaged my chin. "What does your father say?"

"Oh, you know Dad. He shrugs his shoulders and says tiny flying saucers must've landed during the night."

"Well, I'm sure it's nothing to worry about." But for the first time, I wasn't so sure.

"Yeah, well, the thing is, I asked a few of my friends and some of them have noticed the same kinds of things. Like, Mr. Pratt stepped into a pothole in his own backyard and broke an ankle. And Kelly Witherspoon's collie died in his doghouse two nights ago and when they tried to move him, his body was all stuck to the ground and they had to use a shovel. And that big elm tree next to the Donovan's patio lost all its leaves and a couple of days later the trunk just split in two and half of it fell on the roof of their garage."

I raised my hands to stop the tide of words. "What do these things have to do with one another, Rianne? Trees die, so do dogs. And people have accidents."

She sighed theatrically and glanced up at the ceiling. "I'm trying to tell you, Uncle Bob, that there's something wrong in the ground around here lately. There's lots more things I haven't told you yet, like Mr. Whalen's swimming pool collapsing and the sewer lines backing up into the school basement and stuff like that."

I wasn't convinced but I was disquieted. "Rianne, this sounds like a lot of coincidences to me, but I'll tell you what. I'll ask around and see what I can find out."

"Great. And I'll keep gathering evidence." She held up a small notebook I hadn't noticed. "I've been writing everything down and Daddy said he'd bring me home a town map from the office so I could plot them all. I know something's going on, Uncle Bob. I just know it."

* * *

I did make a few inquiries. Chief Connors and I went to school together and we still played cards occasionally.

"There have been a few complaints," he admitted. "Andrews called down to the university and they had some people come up and take samples. They couldn't find anything wrong, just poor soil, they said. The Printworks people deny they've been dumping anything and Matt Carson's a pretty square guy. Could be they had a leak they don't know about, but Bud Nelson found a bad spot in his hay field and that's uphill and way the other side of town."

Dr. Gates, the veterinarian, admitted the state of the dog's body was unusual. "If you ask me, he'd been dead a couple of days, not just a few hours. Too much decomposition even if it was a warm night."

Andrews, the Town Engineer, was openly skeptical. "People are too quick to blame pollution for everything that goes wrong. I had some samples taken to calm things down, but if you ask me, there's nothing to it. But you know how these things take on a life of their own, Bob. One person remarks on a coincidence, and everyone else starts making connections in their minds and the whole thing grows on itself until you have a panic."

* * *

Two days later, little Mickey Walker wandered away from his yard when his mother went in to answer the phone and forgot to watch him. He was only four years old and the wood lot was less than a hundred acres, but the search parties found no trace of him at all. What they did find was a churned up piece of ground about ten feet in diameter where all the grass had rotted to dust and the surrounding brush had died back.

Carl Cellucci told me about it that same evening. "Looked like someone set a fire there, except there wasn't any ash or anything. But the ground sure looked burnt all to hell, and it felt funny walking on it. Spongy like."

Kidnapers were suspected, but there was nothing to hint at their identity. No strange cars or people in the neighborhood. Rianne called to tell me that half a dozen pets had disappeared during the week, and that she was plotting everything on the map her father had brought home.

"I've got it on the wall in my bedroom and there's red pushpins where things've happened."

"Sounds helpful," I said calmly. The truth was that I was getting concerned. Independent of the possible existence of a real danger in the soil was the threat of mass hysteria. Dunwich and Managansett had erupted into violence when strings of apparent coincidences were woven into a consistent though irrational pattern. I would hate to see the same phenomenon repeated at first hand.

* * *

I woke up the following morning to find myself without power or telephone. Unshaven, unshowered, and uncoffee'd, I drove toward town to file a complaint, but ran into the work crew two blocks from my house.

"Morning, Mr. Crane." Harry Feldon waved at me. "Had a little problem here this morning." He gestured toward the utility pole, which lay crumpled across the road. "We'll have this out of the way in a couple of minutes. It'll be a while yet before we can get a new pole in, though."

"What happened?" I had pulled over and leaned out through the car window.

"Damned if I know. The pole just went right over. Bottom's all rotted out, looks like. Don't you worry, though. We'll get it all fixed up before you know it."

It was noon before the power was back on. They had to sink the new pole four times before they found a spot where the soil would support its weight.

I drove over to my brother's to use their shower and sink. Rianne was out already and her mother seemed concerned.

"I don't know what's gotten into that girl lately. She hasn't played tennis in days, she's on the phone constantly, and when she's not on the phone she's acting mysterious and writing things in her new diary."

"School starts back up in another couple of weeks, Erin. She's just trying to cram a whole summer into the last few days. She'll be fine."

I hoped.

* * *

Uncharacteristically, I never even entered my office during that day. The power loss had thrown my schedule sufficiently off that I devoted the afternoon to grocery shopping, dropping off my shirts to be laundered, and running various other errands. I ate out and stopped by Twin Elms Tavern for a drink that expanded to three when Del Scott walked in. I was in bed half an hour after arriving home.

The phone wakened me just before eleven. It was Erin.

"You haven't heard from Rianne today, have you, Bob?"

"No, she hasn't been by. Is something wrong?"

"Well, she's past her curfew. I called Tim and Julie and some of the rest of the kids but none of the ones I reached know anything."

"Did she say where she was going?" I asked inanely.

"No, she rushed out this morning and came back sometime during the afternoon while I was shopping. She was already gone again when I came home."

"Probably just lost track of time." I struggled to keep the concern out of my voice.

"I suppose so. But she's been so preoccupied lately. Sorry to have bothered you, Bob."

"Nonsense. And give me a call when she comes in, will you? Just so I won't worry either."

Unable to sleep, I brewed some tea and wandered into my study, and the brink of nightmare. Rianne had left a note on my desk, anchored by my gargoyle paperweight.

"Dear Uncle Bob," I read. "I think I found something. The bad soil all points to one place. We're going to check it out. We waited for you but it's going to get dark soon so we have to hurry. Love you. Rianne."

Ten minutes later I was dressed and driving.

"Bob?" Erin's face dropped when I got out of the car. Obviously she'd been hoping to see someone else.

"Where's Frank?"

"He's out," she answered vaguely. "Trying to find her. Tim Krenkle is missing too." Tim was Rianne's current boyfriend.

"I need to look at something in her room." I brushed past without waiting for an answer.

The map was bigger than I had expected, a large plat map from her father's realty office. As she had described, there were pushpins marking all of the "incidents" she knew of.

The pattern was obvious.

All of the pins could be grouped into straight lines, each radiating from a common center. Judging by the scale, they extended as much as five miles from the source, reaching almost to the town limits in every direction.

"What is it, Bob?"

"I don't know. I'll be back in a while, Erin. I need to check on something."

And then I was driving toward the dam.

* * *

I parked on the road just downstream from Stauley Dam and climbed the fence designed to keep people from falling into Murly Chasm. The incline was steep, but I'd climbed it scores of times as a boy. It was a bit difficult now that I was in my forties, and the darkness didn't help any, but I managed to reach the bottom with nothing worse than a bruised hip.

The dam towered over me. The sluice gates were closed on this side; they hadn't been opened in four years that I knew of. Murly Chasm was the emergency outflow to bleed off excess water, and we'd had a non-critical shortage for that period. A lot had happened in that time. I resigned as town engineer after Elaine died, made my living as a freelance writer and occasional consultant to the town council. No one knew the dam and the immediate area as well as I did; I'd been project engineer when it was constructed twenty years earlier.

So I knew right away that something was wrong.

This part of the chasm should have been a gently rolling flatland overshadowed by the steep walls to either side. The walls were still there, but the ground had changed shape. Instead of a concave swelling, it was convex, a depression leading off into a declivity I'd never seen before. I stepped forward and the ground felt unnaturally soft under my feet. My feet seemed to sink into the soil as though it were made of pudding.

There was a cave in the side of the hill to my right, a cave that had never been there before. I flicked on my flashlight and descended into darkness.

* * *

For the most part, the passage was high enough to walk normally, although occasionally I was forced to duck under obstructions. I found their footprints right away, although the soil was already dissolving and flowing in to fill the depressions. Rianne obviously wasn't alone because I read two different brand names in the patterns.

I thought to call out her name, but refrained, perhaps warned by some instinctive sense of self preservation.

The decline steepened as I continued.

* * *

I found Tim Krenkle ten minutes later. By that time I had descended an unknown but not inconsiderable distance into the Earth, and I had lost the last vestiges of my former skepticism. This was no natural phenomenon, I knew. The tunnels were purposeful, artificially straight. I paused once to examine the walls and found thick striations of desiccated soil, veins of earth that had been somehow transformed, lessened, robbed of some vitality of content that left them spongy, crumbling, and subtly foul.

Tim was lying at the first intersection of the tunnel I followed with a second, and I literally stumbled over his remains. "Remains" is the operative word here, because part of Tim Krenkle was undeniably missing. His flesh had fallen in over his bones; his face was a terrifying parody of humanity, lips drawn back from the teeth, eyes sunken. I crouched and touched his chest and the ribcage gave way even though my touch was tentative, an indentation that remained when I removed my hand.

Footprints led off to the right.

I was remembering some of the claims made by survivors of the "quiet riot" in Managansett, the insane insistence that a creature or creatures had emerged from beneath the Earth to claim victim after victim, a charge that could not be supported by fact. Thirty-eight people died in Managansett that night, and another dozen disappeared, but there was no evidence that their deaths could have been attributed to anything other than the mass insanity of their neighbors.

But I remembered references to a chthonian race and their dread god Shudde-M'ell and I felt the sweat breaking out all over my body. My steps faltered and I hesitated, telling myself that I was better off summoning help than proceeding unaided. There could be vast caverns down here, and I could not hope to search them myself.

Almost I turned and retraced my steps, but at that very moment I heard a sound, something between a sob and a sigh, and I shrugged off my shameful fears and plunged forward.

The footprints led me through two more intersections. At each, the trail grew momentarily confused, as though Rianne had hesitated, trying to decide how to proceed. In each case, she had continued straight ahead.

There were other tracks as well, though I didn't recognize them at first. There were lines in the soil, as though metallic cables had been dragged across the ground. At first I dismissed them as a natural formation, but at each divergent path, they unerringly turned to follow the Nike prints.

I followed them both.

And emerged into an enormous chamber. I am tempted to call it an amphitheater, because that's what it most closely resembled. I was standing in a kind of balcony level, a narrow ledge that skirted the main chamber. There was a second balcony below me, halfway to the floor, and crumbling slopes analogous to staircases connected each to one another and the floor.

Two levels below me, a diminutive human body lay in a tangle. From this distance, my flash couldn't illuminate enough for me to make out the details, but the body was prone, covered by a mesh of ropes or tendrils or something similar. Every few seconds the body would heave and an arm or leg would thrash about briefly, then subside.

I almost fell as I ran down to the main gallery.

From near at hand, I felt my gorge rise. What I had taken to be ropes were revealed to be much more animate, pale elongated worms whose outer integument was covered with wiry filaments. Their victim was so completely covered that I could no longer see her features, and it was clear that the fibers had penetrated her flesh. They throbbed with obscene life as they drew from her body the same essence they apparently extracted from the very soil around them.

"Rianne! My God!" My whisper was hoarse, horrified.

"Uncle Bob!" The voice was unexpectedly vibrant, and it came from behind me. I whirled and saw her emerge from a side passage.

"Rianne?" I took a hesitant step in her direction.

"Run! Oh, please run, Uncle Bob!"

Even as she spoke, the body beside me gave one final heave, then subsided, sinking into itself, into the soil beneath it. And those horrid, worm-like tendrils withdrew and began questing for fresh sustenance, cilia testing the air as if to smell out their prey. I swept the area with my flashlight and discovered to my horror that neither were they discrete individuals, but rather that their individual threads all led into a single side tunnel, in the depths of which I caught only a passing glimpse of unimaginable horror.

Something lurked there, some central body from which these worm-like things emerged, something so obscenely unnatural that its very appearance was an affront to nature. There were angles to the thing that seemed to twist in impossible directions, into other dimensions.

I ran to Rianne's side, barely able to control my rising gorge.

"Who?" I whispered, nodding back at the now motionless corpse.

"Julie," she answered tearfully, catching hold of my arm. "Uncle Bob, I'm so scared."

"Let's get out of here." I nodded back toward the way I'd come.

"They won't let us leave." She was shaking her head distractedly.

"Nonsense." Had I been on my own, I might have descended into gibbering panic. But I had Rianne to worry about, and I refused to let her down. "Let's go."

I led her back up to the first balcony level. Below us, the fibrous tendrils had spread across the gallery floor, a carpet of giant maggots questing for warm flesh.

We had nearly reached the top level when I sensed rather than heard something above us. Rianne's fingers tightened painfully, pressing into my arm, and I paused, raising the flashlight.

Something moved above us, waiting at the topmost level. I didn't see it clearly, but it recoiled from the beam of my light, retreating into the passageway behind it.

"They're afraid of the light, but I lost mine when they caught Julie." Rianne's voice sounded unnaturally calm.

"Well, we won't lose mine then, will we?" I advanced toward that unseen horror, leading Rianne away from the pit.

I don't remember everything about our retreat from that pit of Hell. Every time we passed a side tunnel we heard movement, but I flicked my light toward those sounds and they quickly retreated. All but the worms.

They nearly caught us at the last intersection, emerging from the right and pouring over the side walls. I saw the soil shrink away where they landed, but only briefly. With Rianne's wrist in one hand and the flashlight in the other, I broke into a run, never stopping, never looking back until we reached the mouth of the cave.

There was a rushing sound behind and below us, almost like water pouring through a tube, but I knew that it was something very unlike water.

Rianne started toward the chasm side but I held her wrist, pulled her in the opposite direction.

"There's a ladder up ahead," I explained. "We'll climb the dam."

At that moment, I was thinking only of rapid escape, but on our torturous climb up the concrete face of the dam, another thought occurred to me. By the time we reached the top, I had made a decision.

"This way."

I led Rianne to the main control room. The door was locked, but I had never returned my key when I resigned and I used it now to open the door. We secured it behind us, and Rianne collapsed into a chair as I approached the sluice gate controls.

It had been a while, but there'd been no reason to change anything. It took no more than five minutes to override the safety interlocks, and then I pressed down hard on the Execute button.

The sluice gates opened wide, and water began flowing into Murly Chasm. And into the cavern from which we'd escaped. We didn't leave until the chasm had turned into a small lake, from which bubbles of unclean air emerged periodically with bloated, popping sounds.

* * *

Officially, I was charged with vandalism, though I have enough friends in town that there were never any legal repercussions. Rianne is now attending private school in Providence and aside from a severe claustrophobia that doesn't seem to respond to therapy, she seems unaffected by her experiences. Indeed, she never alludes to them and her mind may have protectively shielded those memories away.

The disappearances of Julie Evans and Tim Krenkle have never been explained.

There were no more odd problems with the earth in our town after that evening, though none of the dead spots have yet regained their ordinary vigor. There have been rumors of strange soil deficiencies from a remote area of New Hampshire, but I have not investigated and do not plan to do so.

And my book? Well, it hasn't proceeded a single word beyond where it was that night. Because my thesis was that mass hysteria had been responsible for the panics that tormented these two disparate communities, panics with no basis in reality.

And now I'm not so sure.

The Temple of Yig

by Donald R. Burleson

Carlos squinted across the chaparral, raising a hand to shield his eyes from the desert sun and watching as distant, indistinct figures labored to raise large canvas tents against a turquoise sky. It was a curious sight. When you thought about it, it wasn't very often that a carnival came to this part of New Mexico. A carnival, or a funfair, as they were called in England.

Which in fact was where this one was from, he happened to know. He knew other things about it as well. Darker, stranger things.

His cousin Paco from Tucson had come to Socorro to visit a few weeks ago, mentioning that the carnival had stopped in Tucson recently, pitching its tents in the desert a couple of miles outside the city limits and sending up a medley of odd sounds, weird lights, and peculiar odors to swirl aloft in the night sky. Over dinner with Carlos at Geraldo's Cafe in Socorro, Paco had related a chance conversation he had gotten into in a Tucson bar, soon after the arrival of Hodgson's Funfair outside of town.

"Yeah," Paco had said, "this Anglo at the bar said he lived in Yuma and was in Tucson on business, said the carnival had stopped in Yuma about a month before, and had been in southern California someplace before that. It was working its way across Arizona, heading into New Mexico and Texas and wherever. The guy from Yuma said there was a lot of odd talk around town about the whole affair. Some carny workers had come into town, had a few drinks in the bars, dated some of the local women, talked a bit, and stories started going around, strange stories about the carnival. There was supposed to be a tent called Tomb of the Old Ones," Paco had said. "That much is true at least, because I saw it myself when the show came to Tucson." Paco had wiped beer foam off

his lip and had added: "Saw it from the outside. I didn't have any han-
kering to go inside."

"Why not?" Carlos had asked.

"Because I remembered the fellow from Yuma said one of the stories making the rounds was, that some people had gone into that tent
and had never come out."

Carlos had laughed. "Come on, *pendejo*. That's the kind of rumor the
carny people themselves like to start. It's good for business, crazy talk
like that. Makes people want to come out and see the show."

"Yeah, well, I'm not so sure," Paco had replied. "You can laugh all
you like, but that carnival wasn't in Tucson a week, and there were some
people missing. I saw it in the papers. Nobody was saying it had
anything to do with the carnival, but with the reputation the thing
already had—"

"What do you mean, reputation? Those Yuma stories?"

"No. From before," Paco had said. "Some of what the guy from Yuma
had heard was about the carnival when it started, in England some years
before. Even then, everywhere it went, rumors would start up, about
people going to the fair and not coming home. Sometimes people were
never seen again. There was supposed to be something about sacrifices
to ancient gods or some such stuff. I don't half understand it. Eventually
the carnival couldn't get a permit anywhere, from any of the townships
or cities in England, to put up their tents. Nobody would lease them any
land either. So it was like they were being told to shut down or leave the
country. They left the country. From what I heard, they wandered across
Europe for a while, and were in Asia for a time, and ended up in
California. Now they're making their way across the U.S."

"Well, hell," Carlos had said, "it's too bad for them that more people don't hear all the stories and the rumors. It sure makes *me* want to
go see them."

Recalling this exchange now, he leaned against the open door of his
truck and gazed across the dusty plain, watching a distant swarm of
workers toiling ant-like to thrust those tall, intriguing tents against the
late October sky. He felt a little less flippant about the whole subject
than he had been when he was talking to his cousin. There was something disturbing, even with the carnival not completely set up yet, and
even from this distance—something weird about the feeling that the
scene imparted, a feeling that eluded him somehow, but bothered him
nevertheless. And because it bothered him, he knew that when the carnival opened, he would be there.

* * *

Hodgson's Funfair opened the next night.

Carlos had tried to get Angie, who waited on tables at Geraldo's, to go with him, but she had a date. So Carlos was alone. Before driving all the way up to the parking area, he stopped his truck on the roadside and got out and looked across the night-black desert. Perhaps a quarter of a mile off the road, the carny people had set up a large parking lot in a flat stretch of sand fairly free of sagebrush and chamisa. Cars gathered out there now, their taillights winking like odd phosphorescent insects in the gloom. Beyond, the carnival itself reared its canvas corners amid a strange blur of light and muffled sound—strange, at least, for out here in the desert, where usually the only sounds at night were the cry of the owl or the coyote, and the only lights were the stars.

Carlos bumped his truck up the approach to the parking area and edged into a space on the near end. There were a surprising number of cars and trucks, given the lonely location of the site, but he guessed that Belen and even Albuquerque weren't too far away for people to drive down to see the carnival, and of course a number of people from Socorro would come out. He made his way to the entrance, gave the woman at the gate three dollars, and followed the crowd into the funfair.

On the fairgrounds themselves, he felt oddly disoriented, and not just because of the strings of garish bulbs festooning the walkways like bizarre Christmas tree lights, or the din of organ music or the raucous shouting of barkers announcing their bewildering array of sideshows: the Mirror Maze, the Fire Jugglers, Madame Zala the Gypsy Fortune Teller, Lili the Exotic Belly Dancer, Capro the Amazing Goat Boy ("eats tin cans before your very eyes"), Magnus the Magician, and on and on the litany went, into the dusty distance, sideshows lined up out to the limits of sight. No, it wasn't just this cacophony of impressions.

It was the place itself, this particular spot of ground—because it was familiar, or had been familiar. He had grown up in Socorro, had spent his youth in these desert lands, hunting jackrabbits and chasing coyotes and spotting rattlesnakes. The land had, overall, a sense of familiarity that stretched back years in his memory. He had walked over every inch of this land before, had even camped here at times, smoking cigarettes and eating beans from a can, in the flickering light of a campfire.

Now the sideshows, the milling people, the tents lifting their gaunt heads to the sky, all made it difficult to maintain a sense of where he was. The tents, the awnings, the lights, everything made the place look different. What had been wide open space was now contracted, distorted, changed. He remembered what Paco had said, and sure enough, up ahead, a large tent proclaimed in gothic letters: TOMB OF THE OLD ONES. (A barker exhorted the crowd: "See secrets older than the pyramids of Egypt! But beware—people have gone inside, never to be seen again!") Standing outside this tent, Carlos tried to remember: When he had camped that time and sprained his ankle, was that here where he was standing, jostled now by carnival-goers, or was it over there where the tent itself obliterated the land?

And wasn't there a shallow arroyo nearby, a dry wash? Looking around, he thought he could make out a dim trace of its beginnings, farther down the midway, just a barely discernible irregularity in the sand. He walked in that direction, following the traces of the arroyo with his eye. The dry wash gradually deepened, but was still only a foot deep when it vanished under the canvas edge of a large tent.

Carlos, concentrating on the little arroyo, had scarcely even noticed the tent, and scanned it now to find its upper reaches emblazoned with the sign: TEMPLE OF YIG.

Whatever the hell *that* meant, it struck Carlos now that this was a pretty strange place to pitch a sideshow tent, and not only because the tent squatted over a deepening arroyo.

He remembered now what was a little farther back. When he had played here as a kid, he and his friends used to walk just a few yards up this wash, to a place strewn with large rocks. In and among and under those rocks, a good number of rattlesnakes could always be found. Enough rattlesnakes to keep any young lad on his toes, and a few to spare. He hadn't been out here for a long time now, three or four years at least, and he couldn't be sure that the rattlesnake den was still there, but he supposed it would have been, most likely, before the carnival came, and surely these people had insisted on its removal before pitching their tent. In a way, that made him mad; what right did they have to just come through here and alter the landscape for their own convenience, even if they had permission from the landowners? Even rattlesnakes were a natural part of the terrain.

In any event, this didn't seem to be the most popular show on the midway, by any means. Only a few people were standing around nearby to hear the barker in front say, "See the Temple of Yig. Sacred temple older than all of time. One dollar. Come and behold the One True God." The barker chanted this over and over in a tired but insistent monotone, and Carlos, though himself not pious by any means, could only suppose that that "one true God" business must be offensive to religious-fundamentalist ears. In any case, when you got right down to it, the Temple of Yig just didn't sound as fetching as Lili the Exotic Dancer, or even Capro the Goat Boy, so Carlos was surprised to see even a few people here, paying their dollar and going in to see the Temple of Yig.

Among the takers, he noticed, was Angie, from Geraldo's, and she was with Joel, the mechanic at that gas station next to the cafe. What Angie saw in this lout, Carlos could never understand. They were standing several yards away, but he overheard their exchange now as Angie headed into the Temple of Yig sideshow. Or rather, he overheard Joel, who always seemed to do all the talking.

"You go ahead, babes. I'm gonna go see the belly dancer. Meet you back here." He slapped her on the behind. Wincing a little but still managing a smile, she waved to him and went inside the tent, and Joel went off down the midway.

After a while Carlos did too, and found himself back in front of the tent with the sign TOMB OF THE OLD ONES. He hesitated a few minutes, listening to the barker's endless repetition—"Secrets older than the pyramids of Egypt!"—and finally handed the man his dollar and followed the others inside the tent.

He had expected it all to be overblown nonsense, and it was. In the dim illumination of blue and green bulbs, the center of the tent's interior was occupied by a rough circle of what he first took to be large stones, with objects atop them. The stones, on closer inspection, were some dense, spongy stuff painted a mottled gray, and the objects surmounting them seemed to be an odd assortment of small statues, all on the same theme: an octopus-like winged creature whose forearms terminated in clawed hands, and whose great pulpy head bristled with tentacles. One of the pseudo-stone pedestals bore a sign saying: GREAT HLU-HLU, HIGH PRIEST OF THE OLD ONES. Another sign said, incomprehensibly enough: M'WGRRH Y'HAI NG'A-R'LYEH KH'NARR-WA HLU-HLU M'LEI FHTAGN.

Say that ten times fast, Carlos thought, *and win a prize.*

He noticed that despite a few whispered snickerings and asides, most of the other patrons seemed to be rather awed by this display, lingering over the carven forms, examining them with, to judge from facial expressions, a commingling of fascination and loathing. A woman nearby was reading one of the display signs aloud to her male companion: "Listen to this, hon. 'Great Hlu-Hlu seeped down from the stars in the Dream Time, and lies waiting in His watery tomb, undead, ready to come forth and claim His own. In the fullness of time, the stars will come round right, and He will reign.'" The woman essayed a laugh at this, but it came out rather hollow, and she eyed the squid-like figures of Hlu-Hlu with clear distaste.

In truth, there was indeed something repellent about the statuettes, and it was with some relief that Carlos turned away from them, only, however, to face a large oil painting propped in one corner, showing apparently the same mythic figure Hlu-Hlu, rising from the churning ocean in a voracious frenzy, great eyes glistening hungrily, obscene talons ripping to pieces several wild-eyed sailors who seemed to have been try-ing to return to a ship all but swamped in the nearby convulsion of waves. The caption of the painting: HE IS RISEN, HALLELUJAH. *That*, Carlos told himself, *will delight the area Born-Agains no end.* Turning to leave the tent, he noticed, further, only some stone shards piled in a corner near the exit, with a sign: FRAGMENTS OF SUNKEN TEMPLE AT R'LYEH. Sighing, he shook his head on behalf of those other patrons who were really taking this load of crap seriously, and left the tent.

Back out on the midway, he wandered up and down for a while, lis-tening to the harangues and pitches of the barkers selling their various sideshows, and finally ran into Joel, down near the Temple of Yig.

"Hey, man. You seen Angie?"

Carlos shook his head. "Just when she was going in there," he said, pointing to the tent near them.

"Yeah, well, she went in there nearly an hour ago, man, and I haven't seen her since."

"Maybe she's still in there," Carlos said. "Did you go in and look?"

"No."

"Well, I'll tell you what," Carlos offered, "I was kind of thinking about going in there myself. I'll look around for her, and if I see her I'll tell her you're waiting for her."

Joel eyed him narrowly. "You just be sure you tell her to come right out."

"Yeah, okay. See you." He paid his dollar and followed four or five other people into the Temple of Yig.

Inside, though Carlos found others already drifting about the dis-play, Angie was nowhere to be seen. It was the display itself that instant-ly captured his attention. Even in the wan illumination of the weird orange bulbs that hung overhead, he could still see the lines of the dry wash, shallow but discernible in the desert sand beneath his feet, and the wash did after all run back to a rubble of large stones at just about the

center, now, of the interior of the tent. Damn, they had left the spot
intact. As a matter of fact, the display seemed to consist of the rock pile
itself. Surely the owners of the land would have mentioned to them that
the place was infested with rattlesnakes—but here the stones still lay,
and if the stones were still here, Carlos would give good odds that the
snakes were too. Were these people crazy, or just stupid, to pitch a
sideshow here?

His thoughts were interrupted by a new arrival. From somewhere in
the dark depths of the space that the tent enclosed, a man stepped forward in the orange light. He was wearing a kind of quasi-Oriental garb
evidently made of silk but patterned to look like snakeskin. He was carrying a sort of staff, evidently made of wood and painted to resemble a
serpent. So that was it, then—the carny people not only knew about the
rattlesnakes, but were managing to capitalize on the theme, Carlos
thought. Now he'd seen everything.

"In the time before the world," the serpent-man intoned, standing
beside the tumulus of stones, "in the time before time, when Great Hlu-
Hlu had not yet oozed down from the icy stars, when the primordial
Ash-Ha-Thoth had but begun to thrash and writhe in the center of all
chaos, when the unspeakable Yogge-Hsiu-Thoth had but begun to stir
in the void, even then did Yig, the Father of Serpents, come forth.
Behold His children!"

The man levered the wooden staff between two of the large stones
and pried at one of them until it rolled aside. Beneath, several uncovered
snakes coiled and rattled. A shock went through the crowd, and they
moved back. *God*, Carlos thought, *these carny people really are crazy.*

"Do not be afraid," the serpent-man said, prodding the snakes and
making them coil, rattling and striking at the stick. "None of you will
be harmed. See," he said, pointing to a moist spot atop a particularly flat
stone, "see where the sacrifice to Yig has already been made."

The little pool of liquid on the stone did look like blood, but it
might have been water; in the orange light, it was hard to say.

"And because the sacrifice has been offered and accepted, behold
now the face of Yig Himself."

The serpent-man withdrew into the shadows, and all was still,
except for a lingering spiteful rattle or two from the snakes, but they
soon slithered away beneath the rocks and were quiet. Carlos noticed
that no one in the crowd was getting any too close, and a few people had
left. But something else was happening now.

From deeper inside the tent, almost beyond the glow of the orange lights, the very darkness seemed to be thickening into a shape.

God in heaven, what was this?

The shape, at first only a sort of hood or mantle of blackness, rose huge and tall in the air of the tent, nearly scraping the canvas ceiling far above with what increasingly began to look like a head, out of which two baleful slitted eyes shone with a sickly yellow luminescence. The thing took sharper form, and instantly the air turned noxious with an odor that Carlos could never before have imagined. Atop its vast serpentine body, the great angular head turned with shocking rapidity and the dreadful eyes surveyed the crowd with a kind of pitiless nonchalance. After the first stunned moment, the people in the crowd were not long in reacting, bolting in a screaming panic, falling over each other to get out of the tent. Carlos fled with them, but turned at the last second to look back at the horror that hissed and jerked and writhed in the diseased orange light.

At that moment the eyes of the thing met his own.

And more than just their eyes met. For an insane few seconds, their minds met, and Carlos found himself frozen in a mental embrace with the thing. In a soundless exchange that threatened to shatter his brain with its sheer power, the thing told him everything—all the primordial secrets of all the dizzying ages before time, before the universe, all the black and soul-annihilating terror of all the corpse-cold darkness of the void. As suddenly as it had begun, the exchange ended—the loathsome shape that hung before him in the giddy orange air withdrew its hold upon him, and he stumbled back and wheeled and ran, ran out into the open air, where all the others had run before him.

Somewhere close to him a man was saying, "Boy, they had *me* going there for a minute!" And a woman was asking, "How do they *do* that?" And someone was replying, "Aw, they can do anything these days, with computers. Let's go get some popcorn."

Carlos felt someone poke him in the arm. It was Joel.

"Well?" Joel said.

"What?"

Joel looked annoyed. "C'mon, man. Did you see her?"

"I—" For a moment Carlos couldn't fathom what Joel was talking about, but then he remembered. "Angie. No. No, I didn't see her." Was that entirely true? He didn't want to think about it. "She wasn't in there."

"Well, where the hell did she go?" Joel asked, his face ruddy and quarrelsome.

But Carlos could only wander off down the midway, passing among the currents of sound and light spilling from the blathering sideshows, could only drift with the crowds, finally ending up somehow in his truck, driving away from the fairgrounds, into the New Mexico night.

By the next day the carnival was gone, probably to Tucumcari or Roswell or Amarillo, who knew? It was gone, and when Carlos returned to the place where it had stood, the desert was again just desert, broken only by occasional mesquite and sagebrush and prickly-pear cactus.

And—the little arroyo, that meandered back to a tumulus of sun-baked stones.

He sat on the sandy floor of the wash, near the stones, and tried to feel that everything was normal, that everything was all right, but could not escape the conviction that the very sand, the very sage, the very sky would never be the same. He cast his gaze out over the eastward desert lands, where the great mystery of Hodgson's Funfair had vanished, and tried to form words around the great aching hollowness within him, but could not.

When darkness began to gather, he was still sitting in the arroyo, and when the stars came out, he did not move, and when the snakes came out, he still did not move. And when they struck at him, rattling and recoiling and striking again, he felt only the momentary touch of fangs, only the timeless and ecstatic caress of the sacred children of Yig.

Not to Force the Rhymes

by Benjamin Adams

For Jay Bonansinga
Grateful thanks to Bob Smith for encouragement and advice

1996

Can it possibly have been twenty years ago? It seems as if it happened only last month; last week; *yesterday*. During that terrible, cruel summer of 1976. Everything changed that year; for many, struck down by the oppressive heat, it was the end of all they knew. For others, like myself, it marked the realization that the world was capable of infinitely more savagery and mercilessness than they had previously thought. Scotland—all of England—changed that year, and nothing was ever the same.

Was I ever that young? I can't believe I was ever such a fool.

I was there at the center of it all, you see. I set free the greatest evil mankind has ever produced.

But, God help me, I know that even the worst, most corrupted harvest of the human soul is as nothing to what waits beyond. And I saved us all. I exchanged the greater evil for the lesser.

I just wish I knew whether we were worth the trouble.

* * * * *

1976

The dream began as it always did.

I found myself descending the stairwell at Oakdeene. The light was dim and watery, and great strips of paint hung peeling from the walls; the exposed surface beneath looked raw and damp and red, like a bloody abrasion.

—Hhrm, *I heard.* —Hhrm. Come closer.

I floated through the heavy double doors into the Hell ward. Its floor was soft and pulpy, pulsing with some kind of hideous life. The cell doors were open, and as I passed them I looked inside each one. Their rear walls were gone; beyond the physical confines of Oakdeene, the cells opened onto a shadowy plain dimly illuminated by a dark green sky.

In the second cell from the left, the brain-damaged patient sat on the edge of his kip, head hung low as always. But then his head turned toward me, and I saw that his mouth was sewn shut with heavy black thread. From his pleading eyes rolled thick, viscous tears, like gelatin.

—Hhrm, *judged the speaker.* He knows the secret, and look what happened to him.

And then I saw that the patient had my face—

I jerked awake, finding myself in sweat-soaked sheets with a pounding headache. By the clock on my bed stand, the time was already past noon. Another damn hot morning promised another shite-hot day in Glasgow. Not the best situation to wake up to from a night out with Potato-man.

Through my open window I heard disco music playing from the flat opposite mine, across Argyle Street. Abba's "Dancing Queen." I fairly shuddered in revulsion. Anne MacDonald had nearly worn the damn record out since she'd gotten it a few months earlier. I finally decided enough was enough.

I staggered off my kip and shambled to the window, sticking my spiky-haired head out. The song began fading away, Anna-Frid and Agnetha's harmonies twisting around and around and piercing my skull with their banality. As silence fell, I bellowed, "Get a new fuckin' record then, Anne!"

"Yer a bastard, Davey Bremner!" Anne's voice trilled back. "I'll play wot I like!"

"Not when I can't shut my bloody window, yer won't!"

"Piss off!"

I pulled my head back in. All this shouting was just making my head hurt even worse than it did already. *Damn Potato-man, anyway ....*

I hadn't meant to get drunk the night before, but I'd run into Potato-man at the Damned's gig at Charing Cross. Now, *that* was music—real punk rock with hard-ass attitude and energy, not this disco bollocks to which my old group of friends still listened. I'd even gone out with Anne MacDonald a few times last year, when we were still at Glasgow University together. Done her right good, I had, and for a while things had looked fairly serious. But now I found myself drifting away from Anne and the rest, drawn instead to this new music, its excitement and energy and dangerous glamor. The Damned, the Sex Pistols, Eater, the Stranglers—punk rock was where the action lay, and Potato-man was king of the scene in Strathclyde, man, king of the scene.

And to be one of Potato-man's mates—one had to drink like a bleedin' fish.

That was all right, though, wasn't it. Nothing wrong with sinking back some pints of a Friday night.

Except, I realized, my stomach lurching, when I had a shift at Oakdeene Sanatorium this afternoon. Good Christ, and if I didn't get a move on I'd be—

*   *   *

"—*late*, Mr. Bremner," said Dr. Colwyn Jones, impeccable in Harris tweed, tapping the end of a Bic pen against his ever-present clipboard. "One does not believe one has to spell out for you what will occur if this happens one more time. The present employment situation is bad, quite bad. One would think you would bear that in mind."

"Yes, sir," I said, my head bent forward in what I hoped appeared a conciliatory and contrite manner. "I'm sorry, sir."

The words were difficult for a punk rocker like me but necessary. Jones was a right bastard, perhaps the harshest of the doctors at Oakdeene, and a real stickler for protocol. The word among my fellow nurses was that Jones would probably be better off as an inmate of the sanatorium, not as a doctor; it was eerie, the way the man never referred to himself in the first person.

Jones' severe gaze traveled up and down my white nurse uniform, stopping at a slight yellow stain on the left chest. "And do try to take better care of your uniform, Mr. Bremner. Any replacements will, of course, come out of your salary."

Bleedin' chicken vindaloo, I thought morosely. The stain had stubbornly resisted all frantic efforts I'd made at removing it, withstanding even bleach. Indian food is made to last, especially when it's from take-away.

"Come along, Mr. Bremner," ordered the doctor. "One wishes you to assist on rounds."

I followed Jones to the dank stairwell. At some point in the last few years, an attempt had been made at painting the stairwell Institutional Green. But the surface hadn't been prepared properly, and the constant warm humidity in the air made the latex paint bubble away from the walls, in places peeling away and showing the dirty gray paint of years past.

A bead of sweat tickled down my spine. Like most other buildings in Scotland—in all of England, for that matter—Oakdeene Sanatorium had been constructed without concern for hot weather. The temperatures this summer were unfathomably high, and only seemed to be getting worse. I'd heard tell of old folks, trapped in their flats, dying like flies because of the heat. Here at Oakdeene, it had become necessary to walk rounds with a large spray bottle filled with cool water, to mist down overheated loonies. And *oneself*, of course—as Dr. Jones would say. By the end of my shift, my uniform would be thoroughly drenched.

We were headed downstairs now, and although the air actually grew a few degrees cooler as we passed underground, the sweat rolling down my neck only increased.

Dr. Jones was leading me into Hell.

* * *

The ward known as Hell lay in the basement of Oakdeene Sanatorium. Once, a long time ago, it had been home to many of Britain's most dangerous and terrible madmen. That had been during a less enlightened era, before new techniques in psychological treatment—combined liberally with chemical therapy, of course—made such a ward as the original Hell unnecessary.

Now the occupants of Hell were primarily catatonics, people who had withdrawn into their own minds to escape the awfulness of a world in which they could not function. The basement ward was practically silent, except for slight rustlings of skin against sheets, grunts and moans passing through disused, rusty throats.

These poor souls were the bane of my existence. I saw their blank, staring gazes in my worst nightmares. There were times, in my dreams, when I knew that if I looked on the occupants of the basement ward one moment longer, their mouths would creak open and they would begin speaking, telling me the awful secrets which had driven the loonies deep within themselves. At that moment I would invariably awaken, drenched in sweat, gripping the edges of my bed so tightly my hands ached.

As I had this morning.

Hell seemed a perfectly appropriate name for the place, even if Dr. Jones and the rest of the psychiatric staff highly disapproved of that appellation.

The stench of human feces and misery hit me like a lorry as we passed through the heavy oak door at the bottom of the stairwell. "You know what to do, Mr. Bremner," Jones said shortly.

I nodded unhappily. *Slopping the hogs*, the nursing staff called it. Roll the bedridden patients. Check them for bedsores. Clean up their shite and urine, replace their soiled sheets with fresh ones from the linen closet by the ward entrance.

In severe cases, wash the loonies down by hose.

I found my headache returning with vigorous force.

Jones wandered down the ward, glancing through the small, barred spy-holes in each door, checking the labels bearing the case history of each cell's occupant against the comments on his clipboard. Occasionally he would make some notation with his Bic, noting some small change in a patient's condition. But he never passed directly into a cell, leaving that distasteful task instead for me.

With a sigh that was more like a groan, I buckled down to my work. The first two cells on the left and right were vacant, stripped even of their soft padding.

But the second cell on the left held a sixty-five-year old man who had spent more than half his life in Hell.

This patient, Martin Spellman—I couldn't bear to think of him as a loonie—held a special, weighted significance for me. Once, years and years ago, he had been, like myself, a nurse, here, at Oakdeene Sanatorium. Something had happened to Spellman, some kind of psychological *reversal* that had reduced him to this sad, catatonic state. Some of the other nurses claimed that Martin Spellman had still been capable of moments of lucid conversation—interspersed with wild, screaming fits of terror—until 1974, when Dr. Colwyn Jones had prescribed the man a new medication. No one was exactly sure what had happened—lips were shut tight against the admission of such a botched deed—but apparently Spellman had been given an overdose of this unspecified medication, leading to some kind of organic brain damage.

Now Martin Spellman merely rocked back and forth on his kip, staring at the wall with wide, sad eyes that seemed to peer across miles of empty space.

I couldn't understand why, but I felt some strange kinship with the poor man. Something about his condition touched my heart. That could be me in there, I thought, every time I saw him.

That could be me.

No sooner had I unlatched the cell when Dr. Jones, down at the far end of the ward, made a sudden, uncharacteristic cry of alarm and surprise. *"Good Lord!"*

"Doctor?" I stood by the door I had just unlocked, uncertain what to do.

"Mr. Bremner," snapped Jones. "Come here. Quickly."

"This one's *awake*!"

* * *

John Baker peered at me with hard, bright eyes. Hardly the eyes of a man who has been catatonic for forty years; rather, he looked as if he'd just awakened from an afternoon nap, ready for tea and the *Evening Times*.

"You say the year is 1976? Hhrm. Hhrm. It's been quite a long time then, hasn't it. Hhrm."

His voice was thin, raspy and reedy, and he couldn't even lift his head to look at me or Dr. Jones. The nursing staff had kept his thinning white hair trimmed close to his leathery head, and in his standard-issue hospital gown, the man looked like a skeleton wrapped in crinkled papyrus.

Dr. Jones circled Baker warily, almost like a lioness stalking her prey on the savannah. The image startled me with its vividness. Yes, Jones seemed like a beast about to bring down its supper. "Mr. Baker, what is the last thing you remember?"

The old man's glance flickered from Jones to me. I could swear I saw a flash of humor in those unclouded, icy blue eyes.

"Call me Jack. Hhrm."

The doctor blinked. "Ah—yes. Of course. *Jack.* What is the last thing you recall?"

"I remember going to sleep. Hhrm. I had the strangest dreams. Hhrm. Hhrm."

Baker broke into a spasm of coughing; my hands immediately found their way behind his head and lifted it from his pillow, to clear his air passage. His skin felt strangely distasteful to me. I'd long ago shed any aversion to touching the unwell and infirm—being a nurse of any kind would be tough if you couldn't touch a patient—but I couldn't wait to pull my hands away. Something about Baker's dry, fragile skin put me in mind of a moth's pupa before the adult insect emerges.

Jones was clenching his fists, a sure sign the good doctor was feeling undue stress. "No—no—there must be something more. Some kind of trauma that caused you to recede into your own mind. What happened to you that night, forty years ago?"

"Hhrm. A bit of bad pudding. Mayhap a—hhrm—spoiled potato."

"Well. Well. One is uncertain how to proceed," Jones finally admitted.

"Hhrm."

"Bremner here will return and see to your needs. Your case requires some study, and one will come back as soon as possible." Without waiting for a response from Baker, Jones laid a hand on my shoulder and steered me out of the cell, which he then locked behind us.

As we left the Hell ward, Dr. Jones spoke to me, his voice soft and clear.

"You are not, under any circumstances, to mention this case to anyone else on the staff. Is that understood? Mr. Baker will be moved to new, secure quarters; one will tend to him without the prying aid of others."

"But—but this is huge, Doctor! I've never heard of anything like this!"

"That is why it is imperative that certain facts are known before anything further is done. You never saw this man awake, Mr. Bremner. You never spoke to him. Do not mention him to anyone; none of the nursing or psychiatric staff, or even the administration. Your cooperation is vital. Do you understand?"

"Sir, I don't—"

"*Do you understand?* Earlier one warned you about your work habits: your tardiness, your slovenly manner. You are on very thin ice at this institution, Mr. Bremner. Any further skating upon this rapidly weakening ice is—inadvisable."

I nodded slowly. Jones had made himself perfectly clear. And at that moment I realized I hated him more than anyone in my entire life.

* * *

Potato-man took another gulp from his pint of Guinness Stout. "Yeah, awright. I gets the scene. This geezer, he's, wot, been locked up in the loonie-bin fer God's own time, ain't said a bleedin' word fer aroun' forty years."

"That's right," I said, still shaking my head in amazement. "It's a bleedin' miracle, is wot it is." My voice was slurred both by drink, and by my habit of slipping into street-talk when around Potato-man.

"I could give more 'n a shite," Potato-man grimaced. He took a drag off his cig—good American Marlboro—and exhaled with a flourish. "Wot you wanna work in that place fer, ennyway? Locked up with them loonies all day, enough to make a man go off 'is nut. You goin' off yer nut, Davey-boy?"

We sat in the Red Lion, a working-class pub on Bath Street, in the heart of Glasgow. A noisy pub-rock group called the 101'ers were on the stage, playing catchy little toe-tapping numbers. They weren't bad for their ilk, though I liked something with a little bit more energy. But the 101'ers' lead singer had an undeniable charisma in his raw, throaty vocals. Set that bloke up with a proper punk group, I thought, and you might just have something.

The 101'ers finished their set to scattered applause. Some of the old gaffers in the Red Lion looked downright pleased to have the rock band off the stage. Piped music began playing from speakers located in the pub's rafters, and I cringed. Bleedin' *Abba* again! "Waterloo", my baboon's big red arse.

"I dunno," I finally said to Potato-man's question. "It's good wages, an' I spent all that time in university tryin' tae learn somethin', tryin' tae make somethin' of meself."

"Har! Tryin' to make somethin' of yerself, are ya? Yer a punk, pure n' simple, just like me." The Irishman swigged some more Guinness and wiped his mouth with the sleeve of his leather jacket. At twenty-five, he was old—positively ancient—for a punk, and had two good years on me. His broad face, with a nose that had been broken too many times to count, looked like a lumpy potato. "Well, maybe not jus' like me, but then, who is?" He laughed boisterously.

"These bleedin' sots aroun' us are the ones wot made this fucked-up world the way it is, Davey-boy. We never asked fer things ta be this way. They owe us a livin' and I, fer one, am just as happy to take it on the dole as I'd be slavin' away fer some twit wot thinks he's better 'n me. But maybe yer too old t'appreciate what I'm sayin', wot with goin' ta university n' all."

"Nice life, ain't it?" I said with a touch of sarcasm.

Potato-man's eyes narrowed. "Wot the fuck d'ya mean by that?"

I thumped my index finger against the sticky surface of the table. "I've worked hard to get tae this point in me life. I hae a good job and support meself wi' it. I may nae be a teen anymore but I hae just as much right tae this scene as anyone. I goes out and hae a good time on the weekends and I'm just as much punk as ye. I got too much pride tae go suckin' off hind tit."

"Suckin' off—" Potato-man's hand snaked across the table and grabbed me by my collar. "Yer ain't nothin' less I say so," Potato-man hissed, "and you'd best remember that. I don't care shite about whether or not you slave away fer a quid or two. But don't you *ever* say I'm suckin' off hind tit. I gots just as much pride as you. More."

I nodded. I'd been through this before. The only way to keep Potato-man's respect was to mouth off to him every now and then, act like you weren't scared of him. Which would allow Potato-man an opportunity to remind you of your true position in the scene.

Not for the first time, I wondered exactly why my friendship with Potato-man was so important. The Irishman was a lout and often showed signs of veering into sociopathy. He claimed, when deep in his cups, to have murdered a man in Belfast. But he was my ticket into a new world of excitement and thrills, and after being cooped up with the loonies all day, hanging with a different kind of loony was exhilarating.

"Well, well," a snide voice announced. "Look wot we got here. Two faggot punks gonna kiss n' make up fer us, ay?"

A kid with a slicked-back quiff who looked like nothing more than a malnourished clone of Elvis Presley stood by our table, a couple of look-alike pals by his side. They wore blue suede creepers with wild red socks tucked into drainpipe jeans. Confederate flags were painted on the backs of their jackets. Teddy Boys, rockabilly fetishists who looked like they were stuck back in the 1950's.

The Teds hated us punks. They felt we were desecrating everything for which rock n' roll stood. They couldn't have been more wrong—we were just out to kick rock in the arse, bring some life back to it. Eddie Cochran and Gene Vincent would have been punk rockers if only they'd been born twenty years later. The Teds didn't see it that way. We offended them by our very existence, and they wanted to erase us.

"Blue Gene," Potato-man said between clenched teeth. His face went pale, and he released my collar, his muscles tensing for imminent action.

"Ach, come on n' try it, then," Blue Gene laughed. "Yer head'll be bashed in before ye can say 'Erin go bragh', ye Mick bastard."

Beneath the table, I gripped Potato-man's skinny knee, desperate to provide the top punk with any other stimulus besides Blue Gene's taunts. If anything started in here, we were dead. A couple more Teds stood over by the bar, idly munching on crisps and watching Blue Gene's lead.

"Piss off," Potato-man said after a long moment, color finally returning to his face.

"We'll be seein' ye. Later," promised Blue Gene. He stalked back to the bar with his chums.

Potato-man turned back to me and hissed, "Take yer fingers out me fuckin' kneecap before I break 'em all."

"Bleedin' hell, I was only tryin' tae keep ye from gettin' our throats cut."

"They wouldna tried anythin' in here."

"It's not in here that's worryin' me. That bunch are out fer stompin' punks tonight, and ye'd be a right prize for 'em. You'd best watch yer step."

Potato-man raised his left eyebrow in amusement. "So it's me yer worried for? It's not yer own skin yer tryin' to protect, then?"

"That's nae it, and ye know it."

"It seems ta me, Davey-boy, that yer not a blessed bit happy right now. Not really."

"And how is that?"

"This bleedin' Doctor Johnson—Jagoff—"

"Jones," I supplied, feeling a grin break out on my face although I tried to suppress it.

"Yeah, 'im too," Potato-man said, rapping the table. "'E's gotcher over a barrel. An' where there's a barrel, there's a bunghole—an' yer the bunghole, Davey-boy."

I shoved myself away from the table and stood, a bit woozily, but at least upright. "That's it. I've had enough o' ye tonight. I'm goin' home."

Potato-man grabbed my wrist and roughly pulled me back down. "Shurrup and listen, laddy. Doctor Jagoff threw some kinda fit over this ol' geezer wakin' up. 'E's usin' it agin ye, makin' ye keep yer mouth shut about it."

"An' maybe I shoulda kept me mouth shut even tighter," I hissed, "Instead a' blabbin' it tae ye."

"Nah, dontcha see? Ye sure a hard-headed one, Davey-lad. Yer precious Doctor Jagoff's got a *secret*. Use it agin' him. Fight back!"

I've heard it said that moments of epiphany are like thunderbolts. In my case, it was more like a crashing wave of seasickness. Potato-man's face swam before my eyes like a bobbing buoy on storm-tossed waves.

I'd never thought of Dr. Jones as possibly having any kind of emotions whatsoever; his ice-cold demeanor kept such thoughts from anyone on the Oakdeene nursing staff. Jones may as well have been an automaton—a mean-spirited automaton, to be sure—but now I saw something else behind it.

The bastard was frightened.

And whatever—whomever—had Jones scared, was my ally in a war I had just decided was worth fighting.

The pints I'd downed earlier seemed to fade away. My focus grew sharp and I gazed on Potato-man with new respect. Like the Burning Bush had with Moses, this Irish lout had given me new purpose in life.

"Yer right, ye bleedin' oracle!"

He looked at me blearily. "'Bout wot?"

* * *

"Hhrm. I am not terribly pleased with my treatment. Hhrm."

I had to agree with Jack Baker's assessment. Dr. Colwyn Jones had stuck him on the third floor of Oakdeene's practically abandoned west wing. The temperatures were even worse up here, and Jones sent me up several times during my daytime shifts to make sure Baker was kept cool.

"I'm sorry, sir," I told the old man, and gave him another spray of mist from my bottle. "I wish there were somethin' I could do, but I canna."

"Please—hhrm—call me Jack," he croaked through his rusty throat.

"Aye. Jack it is."

"You'll remember this time?"

"Aye."

There was something about the old man that disturbed me, made my insides go all strange when I was near him. My gut tightened up, and I felt cold—honestly cold, almost chilly—despite the temperature.

"Hhrm. You know, you're a good lad," Baker wheezed.

What could I possibly have to fear from this poor old man? His muscles were so atrophied from decades of disuse that he could barely move. He was never any less than polite to me, and he genuinely appeared to have an interest in what I could tell him about the world outside. Everyone he'd ever known was long dead.

Odd. How very odd that I couldn't bear to be near him and his icy blue eyes.

Dr. Jones apparently couldn't bear the man's company for long, either, spending no longer than necessary with Baker than it took to check the man's condition and question him about that fateful night forty years ago, when Baker had gone catatonic.

But Baker had nothing to say to Dr. Colwyn Jones. In fact, the old man appeared to dislike the doctor even more than Jones disliked Baker.

And I couldn't stand being near either of them.

"Hhrm. You know, I was once a poet. Hhrm."

"Were ye now?"

"Oh, yes. Hhrm. I have been composing poetry once again. Hhrm. Here, in my mind—since my body won't cooperate. Hhrm. Would you—would you care to hear it?"

Christ's sake, no, I wouldn't.

"Of course," I said with a smile. Hopefully it looked authentic.

Jack Baker cleared his throat with a royal *Hhrm!* and began reciting:

> An evening's leadership ignores,
> Your mother takes things from Hell.
> But the chameleon quarrels awhile—
> The deadline pilfers
> Desire
> Is
> The ageless mysterious animosity of your abdomen.

Silence fell. I stared at Baker, who had the faintest expectant smile playing around the corners of his paper pale lips. The man was absolutely mad. Forty years in a coma is not a recognized cure for insanity, and he had obviously been quite the madman to be consigned to the Hell ward.

"That—that was verra nice," I finally said, forcing the words past my suddenly dry palate.

"I rather like it myself. Hhrm. Am I not a clever fellow?"

"Oh, aye, that ye are."

"Hhrm. I used to—force the rhymes. Hhrm. You should have heard some of the doggerel verse I produced. Hhrm."

"But now ye know ...."

"Now I know not to force the rhymes. Hhrm."

* * *

I sat in Dr. Colwyn Jones' sparsely decorated office, poring over the historical records of Oakdeene Sanatorium. His shift had ended hours ago. I had prowled the dimly lit halls for a while, to make sure he wouldn't return, then sequestered myself inside.

The large, leather-bound books on his desk dated back to the turn of the century and were filled with the names of patients and doctors long forgotten. The musty scent of decay wafted from them, an inescapable, depressing miasma befitting their contents: a history of human pain and misery bound by madness.

I found Jones' personal journals, and by cross-referencing them with the moldering hospital records, began putting together the pieces of a very large, very ugly puzzle.

Something had happened here at Oakdeene, something awful that had been sealed away, hidden from memory. None of the staff now employed at the sanatorium had been here that fateful New Year's Day in 1936, and only two of the patients were still alive.

They were both in the Hell ward: Jack Baker and Martin Spellman.

Dr. Jones had heard enough of Martin Spellman's ravings to have an inkling of what had actually happened forty years earlier, and had taken steps to ensure that no one else would ever hear what Spellman had to say: lunatic ravings regarding some kind of outside deity called Yibb-Tstll and a book called the *Cthaat Aquadingen*, which contained chants—the Sathlattas—to bring this Elder God into this world.

No, it wasn't murder; Jones slept well at night secure in that knowledge.

And, after all, Spellman had been hopelessly insane, by any reasonable standards.

So the little chemical *push* Jones had given him was nothing more than mercy, really. Martin Spellman was now permanently on the far side of madness, and there would be no return to the green fields of lucidity for him. The higher functions of his cortex had been neutralized.

It was, in effect, a chemical lobotomy. Untraceable and without visible motive.

Now, Jack Baker had been in a catatonic state during those four decades, and had never shown any sign of response to stimuli. Yet his heart beat as strong as ever, and electroencephalograms still showed undeniable activity in his brain. So he was kept on at Oakdeene, his muscles periodically exercised by the nursing staff, kept clean and fed well. Dr. Jones had never seen any need to *attend* this other survivor of

the New Year's Day disaster. Never seen any need to take Baker out of
the equation, like Martin Spellman.

I rubbed my nose tiredly and blinked imaginary grit from my eyes.
Dr. Jones was clearly insane, leaving these incriminating notes in his
office like this. But he was a respected psychologist, a fellow of
Oakdeene, and it was unimaginable that someone—like myself—would
have the audacity to break into his office.

The final pages of Jones' diary set everything forth plainly. In the
grips of his own undiagnosed psychosis, Dr. Jones sat in his office at the
center of Oakdeene Sanatorium, secure in the knowledge that his madness was wholly and totally logical. As a doctor, his job was combating
and destroying insanity. But since he had begun working at Oakdeene,
he had come to the realization that the entire world was insane, *the result
of the evil influence of creatures from beyond the spheres we know.*

Jack Baker's awakening was the last sign Jones had needed.

For Yibb-Tstll waits, the doctor had written. *He turns in darkness,
awaiting His chance to enter this world and wipe it clean.*

To Jones, the key was Jack Baker. The outside entity Yibb-Tstll
would use this man as a gateway to enter our world and wipe it clean.
Destroy all life in preparation for the coming of more creatures known
as the Old Ones, who had once ruled our world and had lain in wait for
untold millennia until they could possess it once again.

And Dr. Colwyn Jones believed he was the only person in the world
who could stop this event from happening.

Obviously, Dr. Jones had suffered some kind of schizophrenic break
with reality. He showed all the signs of having developed a messiah complex. His ramblings about this Yibb-Tstll creature, and Larner's imaginary book, could scarcely be given any credence. This entire elaborate
cosmology was the product of a sick mind. And right here, in Jones' own
writing, was the admittance that he had given Martin Spellman an overdose, the effects of which Jones knew would cause permanent damage to
the poor man's brain.

If Dr. Jones was obsessed with Jack Baker, I had to learn why the
old man was so important to Jones' psychosis.

The answer was buried a few pages deeper in the journals.

But I couldn't believe it. Oh, this was sheer madness. Utter lunacy
on a scale which I'd never before seen.

It was apparent that even Jones had trouble believing his own
conclusions, for there were copious amounts of notes confirming his
hypothesis.

I had what I needed. The final, incontrovertible proof.

Dr. Colwyn Jones was mine.

But now that I had him, what would I do?

* * *

The old man took my elbow in one of his gnarled hands and led me beyond the confines of his cell, into the twilight emerald landscape. Around me grew strange, obscene plants that shone with a sickly gray light. Trees that looked like nothing as much as prehistoric cycads scratched, weakly, at the sky.

—Hhrm. And so now you also know the truth, *spoke my guide.*

—Where are we?

But he chose not to answer my question. Instead, he gave me a riddle.

—The butcher, the baker, the candlestick maker. Hhrm. Which am I?

He roughly turned me to stare into his icy blue eyes. —WHICH AM I?

—The baker! *I cried.* You're the baker!

—No. Hhrm.

And I knew, I knew which he was.

—The butcher ... the butcher ....

Thud! Thud! Thudthudthud!

At first I thought the frantic pounding was within my disjointed dreams, but then a familiar, rumbly voice reached my disoriented ears.

"Davey-lad! Open up!" Potato-man called thickly. "Dammit, I need yer! Open up!"

"It's 2:30 in the bleedin' mornin'," I moaned. "I need me sleep. Go away!"

"Davey, I'm in some bad trouble. Yer gotta open up."

I slogged across my bedsit, cursing all the while. Why should it surprise me that I wound up having Potato-man banging on my door in the middle of the night? I was getting too old for this kind of shite. On the other hand, at least this was a respite from the weird dream I'd been having, which I could only attribute to having read Dr. Jones' weird ravings the night before.

I wasn't prepared for the sight that greeted me when I flung open the door.

Potato-man leaned against the jamb, his head resting on his arm. He stank of sweat and fear. His torn white Sex Pistols T-shirt, from Malcolm McLaren's Sex boutique in London, was heavily splashed with a drying brownish substance that I recognized from clean-up duty at Oakdeene.

Blood. And I immediately knew that not all of it was his.

He turned toward me, and I recoiled. Potato-man was in terrible shape, his face turning black and blue from some kind of awful pounding. A two-inch cut on his right cheek put me in mind, absurdly, of the scar on the cheek of an Action Man doll.

"Aren't yer gonna invite me in?" he mumbled through thick, split lips.

"Uh—yeah! Yeah. Come on over tae my kip. D'yer wanna drink a'water?"

"That'd be nice, Davey." He staggered inside and sank down heavily on my bed.

I grabbed a fresh glass from the cupboard and drew him some tepid water from the tap. He drained it back so quickly that he choked and coughed on his last gulp.

"Ah. Ah, God, that was good, Davey. Thanks."

"Look, mate, what happened tae ye?"

His eyes were nearly swollen shut, but I could still sense them gauging me somehow, sensing whether or not he could fully trust me. Finally Potato-man drew a deep, shuddering breath and said:

"I killed 'im, Davey."

For a moment this didn't make any sense to me; the words buzzed around my head like tiny black insects, impossible to catch.

"God help me, I *killed* 'im," he repeated.

"Killed—killed who?" I finally managed.

"That wanker Teddy Boy. *Blue Gene.* I cut 'im. Cut 'im right open, I did. I didn't have a choice, Davey. I killed the bastard."

* * *

His voice shaking with exhaustion, Potato-man told me what had happened, and I found myself thankful I'd decided to spend the evening at home.

Unlike me, Potato-man and a small group of his mates had spent the evening in the Red Lion, sinking back pints and bitching about the ungodly hot weather. Either bar bitching hadn't been providing enough entertainment, or for once Potato-man had had the sense to call it an early evening. He bid goodnight to his mates and clomped out of the Red Lion, heading for the Queen Street Station.

About halfway there, at the intersection of Renfield and St. Vincent, Blue Gene and a half-dozen Teds emerged from the shadows. Blue Gene slowly swung a homemade set of nunchakus, a length of heavy iron chain with two quarter-meter shafts of steel pipe welded to either end. The martial arts appealed to the Teds, since their beloved King of Rock n' Roll—Elvis Presley—was an aficionado of the form.

Potato-man knew he didn't stand a chance against this bunch. He began sprinting down the middle of empty Renfield Street, but his heavy Doc Martens work boots weighed him down. Blue Gene's swirling nunchakus hit the rear of Potato-man's knees, and he went sprawling to the pavement.

The rest of the Teds caught up to Blue Gene and his victim then and took turns kicking the shite out of Potato-man, who tried curling into a ball, to lessen the amount of his body left open to their steel-toed creepers.

The only thing that saved his life was the approach of his mates. From up the block, they saw the Teds kicking the shite out of some-one—probably couldn't even tell it was Potato-man—and decided to get in on the action.

Within seconds, a full-scale street brawl was in progress.

Potato-man staggered to his feet and reached into his pocket for the switchblade he always carried. He'd never had cause to use it before, never in a fight, but what Blue Gene had just pulled was beyond the pale.

A matter of seconds later, the blade plunged deeply into Blue Gene's back. And again, and again, 'til the Ted leader lay motionless in a pool of his own blood. The rest of the combatants hadn't even noticed. Blue Gene's cries were nothing out of the ordinary in a bit of street action like this.

Potato-man looked at his bloody hands, then at the crimson knife blade, and back at his bloody hands. This wasn't what he'd wanted. But it was either him or Blue Gene, right? It was self-defense, right?

The approaching scream of a siren finally reached him; he looked up in shock and saw the Teds and punks scattering. The switchblade almost fell from Potato-man's bloody hand, and then he found himself running, running, running until he discovered himself in Argyle Street.

Outside my door.

* * *

"I dunno what ta do, Davey. I never been in this kinda trouble before."

"But we thought ye was a hardass up from Ireland. Ye said yer killed a man in Belfast fer lookin' at ye sideways."

Potato-man lowered his head and looked away from me. "Never happened. It was a lie I told."

"Why?!" I exploded. "Why the Hell would ye go an' say somethin' stupid as that?"

"Fer my image, Davey-lad."

What could I say to that? It was absurd. He'd lied to us; said he'd murdered a man in Belfast. And it was just for his image. So we'd treat him with ... what? With respect, with awe, with reverence—as if he were some kind of bloody punk rock saint?

From where I sat I could see Anne MacDonald's darkened window. All I could think was that if I'd played my cards differently—if I'd any damn sense at all—I could be sleeping in her bed tonight, instead of nursemaiding a murdering idiot like Potato-man.

I'd had a good upbringing. I was intelligent enough to finish university and gain a nursing job at Oakdeene Sanatorium. Why did I have to go and throw it all away just for a bit of excitement, for the sake of some loud aggro music and a bunch of brain-dead yobs who spent their time kicking in each other's heads?

What was I doing with my life?

I turned back to Potato-man. He'd slumped back against the wall, his chin leaning against his chest. His breath came in short gasps, and I realized that he was crying.

"Come on, then," I said, shaking him by his right shoulder. He looked up at me with swollen, uncomprehending eyes. "Let's get movin'. I gotta getcher patched up and on yer way, and there's only one place I can get that done."

"Wha—where we goin', Davey?" He wearily pulled himself from the bed and stood on shaky legs.

"Oakdeene," I said. "We're goin' tae Oakdeene."

* * *

At the rear of Oakdeene Sanatorium was a seldom-used door meant for deliveries. A larger, sliding delivery portal for lorries had been installed on the building's east wall at some point during the 1960's, and now the smaller door was used mainly by staffers who wanted to escape outside on a sunny day and have a smoke or two without being pilloried by the doctors for polluting the atmosphere.

With a sheet over his head, I snuck Potato-man through this door and into Oakdeene Sanatorium without incident.

There were medical supplies on the third floor, in the disused west wing, and I could have some peace and quiet while I attended to his wounds.

With some relief I saw that the walls in the stairwell were just as I'd last seen them, and showed no sign of the distortions they'd undergone in my disturbing dream.

"Careful—careful—here's a step up, another—"

"Are we almost bleedin' there yet, Davey-lad?" Even through the sheet, Potato-man's wheedling annoyance was loud and clear.

"Aye," I hissed. "And quit yer wingeing. I'm tryin' tae help yer here, remember?"

He grumbled unhappily.

I guided him onto the third floor and straight into the first cell on the right down the west wing. "Just lay here," I instructed. "I'll be right back with some stuff ta clean yer up."

It was still stifling hot; the thick brick walls of Oakdeene, so good at withholding winter's cold, also held in this strange heat. My plain red T-shirt lay plastered against my back with sweat.

As I headed toward the medical supply closet, I reviewed my plan. Once I got Potato-man patched up, I'd cut off his remaining hair, loan him a few of my clothes, and send him packing out of Glasgow. Maybe to London; hell, where he went didn't matter, as long as it was far enough away from me. This was the last favor I'd ever do for the lousy, bleedin' sot.

I was through with Potato-man; I was through with trying to live a punk lifestyle that just wasn't me during my spare hours.

"I'm done with it," I muttered as I gathered up alcohol, antibiotics, and bandages in my arms. "I'm done with the whole damn lot."

"That's very interesting, Mr. Bremner." Despite the warm temperature, that voice sent shivers down my spine. I slowly turned and faced its owner. "Exactly what are you done with? Your job here, perhaps?"

For the first time—and very likely the last—Dr. Colwyn Jones smiled at me.

"Stealing supplies. One had expected so much more from you, Mr. Bremner. That perhaps you'd accidentally kill a patient, for instance.

Now that would have been an impressive way to lose your job. Most impressive."

His right hand snaked out and caught me by my shoulder. At his touch I flinched and dropped the supplies. They appeared to fall in slow motion toward the stained tile. Seconds became hours. Hours during which my body held an internal debate, my muscles twitching with detonations of adrenaline: Fight or flight? But there was nowhere I could go, nothing I could do. I'd really done for myself this time.

"Come along, Mr. Bremner."

Suddenly nerveless, I allowed him to steer me away from the supply closet. The enormity of the unpleasant situation seemed unreal. Theft of hospital supplies ... *harboring a fugitive* ....

The Strathclyde police would be quite happy to see me. I wondered how long they'd lock me away.

But then I remembered Jones' notes. Good Christ, I still had the upper hand.

"No," I said, yanking my arm away from Jones' grasp. "Get yer bleedin' paws offa me!"

Dr. Colwyn Jones pulled up short and stared at me, not believing I'd show such insolence to his face. "You're only making this worse on yourself, Mr. Bremner."

"Ah, ah," I said, wagging a finger at him. "I know what ye did tae that puir fella, Martin Spellman. Ye destroyed 'is mind."

"*What?!*"

"Ye bleedin' rotter! Don't play coy wi' me."

Dr. Colwyn Jones cocked his head and regarded me oddly. Once again I was reminded of the movements made by a beast of prey. "You're a fool, Bremner," he finally offered.

"I think that's a matter o' perspective. I wonder what the Board of Trustees will think o' ye once they hear 'bout your notebooks, and all this crazy nonsense about Yibb-Tstll or whatever you call it. Not tae mention the admission in yer own writin' about poor Spellman. Likely as not they'll put you in one o' these cells, doctor."

"You've read ... the journals."

"Oh, aye."

Jones looked deflated. When he again spoke, his voice was a whisper. "What if one could prove to you that every word is true—that Yibb-Tstll exists. That such a vile creature waits to enter our world and wipe it clean."

His voice grew stronger again with every word.

"It's taken years to reach this point, Bremner! Years of agonizing study and watching for signs and portents. But now there's no doubt. Yibb-Tstll is coming and only we can stop it!"

We? The good doctor's psychosis had expanded to include both of us. I decided to humor him. "And how's that?"

"The old man who awoke yesterday—John Baker—he's the key. He's the one Yibb-Tstll wants."

I flinched as a chill hand of insight touched my heart. John Baker. *The baker.*

The butcher.

Doctor Jones saw the change in my expression and pounced. "You know! If you read my journal, you *do* know!"

"He's—he's the butcher."

"Yes."

"The Ripper." And as I sighed the word, I knew it to be God's own truth.

* * *

Inspector Frederick George Abberline, who had been in charge of investigating the murders in Whitechapel, never knew what happened. In the late fall of 1888, Abberline was visited in London by Sir Robert Anderson, Assistant Commissioner of the Metropolitan Police CID. At the time of Anderson's visit, there were four suspects in the Ripper slayings: Montague John Druitt, Michael Ostrog, a Polish Jew named Kosminski—and John Michael Baker.

When Anderson left his meeting with Abberline, there were only three suspects. Baker was not among them.

In fact, Baker no longer seemed to exist at all.

A loner on the streets of London, Baker had no family, no friends, and no background. It was as if the man had appeared from nowhere—and begun killing women, butchering and eviscerating them. And once Scotland Yard apprehended him killing Mary Kelly, Baker vanished once again.

No capture was reported in the press.

Abberline never knew why. With the pressure of the Crown behind his orders, he kept silent.

The Crown took a special interest in Baker. The man was spirited away to Oakdeene Sanatorium near Glasgow—in those days, the arse end of nowhere. There Baker was kept and observed by an elite group of doctors and scientists. But as the years dragged on, and the century rolled over, whatever the doctors expected to learn from Jack Baker never materialized.

Their interest waned. By 1935, Baker was forgotten.

Typical of a bureaucracy, really.

* * *

"He's damn well preserved for bein' 111 years old," I told Doctor Jones, still not wanting to believe what I *knew* was truth.

"He's not human," the doctor said. "Or perhaps he's too much human; that's the problem. You see—they knew what they had when he was captured. In those days the ancient books of lore weren't consigned to some back shelf. Queen Victoria was still advised by psychics. And the Ripper's coming was foretold in many volumes—the *Cthaat Aquadingen*, Ludwig Prinn's awful *De Vermis Mysteriis*, the *Necronomicon* of Abd Al-Azred—all spoke of this being's eventual formation. Once any race reaches a certain critical mass, its collective evil splits off and forms an entity, a gestalt creature that acts as a wolf in the fold, thinning the herd, so to speak."

The awfulness of these concepts sent my mind spinning. I could barely comprehend what Jones was telling me. If I hadn't already read his journals, I wouldn't have been able to digest any of it at all. "But— why only the evil? I dinna understand why only the evil part o' mankind would form into this—this gestalt."

The doctor shook his head. "Not only the evil. The good in mankind has also coalesced into gestalts, many times. Jesus, Buddha, Mohammed—all these are names of the unconscious gestalt of mankind's good essence. Just as Jack Baker is not the first manifestation of our evil gestalt. Witness Gilles de Rais and Elizabeth Bathory, for instance.

"Unfortunately, Baker has drawn the attention of Yibb-Tstll to this place. Yibb-Tstll is a creature from outside of our reality who harvests our evil gestalts in order to increase its own powers. It wants to wipe our world clean in preparation for the coming of more of its own kind. It once attempted to break through to Oakdeene when the stars were right, working through a madman named Wilfred Larner, who used a formula called the Sixth Sathlatta from the *Cthaat Aquadingen* to open a doorway for Yibb-Tstll. But Martin Spellman, the poor bastard, stopped Yibb-Tstll from gaining access to our world—at the cost of his own sanity."

I felt my gorge rising at Jones' statement. "But ye ruined the man's mind!"

"He was remembering the words of the Sixth Sathlatta. One had to prevent that from happening. Killing him was not an option—one is not a murderer, Mr. Bremner."

I shook my head in disgusted wonder at Dr. Jones' self-delusion. Even if all he was saying were true—and I still wasn't convinced of much of it—there could still be no denying that Jones was monomaniacal.

"So what will ye do?"

"The gestalt requires a host. Without one, it will die. If the host is destroyed, Yibb-Tstll will no longer have any interest in Oakdeene, and will turn its attention elsewhere. Haven't you ever felt it, Mr. Bremner? Felt the pall hanging over this place? Nobody ever gets well here. They only grow worse and worse ... until they die."

We stood outside the cell holding Jack Baker. Jones fiddled with the lock momentarily and we entered. A shaft of light through the open door showed us the old man lay peacefully on his kip, his eyes closed, his breathing shallow but regular.

"When ye mentioned 'destroying the host', what exactly did ye mean?" I whispered to the doctor.

Colwyn Jones reached inside his jacket pocket and removed a scalpel. The blade glinted in the light from the hallway.

"This," he hissed, and moved toward the sleeping old man.

I am not a fundamentally brave person, but at that moment there was only one thing I could do. Unfortunately, it was absolutely the wrong thing.

I lunged forward, grabbing Dr. Jones around his middle, bringing him to the floor. He made a kind of chuffing sound as the air was knocked from his lungs, and he squirmed and twisted in my grasp.

"Yer nae gonna kill that old man," I burst.

Jones' right arm moved toward me in a blindingly quick movement.

The scalpel blade cut through my belly, slicing through skin and muscle tissue like a hot butter knife.

I screamed and rolled away from Jones in utter agony. My hand went to the wound and I felt the wet pulse of blood against my palm.

"You—were always—a slow learner, Bremner," he said.

He unsteadily got to his feet and once again approached the old man in his sickbed.

"What the fuck's goin' on in 'ere?" asked a happily familiar voice. "I heard a ruckus—hold on a sec—"

Potato-man's swollen eyes took in my pathetic state, lying like a gutted fish on the white tile floor, and then flickered to Dr. Colwyn Jones, who stood with a blood-stained scalpel in his right hand.

"Yer wanna cut someone, cut me, yer cunt!" Potato-man bellowed. From his pocket emerged the same switchblade that had so recently taken the life of Blue Gene, the Ted leader. It flicked open almost of its own accord, and as I watched in shock, the switchblade seemed to pull Potato-man along behind it through the air—

—straight

—toward

—Dr. Colwyn Jones, who was never able to utter any further insulting remarks to me or anyone else, since his throat was cut cleanly ear to ear. The doctor blinked in surprise and collapsed to the floor, his life's blood spattering Potato-man from head to toe.

The floor was awash in crimson gore, the likes I'd never seen in any horror film or hospital. Potato-man looked at his switchblade, almost as if he were seeing it for the first time. "What'd I do?" he mumbled. "What'd I do?"

"Ye saved me life, ye dumb Mick!"

"Davey—are you all right?"

"I—I dunno," I gasped. "It hurts, it does."

"What'd I do? I din' mean ta kill the bastard. I din' mean ta do it ...." Potato-man staggered backward, against Jack Baker's bed.

The old man's claw-like left hand fasted around Potato-man's wrist.

"Bleedin' hell!" Potato-man burst, and tried to back away from the bed.

Impossibly, Jack Baker's desiccated form hid some kind of awful strength. The old man pulled himself upright, and I heard bones snapping with the strain of moving for the first time in forty years. A piece of tibia abruptly sliced through Jack's arm with a thin welling of pinkish, watery blood.

And still he held Potato-man tight.

Something small, black, and chitinous abruptly protruded from Jack's mouth. At first I thought it was his tongue, but it instead popped from his tissue-thin lips and scurried along his cheek.

If I'd still doubted Doctor Jones' story, the sight of that ebon thing would have convinced me. Because there was no doubt that what I was seeing was evil incarnate—the sum total of everything mankind fears and loathes, but knows is contained within each of our hearts. This was the *gestalt*.

It hopped onto Potato-man's shoulder and, as he screamed, leapt into his mouth.

And in the sudden silence that followed, I fell headlong into blessed, blackest unconsciousness.

* * * * *

1996

The events of that summer haunt me still, and their repercussions still curse England and the world.

Why did Potato-man let me live? I can only believe it was because some small part of him still understood that I'd been his friend. Or perhaps he thought the scalpel I'd taken to my abdomen would finish me off. But it takes a long time to die from a gut wound, and I was found in plenty of time for my life to be saved by the good doctors at nearby Yorkhill Hospital. The police were never able to catch the "mad Irish killer", as they called Potato-man in the pages of the *Evening Times*.

The punk scene no longer held any allure for me; I realized that it was time to put away such childish things. I voted against Thatcher, but that was the extent of my politics. I grew my spiky hair out—not by much, but no longer did I bear any unfortunate resemblance to Johnny Rotten or others of the punk ilk—and went back to university.

There I earned a doctorate in psychology; I accepted a post at Oakdeene and through the years gained directorship of the sanatorium. I ensured that the institution's patients were treated properly, not as guinea pigs for misguided fools like Dr. Colwyn Jones.

The basement ward—Hell—was remodeled under my tenure, and now holds the sanatorium records and cleaning supplies. Bright new fluorescent lighting has been installed throughout the aged building, and the walls are a neutral beige.

We even have air conditioning.

Yet I open the *Evening Times* and read of a stabbing in Lanarkshire; a mutilation in Garnethill; a young woman pushed off a street corner in Muirhead in front of an onrushing lorry; and I know. I had it in my power to stop him, the fiend who now wears the face of my mate. Potato-man. Jack the Ripper. Yet I let him go.

What Dr. Jones told me was only apparently part of the full story; the whole truth Jones held locked inside his psychotic mind will forever remain a mystery. For the obvious questions remain: If Jack Baker—the

Ripper entity—is the gestalt of mankind's evil, what of all the other serial killers who have surfaced since the late 19th century? Among them, the monsters Dahmer, Mudgett, Bundy, Fish, Speck, and the worst of all, Pedro Alonso Lopez—are they merely reflections or splinters of Jack Baker? *How can there possibly be so much evil in the world at one time?*

The fiend is still among us. He sows his cancerous seeds of fear and hatred even now, and a thousand disciples mimic his every move. Things grow worse by the day, out in the world I helped save, and I wonder if it was worth saving after all.

Perhaps it would have been better to allow Yibb-Tstll to wipe it clean.

God help us.

For we are not able to help ourselves.

In His Daughter's Darkling Womb

by Tina L. Jens

In his daughter's darkling womb
Great Cthulhu will be born
And at his birth the Fabric of
Space and Time will be torn
When he casts away Death's shroud
And rises from the Deep
Star of yellow will burn out
Mankind slaughtered like the sheep
Mother/Daughter to the eldritch god
And those attendant at his birth
Will be Judge and Executioner
To the Cosmos and the Earth

"Or, so it is written in the poem."

"That's very interesting, David," Katherine Cullom said sarcastically. "But this is a science lab, not a literature classroom."

David Gaughan did not tell the marine biologist that the poem, or *prophecy*, was written in von Junzt's *Unaussprechlichen Kulten*, but she would not have recognized the title if he had.

* * * * *

Field Journal Dr. Katherine Cullom September 29
    After years of preparation, everything has come
    together!

It was with no little awareness of the scientific
significance of this experiment that I first
observed the giant cephalopod this afternoon.

Reciting the phylogeny can't begin to capture the
emotions of seeing the specimen for the first time.
It was monstrous in size, with what seemed like
innumerable tentacles that could curl around the
length of the tanker. It seemed to radiate, if
you'll forgive the word, an aura of age, aeons, and
absolute Evil.

As best we can measure a live specimen it's 24.3
meters in length, roughly the height of a five-
story building! Its weight, judged by water dis-
placement, is 490 kilograms. Just imagine, this
massive creature weighs less than a standard automobile!

Its skin in its natural state is a deep crimson
with concentric black rings running around its tentacles and body like wild racing stripes. Like its
cousin, the *Octopus vulgaris*, it has the ability to
change color and skin texture in response to its
environment and mood, a fact we learned almost
immediately upon entering the hold of the converted
oil tanker, where the immense aquarium had been
constructed. …

* * * * *

Despite repeated warnings to move slowly and speak softly, chaos
reigned in the lab.

You'd think none of these people had ever dealt with a cephalopod before,
Katherine thought angrily. They'd soon learn their lesson if it inked
repeatedly and they had to climb into the tank and net out the cloud of
black ink and mucous. The filtration system was top of the line, but no
filter could keep up with multiple inkings by a specimen this size.

The presence of David Gaughan only increased Katherine's rage.
Katherine had tried to have him thrown off the boat, or at least out of
the lab, but he had the proper authorization papers from Arkham
Industries Corp. She couldn't fault the staff in the home office. She knew
the techniques that David and Animal Rights Now! used to get such
permission slips. David was an official observer for ARN!. She'd had
numerous run-ins with the activist, despite the fact that she was a
research scientist for a marine institute, not some corporate chemist
looking for a way to dump pollution undetected. She often suspected
David harassed her for purely personal reasons.

No hint of her raging emotions slipped past her mask of professionalism, and it took only a firm hand on the shoulder and a quiet, "Let's calm down, shall we?" administered to the half-dozen people nearest to her to start a ripple effect through the room.

In a voice only a notch louder than normal conversation, Katherine began issuing orders to the team. Despite the immense size of the ship's hold, she had no need to repeat herself.

Only after teams were dispatched to measure, weigh, and photograph the specimen did she allow herself the luxury of turning back to the aquarium tank and studying the creature.

The techs had done a good job of building a giant cave in the middle of the tank, as well as tunnels and perches all along the floor of the massive aquarium.

Katherine was more than a little disconcerted to find it had climbed out of its cavernous lair to press itself against the glass and study her.

Like most Octopods, its eyes were telescopic, and could raise and retract from the side of its head more than two feet in any direction. Unlike most Octopods, it had three sets of eye stalks, far more than necessary given the telescopic range of each eye. All six eyes seemed to ignore the rest of the team and follow her about the room.

The specimen was remarkably calm, exhibiting none of the characteristics of fear common to its family, other than a slight pulsing of color when a skin scraping was taken from the tips of one of its tentacles. The examination revealed retractable claw hooks on the underside of each tentacle, five inches in length, curved, and tapered to a deadly point.

It could climb a mountain with spikes like that, Katherine thought.

There were also tiny growths at the base of its two back legs where the tentacles joined the body. They looked like wing buds. More likely, they were the last remnants of dual dorsal fins, discarded by species evolution, but not quite disposed of by the species' genes.

One of the younger members of the research team climbed the ladder to the room of the enormous tank and unlocked the feeding hatch. Using a wench, he raised a giant crate up to the top, then guided it to the opening and dumped the contents in. He quickly closed the hatch when he was done.

Ten pounds of assorted live fish and crustaceans began swimming about the tank. The young scientist would monitor what the creature ate, in order to determine its dietary range and preferences.

"Remember to lock that hatch securely," Katherine told the Feeder. "The specimen may be a giant, but we shouldn't assume that it isn't every bit the escape artist other Octopods are."

He shuddered and nodded. No one wanted to imagine this creature slouching moistly through the corridors of the ship.

Katherine was beginning to think the early field reports were inaccurate and that this specimen didn't have a protective ink sack, when the creature proved her wrong.

Considering how calmly it had weathered the earlier chaos in the lab, its reaction to the ship's cat surprised her.

The specimen had somehow worked the hatch open and snaked a long tentacle across the floor in pursuit of the cat. There were more than a dozen people in the room, but no one noticed until the feline screeched.

Hissing wildly, the cat scraped its claws down the length of the menacing tentacle. Ichor squirted from the wounds. The specimen thumped two tentacles against the aquarium wall as it retracted its injured arm. A black cloud struck and rebounded against the glass. A high-pitched wail pierced the room as it jetted into the rocky cave.

The scream did not end when the creature reached its lair, and more than one member of the team was on his knees, hands clasped to his ears in pain.

But discomfort did not relieve duty.

Katherine barked orders. "Get that blood sample off the floor, on a slide, and into the lab!"

She pointed at the Feeder. "Grab a net and scoop that ink cloud out before it disperses. Send a sample to the lab and monitor the water chemistry every half hour.

"Someone catch that cat and take scrapings from underneath its nails for tissue samples. Let's get a move on, people!"

Ten minutes later and throbbing headaches all around, the team cleared out of the lab and escaped to the top deck for a half-hour break, a private lecture for the Feeder, and a general briefing.

And still, the high-pitched wail drilled into their brains and continued, for over an hour ....

* * *

Katherine Cullom looked up from her computer as she heard the metal clanging that indicated a visitor at the door. She opened the hatch and greeted her research assistant and second in command of the project.

"Helen, come in. I was just working on my journal."

"I'm sorry, Cassie. I can come back if you're busy."

"No need. Let me just save the file."

Katherine completed the series of keystrokes, then gently pushed the flip-top closed.

"You're up late," Katherine said to her friend.

"Can't sleep," Helen grinned.

"Want a celebratory nightcap?"

"Sure."

Katherine opened her desk drawer and pulled out a velvet-lined box. She undid the clasp and removed two crystal snifters, filling each with a generous measure of cognac.

Helen whistled. "That's a beautiful set!"

"It was a gift from Frank on our fifth anniversary."

Helen searched her friend's face for signs of grief at the memory of her dead husband. She saw none. But then, Cassie was a master at shutting off her emotions.

Helen shrugged out of her white lab coat before accepting the drink.

Katherine grinned as she saw Helen's under-apparel. Blue jeans and tennis shoes—standard field gear—and a red T-shirt with a picture of two giant squids mating, encaptioned, "Cephies Do It in the Sea."

"Where did you get that?"

"Going-away gift from The Boyfriend," Helen said.

Helen went through men so fast that Cassie never bothered to memorize their names. The man of the moment was always referred to as The Boyfriend.

The two women were opposites in every way, which may have been the reason they were best friends. Or in Katherine's case, her only friend. There weren't many who wanted to get close to "Dr. Coldfinger", but Helen had known Cassie back before she'd earned that name. She knew why winter had moved into the woman's heart.

"I just stopped by to drop off the briefing reports. I knew you'd want to see them tonight."

Helen handed the stack of papers over and finished her drink quickly. She'd seen Cassie's eyes glancing back to the computer and knew her friend was eager to get back to work.

Katherine closed the door behind her, returned to her desk, and opened her computer. She took another sip of her cognac and started a new paragraph.

* * * * *

Field Journal September 29

    (Continued)

    Arkham Industries is to be commended for the high
    quality of our floating lab. I had reservations
    about this project when A.I. insisted on having so
    many of their own people on the research team, and
    in handling all the arrangements themselves, rather
    than trusting our expertise in such matters at the
    Institute.

    The work progresses well.

    I have tentatively classified the specimen from
    phylum through genus, with species as yet undeter-
    mined. Or (as I strongly suspect that this is a
    previously undiscovered creature) species unnamed.
    Our records search continues. Meanwhile, I have
    classified it as: Mollusca, Cephalopoda, Octopoda,
    Octopodidae, Octopus … (Species undetermined.)

    However, there are numerous distinctions in charac-
    teristics that separate it from other species in
    this phylogeny. I expect this matter to undergo
    fierce debate ….

Katherine hit the Save command on her computer before picking
up the written reports from the afternoon briefing.

                              * * *

Field Journal September 29

    Addendum: Summary of Specimen's Natural Territory
    and Capture

    After repeated attacks on Devil's Reef, and what
    the more fanciful segment of the population refer
    to as the sunken ruins of Y'ha-nthlei, the specimen
    has, over the last decade, abandoned its original
    domain and established a new territory that is
    roughly bordered by three deep sea trenches in the
    South Pacific and the Great Barrier Reef, where it
    has been observed feeding on semiannual occasions
    on the abundance of sea life drawn there.

    The coral reef has provided excellent coverage and
    protection during these infrequent feeding periods.
    Boats are unable to navigate the shallow waters,
    and divers have been unable to keep pace as the
    specimen slipped through the razor-sharp coral
    structure. Despite numerous pursuit attempts, on
    each occasion the creature was able to leave the
    diving teams behind and slip into deeper waters.

    Once away from the reef, the creature has been
    observed to run for three separate bolt holes, all

deep sea trenches that fall far below the depth to
which equipment and divers can follow, where it
will remain for many months at a time. We know of
no other creature that can withstand the G-pres-
sures at the bottom of these trenches.

Cthylla, as the regional natives have named it, was
spotted feeding at the Barrier Reef at 9 p.m. Sept.
23rd. Three dive-teams were immediately dispatched
southeast of its location, with an additional three
teams dispatched to the north, in the coastal waters
of New Guinea, to assist in herding the target.

The dive teams, and their accompanying motor boats,
chased it for five days. There was a very real fear
it would once again escape to the Mariana or Tonga
Trench, meaning at least six months would pass
before the teams could try again.

It did an admirable job of weaving in and out of the
small South Sea islands, and two of the boats were
run aground on rocks or coral. Finally, calling on
the help of several fisherman and their skiffs, as
well as a submersible, the fleet was able to herd
the creature into open waters and through the
underwater hatch of our research vessel.

                          * * * * *

When she could no longer control her yawning, Katherine turned off
her computer and went to bed. Her dreams that night were graphic and
unpleasant, and filled with high-pitched wails, but it did not occur to
her to record that fact in her journal.

                          * * * * *

Field Journal October 10

We have been unable to put a diver in the tank with
Cthylla as yet. We can't get more than a fin in the
water before she begins inking and bolts for her
lair. Her body turns white instantaneously. The
pale form shooting through the black water resem-
bles nothing so much as a ghost floating through
the darkened halls of a haunted house.

However, Cthylla has become very social, as long as
we remain on the other side of the glass, and has
on numerous occasions suction-cupped her entire
body to the glass wall, almost as if she knows we
want to examine her. In this way, we have learned a

great deal about her anatomy and physiology. We
have determined she is female.

Working from the blood and tissue samples taken
last week during the unfortunate cat incident, and
with the long-preserved blood samples taken from
the creature which foundered the *Sea-Maid* off
Hunterby Head nearly two decades ago, Helen is cre-
ating a biogenetically engineered spermatophore.

Our team of technicians is hard at work constructing a mechanical male. Or at least the parts necessary—four electronic tentacles and a body front—for
our first attempt at artificial insemination.

We're afraid there isn't much time. Octopods have
very short life spans, and we believe Cthylla may
be the last of her kind.

The only other member of this species, that we know
of, was killed in the *Sea-Maid* incident.

The research still hasn't revealed a species name,
but local natives nicknamed that specimen "Dagon."

                        * * * * *

"Excuse me, Dr. Collum?"

David's voice bore into her brain, but Katherine's face was a mask
of composure when she looked up from her computer at her work station in the lab.

"I don't mean to bother you," he said insincerely, "but, can an octopus have more than eight legs?"

"Of course not. The prefix 'octo' means eight."

"Then I think you're going to have to rework your phylogeny. And
you might teach your lab assistants how to count."

"What are you talking about?"

He pointed to the tank.

Cthylla had twelve tentacles.

The research team clustered around the tank in disbelief.

"Is there any chance we miscounted?" Katherine asked.

"All of us?" Helen asked, incredulously. "That's impossible."

·   "Feeder" spoke up. "Believe me, I know exactly how many tentacles
Cthylla has, and exactly where they are, before I open that hatch. I don't
want her grabbing me 'cause she's hungry!"

"Well, she has twelve now," Katherine said. "How do we account
for that?"

"The *Octopus vulgaris* can regrow a partial tentacle if it loses one to a predator," Helen pointed out.

"But not four full ones in a matter of hours!"

"Are there any unusual markings on the new legs?"

"Can anyone distinguish between the old and new ones ...."

The lab erupted in a babble of unanswerable questions.

* * * * *

Field Journal October 12

> Today Cthylla has only eight legs. There is no sign that the other four ever existed. As a result of the disappearing legs, debate rages among the team about her phylogeny. Half the team insists that she must be in the giant squid family.

> But that is based strictly on her size. While giant squids do grow to twelve meters, far bigger than the largest known octopus, Cthylla still dwarfs that to such a proportion the issue becomes irrelevant. And squids only have ten arms.

> I remain convinced that she is related to the Octopods because of her ink sac and her lack of internal shell structure. The squid family exhibits neither of these characteristics.

* * *

Field Journal October 15

> She is eating far more than we expected. Then, little is known about the feeding patterns of many of the Octopodidae family.

> We have hired a family-owned fishing company off the coast of New Guinea to provide one hundred pounds of live fish each day.

> The cost is far more than we budgeted for, but Arkham Industries has assured us that there's no problem.

> It won't be a concern much longer, as all species in the Octopodidae family stop feeding after they've laid their eggs, and die soon after.

> We have discovered that she prefers crustaceans and mollusks, especially prawns and giant clams, but as an economic necessity, we favor the larger, cheaper game fish such as blue marlin, mackerel, sailfish, and tuna. While we keep at least a half dozen of

these large fish swimming in her tank at all times,
she seems constantly hungry, and begs for treats.

Today, when her increasingly insistent demands were
ignored, she shot a stream of water through her filter vent at Feeder. The water struck him full in
the chest, knocking him on his back and sending him
hydroplaning across the floor. Afraid of more urgent
messages, he dropped in the last two giant oysters.

I observed her hunting technique. She crawled
through the "octopus garden" of discarded bones and
shells which litters the front yard of her lair,
carefully sifting among them until she found two
long, sturdy bones. Then she crawled quietly across
the floor till she was just within reach of the
oysters. She waited until they opened their shells.
Then she quickly dropped the bones lengthwise across
the openings, simultaneously. The oysters tried to
snap their shells closed, but it was too late.

Cthylla dragged her prizes into her lair to eat in
privacy. Twenty minutes later, she tossed the
shells out her door. She did not come out for several hours. I can't help but think she was taking
an afternoon nap.

* * *

Field Journal October 17

Mike The Mechanical Monster is done. The mantle is
just a large, red mylar balloon with black stripes
painted on it. But the four mechanical tentacles
are a wonder. Based on current Hollywood FX tech-
nology, the techs have rigged up sleeves and a harness backpack that allow the tentacle to mirror
human arm motion.

I will operate the foreplay arms, while Helen handles the insemination.

We've been practicing on large boulders set up in
the secondary tank, which we have prepared in case
Cthylla shows any signs of cannibalism following
the birth. After two days of practice, we feel comfortable enough with the equipment that we intend
to make our first insemination attempt tonight.

* * * * *

"'The dreamer dying faces death with scorn,
"'And in his seed will rise again reborn!'"

"David, what are you muttering now?" Katherine asked, not really wanting an answer, as she slipped into her harness and checked the controls.

"Just a bit of Alhazred's ancient poetry. Perhaps you've heard his most famous couplet? Seems quite fitting for the evening's event.

> 'That is not dead which can eternal lie,
> 'And with strange aeons even death may die.'"

"Thanks for that bit of literary brilliance. Now will you get out of our way, please?"

Using the winch, the techs lowered "Mike" into the tank. Cthylla had retreated to her lair, but was peeking out, watching the proceedings.

When it became apparent the humans weren't invading, she crawled out and ambled awkwardly toward her visitor.

* * * * *

Field Journal October 18

Intercourse occurred! Now we have to wait and see if Cthylla lays her eggs.

It took an hour of flirting and teasing, with Cthylla frequently bolting back to her lair. Finally, she moved closer and let "Mike" touch her. Her skin changed from the heavy bumps that indicate fear or anger to a velvety smoothness. Her color changed to a pale green, indicating sexual arousal.

Like other Octopods, she expected a period of fore-play, where the male caresses the female, stroking her body. But we had not anticipated this phase would last more than two hours! My arms were aching horribly by the time Cthylla finally allowed "Mike" to grasp and hold her while the scooped tentacle inserted the spermatophore into her mantle cavity.

An hour into the process, one of the techs offered to relieve me, but I was afraid that the break in action might upset Cthylla.

At times I saw Cthylla watching me, rather than her mechanical suitor, almost as if she knew it was me touching her. That's impossible, of course. We stood well away from the tank, relying on video monitors to guide our actions.

I am amazed we were successful on our first attempt. Cthylla has been far more cooperative than most lab specimens. Perhaps her size gives her con-

fidence. When one is as large as an apartment
building, one has few natural predators.

A side note, the cat is missing, and hasn't been
seen for several days. The Feeder thinks it may
have jumped to the fishing boat, lured by the smell
of abundant food, during one of their deliveries.

* * *

Field Journal October 22

Cthylla has spent the last two days actively
engaged in housekeeping. She began by sweeping all
the refuse out of her lair: stray shell fragments,
cartilage, and bones from her many meals. Which
solved one mystery at least—the disappearance of
the cat. Its skeleton was in the "dustbin."

Helen was quite upset at the discovery. She had
become rather attached to the creature. It did not
surprise me overly much. It isn't the only example
of a marine carnivore preying on land animals and
birds.

One of my earliest summer internships was a study
of tiger sharks. Albatross chicks were a favorite
delicacy of theirs. I'll never forget watching the
sharks lunge out of the water to catch the birds in
low flight.

In a move that did surprise me, Cthylla continued
her cleaning efforts, sweeping up the extensive
octopus garden that surrounded her lair into a
heaping pile below the feeding hatch. She moved to
a distant corner and waited patiently as the Feeder
netted the discards out.

* * *

Field Journal October 23

It has been our custom to work though the night and
sleep by day. Cthylla, like all Octopods, is a noc-
turnal creature. We generally retire when she does,
around 8 a.m. We were surprised to discover she had
worked through the day yesterday. When we returned
to the lab this evening, we found she had completely rearranged her lair, repositioning each of the
500-pound boulders to build a new cave, somewhat
closer to the viewing wall, but much taller.

As I had hoped, these domestic preparations were
prenatal in nature. Cthylla began laying her eggs
this evening.

They look like a cluster of giant phosphorous jala-
peño peppers hanging from the ceiling of her lair.
Each oblong egg is roughly the length of a banana.

There is only one strand of eggs, only 200-250
total. We are not sure what to make of this. The
common octopus lays approximately 200,000, of which
only one or two will survive.

* * *

Field Journal October 24

The egg strand hangs well inside the cave, but the
technicians have rigged up spotlights and attached
high powered zoom lenses to the video cameras. We
have captured some spectacular video, and the team
is quite excited about documentary and publishing
prospects.

I can't share their enthusiasm, however. I fully
realize our work will revolutionize this branch of
marine biology, but at present I'm too exhausted to
think about it.

David grates ever worse on my nerves. Today, when
he laughed at the team's discussion of a documentary, I found myself having to defend him physically when one of the junior research assistants took
a swing at him. He quoted more obscure poetry
before strolling blithely into the hall.

The words were nonsense, of course, but they have
stayed with me. Perhaps it was the subtle menace in
his tone. I do not trust David. His poem of the day
was this:

"We lie on a placid island of ignorance in
the midst of black seas of infinity and it
was not meant that we should voyage far.
The sciences, each straining in its own
direction, have hitherto harmed us little;
but some day the piecing together of disso-
ciated knowledge will open up such terrifying vistas of reality, and of our frightful
position therein, that we shall either go
mad from the revelation or flee from the
deadly light into the peace and safety of a
new dark age …."

It is the antithesis of all that I stand for as a
scientist. I can not understand this man's motives
or thinking.

However, it does make me wonder, why has David been
so cooperative? He's annoying, but he hasn't really

interfered with anything we've done. On previous
missions, he's fought my actions at every turn.

* * *

Field Journal October 27

Cthylla has begun the egg-cleaning and care rituals
common among Octopods. Twice daily she oxygenates
the eggs with streams of water from her siphon,
then gently cleans them with her suction cups. The
delicacy with which she handles them, in comparison
with her enormous size, is amazing.

Our Fertility Specialist believes Cthylla is winnowing the eggs, and claims she has discarded at
least three of them.

I have my doubts, however. Egg winnowing is not a
trait common to other species in this family. More
likely, the Fertility Specialist's first count was
inaccurate.

* * *

Field Journal October 29

Cthylla actually pounded on the hatch today. We are
uncertain what this means. Her restlessness is
apparent, however. She paces the confines of her
tank, her tentacles whipping furiously as she
stalks across the aquarium floor.

* * *

Field Journal October 30

Cthylla began wailing in that painfully high pitch
as we left the lab this morning. We are at a loss
for the cause of her cry. The eggs are growing
well, and she continues to treat them with the
utmost care.

I can't believe she's crying for her mate, as the
Fertility Specialist suggests. In no Octopod family
does the mate help care for the young.

We are monitoring the water conditions carefully to
be sure it isn't a chemistry problem.

We are checking the hatch and all possible escape
points carefully, as she is exploring those same
areas from the inside of the tank.

I don't know how I will stand her cries if they
continue throughout our sleep period. I've barely
slept in all the time I've been aboard this junker.

```
And what little I do get is plagued by horrid
dreams. I often regret sleeping at all.
```

```
To make matters worse, Tomorrow is The Anniversary.
```

* * *

```
Field Journal October 31
```

```
    Personal Note
```

```
    Damn Cthylla's cry! I'd finally fallen asleep when
    she started up again, her wails corrupting my
    dreams before I woke. Though I'm not sorry I woke
    when I did! I remember only a snippet of the night-
    mare, but that image alone was more than my nerves
    can take.
```

```
    I was on a delivery room table. I'd just given
    birth. But it was David standing there with me, not
    Frank. He held up our baby. It was grotesquely
    deformed! It had four little legs, and a horrible
    soft beak where the mouth should be ….
```

* * * * *

Helen knocked softly on Cassie's door. It was 4 p.m., hours before lab duty began, but Helen was worried about her friend. She'd watched a deep depression settle over Cassie during the last week that no success in the lab could stave off.

Receiving no answer, she knocked again, louder, and called out, "Cassie, it's me, Helen. Can I come in?"

She listened, heard nothing. She tried the latch. The door opened.

The room was dark. It took a moment before her eyes adjusted and she could see Cassie, still in her night clothes, sitting up in bed, clutching a pillow to her face to muffle her sobs. Helen sat down beside her. She said nothing. There were no words that could take this pain away.

Once a year, the doors to Cassie's heart came unlocked and all the grief she kept imprisoned there poured out. Grief for a dead husband and an unborn child.

Helen pulled Cassie into her arms and gently rocked her back and forth, as one might comfort a child.

* * *

When Helen left, Katherine forced herself from the bed and into the bathroom. She showered and dressed, even applied makeup with unusual precision, all of it with shaking hands and deep breaths, as she tried to calm her nerves. With a Herculean effort of will, she marched to the door, opened it, and stepped out into the hall.

She made it down the corridor and around the first corner before the first sob racked her body. She lurched against the wall. Her back pressed against the cold metal; she slid slowly to the floor. Her head buried in her knees, her arms locked around her legs, she hung on in desperation as the flood gates opened again.

When the tears ran out, leaving only stuttering hiccups, she crawled on hands and knees back to her room.

* * *

David Gaughan prowled the corridors looking for his prey. She hadn't been in the lab at all this work-night. He had thought there was nothing that could shake her resolve, topple her unyielding strength. But there were hidden dimensions to Katherine, despite her near-seamless facade.

David hid dark secrets behind his facade, too. Far darker than Katherine could ever comprehend.

* * * * *

Field Journal November 1

    Personal

    It is possible that I have misjudged David Gaughan.
    Our jobs have too often pitted us against each
    other as enemies (despite my feelings that we are
    each fighting for the same thing—the preservation
    of the sea's rich diversity of marine life).

    Last night I saw the more human side of David.
    Concerned that I wasn't in the lab, he came to my
    quarters. He found me in tears. As there was no way
    to hide them, and he refused to leave until I told
    him what was wrong, I was forced to tell him the
    whole story.

    God! Even now I have trouble writing about it!

    I told him about the artificial insemination proce-
    dures and miscarriages. I told him about my hus-
    band's boating accident and death, on Oct. 28th. I
    told him that I had been pregnant, with the first
    chance to carry a baby to term. I fell apart, lost
    control, when I heard the news. Went into shock. My
    body terminated the pregnancy. The doctors couldn't

```
save the infant. October 31st. How badly I wanted
that child. I can't face this … can't face him.

David comforted me. I let the comforting go too far.
But it's been so long since I was with a man. …
```

* * * * *

There was an urgent pounding on Katherine's door, but she took the time to save and close the computer file before she answered it.

It was … Jim? … she was so bad with names … the Feeder.

"Dr. Cullom, come quick! There's been an accident in the lab!"

* * *

At first Katherine could see no signs of trouble other than the huddle of team members in the corner, whispering and watching her. But at Helen's work station there was evidence of a struggle. The computer, still on, though the monitor was dimming as the batteries failed, had crashed to the floor.

Her voice dead of emotion, she instructed a lab assistant to pick up the computer. "Save her work. There could be important information there."

A box of slides had been swept off the table. Glass splinters littered the area. Halfway down the aisle, the bar stool from Helen's station lay on its side in a puddle of water.

Katherine kneeled down to avoid the glare of the lights on the metal floor. She could just make out the damp, suction-cup marked trail that led back to the tank. The feeding hatch was closed. But a femur, with fresh bits of muscle and tendon still clinging to the joints, lay in the "octopus garden", right outside Cthylla's door.

As they watched, the rib cage was flung out of the lair.

"Kill it," Katherine whispered. Her body began to shake.

Grasping a table leg for support, she stood stiffly.

The Feeder was trying, unsuccessfully, to fight off tears? panic? horror? Katherine couldn't tell. She had little practice reading people's emotions.

He babbled at her. "It … it ate Dr. Hydreah because it was hungry! It's all my fault! I … but … octopuses are supposed to stop eating after they lay their eggs! Why is she still eating?"

Katherine knew no words of comfort. She offered the only advice she could. "Feed her now. Call the fisherman. Sedate her if you have to, but get the body out of there!

"Take pictures first. I want a full autopsy—including blood analysis for toxins. Let's see how that poison works on the human system; and an analysis of the skin abrasion for feeding patterns. Let's at least learn something from this!"

She strode out of the lab, well aware of the angry, shocked looks the team was giving her.

Katherine made it back to her quarters, locked the door, and turned on the radio before her knees gave way and the tears began. She composed herself and turned to her computer.

* * * * *

```
Field Journal November 1
    Personal Addendum
    Helen Is Dead. Because I Was Fucking David Gaughan
    Instead Of Doing My Job!
```

* * * * *

The team avoided Katherine as much as possible after that. In reality, there was no great difference in the amount of contact between her and the team.

Katherine did nothing to try to fix the rift in the weeks that followed, though she felt Helen's loss far worse than any of them, and she desperately needed someone to talk to. She kept her distance because she didn't want them to see that she had morning sickness.

* * * * *

```
Field Journal November 21
    Arkham Industries has sent me a new assistant to
    fill Helen's position. His name is Johnny Depone.
    His specialty is ocean ecology.
    I'm not particularly fond of him, though I can't
    put my finger on the reason why. I sometimes think
```

he's following a different agenda, though I can in
no way criticize his performance or dedication.

Perhaps it is just my changing hormones, or the
loss of Helen.

On the positive side, Johnny and David are old
acquaintances, and get along well. So well that I'd
question Johnny's alliances, if I didn't hear them
arguing so often about marine conservation poli-
cies. I'm pleased with the arrangement, if for no
other reason than it provides a buffer between
David and myself.

* * *

Field Journal November 21

The eggs are the size of a beach ball now. And the
Fertility Specialist was correct. Cthylla is winnowing the eggs, eating those she deems unfit to
continue.

The Feeder, convinced that he's to blame for everything she eats, has upped her feeding to one hundred fifty pounds a day, heavy on Cthylla's
favorite delicacies. Would that the team were so
indulgent of me! There are more fish swimming in
her tank than there are people on board this boat.

* * *

Field Journal December 1

Personal

I have decided to take a brief shore leave and
visit my mother before the holidays. Undoubtedly,
most of the team will want to go home for
Christmas, if only for the weekend.

With no grandchildren in the family, we haven't
made a big fuss about Christmas in years. Though I
dread the reaction my pregnancy will cause. For
Mother, Hope Springs Eternal, and Dies Hard. Each
death is more painful.

But it should provide a welcome respite from our
usual morbid conversations regarding Frank's death,
and my dimming prospects for remarriage.

* * * * *

"Leaving without saying good-bye? I'm hurt!" David said.

Katherine tried to hide her sigh. She'd been so close to a clean get-away. She dropped her bag to the boat pilot waiting below the ladder and turned to answer.

"David, a high-impact, deep-sea oil drill couldn't pierce your heart. What do you want?"

"Nothing much," he said, smiling in a way that made Katherine queasy. "I just had a little bon voyage present for you."

He handed her an envelope, printed with the ARN! stationery.

"A very little one, I see. What is it?"

She took the documents out of the envelope.

"Just a couple of restraining orders."

Katherine looked up, shocked. "For what?"

"To protect two babies I happen to care about."

She sputtered.

"You will not abort our child," David said sternly.

Katherine started to protest, but David cut her off.

"Don't tell me that isn't why you planned this little trip."

Katherine said coldly, "I won't have to go to the trouble. You're well aware of my medical history. I've never carried an embryo to term. The odds don't improve with age. So I wouldn't start calling myself 'daddy' just yet if I were you.

"What's the other little document?"

"It protects Cthylla's baby. I won't allow you to kill and dissect it in the name of scientific research. I have the court's backing on this," he said.

"That's a little premature too, don't you think?" Katherine snapped at him. "Cthylla may eat all the eggs. She's got an appetite that just won't quit."

"Then feed her more—or I'll file a lawsuit against you for animal abuse and neglect, and toss in a wrongful death against you on behalf of Dr. Hydreah."

Katherine's eyes narrowed and she dropped her voice to a whisper. "You are way out of line! You have no right telling me what I can or can't do with my body, or with my project. I will appeal."

"I had no doubt that you would," David said. "But the babies are protected while we fight it out."

* * * * *

Field Journal December 24

It's quiet, with just Cthylla and me in the lab.
Everyone else has gone home for the holidays.

We were in a holding pattern while the eggs developed. We expected it to last several more months.
Cthylla had other plans.

There were only three eggs left when I began my
shift tonight. She was fussing with them more than
usual. She kept prodding them with her tentacles,
until at last, a small tear formed and a small tentacle poked out.

I turned the spotlight on and watched the entire
birth through the telephoto lens. It took over an
hour for the little guy to struggle out of the egg
sack, with Mamma pacing nervously the whole time.

He's a translucent milky color. His pigment sacs
should develop within a few weeks. For now, his
internal organs are clearly visible. It was amazing
to watch his little heart pumping.

He shares his mother's appetite. As soon as he
escaped from his sack, he devoured the other two
eggs.

From Cthylla's egg winnowing, and the newborn's
first meal, I think it's safe to hypothesize that
Cthylla will care for her young, rather than aban-
don it, like others in her phylum.

The timing of the birth is an odd bit of irony …
or was it planned? Perhaps Cthylla didn't want a
crowd witnessing such a private event.

* * *

Field Journal December 25

I have named the baby Cthyhni.

I'm having great fun today dropping small fish into
the tank, to assist Cthylla in her training of the
little guy. He is a natural hunter, and seems to
enjoy the thrill of the chase and kill more than
the meal itself.

I had to pay a premium to get a delivery on
Christmas, especially with the request for some
smaller fish. But I consider it a Christmas present
to myself and Cthylla.

I have decided not to recall the team today,
despite the birth. Let them enjoy their holidays. I
am quite capable of operating the cameras and
equipment for observation. And I think Cthylla will
appreciate a few days of quiet with her baby.

* * *

Field Journal December 31

> Cthyhni is growing like wildfire, and cavorts
> around the tank in a manner more befitting a seal
> than an octopus! He is a delight to watch, and
> we're getting very little work done, other than
> observing his antics.
>
> He is a master escape artist. There seems to be
> nothing we can do to make the tank escape-proof.
> Luckily, Cthylla doesn't let him wander far before
> she gently hauls him back in with one of her tenta-
> cles. The extra tentacles have reappeared. They're
> coming in handy.
>
> The team is having a party in the mess hall. I
> should drop by and toast in the New Year with some
> apple juice. But first, I want to stop by the lab.
> The team won't miss me. They'll probably enjoy
> themselves more with my absence.

Katherine hit the Save command and turned off her computer.

* * * * *

In the lab, the lights were turned down low. Katherine enjoyed the artificial twilight. She walked softly to the window of the tank and gently
rested her forehead against the cool glass.

Cthylla ambled across the floor of the tank until she reached the
window. She seemed to be studying Katherine. They watched each
other, until Katherine felt a wet tentacle on her arm.

There was no mistaking the odd sensation of an octopus' suction
cups. Katherine turned slowly, so she wouldn't frighten Cthyhni, but he
was not there. It was only then Katherine realized the tentacle was far
too large to belong to the baby. She turned back to face Cthylla, unafraid.

The tentacle grazed across her body until it reached the plump curve
of her belly. The tentacle rested there, and Katherine had the eerie feeling
Cthylla was familiar with human anatomy, and knew she was pregnant.

Cthyhni was close beside his mother, her arm wrapped lovingly
around him.

A shock coursed through Cthylla's tentacle and into Katherine's
womb. The scientist fell to the floor, convulsing.

In the tank, Cthyhni jerked and turned a ghostly white.

David Gaughan stepped from the shadows, gently picked the
woman up, and carried her back to her room.

* * *

A medivac arrived within the hour. Katherine was groggy, but still fighting as Johnny Depone packed her things. David sat with her, trying to calm her down.

"You must go to the hospital, for the baby's sake."

"The miscarriage has already started. Nothing can stop that," Katherine insisted.

"The doctors disagree. You have to go to the hospital and try."

"No!" Katherine howled. "The baby is going to die! Why can't you accept that? I want to stay here! With Cthyhni, with the baby who will live!"

"You care more about a sea monster than a human!" David accused.

"I care about what's alive, rather than what's dying in my womb!"

* * * * *

Personal Journal January 7

After much fighting with the obstetricians, they've finally relented and allowed me to have my computer. They got more than their share of concessions in exchange, though.

I am to be confined to bed for the duration of my pregnancy. It wasn't too hard to agree to that, as I still can't bring myself to believe for even one moment that the embryo inside me will live. However, between David's court orders and a doctor with no regard for my medical history, it seems we must all wait and see.

I miss the lab, and Cthylla and Cthyhni. And most of all, Helen.

I am tired of the moralizing, the pompous right-eousness of all these men, who see me as nothing but a cold-hearted bitch who cares more for her work than her unborn child. What do they know of the pain I must endure as I wait, helpless, hopeless, and without distraction, as yet another child withers and dies in my womb?

How can they ever know what that does to your head and to your heart? I can not hope this child will live! My sanity will not hold if I love and lose another child.

* * *

Personal Journal January 15

I am receiving daily reports from Johnny Depone via E-mail. The news from the lab is as dreary as my own.

Little Cthyhni has stopped eating. And Cthylla is neglecting him.

They have asked me what to do.

As a scientist, I should tell them to continue observing them. An autopsy of Cthyhni would answer many of the questions we still have about this species. But there's been enough death on this mission, and chances are good Cthyhni would survive if we released him and his mother back into their natural habitat.

We will not be sacrificing everything. We can tag and monitor the two of them.

I should order a new insemination attempt. Several international zoos could advise us on the problems of captive breeding. All the evidence—from Cthylla's continued eating, to the birth of a single baby—suggests this species goes through more than one birth cycle. But I find I haven't the heart to order the procedure.

If Arkham Industries objects to my decision, I have complete faith in David to file the necessary legal documents to see that my will is carried out.

* * *

Personal Journal April 3

I gave birth to a beautiful little boy two days ago! He was three months premature, but healthy. So tiny and perfectly formed! David was by my side.

To my bitter disappointment, they heavily sedated me. I never thought I would be blessed with childbirth. It eats at me that I could not experience the event fully.

The birth was not an easy one. I had severe hemorrhaging, horrendous pain! In all honesty, I probably couldn't have handled it without the sedation.

There was a lot of tissue damage. I have sixty-five stitches! The nurse told me this was the obstetrician's most difficult delivery in his forty years of practice.

I suffered bizarre hallucinations from the drugs, and, at one point, David tells me I screamed out in abject terror. I remember the vision vividly. There was tremendous pain and a sickening sensation of *wriggling* as the baby passed through the outer canal. (I know that's impossible, as they completely numbed my pelvis and thighs.)

I thought I saw the doctor hold up a limp, wriggly mass of flesh, full of grasping tentacles dripping blood and gore. It emitted a high-pitched wail that drilled into my brain.

I saw David take it and hold it up, like a proud papa. One of the tentacles brushed across his cheek, leaving a trail of blood and slime. Then he handed the thing to Johnny Depone, who whisked it from the room!

I blacked out at that point, possibly from the pain. Obviously, my mind was still on my work, even at such a profound moment! But I can't help but hope Cthylla and her son are well, swimming free and swooping down on some unsuspecting monster of a fish.

But enough of such musings. David and the nurse are approaching. It's lunch time for the little one. Just four pounds and six ounces—how could one so small do so much damage to my womb! He has brown eyes, and just a hint of angel-white feathery hair. And Daddy say's he's hungry! We've named our little boy Keenan.

Quotes on pages 78 and 81 are from *The Transition of Titus Crow* (Brian Lumley) and "The Call of Cthulhu" (H. P. Lovecraft), respectively.

The Reliable Vacuum Company

by James Robert Smith

It was coming up Christmas, and Jimmy wanted his wife to have something nice. For the house, he had figured. So when he opened the classifieds, looking for merchandise, something that might be suitable, he noticed the ad: *Vacuum*, it had read, *The finest in creation*. And there had been a phone number.

Two years before, Jimmy Welk and his wife, Maye, had cashed in his $72,000 in Wal-Mart stock and had bought a mobile home on four acres of partially wooded land in Midvale, North Carolina. That's about fifty miles north of Charlotte for those not familiar with Southern geography. The double-wide had three bedrooms and one and a half baths. Jimmy thought that the half a bath description was kind of silly, actually, since it was a four by four room with a sink and a crapper. To his way of thinking, he had one bath and an extra crapper. But such were the vagaries of mobile home propaganda.

It was Jimmy and Maye's intention, after having liquidated those fifteen years of accumulated Wal-Mart stock, to semiretire. However, they soon found that even with a paid-for roof over their heads, and no payments remaining on either his Ford pickup truck or Maye's Audi Fox (she'd bought it used: 50,000 miles), they were both going to have to keep full-time jobs to sustain the demands for life's necessities and the odd emergency now and again. At fifty-five and fifty-four years old respectively, they had some time to go to start collecting their Social Security retirement. So it was still going to be forty hours a week for both of them. Such was life.

The double-wide was the first home they had actually owned. They'd raised four kids in various apartments over the years, and now that they had 1,500 square feet of heated living space, it was all for them and not their kids. Technically speaking, they had been *Maye's* kids, as the three boys and one girl had been part of the package when Jimmy had married Maye. As near as Jimmy and Maye could figure, he shot blanks, for she'd never gotten pregnant by him in all her child-bearing years with him. He hadn't minded feeding and clothing another man's offspring, and the four had turned out okay, despite the fact that they didn't visit that often. At any rate, they were all out of the house, making their own livings, and that was what counted.

But those 1,500 square feet were sometimes a chore for them to keep up. They only used one bedroom, and the second largest of those was full of Jimmy's NASCAR racing memorabilia. With both of them working all day, it was all they could do to keep up the place. So Jimmy had invited the salesman over when he had called that day; as he'd decided, it was almost Christmas and it would be nice to buy Maye a nice home appliance.

"What was the name of the company?" Maye asked. Her hair was still jet black and thick and reflected the light, something which amazed Jimmy. His own hair was thinning badly and he had taken to rubbing it down with Bryl Cream (they still made that stuff, he was happy to know) and combing it in a strange pattern that covered all the bald spots. People laughed at him when he wasn't around to hear, but at least he wasn't bald. *Look at that idiot*, they would say, *how the hell does he comb it like that?*

"Reliable Vacuum Company, I think it was." Jimmy stopped reading the paper and laid it across his thin, naked legs. His stick-like shins jutted out the far end of the newspaper tent he'd made, his toes pointing east and west in a severe, almost extreme example of his pigeon-toed gait. On the north side of the *Charlotte Observer* shelter he'd formed over his crotch, his gut was a soft pink dome fuzzed in intermittent black. "At least I *think* that's what he said. Guy had a strange accent."

"What kind of accent? He ain't colored, is he?" Maye was knitting a comforter for one of their new grandkids, the yellow and blue and red stripes sprawled over her own nakedness as she worked. Both of them were as nude as newborns, for the first thing they did when they got home was strip down and relax.

"I don't think he was a Negro." (He said it *knee-grow*). "He could be. Who cares, these days? You don't, do you?" His wife's opinions often surprised him, even after thirty years.

"No. I don't rightly care one way or the other," she said. She knitted a bit. "What time is it? We ought to put some clothes on before he gets here, don't you think?"

Jimmy just stared at her from behind a barrier of *Charlotte Observer* sports pages. Maye could see Jimmy's black, squinty eyes looking at her from beyond a big color photograph of someone named Kerry Collins. Collins was a quarterback. "No, Maye," he finally said. "I think we ought to greet the man at the door naked as we are right now. Invite his black ass right on in to tell us all about his vacuum cleaner." He said *ott* for ought, and *nekkid* for naked.

"All right," Maye muttered. "That's enough of that." She stood up, her fifty-four year old breasts hanging pendulously, almost to her navel, and Jimmy quickly looked back at the latest NFL standings. "We'd best get dressed if he's going to be here in twenty minutes," she added.

So they dressed.

At six-thirty, as they were sitting at the dining room table, they heard wheels softly smashing the gravel in their driveway. Jimmy had spent four hundred dollars on a couple of loads of freshly crushed granite for their drive and under the carport. Despite the expense, or perhaps because of it, he enjoyed listening to visiting cars squashing the stuff a little more into the ground. "That must be him," Jimmy said, standing, leaving Maye to sip her hot, black coffee.

At the door, Jimmy looked out in the almost dark to see a shadowed figure scampering around an equally dark auto. He heard a door close solidly and watched as the trunk of the car went silently up. The figure rummaged about there in the trunk, and Jimmy squinted pointlessly, trying to make out the race of their visitor. It was just too dark to tell. As he stood there on the wooden deck he'd recently added to the front of the home, the figure straightened, the trunk thumped down without so much as a hint of a squeak, and the salesman was tramping across the irregular surface of pale granite shards.

Well, Jimmy thought, as the man came into the light of the single 60-watt bulb that made a sick yellow light above his head, *he is a knee-grow*. A brownish face gazed at him as it came up the steps to the deck, a white box in the man's arms. *Well, maybe not a knee-grow; but certainly not a white man*, now that he was closer and in the light. *An Oriental, maybe*. Jimmy had seen lots of Orientals when he had cleaned fuel systems for the armed forces when he'd been a younger man. Maye often thought that it had been because he worked around all of those gas fumes that he shot blanks. Jimmy didn't know and didn't care.

"Howdy," Jimmy said as the dark-skinned little man came close. "You're here about the vacuum cleaner, right? From Reliable?" Jimmy smiled, showing his straight, false teeth.

"Yes," the man said, even that one word coming out with something of an accent. "I am here. To show you our vacuum."

Jimmy opened the door for him and ushered the visitor inside. Maye had moved, sitting so that she faced the door, Jimmy coming in behind the salesman. "Maye. This here's the man from the vacuum company. This here's my wife, Maye Welk. I'm sorry, but I've forgot your name," Jimmy added as the other stooped to place the white box on the floor.

"Oh. My name is Mr. Jeng," he said, extending one plump hand to take Jimmy's. "Mr. Jeng from Leng," he said, giggling.

Jimmy and Maye giggled, too, but only because their visitor had. Neither of them knew what Mr. Jeng had said that was funny, but since he was a foreigner, they were willing to humor him. After smiling a bit, Mr. Jeng spoke again. "Are you ready to hear me tell about the vacuum," he asked. "It is a wonderful vacuum, so much better than any other, and I am certain you would be content to have this one, from our company."

"Reliable," Jimmy said. "It *is* reliable, after all." He grinned at his straw of a joke, but Mr. Jeng did not; nor did Maye, who only frowned into her coffee.

"If that is how you wish to refer to the name. Yes," Mr. Jeng said.

"Well, have a seat with us here in the den," Jimmy told him, indicating the part of their great room that was carpeted, that held their coffee table and easy chair and big, overpadded couch. The television sat on its perch adjacent to the fireplace. "And you can tell us about your product."

Mr. Jeng moved his white box from where it sat before the door to the Berber carpeting, where it descended half an inch or so into the soft stuff. Jimmy noted that the box must indeed be heavy to do that, but Mr. Jeng handled it so lightly that he couldn't imagine it being heavy enough to compress the carpet fibers in such a manner. "You wish to hear about our vacuum," he said. "You wish to know how ours is superior to any other."

Maye leaned forward, eyeing the box. "Better than an Electrolux," she asked.

"Eh. Yes. Superior in every way," Jeng said, raising his plump left forefinger, aiming it to the sky. "Their machines merely *draw*," he said, sucking in a breath. "They only *pull* ... air and ... dirt into a *bag*." He paused, smiled. His hosts noted how *full* his smile was. "*Our* machines, though, create a *true* vacuum. *Our* machines draw *out* the dirt, the *matter*, and one has to trouble himself over it never." He emphasized his points like a good evangelist, Maye noted; she liked his style.

"What do you mean?" Jimmy asked. "What do you mean, *no trouble*? Are you talking maintenance? I know all about maintenance. I clean the machinery where I work, and I understand how stuff breaks down."

"Our machine needs no maintenance," Mr. Jeng said. He emphasized it with all sincerity. Maye's eyes widened. Jimmy squinted, revealing his skepticism. "Is true," Mr. Jeng said, sensing Jimmy's disbelief.

"How?" Nothing worked without maintenance. Jimmy knew this, for when he was a kid, he had thought that he could create a perpetual motion machine and had studied the problem. It couldn't be done. One of his teachers once had explained to him about energy and friction.

"First," Mr. Jeng said, "I must explain to you how a normal vacuum works." He himself now squinted. "Like your *Electrolux*." All three of them laughed. And he pulled a drawing tablet from his coat, and a pen from his shirt pocket, and he began to sketch, explaining himself as he drew. Occasionally, he made notes, as if by accident, little scribbles at the edges of the sheets, something that looked to be letters, but not in English, not in any type of writing Jimmy or Maye had ever encountered. And Jimmy had been as far away as an Army base in Japan.

After almost an hour had passed, Jimmy and Maye knew everything there was to know about the construction and operation of the conventional vacuum cleaner. "Why, they're just little motors that *pull*," Maye exclaimed when Mr. Jeng had put his pad and pencil away.

"You are wise," he told Maye. "You are indeed a wise woman." He smiled again.

Maye was staring now at Mr. Jeng's white box. "That's your machine," she asked. "You brought a model with you, right?"

"A model? No. The actual machine, yes. Indeed. You would like a demonstration." He leaned forward, his hands on his knees.

Before their guest could stand, Jimmy rose and, putting a hand on Mr. Jeng's shoulder, spoke up. He had almost said nothing when his hand seemed to have gouged a bit too far into Jeng's shoulder without encountering anything that felt like bone; almost like a very full sponge, Jimmy considered. "Um. I'm kind of dry, myself. I'm going to have a drink before you start. Would you like something?"

Mr. Jeng looked up at his host, almost as if puzzled. "Eh. What you are having," he said. "I would have that, too. Yes." As if making a grave decision.

"Well. I've got tea. But I don't want no tea. And we have beer, but you don't look like a Bud man to me."

"Bud," Jeng asked.

"See? I thought so." Jimmy looked across to Maye who only shrugged. "What about non-bonded liquor? You like that, Mr. Jeng?"

"Non-bonded? In what way? How do you mean," Jeng asked, showing a little confusion.

"Well. Home brew. Non-taxed."

Before he could continue, Jeng waved, as if waving him away. "I have what *you* have," he said. "Is fine."

With that, Jimmy went to the cupboard and pulled down a large Mason jar filled with white corn liquor. Welk eyed the clear liquid in the jar: pure, distilled, ass-kicking pleasure. He took down three small glasses and poured each of them a shot. He handed a glass each to Maye and Mr. Jeng, went back for his, and brought the big Mason jar to the den and set it on the coffee table.

Holding his own glass out to their guest, Jimmy saluted him with the drink. "Cheers and bottoms up," Jimmy said.

Hesitantly, Mr. Jeng mimicked the action and turned his glass up, draining it swiftly. Maye and Jimmy watched him, his head upturned, the glass at his lips (empty), his eyes seeming to lock onto the ceiling. A few seconds passed and they gazed at one another and then back to Mr. Jeng. He twitched, moved, set the glass carefully on the coffee table.

As the dark, little man fumbled with the box, reaching inside, Jimmy looked at Maye and shrugged. "You liked that, Mr. Jeng?"

"Er. Yes," he said, halting in the midst of his movements. "That is indeed a strange concoction," he admitted. "I enjoy immensely," he smiled, his teeth showing even more than before, if that was possible. Maye giggled.

He fumbled about with whatever was in the box a second or two more. Maye and Jimmy heard metallic clicking there, a kind of whirring that stirred the box lid then quickly stopped as Jeng made a swift movement with his left hand. He stopped again, staring into the space of the dark box, the shadows there into which neither Maye nor Jimmy seemed to be able to peer. He struggled with thoughts, with the strange sensations tingling through him; with orders to blend in clashing with commands to remain *true*.

"In fact," Jeng said. "I would indeed like another sample of that drink. May I?" He reached for his glass and his fingers were already touching the Mason jar.

"Sure," Jimmy said. "Be our guest." He smiled. Maye stifled a laugh.

This time, Mr. Jeng filled his glass to the rim, quickly put the edge of it to his lips, and in a fluid movement consumed the contents. His eyes shone back the lamplight in the room, like a pair of polished agates. He squinted, smiled; showing gums, this time. Maye could not suppress a gasp.

Before either of them could say or do a thing, Mr. Jeng put down his glass, lifted up the Mason jar. And he drained the whole damned thing. When the last of the white lightning had vanished past his lips, after he had put the jar back onto the tabletop, he spoke. "You do not mind, do you?"

Whereupon he promptly fell asleep.

In a moment, after the shock wore off, Jimmy placed his hands on his knees, and with a grunt he stood up. "Mr. Jeng," he said. He edged toward the little man who was now lying back in their easy chair, his box before him (the lid drawing and relaxing in a weird manner), his head thrown limply back with his slick, black hair haloed around it, snoring. "Mr. Jeng?" Tentatively, Jimmy reached out and touched the sleeper. "Mr. Jeng," he asked again.

"What do we do, now?" Maye said.

"Hell if I know." Jimmy shrugged, looking down at Jeng.

"Is he okay?" Maye still did not move.

"I think so. Just sleeping." Jimmy leaned in close to hear Jeng's breathing. "I just don't think he ever had no white lightning before. That's all."

Maye finally moved, bowing her head and clasping her hands behind her skull. She always did that in moments of stress. "But what the heck are we supposed to do?"

"Calm down, Maye. It ain't like we killed him or nothing. He's just out drunk is all."

"But in our *house*. A *stranger*," she almost shrieked it.

"Well, I reckon I can call that number. We still have it? I think I had it on the refrigerator."

Maye looked guilty. "I threw it away. And it ain't in the paper this week, 'cause I already checked. That ad only ran last week." She sighed, looking at Mr. Jeng asleep in Jimmy's easy chair. "What'll we do, Jimmy?"

Jimmy was already thinking ahead. He was on his knees, opening that white box. "I'm gonna go ahead and try this thing out," he told her. "Heck. If it's any good, we can order one. I reckon this is his demonstrator. Wonder if he'd sell the demonstrator," he added. "Might be cheaper."

Jimmy had the flaps of the box opened wide, and there seemed to be a kind of sigh from inside it as he pulled them up and folded them back.

"Doesn't look like any vacuum cleaner I ever saw," Maye said.

"Don't, does it?" Jimmy was lifting it out, his hands grasping the sides of a pale metal cylinder that seemed featureless except for a small wheel on one end and a wide tube that extended from what Jimmy assumed to be the front of the simple contraption. "It's kind o' light," Jimmy said. "I thought it was heavy. Look how the box is squashed down in the carpet. Must be the box is heavy."

"How does it work?" Maye asked, bending in to get a better look. "Don't seem like much, does it?"

"Ain't nowhere to plug it in," Jimmy told her. "Hell. It ain't even *got* a plug. How the hell does it work?" He turned and looked at Mr. Jeng. "Wish he was awake. Now I'm curious."

"Any instructions on it?"

Jimmy turned the thing over, noticing the warmth of the fleshy tube that extended from the front. "Nope. Just this weird writin' on it. Like that stuff he was scribbling on the notebook. Must be some kind of Chinese, or something like that. I cain't read it."

"Any instructions in the box?"

Jimmy, as if struck by the muse, put the machine down and reached back for the box. Propped against one side was a booklet printed on yellow paper. "Sure is," he said, bringing it out.

The two of them stood and took the booklet to the table, where they laid it out. It was a single sheet folded in quarters. "What's it say?" Maye pushed down an unruly corner that was curling back toward the center of the page.

"*Ithaqua*," Jimmy read. "*A spatial connection to the great Ithaqua.*" He looked toward Maye. "That's in New York state," he told her. "I was there once. Passed through on my way to an Army base where I cleaned out a big fuel tank. Two-story job about the size of Eastland Mall," he added.

"I've heard of it," Maye told him. "I just didn't know it was spelled like that. And what's a *spatial connection*? You fix them at work?"

"I don't know," Jimmy admitted. "Let's read more."

*"Calling Ithaqua requires utmost concentration. One must have the correct
desire and appropriate offering. Once called, the connection is made and the winds
can be commanded, controlled by one adept."* Jimmy scratched his head,
upsetting his carefully groomed scalp so that bald spots appeared; he
looked back at the machine. "What the hell does *that* mean?"

"What's the rest of the instructions say?" Maye again put the palm
of her hand on the page, straightening it out. "I don't understand *any* of
that. What language is that?"

Jimmy stared at it. *"R'lyeh cfaugh n'tlni* ... what kind of shit is this?
This ain't gonna do us any good. It must be whatever language they
speak where Mr. Jeng comes from."

"What about that picture there?" Maye was pointing at a diagram
in the bottom left corner of the page. It showed a pair of hands adjust-
ing the metal wheel that was attached to one featureless end of the cylinder. "Why don't we try that? Maybe that'll turn it on, or something."

Jimmy refolded the instructions and tossed them back into the box.
"It's worth a try," he said. Bending back to the cylinder, he took the
wheel and turned it until it clicked. Up close, you could see a series of
notches on the cylinder wall and corresponding marks on the wheel. He
turned it to the first notch. Something happened.

"What the hell was that?" Maye said. She rarely cursed. Outside,
the wind had picked up.

"Sounded like a tree fell over. Wish the floodlights in the back yard
hadn't gone out." He bent back to the machine, felt at the end of the
six-foot tube, noticing again its flesh-like warmth. He thought of his
penis, for some reason. "Don't feel no suction," he told Maye. "I'm
gonna try the next setting."

Jimmy turned the wheel another notch, and they *felt* it again.
"What the *hell* is that?" Maye asked. The wind was rattling the bare
branches outside. Dry leaves were playing a parched tune against the
side of their home.

"Feels weird," Jimmy said. He put his hand on the end of the tube.
This time there was something: a slight pulling, air going in. "I think
it's working," Jimmy told Maye, smiling up at her. "Must be some kind
of battery inside it."

"Make it go," Maye told him. "I wanna try it out."

Squatting on the floor, Jimmy turned the wheel three notches up.
Because the tube suddenly lengthened, became even hotter in his grasp,
because it resembled something strong and fleshy and somehow *naughty*,
Maye did not remark when the wind outside correspondingly shrieked

and did not quite shake their home like a rudely nudged cardboard box. "It's *working*," Jimmy announced. "Man, it's really got a pull." The tube was drawing visibly, now. The Berber carpet was stirring at the tube's open end, and they could actually see dirt coming up from within the tightly packed fibers and vanishing down into the cylinder.

Maye got up and took the tube from Jimmy's hand. "Oooo," she exclaimed, feeling it stiffen in her hands. "Really pulls, don't it?" She went round and about the carpet, seeing specks and flecks and bits of leaves and trash going into the tube. "Lordy. I didn't know this carpet was so dirty." Round and round she went, until the carpet had been vacuumed. Mr. Jeng continued to sleep soundlessly.

"Want to try somewhere else? Might as well take advantage of it while he's asleep," Jimmy told her.

"What about around the washer and dryer," she said.

"It's pretty dirty back there," he said. "Let's do it." But as Maye began to lift up the cleaner, Jimmy stopped her. "I'm going to turn it up." He knelt and turned the wheel up to almost its highest setting.

This time, they could not ignore the sound of the wind screaming outside. This time, the winter winds had definitely uprooted one of their big pines and had lain it flat. They felt the impact and Jimmy hoped his storage shed was still in one piece. "Lord, what a storm," Jimmy was saying.

But Maye did not hear him. She was screaming. The tube had stiffened yet again in her grasp, had lengthened, and she could not hold it. One of the cushions from the couch leaped toward the end of the tube and stuck fast there as the machine strained to suck it down. "Turn it off, Jimmy. I think it ain't meant to go this fast. Not in a home, anyways."

Before Jimmy could touch the wheel that seemed to regulate the machine, he watched in a kind of frozen horror as the couch cushion bent impossibly and *vanished* like an old memory down the tube. He heard a soft exchange of air as the tube bulged slightly and the cushion went into the cylinder. "How the *hell*?"

And then the couch was slowly creeping toward the end of that tube; that tube that Maye was holding as if it were the tail of a large and slowly growling tiger. "Jimmy! Make it stop! It's sucking the *couch*!"

It can't be. That thought went around in Jimmy's head a few times before he bent back to the little wheel. His fingers fumbled at the simple control, but now it seemed locked, stuck in that next to last notch. "I cain't turn it off, Maye. It won't move!"

Slowly, inexorably, their couch was inching toward the end of that tube. Maye still held fast. What else could she do? "Mr. Jeng," Jimmy screamed. "Mr. Jeng, wake up!" Mr. Jeng slept on.

"Point it away from the couch," Jimmy told her. She did, aiming it up a bit, and the drapes above the couch came loose without so much as a pause and went hurtling down the tubing. Jimmy thought he could see their window glass bulging toward them. He pushed Maye's hands until the tube was aimed once more at the couch, which skidded along the carpet toward them.

"Jesus and Mary," Jimmy said. "Wake him up, Maye. Let go and wake him up."

"I'm afraid to let go," she told him. Indeed, she was a wise woman.

"Hell with it," Jimmy said. He knelt again to the little wheel.

"What are you going to do?" Maye asked, watching their couch coming closer.

"I'm gonna turn it up all the way. Maybe the wheel just goes all the way around and starts back to the 'off' switch. I've seen switches like that. In the Army," he added, remembering a big explosion and a nasty fire (but too late to stop what he was doing). He had was already turning the wheel a full turn, where it stopped fast.

Outside, trees snapped like small, dry sticks in a strongman's grasp. The house shuddered. There was a strange wailing coming from the sky, like a wind, but also like the scream of some gigantic human. At that moment, Mr. Jeng stirred in his seat, brought his hand to his face, and seemed to realize that something had gone terribly wrong. Seeing the couple struggling with the cylinder and its obscenely distended tube, he rose and staggered toward them. At that moment, the couch came *flying at them* and Jeng seemed to throw himself between the sucking tube and that couch. Seeing his error, he screeched, Maye and Jimmy decided, in his native tongue.

And the lights went out.

In the dark, something struck the end of the now iron-stiff tube Maye and Jimmy held. It hit with such an impact that they assumed it was their couch. But there was a soft, sucking sound, as of a boot being pulled from exceptionally thick and clinging mud. Mr. Jeng screamed again, then sighed, and something quite considerable went sluicing down the tube, and there was a sound like a rubber mud flap caught in a high wind.

"Jimmy!" Maye screamed, finally releasing the thing she had held to so tenaciously.

The cylinder had ceased to operate. Outside, the wind had died, and there was a final thumping, as of something large smacking the earth. Maye and Jimmy huddled together on the floor, afraid to move as something not unlike a gigantic voice roared, as a sound they both could think of only as *trees walking* boomed around their little house. The sun found them still on the floor, in a tight clench. Mr. Jeng seemed to be gone.

When the sun was finally up, and they felt courageous enough, they went out. A severe but weirdly limited storm had menaced them during the night. The couple had lost a number of trees, one of which had severed both their power and phone lines. Jimmy had to go to a neighbor's house to ring up the repair crews, who had their services restored by midday.

In Mr. Jeng's automobile, they found a notebook with the phone number Jimmy recognized as the one he had called the previous week. He dialed it and someone answered. "This is Jimmy Welk," he told the person on the other end. "Your Mr. Jeng was out here last night, but we don't know where he is now. We have his car here. And the vacuum. You probably should send somebody out for them."

"Yes," the voice answered, sounding very much like Mr. Jeng. "Will be someone there very soon." Then there was silence.

In a while, shortly before nightfall, someone arrived—two men in a car very similar to the one Jeng had left. Jimmy had the box with the vacuum in it out on his deck. He didn't want the two coming into his house. "Mr. Jeng disappeared," he told them. "You might want to call the police. We don't know where he went."

One of the men, who looked a lot like Mr. Jeng, quickly answered as the other jumped in Jeng's car and drove away. "Eh. We know where Mr. Jeng is," he said. "There will be no need of police officers. Is all right," he added.

"I guess he wandered off because he was so embarrassed," Jimmy decided aloud.

"Yes. Is true," the man said, lifting up the white box with the cylinder inside. Just before he turned to leave, he asked, "You did not *see* anything? Out here? Last night? Something in the sky?"

Jimmy looked into the black, staring eyes of the small Oriental man. "Um. No. It was very dark," he told him. "The lights went out and we didn't see a thing."

"Is good," the man told him, descending the stairs to the ground. "Is very good for you. Lucky." Without another word he slid into the front seat, the box alongside him. "You should go inside now." Jimmy obeyed, watching them from behind the sheet Maye had put up to replace the vacuum-eaten drapes.

From behind that cover, he watched as the two stocky men ran around, until one of them pointed high into a tree. Jimmy looked up to see what excited him, and he almost thought he saw a body up there. A human body. Mr. *Jeng's* body? Impossibly, the two scampered up the tree like a couple of squirrels. Whatever they brought down was stiff, as if frozen, and somehow broken, like a block of ice. But ice wasn't red.

Soon, they stuffed the thing into their car. Jimmy never saw them again.

But that evening, as he walked about his property, surveying the damage the severe, if small, storm had inflicted on his four acres, he came upon something in the soft loam. Jimmy was standing at the upturned roots of what had been his largest pine tree and he realized he was in a shallow depression. Moving back, about twenty feet or so, he realized that what he'd been looking at appeared to be a pair of gigantic footprints, not unlike those he himself might make. If he were a hundred feet tall and had rounded, splayed feet. He didn't tell Maye.

But when Christmas came, among the gifts Jimmy's wife found around their small artificial tree was a new broom. And a dustpan. And she had bought him a fresh supply of non-bonded liquor.

They counted their blessings.

The Nullity of Choice

by John Tynes

"Now here's an odd one, sir."

"I'm inclined to agree, sergeant. Not often that people assassinate a mental patient, after all. What's all that racket?"

"The other patients, sir. They were all out here in the exercise yard when the killer fired—saw this man's brains blown out right in front of them. Delicate sensibilities and so forth, you know."

"I'm sure I would."

"Who would want to go and kill this poor old mad bastard?"

"We won't find out 'who' from this, sergeant. But we might find out why."

"Why, sir? This man's been in the booby hatch for sixty years. Why would anyone want to kill him now?"

"Answer that question, sergeant, and you'll answer your first one."

"Sir?"

"Never mind. Bag him."

* * *

May 8 (#1): I took the .303 Lee-Enfield out of its case and drew a bead on the sun. BANG, I pretend. Were the rifle capable of firing at the speed of light—and were my cartridges capable of withstanding such travel—the sun would have a hole in it, courtesy of me.

Shame that such things aren't possible, lest I leave a mark the world would never forget. Instead, 'tis a whimper I leave behind. Who would care, after all, should an eighty-five-year-old mental patient have his head blown off from long range?

Work the action. Load the shell. One will do; a second shot only sig-
nifies failure, so best get it right in one. The exercise yard of the sanitarium in Oakdeene Village lies before me from my vantage point within this tree. He'll be out at any moment, the occupant of the second cell
on the left in Hell—that's what they call the basement level where the
untreatables reside. These folks are beyond Prozac; for that matter,
they've all been mad for far longer than Prozac has even been around.
Spellman's been in since 1935, poor old mad bastard.

Martin Spellman, to be precise. He was a nurse at the sanitarium
until that night when the Hell ward went nuts; come morrow, he might
as well have been serving tea in Wonderland and so they locked him up
in his former place of employment. Mad, raving mad, shouldn't have
survived this long in such conditions.

Won't, much longer.

There he is now. Sanitarium whites on pale, too-scrubbed skin.
Little old man, wobbling about. His legs won't last long; then he'll take
a seat and make a perfect target.

Like so. Seated upon the bench, the madman known as Martin
Spellman unknowingly surveys the exercise yard for the last time. I raise
the Browning Hi-Power to my shoulder, take aim at the back of his
head, and gently squeeze the trigger.

BANG.

Martin Spellman's mind, or at least a sodden portion thereof, blows
out through his forehead as the cartridge impacts, mushrooms, plows
through his brain, punches through the far side of his skull in a spray of
blood and tissue, and then strikes the ground six feet in front of him.
The bloody, chunky hole in Spellman's head as he sort of turns and slides
to the ground reminds me of nothing so much as the horrible anus in the
forehead of my lord Yibb-Tstll, from whose similar region black wastes
are urged out after the brain has had its fill.

The rifle goes back in the case, I drop down to the ground, the car
welcomes my hurried presence, and I am gone. Scratch one aged mental patient. Scratch Martin Spellman.

* * *

*Few would have the capacity to understand the business which I am about—or
do I delude myself? Perhaps my methods are not so obscure as they might seem. My
lord Yibb-Tstll sees all of space and time as he rotates slowly, his terrible eyes fix-*

ated on the least significant atom of the universe, understanding both form and function in bold defiance of Heisenberg. Those who invoke my lord Yibb-Tstll undergo a reversal, becoming in some fashion unlike themselves. Sanity become madness; order become chaos; life become death. Or vice versa.

* * *

"Now here's an odd one."

"Consistency is the hobgoblin of small minds, sergeant."

"Sir?"

"Never mind. What's the victim's name again?"

"George Baker, sir. Strangled with a wire, it would seem. Wife out shopping."

"She the one that found the body?"

"No, sir. The postman. Came with the mail and the door was standing wide open, as it is now. Baker's body was lying just inside the foyer."

"So odds are the killer just walked up and knocked, then attacked Baker when he opened the door."

"Makes sense, sir. Folk are trusting hereabouts, they'd open the door to Jack the Ripper like as not and offer him tea."

"Delightful to hear."

"It's not like London, sir."

"But then, what is?"

"London is, sir."

"That was a rhetorical question, sergeant."

"Pardon, sir."

* * *

May 17 (#3): George Baker suffered from a hail of frogs during the days leading up to Christmas, 1964. It lasted three days, albeit intermittently. The case was documented extensively by the local press and by a meteorologist who lived nearby. No cause was uncovered and once the frogs stopped, so did interest in George Baker's situation.

Which is a pity. Poor Mister Baker was game; he stuck the frogs in bottles and tried to sell them at local shops as "miracle frogs." They were not a rousing success, and in fact were an abject failure. Three years later he went to great pains to attract a family of boarders that included a fourteen-year-old-girl to his house; subsequently, he staged poltergeist phenomena in the hopes of bringing attention back to his door. Unwisely, perhaps, Baker did not cut the family in on the deal and they quickly disputed his desperate claims.

In 1975, Baker gave it one more go. Securing a number of statues of the Virgin Mary, he rigged them with simple reservoirs that would allow them to bleed periodically. For the better part of two weeks, all was well: Local believers beat a path to his door, and the media followed. The church quickly exposed the "miracle virgins" as fakes, however, and Baker resigned himself to a life of drab anonymity.

The damnedest thing, of course, was that the hail of frogs was for real. Baker didn't fake that. So it was that I found myself on a lovely spring morning with a garrote about Baker's neck while his wife was at the shops. He sputtered and clawed arthritically at my hands but in the end could do nothing but asphyxiate at my convenience.

When we were done with our little procedure, I lowered his body to the floor and pulled up the grimy T-shirt he was wearing. Fastening my lips upon Baker's right nipple, I suckled briefly but harshly, as long as I dared, and envisaged myself as a night-gaunt suckling at the gangrenous, engorged nipples of my lord Yibb-Tstll.

* * *

I shall become as my lord Yibb-Tstll. The world I dwell in cannot help but experience me, and so undergo a reversal of its own. The corners shall be smoothed, the rough surfaces hewn clean. That which makes no sense shall be urged to rightness in a blinding moment of singular perfection. The dustbin of science shall be emptied, leaving only that which fits into the natural order. I shall remove every trace of that which should not be from the surface of the planet, that men may live with no questions in their hearts.

* * *

"Now here's an odd one, sir."

"Is that the customary greeting one extends to corpses in Oakdeene, sergeant?"

"Pardon, sir?"

"Forget it. What's her name?"

"Sarah Dunwoody, sir. The cuts were administered after she was suspended from the ceiling, near as we can tell. The blood on the floor's been messed with."

"How so?"

"See the footprints? The coroner believes the killer stood beneath the corpse and, um, played in the blood, sir."

"Played in the blood?"

"Well, I'm not sure how you'd describe it, sir. There are spatter marks all about that didn't come from the cuts; they came from the killer having the blood drop on him from above and then moving about rapidly."

"So he was singing in the shower?"

"The neighbors didn't hear any singing, sir."

"I didn't mean that literally, sergeant."

"Of course, sir."

* * *

April 3 (#7): When Sarah Dunwoody was twelve years old, she was staying overnight at a friend's house. The other girl dug out a Ouija board, and the pair—giggling—did their best to contact the spirits of the dead. The other girl's older brother snuck in and took a photograph of them, in the hopes of getting them in trouble later by showing the girl's absent parents what their daughter and her friend Sarah had been up to.

When the photograph was developed, Sarah didn't look herself. The image of another person altogether, a woman in a dress thirty years out of date, was translucently superimposed over where Sarah sat. The woman had a cadaverous look to her, and yet a wistful one; the photograph caused a minor sensation (in the town, at least) and is now a staple of Strange But True books: the Dunwoody Spirit Photograph, one of the few examples of ghost photographs whose negative has held up under repeated scrutiny for signs of forgery.

Sarah Dunwoody, age twenty-four, is unconscious and near death, suspended from the ceiling. Standing beneath her, I scrub my naked form in the blood dripping from the numerous small wounds I have given her. I become as one with the blood, smearing it across myself. Above us, perhaps the spirit of the mystery woman dances about the body of Sarah Dunwoody as it draws its shallow breaths. I wonder who that ghost woman was, and what she might think of the proceedings I have initiated this night. Is she pleased, perhaps, that this callow youth who disturbed her rest has met this fate? Or is she sorrowful, her spectral heart awash in ectoplasmic sympathy?

Dream, ghost, dance and dream in the space above my bloodied head. I could not care less; I am one with the blood. When my lord Yibb-Tstll bleeds, his blood is known as the Black to those who call it. I am one with the Black, one with my lord Yibb-Tstll, one with the sweet juice that courses through his atrophied veins and nourishes his sallow flesh. I am the Black. My only enemy is running water, and here in this room nothing runs but the blood, the Black, and we are as one.

* * *

It is the question of anomaly that vexes us. It is that which we do not understand that unsettles us. It is the presence of uncertainty in our lives that leaves us gasping for reason. Would that we suffered not from unreason, we would become as gods. Devoid of bewilderment, we would walk proudly in the cold light of fate and accept the destiny that is due us. The course would be straight, the road less traveled revealed for the illusion Frost intended, the nullity of choice constrained to the certainty of the absolute.

* * *

"Now here's an odd one, sir."

"I beg pardon, sir?"

"I'm sorry, sergeant. Whenever I see you these days, that phrase pops into my head. I can't imagine why."

"Well, anyway, Inspector Hawthorne sir, I just came to tell you that we have a match."

"A match?"

"The saliva found in the bite marks on George Baker's nipples match the semen in Sarah Dunwoody, sir."

"You bowl me over with incident."

"I'm sorry, sir."

"Don't be. 'Though the mills of God grind slowly, yet they grind exceeding small.'"

"Sir?"

"'Though with patience He stands waiting, with exactness grinds He all.'"

"Sir?"

"I just mean that the devil is in the details, sergeant. It's our job to ferret him out, no matter how dull he may prove to be."

"I don't follow you, sir."

"Good on you. I'm full of good intentions, after all."

* * *

April 23 (#10): Melissa Trokay has already experienced the unusual phenomenon known as alien abduction, or so she and her therapist claim. More tellingly, the local hospital confirmed that she underwent surgery recently on her cranium—an anomaly that she nor her employer (who would have had to let her off from work to undergo and recuperate from such surgery, were it performed by a human agency) can explain. Incisions, scars, these are the manifestations of uncertainty that have left their mark on Melissa Trokay.

Today she undergoes abduction of a terrestrial sort. Tied and gagged in the back of my van, she whimpers feebly as we drive out to the farms surrounding Oakdeene. Great fields of green extend around us on all sides. Upon a nearby hillock, the standing stone known as Laughing George waits and watches, its secrets buried in time and inscrutable to all. Were there a single living witness to the erection of Laughing George, it would be that witness rather than Melissa Trokay in the back of my van at this moment—but such a witness would need be thousands of years old. Melissa Trokay is thirty-four, well within my range of opportunity.

As the sun dips down, I pull the van off to the side of the road and into a copse of trees. I step out and head for the back of the van, then remove Melissa Trokay, ignoring her struggling and plaintive whelps, and place her upon the picnic table erected here by some helpful branch of the civil service.

Her small, gagged cries vie for prominence with the babble of the creek nearby. I shall wash my hands in that creek when this is done, I tell her, leaving open the outcome as to whether or not she will survive the encounter. She won't, of course, but I'm not going to address that topic directly. Not now. Not when so much remains to be done.

She is so proud of that head of hers. So proud of those inexplicable scars, so proud of the lurid X-rays and the baffled doctors. Her very flesh exudes anomaly, in a cacophony of shrill voices crying "Explain me!" and "I cannot be!" I would silence such voices, and remove from them their validity. Divorced from direct experience, they shall enter the halls of hearsay and folklore and shall trouble science no more. Severed from her living witness, they shall be as dust in the halls of the dead. When she is quite gone, I will peel the flesh from her body, turn it inside-out, and put it back in its place. Melissa Trokay will undergo a reversal of her own, a microcosm of the greater whole, a mere detail of the canvas that I work from. As one with my lord Yibb-Tstll himself, I shall affect upon Ms. Trokay a model of that which will soon affect all of human existence.

* * *

Uncertainty begets confusion, confusion begets fear, fear begets malice, malice begets violence, violence begets death. Millions of innocents suffer death year to year. Lacking death, ascension may occur. We may migrate to a higher level of being, leaving these fleshy enclosures behind. Lacking violence, we lack death. Lacking malice, we lack violence. Lacking fear, we lack malice. Lacking confusion, we lack fear. Lacking uncertainty, we lack confusion. Send Heisenberg screaming to his grave! Send the Forteans and the parapsychologists and the cryptozoologists and all those whining, shrill naysayers of the natural order to their graves! Resolve that once and for all the universe moves in the way which man understands, and no other! Make sense of the world and we shall leave the world behind!

* * *

"So this woman was seen in the van?"

"Yes, sir. Another driver spotted her in the back through the windows with tape 'round her mouth and called it in."

"I hope this isn't just someone's overactive imagination."

"There, sir! In that copse."

"Right. Pull over, sergeant."

* * *

The car comes to a stop. I pull the knife out, climb off the table, sidle to one side amidst the branches. The men pile out. Some are wearing uniforms. They shout something. One has a gun, levels it, fires. I feel nothing. I am the Black. I am the blood of my lord Yibb-Tstll. I am fluttering shadows, unearthly winged beasts, I am no longer human. The Black sings, the Black calls, the Black cries, and I sing, I call, I cry. My corporeal form dissolves into a hundred fluttering things, the servants of Yibb-Tstll, the whispery, flapping components of the Black. I cannot be hurt. The man's bullet passes through the spaces between my selves, screams off into the horizon. I remain whole, inviolate. Then there is water at my ankles.

* * *

My lord Yibb-Tstll, would that I could work such a reversal the whole world would be as new. Would that I could stem the tide of my life, sending it screaming back into the firmament of creation itself and then bring it rushing back toward consciousness, becoming as one with your great work. I could right all wrongs, remake all that was sundered, avoid all mistakes, become perfection incarnate. If only a reversal could occur, and that I could live my life over again, all would be well. I would not hurt a fly, nor need to, for all would be as it should in your divine image.

* * *

"Now *here's* an odd one, sir."

"Emphasis, sergeant. It's a novelty. You are to be congratulated."

"Sir?"

"Get him up. He's just hit in the leg, for God's sake. Get him out of the water. And get that woman untied so she'll stop screaming, already."

* * *

The fluttering components of self that were my feet are immobilized in the running water of the creek, sole foe of the Black. My feet will not move. I look down, will myself to see the flapping shades of my self as a lone corporeal form and there, below the knee, is the hole in my pants leg, wetted with blood. I am mortal and immortal at once. I am human and I am the Black. As human, I am wounded with the strike of a bullet. As Black, I am immobilized in the running water. I am lost. I am undone. I cry out in pain and collapse into the waters, surrendering to my weakness.

* * *

My lord Yibb-Tstll, deliver me from mine enemies. I would be as one with you, the keenness of two alike felt as one, the sanctity of your divine spirit, your divine anus, your divine breasts. Allow me to merge with you, to achieve my aim, and take me away from this place of water and pain.

* * *

"He's dead, sir."

    "What do you mean, he's dead? I just shot him in the leg!"

    "I know that, sir, but he's dead. No pulse, no nothing."

    "Christ!"

    "Yes, sir?"

    "Shut up, sergeant. I was talking to myself."

* * *

I am aware of every sensation as my body falls into the brook. The cold of the water, the heat of the wound, the electricity in my brain—all combine in a chorus of mourning. I am lost. I am undone. My body lies in the water, returning to its corporeal form and abandoning the beauty of the Black once and for all. Let me ascend, my lord Yibb-Tstll! Let be suckle at your breasts, and draw the wastes from your brain, and scrub the lowliest threads of the green cloak that envelops you. Let me be as one with you, my lord, or let me be as nothing.

* * *

The foliage parts, and I see him in the clearing. He rotates slowly on feet unglimpsed beneath the robe. The cloth about his chest throbs with the movements of the faceless beasts that lie beneath, feeding on the power that resides within. I float into the clearing, feeling the features of my face drop away and the flesh of my back split to admit the extension of my great wings. Lord Yibb-Tstll, I come to you.

* * *

"That's it, then, sir."

"You're a master of understatement, sergeant."

"Sir?"

"My point proven. It is so rare that we can excel at that which we seek to be. You are to be congratulated."

"I don't follow, sir."

"Those who eschew following have little choice but to lead, sergeant. You've chosen a bright path."

"Thank you, sir. I think."

"Take the lead, sergeant. Get me some coffee. And get that bastard's body out of the creek."

Where I Go, Mi-go

by Lois H. Gresh

It was a catatonic summer, still as if the world was grinding to a halt. The only sound was the drone of endless rain. I peered from the cabin window at the swing of the Miskatonic River as it swelled and arced and beat the ancient trees. A canopy of black clouds hung over the forest.

When would Thaddeus show up?

"He'll come when summer bleeds into autumn." My aunt's voice was sharp. She was tired of my questions.

It wasn't my fault that she read my mind.

"But if I didn't read your mind, Mirabella, how else would I know you?"

"If you knew me, Auntie, you wouldn't keep me here, alone like this, on the edge of nowhere." Angry, I turned and faced her, ready to tell her for the millionth time to stop invading my mind.

She was in her rocker by the eating table. Fingering a letter damp from tears. Withered, thin, sunk into that hard wooden chair as if her bones were part of its structure. Tiny green eyes, sparse gray hair, a mass of wrinkles.

Aunt Gertrude was all I had, and she had been very good to me.

"I'm sorry, Auntie." I walked across the dirt floor in bare feet, and stooped and lifted one hand from her lap. It was cold, and shaking.

She smelled of old age, as a leaf that falls into dew and slowly rots. Her voice faltered. "My time is nearly done. My only curse was to read minds. I thought you might be spared, that your cousin could save you before …. But now I know … your curse will be much greater. *The letter ….*"

Her other hand held it out to me, and I caught it as it fell to the floor. "Read it," she said.

Her trembling told me that whatever was in the letter would not please me.

I unfolded it, settled onto the dirt, and hugged the thin flannel shirt to my body. My hair, dark as the sky, fell across my face to my chest, and in this shroud of black, I read:

"Gertrude, you are the last Akeley. The child, Mirabella, is the last Wendigo. The boy, Thaddeus, is the last Derby and brings the Spawn of the Wind. *N'gai, n'gha'ghaa, bugg-shoggog, y'hah*; Yog-Sothoth, Yog-Sothoth. The gate, the gate, the whippoorwills, the gate. The Crawling Mist, the Dweller in Darkness, *Nyarlathotep!*"

It was signed Walter Gilman-Smith, Professor of Neurobiology, Miskatonic University.

I laughed. "This professor guy is nuts. What a bunch of stinking gibberish."

"You don't understand, Mirabella. You're too young, only sixteen! Too young to hear the horrors, to know your past, to know what is meant to be."

I *didn't* understand. I didn't know what to say.

For a moment, we sat in silence.

The rain slowed, then ceased.

The hum of bumblebees rose.

The dead summer was changing, coming alive.

"It's happening," my aunt said, and then the cabin door opened, and a boy, several years my elder, stepped into the one room we shared as home. Behind him, the black sky glowered, then retreated, and a blue mist rolled from the river into the forest. Behind him, whippoorwills and warbling wrens flitted through the trees. Black flies swarmed around his head, probing for a blood feast. He swatted them away.

Finally, he was here.

Cousin Thaddeus had come to take me away.

* * *

We lay by the river on a carpet of pine needles. Worms poked from the damp soil. Moths nibbled the leaves of sun-sprinkled maples.

I gazed at my cousin. His lips had been soft on mine, too many times, as many times as we could escape from Auntie. His eyes were

huge and hazel; they looked like the mist that rolled on the Miskatonic
River. His hair: red and brown, billowing in loose waves to his shoulders.
And his arms, I lived for the times when he wrapped me in them and
held me closely.

And yet, we were cousins. I would do nothing more than kiss him.

"You will come with me to Boston?" he asked, stroking my cheek.

I shivered. I could not resist. Of course, I would go to Boston.
Anything to be away from here. "School starts in a few weeks,
Thaddeus. Auntie's only looking out for me, but she'll let me go before
then, I'm sure."

I'd never lived anywhere else. As a baby, my parents died in
Innsmouth, where I was born. My only adult relative, a distant one at
that, had taken me in. Aunt Gertrude. The last of the Akeleys.

And now there was Thaddeus: an adult at eighteen, on his own,
having been raised in foster homes, the product of my dead uncle,
Ephraim Derby, and his wife, who killed him with her own hands.

"Thaddeus, why does my aunt fear you so much? Why does she
delay letting me go with you to Boston? Why does she say you're the
Spawn of the Wind? What does that mean?"

He rolled away from me onto his back and frowned. "I don't know.
She's old. It's nonsense. This Gilman-Smith is a lunatic. It's best for you
to leave this place."

Then the frown left his face, and he smiled again, and I remembered
the catatonic summer, how dead everything had been before my cousin
came, and how now, the world was alive, and birds sang, and bees
hummed, and the river flowed gently again through my woods.

For the moment, I was happy to forget the strange letter and my
aunt's terror at letting me leave with cousin Thaddeus.

But the moment was short-lived. As I felt warm breath upon my
neck and a strong hand within my hair, I felt something else, as well.

The earth shifted beneath us. The sky went black, like the polished
surface of a glass marble. A bang of thunder made my breath stop and
my body freeze.

Thaddeus leapt to his feet. His face twisted. "No, I won't let it happen!"

I was too cold to scream. My lips were frostbitten, my teeth chat-
tering. The summer had bled into autumn; it had bled into ice-black
winter. A wind raged the trees, stripping the leaves from the maples,
scattering the needles from the pines. They scraped my face, and I bled
in a hundred pinpricks of pain.

The birds screamed *for* me. The river rose in a mighty wave, some ten feet tall, and crashed back down, as if the water itself was fighting some unknown, unseen horror. And then, overhead, I saw the stars—

The stars!

Droplets of light falling upon them in the black sky, the twinkling magnified, the stars spinning madly, like ice skaters gone wild.

Spinning, *spinning* ....

I lay on the needles, unable to move, my breathing like the pounding of drums above the crash of the river and the screams of the birds. My eyes saw nothing but those stars, and they were turquoise, and they danced and cavorted and mated, in some odd heavenly orgy, and then their spawn showered down upon me in a cloud of black dust.

Thaddeus fell, limp, and his mouth opened, and the words tumbled out in a voice I did not know: "The Crawling Mist ... the Dweller in Darkness ... Nyarlathotep ... Cthulhu comes from beyond when the stars are right: *N'gai, n'gha'ghaa, bugg-shoggog, y'hah*; Yog-Sothoth, Yog-Sothoth."

The words of Walter Gilman-Smith.

I thought Thaddeus had gone mad, or perhaps that I was just so dizzy that I didn't know what I was hearing. But later, while wrapping me in bearskins and forcing tea through my bleeding lips, my aunt said, "When the stars are right, *Cthulhu comes.* Find the professor, Mirabella. Nobody else can save you."

Thaddeus knew something; he knew whatever it was that scared my aunt.

But Thaddeus was in the woods, meditating alone, as he always did, twice a day.

I said, "You've got to tell me what this is—"

But it was too late for words. My aunt dropped the tea cup, the burning liquid searing my chest, and she collapsed in a great spasm of pain upon the dirt floor.

I cried. I tried to lift myself from my cot, to pull her up and revive her, to bring back the only love I'd ever known; but I was too weak and feverish, and the best I could do was roll from the cot and crawl to her, holding her head in my arms and praying that she be released from whatever hell had devoured her.

I cradled her until Thaddeus came home, and then together we buried her by the river beneath the carpet of pine. The tea burns on my chest steamed with infection, and it hurt to move my arms, to breathe, to walk. The pain was a steady blade, muted only by the pain I felt from losing my aunt. I was left with only one source of comfort: Thaddeus, the Spawn of the Wind.

For days he tended to me, placing cool cloths on my forehead and trying to cheer me with inane chatter. But he would grow moody as he looked at my burns, and once he commented that they formed the shape of the Big Dipper, "home of the mi-go," he said, "from Yuggoth."

When I asked what he meant, he would not tell me.

It was shortly after, when my fever subsided and the dizziness left, that my cousin and I trekked to Arkham, in hopes of finding Professor Gilman-Smith. I'd been to Arkham many times to buy food and other household items, though my school was in the forest, three miles north on the Miskatonic River.

I didn't like Arkham. It was worse than Auntie's cabin. The winds surged through the narrow streets in billows of soot. The houses were tall, yet tottering and crumbling to waste. The smell reminded me of Auntie's outhouse. And the people, those few who ventured into the streets, had vacant eyes, shuffling gaits, and filthy faces that bore the marks of alcohol and pain. These were people who had given up on life, who expected the worst and always got it, who cowered, as if waiting for the whipping or the knout.

I didn't like Arkham.

Thaddeus put his arm around my shoulders. He told me that the only thing that mattered was the future, getting out of Arkham, returning to Boston, blotting out our pasts.

I knew he spoke the truth. He had lived much as I had: alone, without real family, without friends, his schooling as raw and shallow as mine.

I felt safe with him. I finally belonged, I was finally loved, not in the way that Auntie loved me, but in some new way that was deeper and more comforting.

We were the same.

Thaddeus drew me closer, and a great warmth enveloped me. I put my arms around him, wanting to return that warmth and comfort. "Thaddeus, after we see the professor, we should leave at once."

He hesitated, untwined my arms from his body. "We may not be *allowed* to leave Arkham."

"But ... *why?*"

He took my elbow and steered me to a splintered wooden stoop in front of a church that looked like a morgue.

"St. Stanislaus Church," he said, "a place where people like us are worshiped."

"Worshiped? Whatever for?"

"Your aunt wrote to me a few months before her death. She wanted me to get you out of here before they came."

"They? You're making no sense."

He pointed at the church. The front door was embellished with Gothic script, the letters unknown to me, the knocker carved into the shape of an octopus with bat wings. "*That* is Cthulhu. *They* are the ones who have served him since the beginning of time."

"You're talking nonsense. I'm going to see the professor, and then I'm getting the hell out of here." I rose to leave, but he grabbed my arm.

"It has long been said that Cthulhu would return when the stars are right, and the stars are *weird* right now, spinning—"

And my aunt died ...

My auntie who read my mind.

And I remembered how Thaddeus had seemed to know that something terrible was happening.

"Why didn't you tell me this before? Why don't you tell me *now*?" I said.

He held my arm firmly, tried to force me to sit upon the steps. But I wouldn't budge. "I *want* to know," I said.

He released me. He ran his fingers through his hair, bent his head, his shoulders. "I didn't want to scare you. I wanted to get you away from here. But Cthulhu and his hellspawn are on the rise—hellspawn that possess a man's soul, drive him mad, drive him to murder. I believe that this Gilman-Smith has evidence that Cthulhu has come for *you*."

I jerked away from him. How could I trust someone like Thaddeus, who insisted that demon-gods were after me? It was ludicrous, insane; it was ... *unforgivable.*

"You're out of your mind!" and I tore down the street, the tears burning my face, the cobblestones hard on my bare feet. Thaddeus raced after me, but I whirled and shoved him against the granite wall of a building that bore the name Miskatonic University, Department of Neurobiology.

He recoiled from the wall, tottered toward me, arms outstretched. "Ask the professor, Mirabella. The Big Dipper on your chest ... the mi-go, they are fungi from a planet called Yuggoth, out past Pluto, and their home is the Big Dipper. They come in the Crawling Mist of Nyarlathotep, a great demon who serves Cthulhu. It's too late for you, Mirabella. My presence, our ancient fouled genes so close together, the stars shifting—"

"Stop it!" I screamed.

I dashed up the stairs toward Gilman-Smith's laboratory; but my feet were bleeding, they hurt like hell, and I slipped on my own blood and fell. I crashed backward, the spires and pillars jutting above me into the black sky, spearing the spinning stars,

Something warm and solid caught me: Thaddeus' arms. We sank to the stairs, both of us moaning. My eyes followed the trail of blood and then beyond to the double front doors. Massive, wooden, twenty feet tall, and upon each door, a crest in bas relief ... my eyes fixated on that crest and it swam before me ... a crest of the octopus with the bat wings, of *Cthulhu*.

The crest rose from the door, it grew, and the tentacles quivered and reached for me; and my skin, my nerves: everything shot through with fire.

I had to get loose, get away from here, get away from those tentacles, now so close, mere inches from my eyes. The suckers large and luminous, and filled with a pus that fizzed like an angry sore.

But I couldn't move, I was rigid in terror, and beneath me, on the hard granite steps, Thaddeus' breath came in sharp spurts.

And then a horrible keening erupted from the bloated lips of the octopus creature. Black steam shot from its suckers and poured over us, tumbling through the streets. Sparkling steam, winding its way into filaments that encased Thaddeus as mummy wrap, wrenching him from me.

"Nyarlathotep!" he screamed. "The Crawling Mist, the fog of death! It brings the mi-go!"

The steam was alive with filaments, long and slender as fungi tentacles—the mi-go, *the fungi from where?*—from Yuggoth—

The filaments wrapped around me. They tore at my clothes. They were on my skin. Hot, wet, *strong*. They were like black flies, seeking blood feasts. Merging with my skin, digesting it, *pouring into me*—

Oh god, how I strained my muscles, my arms tight against the filaments, pushing, my legs trying to kick—

And then, I heard the flutes. Two of them, in duet, their eerie tones emitted from the pit of hell itself. I shouldn't have known the tune. I had no knowledge of music. Yet the name of the piece flashed to my mind. "Suite Modale" by Bloch. Mezzopiano, medium quiet, then poco ritardo, slowing to a soothing whine.

The whippoorwills and wrens began warbling, soft and quiet: the "Suite Modale."

And behind this backdrop, the bumblebees hummed, "The Crawling Mist. The mi-go come on Nyarlathotep. The gate opens."

Somewhere in the mist, Aunt Gertrude swayed in her rocker by the eating table. She was smiling. Her lips moved in the pattern: "The mi-go come on Nyarlathotep. The mi-go come on Nyarlathotep."

Aunt Gertrude looked happy. Her wrinkles had cleared. Her eyes sparkled. All was right in the world. Beneath me, Thaddeus' muscles relaxed, and a flush swept through me. A flush of peace and calmness, of warmth and ecstasy.

Yes, *ecstasy*, and I sank into it, as the gate opened, and I felt myself being flooded with a million happy thoughts, a million happy desires, and a million tiny lovers.

* * *

I must have slept, for the next thing I knew, I was stretched on a sofa in a laboratory of some kind. Above me, Thaddeus' eyes were huge and round, his face pinched by concern. His hair no longer hung in reddish brown curls; rather, it was short and kinked and gray. His skin had a greenish tint.

A man's voice drifted toward me. "The mi-go are the Spawn of the Wind, released by Yog-Sothoth, the gatekeeper of Cthulhu's hell, and swept upon Mirabella by the Crawling Mist of Nyarlathotep."

The man stood behind Thaddeus, and now he stepped around my cousin to peer at me. He had a clipped black beard and thick glasses. A muscle beneath his eye twitched, jerking his lips up and then back down. He wore a white lab coat smeared with green fluid. A swampy odor filled my nostrils, and it was sweet and pleasant.

"She's coming to ...." The man leaned and rubbed soft fingers down my arms. On his coat were letters in odd script: *Professor Walter Gilman-Smith*.

"Will she live?" asked Thaddeus.

"She'll live, but I don't know *what as*."

"My presence ... this is all my fault," said Thaddeus.

"You were near, yes, and all that was required to release the mi-go was a time when your genes were near hers, when the stars spun as strange quark—"

"My clothes ...." I struggled to my elbows and sat on the sofa cushions. I was naked, my skin greenish and prickled by goosebumps. I was shivering. "My clothes ...."

"Here, here." Thaddeus thrust them at me.

The two men turned so I could dress with some privacy. It was hard, fumbling with the zipper to my jeans, the buttons to my shirt, but I managed. My stomach was queasy, my head ached. My breasts were swollen, and they hurt.

I swallowed, trying not to throw up, and sank back onto the sofa. I peered at my surroundings, hoping to figure out just what it was the professor did here, and how it might help us.

The room held a large machine, some fifteen feet long, made of tubes and gears, and twisting wires of all colors. The machine looked like two gigantic telescopes separated by a car engine.

The room held little else: a few microscopes, of course, and beakers, and various pieces of equipment that looked like sealed vaults.

The professor fiddled with some wires, muttering words like "Quadruple Focusing Magnets" and "Cerenkov Detector."

Maybe Aunt Gertrude had been right: Only Professor Gilman-Smith could save us. My stomach cramped and I doubled over in pain, my head between my knees.

The professor flipped a switch and stood back. "Watch," he said.

Thaddeus sank onto the sofa beside me. He held my hand. He looked as terrified as I felt.

The machine vibrated. A flash bolted from one telescope into the car engine, then crashed into the other telescope.

"Gold nuclei at the speed of light," said Gilman-Smith. "Shoot them at gold foil, and they explode into thousands of particles called strange quark matter. I measure velocities with scintillation counters, the fastest velocities with the Cerenkov detector."

Thaddeus shifted beside me. "That's all very cool, doctor man, but what does it have to do with me being old and Mirabella being attacked by hellspawn?"

Even old, Thaddeus was cute. His hand was still warm in mine, his eyes still held the depths of blue mist, his lips still soft and—

The professor ran a hand through greasy hair. He was highly agitated, his thin body twitching, the tick beneath his eye spazzing like the frog heart I cut open in biology class. He said: "We don't have much time. I was smart. I married a Smith, a girl from *out of town*, a girl without tainted genes. And I had myself sterilized. But you, Thaddeus, are young and fertile, or you *were*—"

"Now, just a minute!" Thaddeus released my hand and leapt from the sofa.

Gilman-Smith laughed, a high-pitched cackling. "Go outside, see for yourself. And when you're convinced that I'm not a mad professor, wait for me at St. Stanislaus Church, wait for me and I will come."

* * *

Gilman-Smith was right. The mi-go were everywhere, the Crawling Mist hovered over the tottering buildings, swirled like vultures, descended to encase the dead-gazed people of Arkham. Women staggered, their children wailing, their men screaming about adultery and incest and the habits of whores.

I clutched my belly, sick with fear. The cramps, my bloated breasts, the nausea—

"I'm pregnant," I said.

"Yes. I know," said Thaddeus.

"But how can this be? You're my cousin. We've never had sex, we've never done anything but kiss."

"A kiss can't make a girl pregnant. Something else did it to you." He wrapped his arms around me.

I looked up at him. "Thaddeus, you don't think that I, that I—"

"Slept with some guy? No."

"Then, what?"

"Mirabella, your pregnancy is not a *human* thing."

A shiver ran down my back, like a long cold finger upon my spine. If I didn't carry a human child, then what was it that grew within me?

We sank once again to the stoop in front of St. Stanislaus Church. The door knocker, the octopus with bat wings, was huge now: at least three feet in diameter. It throbbed as if ready to erupt and spew its children upon the earth.

Thaddeus' hair was silver and falling from his scalp in clumps. Wrinkles covered his face. One withered hand took mine. "All I know is that I shouldn't have come; I should have stayed very far away from you. I knew the stars were shifting; I could sense it, I dreamed about it. Long, intense dreams in which the world stopped and the stars spun and showered down horrible strange matter that destroyed mankind. Terrible dreams ... I came here, had to save you, but *they* were waiting, *they* knew I would come, they waited ...."

I bent and kissed his hand. The skin dry as a birch trunk, the nails black and hard from age. My poor Thaddeus would soon die unless I could put an end to whatever I had started.

But what could I do?

I gazed at my love again, his beautiful hazel eyes ringed with dark circles, puffed by bags; his lips, once soft, now so dry they were cracked with blood.

This was my fault.

My tainted genes.

And within me, I carried the seeds of creatures that would come alive and devour mankind.

Across the street, a man shoved a woman against a garbage bin and slammed a fist to her cheek. I saw blood, and the woman fell, and still the man pounded her face, as she cried and begged him to stop.

The sounds were everywhere, of people screaming, of children crying.

I had done this.

"I think we should go in the church," I said. Perhaps inside we would find a clue, something to help us ....

I grabbed Thaddeus' hand and pulled him up.

"I don't think we should go in there," he said.

"Oh, come on," I said, "what do we have to lose? I'm going, so you may as well come with me."

"This isn't a good idea," he said.

But he followed me up the stairs.

The octopus knocker throbbed as a heart in an open wound. Glistening, a deep maroon, it pulsed with a steady beat, skin stretching to its limit, then shrinking back upon the organ. I heard the flutes again, the "Suite Modale", playing to the metronome beat of that heart, that octopus thing upon the door.

I reached for the knocker.

"*No, don't touch it.*" Thaddeus grasped my wrist, but he was feeble, an old man, and I easily pried his fingers loose.

"You're being silly," I said, and I shut my eyes and touched the thing. It was wet and clammy. I pushed, and a spray of moisture, of blood perhaps, drizzled down my arm.

The door opened.

It was dark inside. Whatever was on my arm was sticky, and stung like acid.

We were in a tiny atrium, the walls elaborately carved from hard wood, perhaps mahogany; the ceiling high and domed; a latch on one wall indicating that there was a larger room beyond.

I reached for the latch.

"*Wait.*"

"What is it, Thaddeus?"

He was standing behind me, his back pressed to the outer door where the octopus knocker throbbed, his breath hot upon my neck.

"We can't go in there."

"Why? *Tell me why.*"

He pulled something from his pocket, shoved it at me. "This. Mirabella, read *this.*"

I paused, torn between the two: entering the church to seek an answer, returning to the streets of Arkham to read whatever Thaddeus offered.

The flutes moaned from within the depths of the church. I wanted to go inside, to hear them—

"If you go in there, Mirabella, they will have you. This is the place where they dwell."

Come to us. Come inside. Have our children here. Come and be one with us, where you belong . . . .

The latch was cold in my sweating palm. I pressed downward.

"No." Thaddeus jerked my shoulders back. "Read the letter. It's from your aunt, the one she sent to me, the one that tells *why* I came to save you."

Yes, my auntie, my beloved auntie . . .

Thaddeus had come for me, to save me . . . .

I turned and followed him from the atrium, and the flute music dimmed to a sigh. Outside, the air was rank with the sickly sweet odor of mi-go, and in something of a swoon, I sank with Thaddeus to the cracked stoop, took the crinkled papers from him, and read.

My aunt wrote: "As a Derby, perhaps you've seen the Wilfred Larner notes. Your mother found them buried deep in the dirt floor of her cell at the Oakdeene Sanatorium."

"Thaddeus, your mother was in a mental institution?"

His head bowed, he did not look at me. His hands twisted in his lap. "Yes," he said, "before she killed my father . . . she was a patient at Oakdeene; she was released to make room for Harold 'The Mincer' Graves, the guy who poisoned his entire family and put them through the meat grinder."

Poor Thaddeus, so dear and sweet, wanting only to save me, yet his past was much worse than mine. I read further: "Larner's notes, though aimed at raising Yibb-Tstll, also contained the following warnings about the Crawling Mist and the Mi-Go."

Here, my aunt's script became feverish, as if written in haste, as if the words had come to her in a dream rather than from thoughtful recollection.

"Yea, and I discovered how the Mi-Go Fungi drop from Yuggoth, from beyond Pluto. They come as Strangelets, as chunks of Strange Quark Matter. They make the Stars spin. They come in the Crawling Mist. They enter a man at the Most Minute Level, at the Quantum Level. If a human man and woman have the Genetic Disposition of the Great Old Ones, the Mi-Go enter and eat and transpose and mutate the egg and sperm. The Mi-Go *Combine All*. Yea, the Mi-Go create the Keys to the Gate of Yog-Sothoth."

Above us, the black mist faded into the midnight sky. The moon sank into a mi-go veil.

My body quaked. "Thaddeus—this means—"

He nodded. "It means you carry the spawn of creatures who will unlatch the gates of hell. Do you need more proof than *this*, Mirabella?"

No, I didn't need more proof; what I needed was a solution. It was hard not to race immediately to the lab, to confront Gilman-Smith and demand help. But the professor had told us to wait here, on the steps of St. Stanislaus Church, so I waited with Thaddeus, until, finally, the professor arrived. I no longer wanted to enter the church. I only wanted help. *Human* help.

* * *

The professor's hands shook. He switched on the giant machine. "A decade ago, my wife died in a boating accident on the Miskatonic River. A sudden storm killed her. I've been alone since, living for nothing but this, the battle against Cthulhu."

Gilman-Smith's only love: gone. I looked at Thaddeus. Yet older now, his breathing raw as if his lungs could barely expel air, brown splotches on his face, lips drawn back over yellow teeth.

The professor turned, his thick glasses smeared by tears. "You believe me?"

"Yes," I said softly.

"Thank God, then you are ready to listen. Have you ever wondered, my dear, what exists between the cell nucleus and the neutron star? Why is there no nuclear matter found between the tiny cell and the giant star?"

I hadn't even had chemistry class yet: What did I know? But Thaddeus answered, his voice the feeble strain of a dying man: "All known matter consists of quarks. A proton has two up quarks and one down quark. A neutron has two down quarks and one up quark. All nuclear matter contains these three-quark entities. But of the unknown matter ... well, we don't know what quark combinations make up a full eighty percent of the universe."

The professor looked startled. "How did you know that?"

Thaddeus knew science that he'd never learned.

I knew music that I'd never heard.

The machine vibrated. The professor returned his attention to it, as a flash bolted from one telescope into the car engine, then crashed into the other telescope; but this time, the flash bolted in the opposite direction. He said, "I'm reversing the process. I'm destroying the strange quark matter that forms the Crawling Mist and the mi-go."

Beside me on the sofa, Thaddeus' body went limp. He fell across me, his right arm dangling to the floor, his left fingers splayed across the pregnant bulk of my lap. Within me, things fluttered. Thousands of claws scratched, something oozed and condensed toward the spot where Thaddeus' fingers lay.

The creatures within me were growing.

"Do something!" I cried.

I kissed Thaddeus' cheeks. His eyes were closed, and I kissed the gray shuddering lids, praying to see his hazel eyes again.

His eyes did not open.

My stomach ached; it kept pushing outward in spasms:

I was about to give birth.

"It's not working. Damn it all, it's not working!" The professor slammed off the machine, whirled to face me. He pointed at Thaddeus. "Kill him *now!*"

Was he mad? I wouldn't kill Thaddeus.

"Kill him!" The professor raced across the room to where I sat with Thaddeus dying in my arms. In his hand was a scalpel, six inches long; the blade: mean.

"One drop of strangelet falling on a star eats it within seconds, devouring all neutrons. One drop, and the star becomes a *strange* star. And a strange star spins like wild—it drops Mi-Go to the earth—"

"Stop already! Stop with the scientific *crap!*" I slapped the scalpel from Gilman-Smith's hand. It clattered to the floor. The professor stooped to pick it up, but I kicked his stomach with my foot and sent him reeling.

He continued muttering from the floor. "The mi-go got into Thaddeus' skin, his blood, his brain. At a quantum level, they entered him and changed his cells. They sucked up his genetic material—his *tainted* genes—and then, at a quantum level, at a strange quark level, they entered you, and now you're pregnant with some weird new creature, spawned of mi-go and of Thaddeus—"

My face burned. The room whirled.

I hated Gilman-Smith.

I struggled to my feet. I fell upon him, my pregnant bulk pinning him to the floor, my hand clamped across his mouth.

His fingers strained for the scalpel.

"No!" I slammed Gilman-Smith's head to the floor. He groaned, and blood appeared on his lips.

I left him there, still alive but close to death, and ran from the lab and collapsed on the hard granite stairs of the Department of Neurobiology.

The black mist of Nyarlathotep shimmered in the midnight sky. Filaments curled around the spires of the university buildings that towered like monuments to the demon gods. The moon was strangled by the stuff; it barely glimmered. But the stars were bright, those mad, spinning stars ....

The night was silent but for the whining strains of flutes. No wailing, no shouting, no crying. The people of Arkham were either asleep or dead.

The music rose and lifted me, and I soared through the mist, feeling the filaments wind around me, hug me, embrace me with such love that all I wanted to do was drop back to earth and release those monstrous children from my body.

"The gate is open. Release them." It was my Aunt Gertrude's voice, and there she floated, beyond me in the mist, swaying in her rocker, smiling, her eyes sparkling.

She was happy. She wanted me to give birth.

"You are the last Wendigo. I was the last Akeley. Release them. Release us so we may live on."

In her hand was a teacup, the very one she had held when she died, and when she lifted the cup to her lips and drank, her smile spread into a warm glow the shape of the Big Dipper.

I was dreaming, I had to be dreaming ....

I felt the cold granite beneath my jeans. I grappled for the torn zipper where my belly bulged. I was real.

Killing Thaddeus wouldn't help. The Crawling Mist had already used him to impregnate me. The professor was wrong, wrong.

But should I kill myself?

Or could I somehow destroy what grew within me?

Yes, perhaps ... a glimmer of an idea, and I didn't know if it would work, but ....

Thaddeus had come to me. Now, I would go to Thaddeus.

I found him in the lab, quiet upon the sofa, his heart beating faintly, his body shriveled as a corpse. The professor had crawled to his machine, where he lay in a heap, sleeping.

I crawled on top of Thaddeus. I opened his shirt. I pressed my lips to his chest, but he didn't respond. I pressed my lips harder. Then I rolled to the floor, picked up the scalpel, ran it gently down his arms. It scratched him, and he awakened and stared at me. "What?" The word was a moan.

My hands groped and awakened parts of him that I had only dreamed of awakening. In my head, I heard my aunt: "Take him, yes, take him and do what's right."

He was my cousin. We had tainted genes. We were the same, Thaddeus and I, and whatever child we formed would be weird and *strong*. It would have the genes of the last of the Wendigos and the last of the Derbys.

The fetus would fight whatever grew inside me. It would expel the hellspawn, destroy it.

Thaddeus opened his eyes. His skin was clear of wrinkles. Reddish brown hair poked from his scalp.

Perhaps I had done what was right. Perhaps only those of us with the genes of the Great Old Ones had the strength to fight them.

And this is why the people of Arkham had lost all hope, why they shuffled endlessly as people doomed to the knout and the whip. The people of Arkham carried the *genes*. And this is why my auntie read minds, why we were all so damned *twisted*.

It was our fate.

But it served a purpose.

Thaddeus and I would take our child to Auntie's cabin, and there he would grow up, alone and on the edge of nowhere.

And far away from those with tainted genes.

Subway Accident

by Gregory Nicoll

He held his head high and tried not to look at them as he passed. It was still early and they weren't all out yet, but the big gray chairs at the edge of the yard were already occupied. Two of the oldest men were perched like misshapen gargoyles on the brick ledge, their spindly legs hanging over the edge. As he walked by, they called to him, begging for spare change and cigarettes, the awful stink of their breath fouling the aromas of coffee and bacon from the Mission House kitchen behind them.

Gentry hadn't slept in the Mission House in weeks, and was damn proud of it. He'd fended for himself just fine for quite a while now, spending his nights alone in the park, wrapped in newspapers and cardboard. After grabbing two pick-up jobs unloading freight last weekend, he'd been able to rent a room of his own across the street at the Clermont. Sure, he'd shared the space with more than a few cockroaches, but he preferred their quiet, skittering company to the grumbles of the human parasites who gave him no peace whenever he stayed in the Mission House.

"Gentry!" called a hoarse voice from the center of the lawn. "Hey, Grady Gentry!"

He turned up the collar of his dirty green Army jacket and felt it brush against the ragged, sandpapery stubble of his beard. Wind whipped through his thin white hair and he groped for the tattered canvas hood which hung limply behind his neck.

"Grady Gentry!"

He stopped and looked over at the man who was calling him. Smedley, he recalled. Theo Smedley. He'd slept next to him in the

Mission through several oven-hot nights during the summer. Smedley was a Yankee, originally from Rhode Island or some such place, and said he'd worked in Boston on the city's subway until some weird accident— or something he saw in the tunnels after an accident—had made him move south.

Until budget cuts eliminated his own position, Gentry had spent seven years maintaining underground rails for the Metro Atlanta Rapid Transit Authority, and he knew how crazy men got after spending all day without seeing daylight, but Smedley had been fine up until midsummer. They'd even talked about going to MARTA and re-applying this fall, when new construction was supposed to open a northeast line.

"G-g-got any smokes?" asked Smedley, his lower lip quivering. A gob of snot hung from his left nostril.

Gentry fished in his jacket pocket for the half-pack of Vantages he'd found in the Clermont lobby. He handed one to Smedley, who placed it greedily to his lips and beckoned for a light, his hands trembling.

As Gentry patted down his pockets for a matchbook, he watched the cigarette wobble pathetically on Smedley's weak lips. The man had gone totally loony over a small poster he saw near here, something tacked to a phone pole to advertise an exhibit by a Boston artist named Pinckard or Pickmund or something. There was little sample—a tiny black and white reprint—of a piece of the artist's work reprinted on the poster. Gentry still remembered vividly how Smedley had stopped in midstride and bent down to examine the handbill, stammering as he read aloud the title, "S-s-subway Accident", and raising his head a changed man.

And it wasn't a pleasant change.

Gentry snapped a paper match against the edge of the matchbook. The tip hissed into a smelly sulfurous ball of flame. Like a moth to a candle, Smedley leaned toward it and lit the end of his cigarette. His red eyes watered and his eyelashes fluttered like insects' wings as he sucked at the smoke.

Gentry blew the match out and turned away in disgust. He walked briskly up the street, pulling the hood of his Army jacket over his head to shield his ears from the cries and moans of the broken, helpless excuses for men lounging in the Mission yard.

"As long as I've got two good legs so I can keep walkin'," he thought, "and two good arms, and enough of a brain so I can find a job and work ...."

He walked several blocks along the gritty concrete sidewalk, passing the old rooming houses and the steel and formica facade of the Majestic Diner, with its enticing early morning aromas of grits and waffles. His stomach growled and he thought of investing some of his precious cash reserves in a breakfast, but he knew how early the MARTA construction crews started work and he wanted to find the foreman and talk about a job before they got too involved in the day's projects. Right about now they'd all be standing around a fire in a 55-gallon drum, each man wearing his bright yellow hard hat and sipping coffee or juice from his steel thermos as they all passed around boxes of sticky, sugary Krispy Kreme doughnuts.

"Maybe," he thought hopefully, "if it's not too late when I get there, there'll be some left over ...."

At North Highland Avenue, Gentry cut across the yard of one of the nice Virginia-Highlands homes and climbed the back fence, scraping one of his hands painfully as he hoisted himself over the sharpened, stake-like points across the top of it. A small dog hidden from view somewhere behind a hedge barked furiously at him as he scrambled through the slushy carpet of dead leaves in the vacant lot beyond the fence, the dry wrinkled brown husks reminding him of dead cockroaches. He stepped over the putrid, stagnant water of a drainage channel which, even in this first bitter chill of the fall season, still swarmed and buzzed with insect life. He reminded himself not to cross back this way if he returned during the warm, late afternoon—unless he wanted to emerge partially eaten.

At length Gentry came upon a wide expanse of cleared ground, where the green-brown skin of the earth had been scraped away to reveal the bright red Georgia clay beneath it. Huge engines of construction—bulldozers, Ditch Witches, earthmovers, steam shovels, and cranes—stood idle at the edges of the lot like yellowed saurian skeletons cast aside by archaeologists eager for greater treasures. Huge metal signs proclaimed the beginning of construction on this, the northeast MARTA line, but smaller red-letter signs dangling from a chain stretched across the site entrance warned, KEEP OUT—NO TRESPASSING.

Gentry stepped boldly over the chain and walked into the site, marveling at the deathly silence which hung over the place. There were no rattles of diesel generators, no shouted orders, no warning beeps from trucks or cranes backing up. Everything was still. All trees had been cleared out for an entire block so there were no natural perches for birds to alight, and none chose to land on the abandoned equipment and vehicles. No security officer confronted Gentry as he made his way through the site; he would have welcomed being challenged by a guard, as it would have been a quick shortcut to a meeting with the site supervisor. But no, beyond his own breath and heartbeat, the only sound Gentry heard was the gooey red clay sucking at the smooth soles of his badly worn shoes. He let out a sigh and sat down on the planks of a storage crate which floundered partially submerged in the clay. He listened carefully.

And then he heard the rumbling.

It came from below—something massive moving beneath the earth, shaking the ground as it went. Gentry thought at once of the MARTA trains but—no—this was not as fast as a train, although somehow it paradoxically appeared to have more force. Besides, construction on the line had just begun this week, so how could trains be traveling on it already? No, this was something else, something different.

He tugged the hood of jacket down, the cool air stinging his exposed ears, and listened more closely.

He recognized a sound similar to an industrial masonry drill, but with a distinctly jaw-like back-and-forth motion instead of a drill's rotating spin. Something was digging—*burrowing*—beneath the earth here.

Gentry smiled. "They're working down there," he whispered happily. "That's where I'll find them."

He got to his feet and, struggling against the sticky clay that clutched at his shoes, he continued through the construction site until he found the passageways leading down. There were several of them, all marked with DANGER—DO NOT ENTER signs, some large and graded evenly enough to drive a truck through, others narrow, vertical, and equipped only with iron rungs as handholds. Eventually Gentry found one with handholds that was unsealed, its padlock shattered on the ground beside it. He lifted the loose grating off its retaining pegs and cast it aside, eagerly climbing down and descending the handholds with the ease of a spider on a strand of webbing.

It all came back to him, his years of inspecting and maintaining the rails. There was a period in his life when three or four times a day he was dropping down a quarter mile or more of concrete tunnel like this in a matter of a few minutes, and sometimes returning to the surface almost as quickly. He was out of practice, yes, and over the years those muscles had weakened, but he could get them back in shape—yes, he could.

"As long as I've still got two good legs and two good arms," he thought, "I can find the foreman on this job and prove to him I can work ...."

The tunnel floor looked as if it was just a dozen yards away now. He slowed his pace. A weird smell, something like sulfur and animal dung, came from whatever machinery they were using down there, and a strange ambient light glowed blue-green. Gentry reached the end of the shaft and let himself drop down easily onto the broken rocky surface of the underground construction site. He shielded his eyes from the colored light and called out, "Where's the foreman? Who's in charge down here?"

The lights shined brighter in his eyes and he squinted against the glare. He felt intense heat coming in bursts like an animal's breath, but with a temperature more like an ore-smelting oven. Gentry's skin tingled at the heat and fear overcame him. He leaped back up to the mouth of the shaft, getting a grip on the iron handholds which were already warm to his touch. As he tugged himself back up, he recognized the distinctly jaw-like back-and-forth motion of the monstrous burrowing thing he'd heard from the surface.

It was right behind him, and coming up fast.

* * *

Dawn broke slowly, the first ribbon of sunlight beaming in through the window of the Mission's dining hall as Gentry chewed his grits. He sipped weak, warm coffee from a chipped ceramic cup as he idly broke a blackened bacon strip into smaller pieces with the edge of a bent steel fork. Then he pushed the plate away and beckoned to Smedley.

Later the two men sat together in the yard, swatting at the first morning flies which buzzed over to their chairs. Gentry fished a crumpled pack of Vantages from his shirt pocket and offered one to his companion, who accepted it wordlessly. The smoke helped keep the flies away.

Seeing the cigarettes, an old man who was new to the Mission ambled over and asked for one. Gentry slowly shook his head.

Disappointed but still hungry for conversation, the old man pointed down at Gentry's chair. "What happened there?" he asked.

Smedley sighed briefly. "S-s-subway accident," he said, after a pause.

Gentry said nothing as, like a parasite, he sucked the last puff of tobacco from his cigarette and then crushed it out on the edge of the chair, where his legs used to be.

The High Rollers

by Benjamin Adams and James Robert Smith

The "gateway to treasure" beckoned the tall ships more than 200 years ago, and modern-day treasure hunters follow in the same spirit. Innsmouth, Massachusetts, promises the finest modern entertainment in a setting of lovely rustic charm. World-class casinos, dining, and performing arts. Award-winning skyscrapers overlooking quaint, reconstructed canneries filled with over a hundred specialty shops ....

—From the unproduced advertising pamphlet,
"Visit Exciting Innsmouth — Massachusetts' Gambling Capital!"

Anthony King looked down from a height of thirty stories and surveyed the rainy twilight coast. The petulant Atlantic sniped at the ancient claws of land that stood adamantly against it. Whitecaps rolled in over the slowly regenerating remains of Devil's Reef, which had been dynamited for unknown reasons by the U.S. Government in 1928. King thought that he could smell salt air, but knew he imagined it, for his great towers were sealed against outside impurities, especially here in his grand penthouse. Somewhere, there was a faint and gentle pulse, a mild sound that indicated he might receive a message if he were so inclined.

His long legs took him across soundless carpeting to a speakerphone, a yellow carapace squatting atop a shining marble counter. He set his crystal down and let the wine breathe a bit more as he answered the lowly muttering mechanical request.

"King here," he said.

"Sir." It was Vagan, the security chief of King Towers, a man in whom King had placed a lot of trust. Relatively speaking.

"What is it? Any word on our missing guests?"

"No, sir. We've not ... located them. Not yet," he added. There was a very brief pause. "But we have heard from Mr. Steinberg. He—"

"Put him on," King ordered.

"Well, sir ...."

"Yes? What's wrong?" There was actually concern in the rich man's voice. Robert Steinberg was, these days, King's closest friend; perhaps his only friend now that his wife and children were estranged from him. The thought caused a bitter taste in his mouth.

"Mr. Steinberg doesn't seem to be ... he doesn't seem to be completely well, Mr. King."

"What do you mean?" Anthony placed his right hand atop the black marble, surveying his fine, long fingers, seeing their dark analog reflected there on the polished surface.

"We've received a couple of messages from him—we've recorded them for you—but they don't seem to make a lot of sense. I'll play them back for you, if you wish." The voice seemed nearby, although King knew the security chief's office was twenty-nine floors below, not far from the main gaming rooms where gamblers were supposed to be coughing up their hard-earned bucks into his accounts.

King held back an urge to lose his temper, to snap and break the illusion of his calm demeanor, the mask of the consummate deal maker. "Of course." *You fool*, he wanted to add, but did not. He preferred believing that he had self-restraint when dealing with his employees. An iron fist in a velvet glove, so to speak.

Without another word Vagan played back the message he'd received from Steinberg, called in from some location the security man had not yet placed.

Tony, the voice began. Only King's family and close friends called him that. Four or five souls, these days. *The buyers. Those fine fellows from the coast.* Steinberg giggled, then. *I don't think you should deal with them. I mean.* Here he giggled again, although the sound seemed to be broken by both sobs and grunts. *They drive a hard bargain, but I'd turn them down, if I were you.* A pause. *Which I'm not, I'm quite happy to say, you doomed bastard.* This was followed by a sound King thought sounded almost maniacal; a kind of laughing/sobbing that was suddenly cut short by the electrical click of disconnection.

"There's another message," inserted Vagan. "It came about thirty minutes later."

Again, Steinberg's voice. *These ... people have shown me things, Tony. If it's a deal you're after, this is such a deal! Um. If it's all the same to you, I don't*

wish to negotiate with them anymore. I can't do it. I didn't like their offices.
Here he laughed, a short guffaw that seemed painful. *However, if it's real
estate you want, they have as good a deal as you're going to find. A lot for a little, in your case.* Wherever Steinberg had been, his phone went dead. This
time, not even with a click, but rather a subsidence into faint static, in
which King could almost hear the whispering of a million voices at once,
a susurrus of sound that only ended when Vagan shut off the tape.

"That's all we have, sir. Mr. Steinberg did not call from his office,
nor from that bookstore of his. We checked. His store is closed, has been
for about a week according to nearby merchants and some of his clients.
His manager doesn't know what to do, so he's keeping it shut until he
hears from Steinberg."

Vagan waited for orders.

"Keep looking for him," King replied. "I need to see my friend
before I think about closing any deal with these people." He broke the
connection, not waiting for Vagan to answer. A man such as his security chief usually answered with action, at any rate. It was why King had
hired him.

King stood there for a moment, regarding his glass of red wine and
thinking about it not at all. The first offer had come three months ago,
just before King Towers had been completed, the first gaming casino to
open on the rocky Innsmouth coastline. He had been fortunate, he'd
thought, to have paid the highest bribes so that he had been awarded
the first license to open this establishment. But Anthony King was nothing if not a high roller. He had started his professional life with a mere
seventy thousand dollars in assets, and had built it to over two billion in
less than twenty years. High roller, indeed. He rubbed shoulders with
high-fashion models and heads of state. Power crackled in the air, like
electricity, when he snapped his fingers.

And yet, and yet ... the King Towers project had its share of problems. Construction had been harried by an inbred-looking batch of
locals who loitered around the site and pestered the hard-hat crew. Small
accidents had begun plaguing the site, and work fell behind by an entire
two weeks. "It's them damn locals," said the foreman, a normally stolid
fellow from nearby Arkham. "They got the Innsmouth look, and they're
spookin' the men."

The Innsmouth look. That was the first King had heard of such a
thing. Somewhere along the line some kind of genetic bad apple had
gotten introduced to some of the Innsmouth families, a joker card that
gave them bulging fish eyes and wide, floppy lips. They were disturbing

to the eyes, but obviously these poor, pathetic creatures were harmless. King fired his project foreman and all the other men on the crew who were from the nearby area, and brought in another foreman and crew who had helped construct King's Castle in Atlantic City. They knew nothing of Innsmouth or its peculiar legends, and weren't spooked by the locals.

Construction had gone fairly smoothly after that, although it still seemed the work had more than its decent share of problems.

With what had happened since then, it was no surprise that Anthony King had heard the word "curse" used to describe his hotel. Hell, he was halfway to believing it himself, the way things had been going.

The bidders wanted this place before the doors had so much as cracked to admit the first gambler. Never one to snub an offer, King had read that first mailed bid: a cash offer from a group of investors of which he had never heard. The Newquay and Raleigh Establishment, the letterhead had indicated. While the offer had been a healthy one, King had dismissed it with little fanfare. That had been shortly before the tower was capped and his penthouse was finished, before the casino doors swung wide.

Then a second offer had arrived, less than a week after King Towers had opened for business, much less business than they had anticipated when a rogue storm had surged up the Gulf Stream to batter the New England coast with sustained winds of 120 miles per hour. The power had been knocked out to the peninsula on which the Tower was built and had not been restored for almost a week, despite his stature as a deal-maker and his place as an employer in the Innsmouth community.

It had been during the storm that the first guests had vanished.

King and Vagan and the local police were quoted as saying the poor souls must have ventured out on one of the rocky jetties to observe the storm, not knowing what they were getting into. And the sea had merely dragged them to the bottom.

However, King thought differently. He had seen the guest logs, and Vagan himself had said that he had seen one of the three missing guests shortly after the storm had passed. The security chief didn't believe they had been foolhardy enough to risk an idiot's adventure in a hurricane.

"What do you think happened to them?" King had asked.

"I'm working on it," was all Vagan had said.

After that, King had shown the second offer to Steinberg. And it was then that his friend had mentioned something.

"You know, Tony," Steinberg had said, stroking his salt-and-pepper beard and gazing at the letterhead. "I thought the name of this investor's group looked familiar, and I think I've read something of them. Or at least on what the group bases their name."

"Newquay and Raleigh, you mean? What is it?" King had been more interested in the inflated offer for the Tower than in the origin of the name of some obscure investor group.

Steinberg had raised one hand, still holding the printed offer in the other. "I'm not quite sure," he'd said. "I'll have to check in some books I have at home, and in one I just acquired at the shop. But I know I've run across Newquay and Raleigh. Although—I think the second is a variant spelling of another, older place name with an Innsmouth connection: *R'lyeh*."

To King the word sounded like mere gibberish. "Never heard of it," he said bluntly.

Steinberg lowered his glasses and peered bemusedly at King. "That doesn't surprise me. The Innsmouth folks are notoriously close-lipped."

"Where on Earth do you get this stuff?" King said.

"Oh, here and there. Old books and hearsay. You ought to come up to the shop sometime; I'll be glad to show you a few things that would surprise you. I think."

"Your shop, Bob. Why the hell do you waste time with that place?" It was a sore point between them. Hobbies were one thing, but something to reconsider when they sapped valuable time.

"Don't knock my bookselling business, Tony. You've seen the bottom line. It's a money maker."

"Yes," King admitted. "You clear a respectable amount there, and it would be just fine if you were merely some middle class merchant. But you aren't. You're one of the best advisors I've ever had and if you put the time in with me that you do in that store, you'd be as wealthy as I am."

Steinberg had chuckled, enjoying an inner joke King would never fathom. "Sure, Tony. But then I wouldn't ever have heard of Newquay and R'lyeh, would I?"

They had shared a short laugh.

King had decided to turn down that second offer, and shortly thereafter three more guests had vanished from the place. This time, no one could blame it on some fools wandering into the jaws of a hurricane. This time, there was no reasonable explanation. It seemed the three guests, with no connection anyone had so far been able to make, had checked in, done a little gambling, retired to their rooms ... and that was all. No one had again seen any of them. Not the maids. Not a single porter. They had not again emerged into the casino proper, nor had they been spotted in any of the bars of in the parking lots or in the long and winding hallways of King Towers.

There had just been one image captured on video tape, outside the room of one of the missing gamblers: A Mr. Woodring who had been recorded in a brief moment. The middle-aged radio executive was frozen in grainy black and white with his access card jammed in the door lock, his head turned to peer into the shadowed hallway behind him. That was all. Except there had been something more when Vagan had run the bit of tape through a video enhancer. There in the shadows had been at least one other figure, something vaguely ape-like in its general outline, something which King had finally dismissed as an obvious anomaly in the tape. After all, nothing like that existed outside a zoo.

King found himself thinking often of that twisted expression on Woodring's face. He assumed the bottomless sensation in the pit of his stomach must be pity. It was an emotion almost as alien to him as fear.

Once more King looked around him, looked across the huge central room of his penthouse, at the gigantic plasteel window that afforded him a view of the snaggletoothed shoreline and the frothy ocean beyond, stirred up by the savage winter storm now lashing the coast. Sometimes, he missed his family, his wife and his two children. Female companionship was not a problem—he had the pick of the most beautiful women position could buy. But he missed his family. Everyone thought he was basically a bad man, full of greed; ruthlessness filed to a keen edge. A robber baron for the new millennium.

Well, that may be, King thought sometimes. Then he'd dwell on it, and he'd reconsider. *At least I wasn't always like this.* And he'd rub his hands together and think of himself as some great modern Shylock.

There'd been a time when that wasn't so—at least not quite. He recalled times when he had lived with Irena and the twins, Jeremy and Sabrina, in their various apartments. His favorite had been in New York, overlooking Central Park, where he had been able to take the kids in days when his face had not been so well known. Those were grand days—golden days—salad days they were sometimes called.

He hadn't been terribly greedy or terribly selfish in those times. Jeremy, Sabrina, and Irena with him, he had lavished them all with whatever they'd desired, and with his time.

King smiled, briefly, remembering. *Can I have a sandwich, Dad?* Jeremy, only five years old, had crept into the master bedroom much past bedtime craving a snack. *No problem*, his father had replied, looking up from some financial papers. Irena lay asleep on her side of the bed, a sleeping mask covering her eyes against the light King needed for his work. It had been no trouble. No trouble whatsoever. Sighing, he missed them, wishing Irena had not imagined herself secondary to his business.

But now the business was all he had left, and he poured himself into it with every ounce of his being.

The bittersweet smile quickly fled as he recalled the arrival of the third offer. There had been a knock on his office door, here in the penthouse, and he had assumed it had been either a security man unfamiliar with regulations or, more likely, another of the snoopy reporters from Arkham or Boston who were still skulking about the place. "Come in," he'd shouted, and the door had opened with a breath of vaguely fishy air to reveal a singularly repulsive individual lurking at the threshold.

"Who the hell are you?" King had asked, not a little angry at this intrusion.

"Eh," the man's wide, fish-like mouth had opened, a crack in his pasty, almost featureless face. "I am most sorry, sir. But you have chosen to reject our previous offers and so we find we must ... address you ... person to person ... to seal a deal for this ... property."

"What?! Who *are* you, I asked!" King had stood, reaching for the 9mm mounted beneath his desk, having already alerted security with the simple press of a button at his knee.

"I—" and the man had come forward, his white, doughy hand out in supplication, "—represent the Newquay and Raleigh Establishment," he finished. "We wish very much to secure this property. These King Towers." The man produced a document from the pocket of his coat, placing it on the desktop after King had reluctantly taken his hand in greeting.

Then they had talked for a while. King had later raged at 'Vagan, who had never received notice of the alarm his employer had activated. When they had inspected the wiring, nothing had been amiss. It had just not operated as it should have, King had been told. "These things don't happen here," King had told them. But what was done was done. Now Anthony King had the third and final offer and there was nothing to be done for it.

The money wasn't in question. He had checked the accounts of the Newquay and Raleigh Establishment, and they could back up the ridiculous cash offer they had made. "We need this property," the pale, fish-eyed intruder had told him. "You bought it before we could act. It was ... ah ... an error on our part. One we now must correct."

Now, it wasn't the cash that concerned Anthony King. It was the unspecified real estate to be given to close the transaction. They had offered the cash, which had actually been enough, especially due to the problems the Tower was facing because of the combined blows of the storm, the missing guests (the number was up to nine), and the lurid headlines playing out on supermarket tabloids and on those horrid newsmagazines on television. There was now the real possibility that King Towers might actually never turn the corner toward profit. There was the real possibility that, for the first time in his life, he might actually fail at business.

He wished he could talk again to Bob Steinberg. *If only you were here,* he thought.

With that thought, the phone muttered again. He knew it was them, the Newquay and Raleigh people. All of his calls were filtered first through Vagan's office, so he usually expected to hear the familiar voice of one of his security men.

"King here," he said.

There was a liquid sighing, as of some hollow pipe being cleared of blockage. "Mr. King," the voice said. King's mind was filled with images of that flat, fishy face, those sausage fingers extended to him to make the offer. "We will meet ... now?" Somehow, it did not seem like a request.

"Yes," King told him, not wishing to wonder aloud why Vagan or one of his other subordinates had not screened the call. "We can meet any time today. When can you come?"

"I am ... here ... now. I am awaiting you in your lobby." Silence.

Damn, King thought. This was strange. Very strange. Why hadn't Vagan alerted him? "Wait there for me. I'll be down shortly." He thought of the weird, doughy figure sitting in the lobby, frightening off guests, perhaps being photographed by someone, his disgusting image destined to appear on the front page of one of those tabloids that were now touting King Towers as some kind of horror palace. He hung up on the stranger and punched in Vagan's line.

After ten rings he slammed the phone down, picked it up, and once more punched in Vagan's number. Again, no answer. "What's going *on* around here?" he raged to himself.

He allowed himself one last glance out of the penthouse windows.

The storm had heightened in intensity, blinding sheets of rain driving against the plasteel windows. The coast was invisible, and far below South Street was a blur of dim light. But not a sound pierced the sanctity of King's retreat. The gale might as well be happening on another world, viewed dimly through an immensely powerful telescope.

Leaving his office, King padded across the wide expanse of carpet to the door of his private elevator. He jammed his thumb at the button, half expecting the thing not to respond. But the doors yawned silently and he let himself in, punching L to send him down to the Lobby.

* * *

The elevator chimed softly at each floor it passed, and King took a quick moment to check his reflection in the overhead mirror. The lean planes of his face seemed even harsher than usual, most likely due to the stress he'd been under lately. The skin under his striking, pale blue eyes was dark and slightly puffy. He patted his salt-and-pepper hair, lightly lacquered in place with styling gel. Was there more gray there lately? Vanishing guests, troubled construction, the loss of his family ... as much as he hated admitting it, the cumulative effects were taking their toll.

He must not appear weak in front of the Newquay and Raleigh representative. This casino represented everything King had left, all he could truly call his own any longer. He had sunk more than a good chunk of his fortune into King Towers. He had also invested his soul.

He would not sell. It had never really been in question.

The elevator began slowing, and King turned his gaze resolutely toward the doors, intending to present a determined, firm countenance to the Newquay and Raleigh man.

The soft, indirect lighting spaced around the elevator's ceiling flickered momentarily, causing strange mottled spots on the rich walnut paneling. King blinked. *That shouldn't happen*, he thought. Not with the amount of money he'd invested in power back-up systems after that first storm.

Then the lights faded completely.

In darkness, King stumbled as the elevator ground to a halt. His hands slammed against the door, sending a jolt up his arms. Muttering under his breath, he found his footing. "Dammit! What the hell is going on around here?"

His voice sounded tinny and petulant in the enclosed space.

Where were those damned emergency lights? They should have kicked on as soon as the main power was interrupted.

The darkness enveloped him, embraced him. It almost seemed like it had a life of its own.

The only thing to do was remain calm. A situation like this couldn't best Anthony King. All right. He took several deep, cleansing breaths. What to do? Call for help. Damn, he didn't have his cellphone on him; it was on top of his dresser, in the penthouse.

The emergency phone. Of course!

He groped to the left of the door and eventually found the cool, projecting latch of steel he needed. The emergency phone compartment opened easily. Beneath his questing fingers the handset felt smooth, calming; like a chanted mantra made concrete solid. With a sigh of relief, he lifted it to his ear.

The receiver was dead.

"No! Goddammit, you stupid thing, work!"

King reached inside the phone compartment and checked the connections. Nothing seemed disconnected or out of place. The coiled cord ran from the base of the handset to the rear of the compartment just as it should.

"God damn you!" he yelled in frustration and bashed the handset against the elevator wall, over and over again, until the rage finally slipped away.

His family, gone.

His fortune, invested in a hotel and casino that apparently ate its guests alive.

It was almost enough to make him reconsider the Newquay and Raleigh Establishment's offer.

Lord, it was dark in the elevator.

He imagined he heard noises around him in the pitch black. Soft, hollow liquid sighs and huffs, like the wheezing sounds made by the Newquay and Raleigh representative. Beneath it, a rhythmic pulse like distant waves washing against an unknown beach.

Was it the sound of his blood pumping, rushing through the tight confines of his veins and arteries, echoing in his ears, only audible because of the utter lack of any other ambient noise in the elevator?

Or could it be ... something else? Something in the elevator with him?

Anthony King fell to his knees and began pounding on the elevator doors. "HELP! HELP ME! IS THERE ANYONE OUT THERE? GET VAGAN! GET VAGAN!"

The panels thumped and rattled beneath his blows, and his voice echoed loudly, painfully. He lost track of how long he hammered and bellowed and only stopped when he felt his throat turning rough and raw. But as soon as he stopped, he heard the other sound. The one which he couldn't identify; whether it originated in his own body, or somewhere ... out there. Somewhere in the velvet darkness.

He abruptly pulled away from the doors and huddled in the center of the small space. *I'm losing it*, he thought. *All the recent stress—it's gotten to me. I must be having a breakdown. An attack of some kind.*

Someone had to come soon. They had to come.

Didn't they?

The pulsing noises around him ebbed and flowed, a dark tide encroaching on his soul's shore.

It was quite a while later when he began hearing the voices.

* * *

"Tony? Tony, do you hear me?"

King stirred at the sound of the familiar voice. It was coming from out there somewhere; somewhere in the world beyond his new black universe.

Irena. She had returned to him, come to rescue him from this walnut-paneled tomb. He didn't ask for a moment how or why. He was beyond questions and rational thought now.

He rushed toward the elevator door and laid his palms against it. "Are you there?" he croaked, his tortured voice a pitiful remnant of its stentorian glory. "Irena, are you really there?"

"Do you need me to be here?" she replied calmly.

"Oh, God, yes! Listen: You must find Vagan. Tell him I'm trapped in my private elevator. Tell him to get a crew up here and get me out. Please—hurry!"

"You really need me to do this for you, don't you?"

He couldn't understand what she meant. Why was she playing games with him? "Irena, please—"

"Where were you when I needed *you*, Tony?"

His bewildered mind couldn't make the leap necessary to comprehend her question. A small choking sound that might have been her name escaped his wounded larynx.

"I'll tell you where you were," she continued. "You were with your-self. It's always been about you, Tony King, and nobody else. How high you could climb the ladder of success. I was just a trophy. A beautiful bride, two lovely children, and you could barely spare us a moment of your previous time. But we looked good by your side. Tony King's ador-ing family, the American ideal."

"But—but that's not how it was—"

"If you think anything different, you're deluding yourself. But then you were always good at that. In the grand scheme of things, you're nobody important, Tony. No matter how much money you make in this lifetime, how much land you acquire, you still have to eat and sleep and pee just like anyone else. And die, Tony. You still have to die."

He thudded a clenched fist against the door. "Goddammit, how *dare* you speak to me that way? I provided well for you and the children. I was there for you when you needed me!"

"You were *nowhere*. Just like now. Nowhere to be found. Never around. Nowhere ...."

Irena's voice drifted away gradually, a fading echo in his head. *Nowhere*, he thought numbly, *I'm nowhere and nobody. I'm destined to die here, alone and unwanted.*

He thought he heard children's voices now, chanting some kind of nursery rhyme. It sounded like ... like Jeremy and Sabrina ....

"Humpty Dumpty sat on a wall.

"Humpty Dumpty had a great fall.

"All the King's horses and all the King's men

"Couldn't put Humpty back together again."

All the King's men. He giggled. *I'm King, Anthony Humpty Dumpty King. I sat on a wall and had a great fall and I can't put myself back together again.*

"Go away!" he suddenly shouted hoarsely. "Stop it—just leave me alone! Just leave me alone ...."

His voice trailed off as he realized what he was saying. These were his children, whom he had already lost once when Irena took them away. Now he was rejecting them.

Dear Lord, she'd been correct. He was just as bad as Irena said. Was there anything at all left that he could do to make it right?

"No, wait! Please, please—I—I didn't mean it. Jeremy, Sabrina, come back! I want you with me. Come back!

"COME BACK!"

But the children's mocking voices already had faded away into nothing, just as Irena's had. No, something both less and more than nothing: that same damn soft maddening pulse coming from the darkness around him.

And in time with that pulsing, a dim aquamarine glow began suffusing the inside of the elevator.

"The lights ... the emergency lights!" King breathed, feeling an immense wave of relief.

The light grew subtly stronger with each cycle of the pulsing sound. Soon it was bright enough for King to see clearly, though the eerie illumination made everything look almost as if it were underwater. Strangely, the luminescence didn't seem to emanate from the indirect lighting recesses by the ceiling, but rather from every surface; the ceiling, the walnut paneling, the brass control panel, even the soft shag carpeting all gave off the pale blue-green glow.

He didn't think he'd ever seen anything so beautiful before.

A soft whir, a momentary grinding noise, and the elevator resumed its descent.

*　*　*

Bob Steinberg clapped a comradely hand against King's back.

"Tony, we've known each other for ... how long now? Twenty-five years it's been, since we met at Princeton. It didn't make any sense to me that we'd become friends. I was a Jewish kid from New Jersey, lucky as all hell to get a scholarship to an Ivy League school. And you—pfahh! You were rich, good-looking, and had never wanted for anything in your life. Yet we clicked somehow. Am I right or am I right?"

"Ah—that's pretty much on the money," King said.

He was glad his old friend had shown up in the elevator lobby to greet him. The doors had quietly hissed open, and there was good old Bob Steinberg, large as life, waiting for him, a huge smile plastered across his fleshy face. But Bob seemed strangely edgy, and his beard and hair had turned shockingly white, making him look a good ten years older than the hale forty-five he actually was.

"So, Tony, I just want to say to you—and this is as your oldest friend, you understand—that I think you should take these fine fellows from the Newquay and Raleigh Establishment up on their offer."

As they walked toward the hotel's front desk, everything strangely seemed to glow with that same aquamarine light as the elevator. The Art Deco lighting sconces, the waist-high faux bronze ashtrays generously spaced every eight feet, the decorative antique dime and penny slot machines. Drowned blue-green faces smiled from the promotional posters advertising HOT ACTION AT OUR KENO TABLES! and EAT LIKE A KING AT KING'S TOWER BUFFET! and THIS SATURDAY AND SUNDAY ONLY! TOM JONES!

Dimly, King remembered Steinberg's messages that Vagan had played back:

I don't think you should deal with them.

They drive a hard bargain, but I'd turn them down, if I were you.

"But I thought you told me—"

Steinberg chuckled, a wet sound deep in his throat. "I was ... oh, let's just say ... a bit out of sorts when I called you earlier. I've come around to their way of thinking. Tony, they have got what I'd call the mother of deals you can't refuse. You're being offered the most unbelievable real estate deal in history. Actually, I'd wager in the history of the *universe*. Do you understand me? This is a once-in-a-lifetime opportunity. All you have to do—is give them Innsmouth. That's all they want."

"Innsmouth."

"It's very important to them, Innsmouth is."

King felt a surge of uncontrollable anger. "How the hell can you suggest such a thing? Do you have any idea what I sank into this old shambles of a town? What I went through to build this hotel, this casino? My God, Bob, I gave up my life for this place! I gave up my family!"

They had reached the hotel's lobby. In the strange blue-green iridescence, by the front desk, waited the Newquay and Raleigh Establishment's representative. His bulging eyes and puffy lips seemed more appropriate in the aquamarine glow, and for the first time King realized the man showed a more advanced case of what some of the locals whisperingly called "the Innsmouth look." It explained King's initial unease of the man; during the hotel's construction, other area natives with the same fishy appearance had gone out of their way to harass and worry the building crew. It was then that King had first heard whispers of King Towers being a cursed project.

"Believe me, Tony," whispered Steinberg. "This place means far more to these people than it does to you." He indicated the Newquay and Raleigh representative with a wave of his hand. "I know how much this place means to you—but you can't make it work. It's been a battle every step of the way, and you're losing it all. Take their offer. You'll reconsolidate in ways you can't even imagine. Ways you can't even comprehend."

"Bob, I—I don't know. Everything seems so strange, like a bad dream. I can't even trust my own senses. Am I going mad? Is this a nightmare? I ... I feel like I need to wake up, or something."

Steinberg merely smiled. He touched his button of a nose and then pointed from King to the Newquay and Raleigh representative. "Go talk to the man, Tony. He's prepared to give you the *world*."

* * *

The weird rep from the Newquay and Raleigh Establishment greeted King, that moist, flabby hand extended like a starfish made of unbaked Pillsbury dough. King took it, felt that same clammy dampness as before, and turned to say something to Steinberg.

But Steinberg was gone.

"Where did Bob go?" King asked, gingerly disengaging his hand from the rep's dank clasp.

"He ... eh ... he went that way," said the rep, pointing toward the far end of the lobby.

There was no way, thought King. Not that fast. No way. "Just a minute," Tony began, but the other interrupted.

"We go, now. We go to a private place to ... negotiate ... to seal this deal." The expression on his face was probably a smile, but it made King's blood run cold to see it. *My God!*

"We can return to my penthouse. Or to my security man's offices. We have a nice conference room there ... not too large and that would serve fine for our purposes." King extended his own arm to guide the visitor.

"No. That will not be ... eh ... necessary. We have ... secured our own ... eh ... *space* ... here." The stranger was already moving, his left hand at King's back, pushing him insistently, alarming Tony King with the power evident in that left arm. It was almost like being prodded by a very heavy metal bar.

Despite King's own desires, he let himself be led. "What room did you rent?" he asked. "The Queen Charlotte office?" That seemed the most logical spot.

"No. Not the Queen ... Charlotte room." The rep lapsed back into silence as they exited the main lobby. They did not go toward the elevators, but passed through a set of double doors that King knew led toward the entrance to the lower parking garage, or to the lower lobby and subbasements if one was so inclined. There were no decent conference rooms in that direction, and he was about to say as much.

But the light went a strange shade of crimson, and the carpet seemed to *undulate* beneath King's excellent, handmade shoes. He peered down at the carpeting, and could almost have sworn that the pile wasn't fabric at all, but was a tightly passed mass of vibrating *cilia*, like those of an anemone. Blinking, he tried to get the image out of his mind.

Peering ahead, the corridor seemed longer than it had been. It seemed to go on for a much greater distance than it possibly could. How far had they gone? He wanted to look back, to peer in the direction from which they had come, but the rep's hand at his back seemed so *demanding* that King just kept walking, keeping pace with the man from The Newquay and Raleigh Establishment. And he realized he didn't know anything about the rep. Not a damn thing.

"Excuse me," King blurted. "But ... I find I don't even know your name. Only the company you represent. Who *are* you?" And now the faint crimson glow of the light seemed to intensify a shade, and the hallway seemed even longer than it had, and he was suddenly gripped by the idea that the last thing in the world he needed to do right now was look the other man in the eye. Peripherally, he tried to see the stranger's face, and the image he conjured was of a fishbelly balloon expanding until the skein of latex was about to burst in that reddish glow.

"My ... eh ... name, you could not correctly pronounce." The rep paused, and there seemed to be a labored draught of air into his lungs. "Your own mouth is not properly ... eh ... configured."

The hallway ... *this* hallway, was much too long. *This can't be*, King thought. "Where *are* we?" he asked. "I don't recall this corridor!"

"Oh ... this is your building, Mr. King. It should have been *ours*, and, in a way, it is. But not in every way. We ... need what you call ... the legal ownership." He chuckled.

"What? Are you saying The Newquay and Raleigh Establishment represents Native Americans? Are these some kind of tribal lands?" They were slowing down. The other's pace was growing more sluggish. Ahead, in the reddish glow of the lighting, King could make out doorways.

"Oh, no. We are not ... *Native Americans*. We have *prior* claim."

"What are you saying?"

There was silence. Their steps became leaden. They slowed. They took smaller strides. One. Two. They stopped. "Here," the stranger said.

A door stood before Anthony King. He stared at it. It seemed made of something living, not of wood or composites or steel. He made a

motion, as if to touch the door, but the other reached out and stopped
him, stopped him cold with an inhuman strength that was exerted with a
casualness that frightened King more than the physical power exhibited.

"No ... not yet," said the stranger.

"What? Why are we here?" King made another movement, this
time to look back, but again the man from The Newquay and Raleigh
Establishment prevented this. Those sausage fingers gripped the base of
King's skull and aimed his face forward, so that all King saw of the way
they had come was a fleeting glance that froze his soul. The hallway apparently led into infinity. *It can't be,* he thought. *We can't have come so far!*

"This is where ... this is the time and the place ... we finish nego-
tiations. Your ... eh ... your Mr. Steinberg has completed the *legalities*, the
... eh, transfer of funds. We have paid you well for this bit of ... Earth."

King felt what remained of his control, his anger come up from a
tiny wellspring almost frozen completely over by his fear. "But we
haven't ... I haven't agreed."

"Yes ... you have agreed. You agreed in your own manner on the
way to where ... we ... Steinberg and I ... met you. There are things
that you desire ... *more* than you desire this segment of Earth." That
hand remained like a spongy vise on the base of King's skull.

"I ... you have spoken with my *family*? Irena and I can be recon-
ciled?" King could barely force his voice through his fear. He realized
that what he'd felt in his stomach when looking at the photo of the
unfortunate Mr. Woodring wasn't pity. It was a distant cousin of the terror King now felt in the grip of the stranger.

"Eh ... no. That is not what you desire." The strange man began
then to press King forward, toward the door before him, toward the portal that even then was beginning to tear open slowly like a wet film of
bloody tissue. "What you desire ... as Steinberg understood ... is property, Anthony King. You desire ... land ... and we can ... are prepared
... *have now given you ... all the land that there will be.*"

The doorway parted then. It parted like the afterbirth from some
mammalian orifice, and King was jammed through it.

The bottom fell out of King's world.

He felt himself surging in all directions at once, past light, past
things that hurtled by him at a speed he could barely comprehend. He
gazed around, and heard a familiar voice, heard Bob Steinberg screaming his name over and over. His old friend was cursing him.

Still King continued to fall, to be drawn upward, forward, in all
directions, expanding.

You shall have everything you desire, someone, some*thing* muttered to him.

For that small section of our place that is called, by your insignificant race, Innsmouth, we give you all of Earth. All that is left of Earth after we are done with it, after we have wiped it clean.

King tumbled forward, counter to the turning of the galaxy, along with the babbling mass of the Elder Gods. Rolling on high past dimensions and sights undreamt and unseen.

He will ride that wheel of light, is riding it now, has ridden it for untold centuries that turn his mind to sparks of madness, until he finds himself, will find himself, has found himself on the ball of dried mud he so covets.

In time, he forgets how to say the names of his wife and children, forgets that he even had organs to create children. He forgets the pleasures and pains of the flesh entirely.

He has forgotten all save the sun-scoured goal ... that globe of rock. It belongs to him now; the Old Ones have given it to him as his reward.

Earth.

* * *

... updating the news again, millionaire Anthony King has officially been pronounced dead. King vanished seven years ago, an apparent victim of the so-called "curse" that plagues his ill-fated King Towers gambling resort. The current owners of the late Mr. King's property, the Newquay and Raleigh Oceanographic Institute, have no comment about allegations made by Andrew Vagan, King Towers' former security chief, that King was murdered.

In other Innsmouth news, ecological efforts to restore Devil's Reef appear to be paying off, as reports of schools of large fish in and around the reef have been increasing lately ....

WAGL TV, Arkham

A Forty Share In
Innsmouth

by C. J. Henderson

or those of you just joining us here in Boston's venerable Fenway Park, tonight promises to be our most spectacular voyage ever into the realm of the beyond." Marvin Richards, host of the wildly popular show *Challenge of the Unknown*, had to choke back the smile threatening to ruin his carefully manufactured impartiality. It was difficult for him. Not because he was anything but the consummate professional, but because this time, he had really done it.

"For now, as promised earlier, we shall conclude our investigation of the disappearance of Thomas Millwright, Alan Bart, and Ray Nuttall— the three men who vanished from the streets of London nearly thirty years ago. As our regular viewers know, all three men were involved in the supernatural disciplines ...."

"How can he ooze that crap with such a straight face?" asked Marc Thorner, the show's new chief animated effects engineer.

"That's why they pay him the big bucks and we have to pray for overtime," answered his assistant, Larry Spezzi.

The pair were content to leave things at that, but another voice joined in, offering, "No—he can do it because he *believes*."

Thorner rolled his eyes. Spezzi covered a chuckle with his free hand. The speaker, an attractive young woman named Lora Dean, had been with the show throughout its first season. Their last show in the spring had coincided with a massive nightmare that had blanketed the globe. Certainly, one could indeed blame that live presentation for the hundreds of thousands of unexplained deaths which occurred that night. All one had to do was believe in witchcraft and malevolent dwarf races.

"Nuttall's diary revealed a tale of demonic summoning," said Richards, his calm tones echoing through the stadium, reverberating in homes throughout the city, the country, the world. "An ancient god was summoned, Bugg-Shash, the Black One, the Filler of Space—He Who Comes in the Dark—a creature or power of the outer dimensions which only the purity of light might disperse."

"Jeez, Dean," scoffed Thorner, ignoring the voice filtering through the speaker above their heads. His attention focused on his guide board, he begged, "Gimme a break, will you?"

"You weren't here," answered the correct young woman. Watching through the observation booth's thick, darkened plate glass, she reminded him, "The man you replaced was, though. He died that night. Along with twenty-seven more of the crew."

"Hey," interrupted Spezzi, "if you're so worried about what's goin' ta happen tonight, then what're ya doin' here? Why aren't ya stashed away safe somewheres?"

Lora admitted in her mind that it was a good question. She tried to say so, fighting to push the words out of her mouth. But she found she could not. Her lips had sealed one against the other, forcing themselves together all the harder the more she tried to speak. The young woman *had* been there—she *knew* what had happened. Convincing others, though, had become impossible. The more proof people gathered proving *Challenge* was responsible, the more the doubters shouted them down, terrified they might be right.

Happy to answer his own question, however, Spezzi told her, "What do people say when they pass an overturned school bus—that they was lookin' because they was so concerned about da little kiddies? Nah. That'd be a lie. Alla us—we look because we wanta see blood. Small twisted-up broken bodies."

The technician turned from his work for a moment. Staring at Lora, he smirked cruelly as he told her, "You're just human, Dean. An' human beings crave da bizarre an' da horrible." Snorting at his analysis, Spezzi then turned back to his work, adding, "Which is good, 'cause dats why we all got jobs tonight."

"Bart and Nuttall had originally summoned the beast," Richards told the audience—the tens of thousands in the arena and the hundreds of millions at home. "Chanting under the influence of mild hallucinogens, listening to the music of the then-popular rock group Fried

Spiders, the pair somehow stumbled on the exact mood and tone necessary to summon the elder beast from its otherly dimensional lair."

Lora had to admit that Spezzi was correct. After last season's closing episode, the world had become greatly interested in Marvin Richards' weekly productions. No one could actually prove the producer's blind stumbling had unleashed the horrors it had. No one in authority would even give such a notion the slightest credence—that was left to the masses, reading their horoscopes, calling their psychic hotlines, throwing salt over their shoulders. Over the summer they had bought every article and watched any newscast dedicated to the season closer of *Challenge*, and they were tuned in that night, by the hundreds of millions, hanging on Richards' every word—waiting.

"Nuttall and Bart managed to make their way to the light—which as we noted earlier was the only way to repel the shambler—and stay there long enough to involve Millwright, apparently against his will. But, again according to the diary, once thus entangled in the younger men's nightmare, the older, more knowledgeable Millwright was actually able to reverse the spell and repulse the demon now waiting for the three of them ... but only for a time."

Lora shifted uncomfortably from foot to foot. Her job used to be *so* easy. It had been so simple to ignore the legion of guests come to talk about being vampires and witches—about living in haunted houses or having seen a lake monster—about being abducted by aliens, probed by aliens, forced to have sex with aliens—come to show their amulets and monkey's paws and Mothman photographs, to tell their tales of Roswell and aliens corpses hidden in freezers by the government ...

Oh yes, she thought, *the government.*

They had come to the show, had taken Richards away for "discussions" and "debriefing." The producer/star had never spoken of what had gone on after the FBI had come to see him, or the FCC, the Secret Service, the CIA, or any of the dozen others. He had bluffed or made deals or pleaded or defied them with the searing ridicule that they might actually be labeled "believers." A hundred such theories had been put forth, none of which Richards had either confirmed or denied. Conjecture meant publicity, and after having gotten through the bureaucrats, he was not about to throw away a free summer's ride on the Speculation Express.

And now, she thought, here we are again. *Again.*

Lora bit at her lower lip, right hand grabbing her left wrist. Her legs tight, one against the other, she tried to get a grip on her nerves, to stop the dread boiling upward from the lower regions of her brain. She could not, however, for the harder she tried to dismiss what their show was investigating that week, the more her legs ached to bolt for the door.

"Millwright was killed only a week after the events described in Nuttall's diary," Richards continued. "Not by some fantastic, otherworldly thing from afar, however, but in a simple automobile accident. His death was duly recorded by the local coroner, his body removed to the town mortuary. But ... that was not the end of things."

No, thought Lora, her body shaking. Not by a long shot. His body disappeared from the morgue, the same day Nuttall and Bart disappeared as well. Without a trace.

Not true, objected a voice from the back of her brain. Shuddering, swallowing against the bile creeping upward in her throat, Lora agreed. The young woman tried desperately to reject the details forcing their way to the center stage of her brain, but she failed.

"A gelatinous mass had been found on the street halfway between the Windsor Tavern—the last place Nuttall and Bart had been seen— and Bart's own flat." While Lora cringed, rich color coroner's photos flashed on all the screens in the booth, showing those in Fenway and those at home what the young woman was so desperate to forget.

"The bloody slime you see coating the sidewalk proved to have been human in origin. After an extensive examination, both teeth and bridgework matching portions of all three men's dental records were discovered in the blackening pink slop."

Lora's eyes fixed on the decades-old photos. How could everyone remain so calm, she wondered. How? *How?*

She had held Nuttall's diary in her hands. The feel of the battered old thing alone should have been enough to convince anyone that they were dealing with something beyond their comprehension. The cheap plastic binding, the yellowing pages—the thing reeked of human terror. You could feel it in the paper, see it in the garbled, panicked scrawl of the later entries.

Even when the man had been describing his relief that the trio had managed to save themselves, gone was the steady hand found earlier in the book. Compared to the entries made before the fatal seance, the shattered penmanship of the volume's last few pages looked like the work of a lunatic. Thinking to herself of what Nuttall and Bart were supposed to have survived—if even for a time—Lora decided that lunatic might be too kind a word.

How about damned.?, she asked herself. *How's that for a word for people who go mucking around with things they don't understand?* Looking about at the others calmly going about their jobs, she thought, *This isn't some kind of game—for Christ's sake—what are we doing? We're getting ready to demonstrate how the patient died by putting the same gun to our heads.*

"So now," asked Richards, "the question remains, were these three men liquefied unto death by a horror they called down upon themselves? *That*, ladies and gentlemen, is what we will now try to prove, once and for all."

Then Lora Dean shuddered. Involuntarily she moved toward the rear of the room in jerks and starts, one trembling backward step after another. Her shoulders hit the wall, the cold of its tile cutting through her. No one noticed her retreat, however, nor heard the small whimper that passed her lips as her escape was thus cut off. Despite their mocking tones, Thorner, Spezzi, and everyone else in the booth was riveted at that moment, all their eyes pouring forth toward the stage below.

"We can not, of course, supply our audience with narcotics," announced Richards, "but we can duplicate all other aspects of the ritual as described in Mr. Nuttall's diary."

Even at a distance, Lora stared at the stage in the center of the vast arena below her. Trembling, she watched as a somber young man approached Richards. One of the production company's gaffers had been outfitted by the costuming staff with black horn-rimmed glasses and a patch-elbowed tweed suit, television's subtle way of conferring scholarly dignity on the tome he was carrying.

"Tell the audience what you have there, Robert."

"This volume, commonly referred to throughout the supernatural underworld as *Mad Berkley's Book*, is believed to be the only single source for the worst elements of such esoteric volumes as the *Unaussprechlichen Kulten*, the *Cthaat Aquadingen*, and even the long-lost *Necronomicon*."

"And this book was found amongst Ray Nuttall's effects—correct, Robert?"

"Yes, sir ... along with his diary. Both of which were loaned to us tonight by his estate."

Lora went tense, her fingernails digging futilely against the hard tiles behind her. She could feel the thin, pricking fingers of panic tearing at her, jabbing her spine, scratching the sensitive skin along the line of her shoulders. Sweat beaded across her skull, the first stale lines of it oozing down the back of her neck. Her eyes stared unblinking as Richards waved forward the Satanic priest he had hired to read the correct passage. She tried to remind herself that the man was a fool. She had met the so called Reverend Ralaratri during the taping of their show on cults. He had only been interested in being paid and in chasing every warm body in the studio, whether in pants or a skirt.

He's a phony, a clown. He's not a priest; he's just a performer. Just like Richards.

Yes, Richards, the voice from the back of her mind whispered, *the man who summoned the last nightmare.*

"God—"

Lora choked on the word, its power somehow seeming small and distant, and, in the face of what they were doing, perhaps even insignificant. She thought about the word "God." Was that not what they were attempting to contact? Some kind of god? And apparently just one of dozens, all held back from humanity by some veil she could not understand.

She had looked through *Mad Berkley's Book,* tried to read it, to comprehend what it held, but if Nuttall's diary had felt disturbing to the young woman, Berkley's volume had terrified her. Although its binding had been dry—practically desiccated—still the book had somehow left her hands feeling clammy, greasy. She had left off the reading of it cursing her curiosity under her breath. Now Lora wished she had the strength to curse.

A tear formed in her left eye, growing slowly in size, but refusing to break loose. The weight of it dragged at the woman, stabbing at her paralyzed eyes until they finally surrendered and blinked, knocking the repellent moisture free. The tear crashed against her blouse, soaking through to her breast.

Drips, thought Lora, *falling from the sky—even indoors. That was what the diary said. That's how it comes. That's how you know it's here!*

Lora fought her unreasoning panic, shouting within her mind that it had only been a tear. Doing so, she found the strength to move forward, her eyes searching the clear night sky for any dark shapes that might be forming over the stadium. She knew it was not possible—even if the invocation were to work, it had not yet been voiced. But it would be—soon.

On the stage below, Marvin Richards had just finished introducing the members of Fried Spiders—all still alive, gathered together by money and flattery from their lives as accountants, bartenders, and clerks once more to pick up their dusty instruments and prove that entertainment knows no honor—only desperate need and the pitiful ability to delude itself with self-importance. Somehow overweight and somewhat confused men in their fifties dressed in fashions three decades out of date was reckoned as showmanship. Lora might have laughed if the terror did not have her so firmly in its grip. Nor was that the limit of it.

Lined against the inner wall of the arena, an entire battalion of marines stood to the ready. Richards had staged a show consisting of two average comedians and seven even more average dancers for the local Army base. That and a check covering their transportation expenses had gotten him hundreds of armed men ready to defend the world against the kiss of Bugg-Shash.

Lora noted their weapons, tightly clutched, all of it for form only— death-dealers posed like puppets. Part of her mind wondered, *Could their bullets be of any use against the horror to come?*

Can gods die of lead poisoning?

Lora giggled at her joke. Below her the stadium lights were being dramatically shut down one by one. As the cameras switched over to infrared, half of Lora's mind wanted to expand her tiny noises outward into full-blown laughter, simply to collapse into a heap on the floor and to laugh and laugh until whatever was going to happen was over. The rest of her clamped a hand over her mouth and screamed in her ear, clinging desperately to sanity by giving in to the one insane notion in the air—

It's real! she told herself. *It's real and it's* coming!

And then Lora Dean gave in to the helplessness assailing her. What else could she do, she wondered. She knew it was coming—*knew it*. In the depths of her soul, even as the clownish Satanist on the stage stepped between the prop candles into his neon pentagram and began to intone the words on the prompter before him, there was no doubt that some-where beyond the limits of her imagination's ability to dream a black, fetid shape was sputtering free of its slumber and staggering onward toward her world.

She wanted to run, to stash herself "away safe somewheres", as Spezzi had put it. But where was that safe haven? An idiot god that existed only to bring death was on its way, a slobbering vileness that slid through the darkness, a thing that could be turned by the light, but never stopped. There were lights behind the booth's darkened glass, but how long could she stay within their wretchedly small reach?

Then all thought fell from Lora's mind as the first dark drops began to splash against the glass plates.

"It seems something is happening," said Richards, his mike overriding the Satanic priest's. Too busy calculating his overnight ratings, the producer failed to gauge the changes around him, either the slimy grayness of the drops striking him, or the immeasurable cold and blackness following them. In the near distance, a dark but delighted chittering began to trill, and across the stadium, the spectators awoke to the horror that they were about to get their money's worth.

Wet, noxious fingers of invisible blackness stroked heads and bodies, slurping and tasting, coming to those who had called for their touch. Instantly the crowd rose like a mad animal, panic leaping through the pitch black from body to body like electricity. Fright pushed and smote and struggled, jamming doorways and stairwells with flesh, pulling Bugg-Shash free of its dimensional restraints all the faster. Then the shooting started.

All around the stadium, marines lifted their weapons skyward, firing into the approaching darkness that blocked the stars and smothered the moon. Their bullets had little effect, only the red glow of each third round's tracer trail casting a moment of pink-orange light in the way of the hungry god's wanton path.

In the past, the tiniest fires had repelled the chilling slitherer, but not this time. When called by groups of one or two, only the tiniest vestige of the elder thing had ever come forth onto the Earthly plane. This time it had not been summoned by a handful of creatures, but by an entire world! Tied together by cables and satellites, all looking for Spezzi's blood and small twisted-up broken bodies, their desire to be entertained by the forces of Hell had finally been satisfied.

All around the world, in homes and taverns, in television stores and communal rec rooms, clinging uliginous liquid dribbled down out of the above, followed by the almost never-ending length of Bugg-Shash. Across every time zone, in both light and darkness, the rapturous horror sent forth a billion tongues, unable to check its desire to respond to the overwhelming call.

And thus was its undoing.

In tiny bites, answering the isolated summons of this or that magician over the millennium, the Ebony One had always been the relentless lurker, patiently waiting in the darkness until it could escape the hated light and come for its victims in a gelid splash of nauseous blackness. This time the call was overwhelming, pulling the bloated horror in a billion directions at once, stretching it across the face of a world.

Desperate to flee the repulsive light, Bugg-Shash strained to find only those voices in darkness, but there were too many lights and lamps webbing their way to the half world of sunlight. Too much of the shambler's essence pulled forward; the ancient vileness tried to kill enough of the summoning vermin to give it the energy to retreat, but there were too many calls, all of them protected by the glow of their televisions.

Too many ... simply too many ....

* * *

"Are you listening to me, Richards? Have you heard anything I've said?!"

"Yeah, yeah," answered the producer, still trying to talk to both his contacts in Hong Kong and Germany at the same time. "Streets full of rotting gook. Dead people all over the world. Car wrecks, plane crashes, people trampled and crushed. Yatida, yatida ... I heard you."

"But it's our fault," whined the network contact. "*Our fault!*"

Assuring his people he would get back to them, the producer/star of *Challenge of the Unknown* hung up all his phones, shut down his mobile switchboard for the moment, and then turned to say, "*We* didn't do anything. *We* didn't trample anyone. *We* didn't kill anybody. Okay? They didn't put away Orson Welles for the Martian invasion stunt, did they? And that was a phony. This was real—we told everyone it was real. It's not our fault if they didn't believe us."

The network man vacillated between tears and rage, unable to find any chinks in Richards' armor. Frustrated, he pointed to the producer's assistant, Lora Dean. The young woman was still cowering in the corner, hugging herself, murmuring low with her eyes shut tight. His finger shaking, the network man snarled, "*They* didn't believe us? *Us* didn't believe us. Look at your own damn people, for Christ's sake."

Crossing the room, Richards put his arm around Lora and said softly, "Hey, kid—you going to be all right?"

Slowly, Lora opened her eyes and looked up at her smiling boss. Sucking down his callous strength in greedy amounts, she managed a bit of a grin, then stammered, "You know, you know ... I don't know if this is the time to, to bring it up, but ... you don't pay us enough."

Then Marvin Richards' marvelous inner control snapped. Laughing, he bent down and kissed the terrified woman on the cheek. He hugged her with open passion, not as man to woman, but with the joy of an athlete embracing a teammate at the moment of a championship win.

Tousling her hair the way he would a dog's, the man cackled, "You're absolutely right. Your salary is now doubled—starting yesterday."

Still laughing, Richards leapt from his chair newly energized. Pushing the network man toward the door, he levered the annoying worrier out into the hall, promising to be right behind him. Then, in a moment of amazing tenderness, he somehow managed to break off calculating profits long enough to ask Lora, "Look, I've gotta go jump on this thing—you know—deal while the wheel's in motion. But, *are* you going to be all right?"

"I—I think so," answered Lora, shutting off her memories of the recent past like doors to a winter day—slamming them to save what heat she still possessed. "But, could ... could I ask you a question?"

"Sure. What is it, kid?"

"Did we really kill ... a god ... just for higher ratings?"

"Yeah, looks that way—ain't it cool?" Grabbing a cigar from his desk, a reward Richards allowed himself on only the most exalted of occasions, he bit off the end and spat it across the room. Firing the end, he tilted his head to the side and added, "You know, they're absolutely right. There is no business like show business." Then the producer/star disappeared through his smoke, off to battle the kind of leeching horrors he was used to—the reporters and lawyers and government officials waiting in the hall.

Lora watched the door shut, cutting her off from the pandemonium beyond. She had read enough of *Mad Berkley's Book* to know that they might have repulsed or confused the Filler of Space, but killed it? That she was not as certain about. Clutching at herself, the young woman found she was quite content to stay in her chair, legs pulled up, arms wrapped around them. Humming softly. Not closing her eyes.

Not daring to close her eyes.

The next day, when a passing janitor reached in to shut off the office's still burning light, Lora started screaming—a plaintive wail all the raises in the world could not silence.

Shudder Wyrm

by Stephen Mark Rainey

I.

Little disgusts me more than the methods of putting up new sub-divisions—"corrals", as we call them—favored by most of my counterparts in the land development business. My designs cost more than most, true, but what you will not find in a development by my company (Pinnacle Enterprises, should you ever wish to look us up) is the indiscriminate clearcutting of pristine woodland to make room for a cluster of prefabricated shoeboxes, the result of which is then christened Jefferson's Forest, or Lincoln Village, or Commonwealth Green, or some such deceitfully dignified appellation. No, this practice, so widely embraced by my peers, is a blight and an insult, both to my own sensibilities and to the good green Earth, which God instructed us to use wisely, not to rape and disfigure.

No, in a Pinnacle development, you will find homes and streets that blend aesthetically into the landscape with the least amount of damage to the local environment. In my communities, the greater share of the native wildlife remains in place, and I employ only a select crew of plumbing and wastewater specialists, whose top priority is to protect our natural watersheds. Face it, in this environmentally sensitive age, responsible use of our resources is only good business.

It was about six months ago that I was contracted for a new student housing project at Beckham College, a tiny but prestigious entity in the world of academia about twenty minutes away from my home in Aiken Mill, Virginia. It's a private school, as you might guess, since no state-licensed institution would ever pay the prices I charge for my projects. But the Dean of the School, Dr. Willard Vickers, apparently insisted on Pinnacle as the site's builder, and while I professed some bewilderment that he would choose the most expensive company for such a relatively mundane undertaking, I also felt rather honored; being my own alma mater, and the place where I met my wife, Beckham has always been rather special to me.

Dr. Vickers—who, I might mention, is the college's first black administrator—came to my office one afternoon with his drawings, which were passable, if a bit crude, and told me it was imperative that the specifications be followed exactly. He knew Pinnacle would be the one company that would never take shortcuts where shortcuts were not desired.

"I know you've done well for yourself, Alec," Dr. Vickers told me, "and I know you'll do well for us, too. Just like you did back in the classroom."

We chuckled together. Dr. Vickers had a good twenty years on me, for he was a chemistry professor back in the days when I attended college, but a casual observer seeing us together would probably think we were the same age. He stands most of a head shorter than I, and is considerably stockier; but he, at least, has a full head of hair, whereas mine began its migration when I was in his class. His fault, I'm sure, for many was the night I stayed up till dawn studying for his tests. His nickname, "Das Pedagogue", couldn't have been more apt.

"This will be the first of many renovations I hope to see," he said. "Most will follow plans similar to these. First things first, though. This project must be started as soon as possible."

I quoted him a time frame, which included all the necessary permits, the ordering of materials, and surveying; he looked a little disappointed at having to wait more than the month he'd anticipated, and I have to confess that his need for haste struck me as a bit peculiar. In the time since then, however, his reasoning has been made abundantly clear.

The contract was signed, and the project started in May, with a deadline I considered a bit tight; but I assured Dr. Vickers that at least the first phase of the housing project would be ready by the time the students reported for class in early September.

II.

Young Bobby Hoffman found the first of what he called "the Shudders" in my own neighborhood early one morning in June, shortly after the college students had left for vacation and the existing dormitories had been demolished. It was a Saturday, and I'd decided not to work for the weekend, even though I knew that to finish by the completion date, I'd have to schedule extensive overtime. While my wife Maggie started breakfast, I went out to get the morning paper; it was then that I saw young Mr. Hoffman kneeling by the curb across the street, toying with something that for a moment I thought was a snake.

"Hello, young lad," I said, walking over to him. "What's that you've got there?"

"A direful wirrum," he replied, not looking up at me. Bobby was ten years old, with a generally pleasant disposition, though like most children, he could be loud and annoying, especially when in the company of his neighborhood retinue. I noticed dirt on his hands and clothes, and his raggedy blond hair had gone all askew. When I saw what he was poking with a pointed stick, I nearly fell backward in surprise.

"My God, son, you should leave that alone!"

The creature looked to be about nine inches long, worm-like, but with two rows of multijointed legs that twitched erratically with each jab of the boy's stick. Its body was fleshy and gray, like an earthworm, but, unlike a worm, the creature had a distinct head with two black, bulbous eyes that were large enough to see Bobby's face reflected in them. Below the eyes, a pair of beak-like mandibles opened and closed sporadically, emitting a soft, breathy hiss.

"Gracious, I've never seen one of these before," I said. "Where did you find it?"

"In the woods over there," Bobby said, pointing to the dense stand of trees at the end of the cul-de-sac. "There were a coupla others, but they got away."

"How'd you find it?"

"There was a big hole, and when I poked a stick into it, these Shudders came out."

"Shudders?"

"That's what I call 'em. That's the noise they make."

"I see. You know, that thing could bite you—it might even be poisonous."

"I'm being real careful. It won't bite me."

As I started to step back, the animal's head turned to follow my movement. I waved my hand back and forth; the pair of eyes remained locked on the movement. Then, at the back of my skull, I felt a weird tickling, and for a panicked second, I thought perhaps another one of those things had somehow crawled up my back. But when I felt around, there was nothing.

"Tell you what," I said, "I think it would be a good idea to capture that thing and take it down to the college. Maybe they can figure out what it is."

"Can I kill it first?"

"No, no, let's try to get it alive. I'm sure the people at the school would much prefer it not be dead."

"Hokay," Bobby sighed.

I hurried back into my house, found a large Mason jar that I thought would accommodate the beast, then took the tongs that Maggie was using to cook the bacon right out of her hands.

"And what do you want those for?" she called after me.

"A direful wirrum."

Back on the street, Bobby had pinned his prize to the curbside with his stick. He was holding his forehead with one hand, and from his expression of pain, I thought perhaps the thing had bitten him after all.

"What's wrong? Did it bite you?"

"No," he cried. "It's yelling at me!"

"Yelling?"

"It goes 'shudder-meal-shudder-meal' loud loud loud!"

"Stand back!" I said, and, putting down the jar, I reached for the thing with the cooking tongs. To my surprise, it emitted a loud, piercing shriek, and again that weird tickling just behind my ears made me think that something was on me. But I grabbed it with the tongs just behind its head and dropped it quickly into the jar, twisting the lid on right behind it.

"You know, if I were you, I wouldn't go digging around for any more of these," I said. "He looks mighty dangerous."

Bobby shook his head like a dog after a bath. "Jeez," he said. "It sure hurts my head when it talks like that."

I wondered for a second just what he meant, but my attention immediately went to the trapped creature. It stared at me from behind the wall of glass with eyes magnified by the jar's curve. "I'll call down to Beckham after breakfast," I said. "I know some professors are still there for summer school, so hopefully they can tell us all about this fellow."

"Okay," Bobby said sullenly, no doubt disappointed to have me pur-
loin his find.

"I wouldn't go back in the woods," I said cautiously, hoping he
wouldn't do just the opposite. Bidding him a final good morning, I went
back in for breakfast after putting the jar and its evil-looking captive on
the workbench in the garage, where I hoped my wife would not find it
and cause a scene. Her dislike of crawling things is no better illustrated
than by the time she was gardening in the back yard and happened into
a large garden spider's web; in front of several amused and/or embarrassed neighbors, my dear Maggie had in seconds stripped off every last
shred of her clothing and made a screaming, quantum leap into the
house, an incident that earned this family a certain degree of notoriety
in the neighborhood.

There are, unfortunately, worse things than garden spiders lurking
deviously in the darkened corners of the earth, and it was not my wife
this time that had happened upon them.

                                    III.

"Mr. Lang?" came the voice over the telephone. "This is Alicia Sykes
from the Biology department at Beckham. You're the one that brought
in that strange animal the other day, right?" I told her I was. "Did you
say there were more of these in the area where you found it?"

"Well, I didn't see any, but the youngster who found it said he saw
others. Why, is it dangerous?"

There was a pause at the other end of the line. "It would be best to
avoid the area where it was found. Tomorrow we're going to send some
people over to investigate. Would you be able to meet them?"

I fretted a little; I didn't want to be away from the job unless it was
absolutely necessary. But I agreed to see them if they thought I could be
of any help. Dr. Sykes assured me they would appreciate my time, especially if I could see fit to bring along the boy who'd found the creature.

"You're in charge of the new student housing project, aren't you,
Mr. Lang?"

"Yes, that's right."

"Hmm ... interesting," she murmured thoughtfully.

Before I could question her further, she bid me a curt good day,
leaving me curious as to why the school would send what was presumably a team of specialists to check out an odd bug. Could it be that,

somehow, a new or undiscovered species of animal had turned up right here in our own little town? I could think of more appealing claims to fame; I didn't fancy having our community come to be known as Wormwood, or something similarly disparaging.

At the time, I was at my office, jotting down some survey figures from the college construction site. Every time I looked at Dr. Vickers' drawings, I found a new intricacy, some previously unseen nuance that he had obviously taken great pains to infuse into the design. No doubt about it, erecting the project would probably be the most expensive undertaking the college had ever funded, and if the Dean meant what he'd said about future renovations, then I'd hate to be paying the tuition for a son or daughter attending the school.

I had accepted the work on the Dean's word and the college's credit rating. But in the back of my mind, I was beginning to have doubts. Could the whole enterprise be merely some personal eccentricity the Dean had the hubris to charge to the institution? Certainly, though, even having reached the most mature of his professional years, Dr. Vickers could not have let good sense take a back seat to his own ego!

The deep—and I mean very deep—pool in the center of the complex, with its five channels that fed a similarly deep moat around each of the dormitories, would be a tricky feat of engineering. Fortunately, I knew a few vendors that could provide the amounts of granite that Dr. Vickers desired to floor the large, star-shaped common areas in front of each individual housing unit. But it would cost more dollars than I was comfortable dropping above the initial sum the college had paid me.

As I sat at my desk, I suddenly felt a thin vibration at the back of my skull, which crept through my head, seeming to pierce my eardrums. I cocked my head, thinking it a familiar, if disturbing, feeling, and it only took a moment to recall that I'd felt the same thing when I'd encountered Bobby Hoffman and his remarkable discovery. Then, over in the corner of my office, behind my file cabinet, I heard a distinct rustling noise, then a little hiss of breath that sounded like, "Ssshuuudddrrr."

"Daggumit," I said, rising from my seat, realizing that, very likely, one of those vile little bastards had made its way into my office. The idea of being bitten by its vicious jaws sent a shiver of revulsion up and down my spine; looking around for something with which to swat the fiend, I spied an aluminum T-square that I figured would do the job nicely. I confess to being peeved that something so reputedly rare had begun to show signs of a most offensive ubiquity.

I knelt down by the file cabinet and poked the end of the T-square back into the corner where I suspected the thing was hiding. However, my first strike evidently failed to put it down, for a moment later I heard the scuttling sound coming from beneath the shelves next to my desk.

Then I saw it—or at least I saw the tips of its multijointed legs protruding from beneath the lowest shelf. I crept stealthily toward it, then knelt down again to deliver a killing blow. But as I drew back to whack it, the thing wriggled into view, giving me what I can only describe as a chilling look with those monstrous, bulbous black eyes.

This one was at least twice the size of the first. As I backed away from the horrid thing, I felt a piercing whine drilling into my eardrums and, this time, my head felt as if concrete nails had been fired straight into my brain. I cried out in pain and shock, and fell back against my desk chair. I remembered Bobby saying that the thing hurt his head, and I knew that he had surely suffered the same kind of attack.

But my God—*what kind of attack?*

I'd heard the scream of a bat before, its voice so high-pitched that it could actually be felt; this had something of the same timbre, only infinitely more intense. And the ringing echoes in my head ... modulating themselves into syllables, it seemed ....

I backed out of my office into the reception area, which was empty at the moment. I took a few deep, calming breaths and decided that, rarity or not, the beast must die. Sherry, my receptionist, had gone to lunch, so I picked up the phone book and looked up the number for Orkin, hoping they could send someone out immediately so that I might be the proprietor of my own office again before the close of the business day.

IV.

As it was, the Beckham specialists showed up later that afternoon, and I left the exterminator to his own devices so that I might take the team back to my neighborhood. Dr. Sykes, an attractive brunette who looked about ten years too young to be a department head, had three men with her, each carrying heavy-looking cases of instruments; one of them held something that looked something like a metal detector, but which scanned for hollow spaces underneath the earth's surface, so I was informed—certainly a tool that would come in handy in my business. Dr. Sykes, however, seemed loath to give me the name of a supplier.

I had called on Mrs. Hoffman and explained the situation to her; she somewhat apprehensively allowed Bobby to talk to the Beckham crew, but insisted on remaining with him. Mainly, Dr. Sykes wanted him to show her the exact spot where he'd found the creature, but when she asked him if it had made any noise or done anything that made him "feel funny", my skin suddenly crawled as if one of those things had leaped upon me.

"It screamed," Bobby said. "It made my head hurt. It was talking to me, I think."

"It talked?"

"Not with a voice, really. But inside my head."

"He has a point," I interjected. "The same thing happened to me today." I explained about the unwelcome visitor at my office.

"You saw one today?" Dr. Sykes looked pained that I had not broken the news to her sooner.

"Yeah, it was bigger than the one Bobby caught the other day."

"And you called an exterminator?"

"I do have to work, you know."

She sighed. "Once we're done here, we must go straight to your office." Just then, one of the men in the woods called to her and she hurried to see what he'd found. I followed at her heels, leaving Mrs. Hoffman—apparently nonplused by the hubbub over Bobby's direful wirrum—to take her son hastily home.

The man was standing before a wide, deep-looking hole near the base of a stout oak tree, holding two halves of what appeared to be a hollow, spherical object the color and sheen of a pearl, but roughly the size of a cantaloupe.

"Is this the only one?" she asked.

"So far."

"Definitely chthonic."

"Yes."

"Well, let's clean the nest. There may still be others down there." Dr. Sykes then surprised me by pointing to the fire hydrant at the edge of my yard. "Let's hook up over there," she said.

"Right away, Doctor," the man said, and he hurried off toward the featureless black van in which they'd arrived. A moment later, he and his partners had removed a heavy, coiled fire hose from the van and attached one end to the hydrant; once it was connected, two of them carried the nozzle end back to the hole in the ground and immediately opened fire. The powerful gush of water sounded like thunder as it flooded the cavity, and the flow continued for a long time without backing up as I expected. Evidently, this aperture in the earth went deep indeed!

"So what gives?" I asked Dr. Sykes. "I think some answers would be in order here."

She began walking back toward the van, seemingly uncertain about how much of her esoteric knowledge she should reveal to me. Finally, she said, "The fact that these creatures appeared near your house, and at your office, is more than a coincidence, Mr. Lang. I would be very surprised if the portal we just flooded is the only one around here."

I stopped in my tracks. "You're telling me these things were *planted* by someone—with the intent to do me harm?"

"That's only a slightly erroneous assumption," she said. "Planted, yes, but not by *someone*."

"Do tell."

"Your experiences with the creatures have been, shall we say, out of the ordinary, have they not? The feelings you've had that they are actually 'attacking' you. The sensation that they are almost 'talking' to you. As they grow, their ability to affect you—to affect your *mind*—increases. I know this sounds very strange to you, but you must trust me. They know who you are, Mr. Lang, and what you are doing."

I couldn't suppress the snicker and the shudder that came upon me simultaneously. "And what am I doing?"

"You are constructing a complex that is designed to hold them at bay. The chthonics are not widespread on the earth, Mr. Lang, but where they exist, they do so with a tenacity and a ruthlessness that is frightening to behold. It is the ambition of the organization to which I belong— apart from Beckham University, as you have no doubt guessed—to eradicate this blight. Admittedly, it is a tall, almost impossible order. Yet one that we seek to carry out with all possible haste and thoroughness."

"Dr. Sykes," I said, scarcely able to swallow the amount of information suddenly being fed to me, "what the hell are these ... 'chthonics', as you call them?"

"Old ones," she said softly, as if afraid the air itself had become a threat. "Beings that were old when the dinosaurs walked where you and I are standing. Beings that came here from places beyond—and between—those that make up the physical universe as we know it. Their types are as diverse as the earth's own indigenous life. These that we encountered here are among the more common ... descended from a being whose name can be approximated by the term 'Shudde-M'ell', a monstrosity that exists *somewhere* below us. Its reality includes dimensions of time and space that to us are unreachable, unknowable. But from time to time, it invades the reality we occupy, and there is every indication that it has done so quite recently."

"Dr. Sykes, if I hadn't seen and experienced what I already have, I'd think you needed to be committed."

She laughed lightly. "So would most people, Mr. Lang, which is the very reason that our organization operates surreptitiously, inasmuch as possible."

"And just what is your organization?"

She smiled wryly. "For now, let's let that remain my secret."

"Tell me," I said, after several moments of thoughtful silence. "What was the point of flooding that hole?"

"For all their unique, deadly properties, the chthonics of this variety have a few crucial vulnerabilities. Water, of all things, is one of them."

"My God," I said, "if that is the case, the answer to wiping them out seems relatively simple."

"It might be, if these creatures traveled in the open ... or always in the same space-time continuum as us. And as I said—this is only one variety, Mr. Lang. What if I told you that an entirely different breed inhabits the waters of the earth?"

"If that were the case, why would their existence not have been discovered and reported by now?"

"But it has, to the degree they have allowed it. Think about that."

"That they have allowed it?

She nodded. "There are instances throughout history of encounters with them, most of which are discounted by rational men. This again is one of their most significant advantages."

"Then why not take what you know to the public? Present all the evidence, convince everyone the way you wish to convince me?"

She smiled again. "The main point you need to consider, Mr. Lang, is which race in reality holds dominion on this planet. And which suffers whom to coexist with the other, according to its own best interests."

I felt a frigid finger of dread brush up and down my spine at the implications of her statement. At that moment, I wanted nothing more than to believe that this woman, so young, whose main concerns should by all rights be about a healthy career in the academic world, about romance, or about raising a family, was merely a silly, misguided individual whose imagination had gone completely awry. Yet, after what I'd seen—the creatures themselves, these men with their equipment, Dr. Vickers and his outlandish architectural plans I had committed to developing—there was no way to write off what was happening as some kind of mad game.

"So, Dr. Sykes," I said, "What shall I do to defend myself? Get a water pistol?"

Her little laugh brightened my mood, yet at the same time chilled me with its confirmation of all that she had revealed to me. "If you wish," she said. "However, I recommend a heavy-duty, double-barreled water gun with a battery-powered compressor and at least half-gallon capacity. I believe they carry them at Wal-Mart."

V.

From there, I took Dr. Sykes and crew to my office, where Sherry informed me that the exterminator had found no sign of undesirables, but had sprayed anyway. The stink of insecticide was strong, and as most of the working day was already shot, I told Sherry to go ahead and leave, giving the Beckham team an opportunity to examine the premises thoroughly. I was relieved when they informed me they couldn't find any signs of a portal that posed an immediate threat.

That evening, I managed to spend a few pleasant hours with Maggie, complete with dinner out—her suggestion, because I seemed so vexed and fatigued. It was certainly easy enough to blame the pressures of the Beckham project, what with the tight deadline and the sheer amount of work to oversee. We both retired early, and I hoped to get a good night's sleep, since I intended to be at the construction site by seven in the morning.

But as I lay by Maggie's side, listening to her peaceful breathing, I thought I felt the faintest vibration at the edge of my perception, as if something very far away was *tugging* at me, trying to get my attention. Shortly before midnight—I remember because I looked at the clock— the bed began to quiver slightly. Even the lamp on my nightstand shifted and shook, and after a few moments, I could hear a deep, distant rumble that inexplicably sent a thrill of horror through my entire body. I began hyperventilating, and only recovered when my wife began to stir next to me.

It took a good hour after the distant sounds had fallen silent for me to drift into an uneasy sleep—though using the term "uneasy" is much like calling the Grand Canyon a little wormhole.

VI.

Pulling me pulling me pulling me pulling me pulling me pulling

VII.

"I felt it too," Dr. Sykes said. "Distant, but distinct. If I were you, I would prioritize the completion of the star formations. Dr. Vickers configured the pattern to preempt a strike from below on the students, but they will also protect you while work is completed on the dorms and the water basins. No one is completely certain why the symbol is effective, though the prevailing theory is that the Old Ones' aversion to what we call the Elder Sign may have actually been 'programmed' into their psyches by their own creators—who themselves, we believe, required a means of defense against them."

Drs. Sykes and Vickers had come to pay their respects at the construction site, where I'd been since dawn, as sleeping had become a thing of horror. It was now near lunch time, and I was pleased to see that my work crew was going full bore, with the foundations for the five, five-pointed star patterns of granite now finished. Completing the basin for the star-shaped pool in the center of the complex would still require several days, due to its great depth.

"You know the specimen we collected from you?" Dr. Sykes asked. "What would you say if I told you it was now six times the size it was when your young neighbor found it?"

"My God, that's unbelievable!"

"We have it housed in a relatively safe facility, though at this point, nothing is foolproof. I believe it is going to be necessary to dispose of it to ensure our own safety. The fact that these creatures are able to communicate over great distances with each other—not to mention their unpleasant habit of completely disintegrating upon their expiration—makes them almost impossible to study. There's still so much about them we do not know."

Dr. Vickers put his hand on my shoulder. "Alec—are you prepared to witness something unlike anything you've ever imagined? Be warned: It might be considered gruesome, by some."

"You're asking me to witness the destruction of the creature."

"Yes."

I nodded thoughtfully. "I think I would, yes."

Dr. Sykes was leading us down the path through the trees toward the main campus, and, for a moment, the whole world seemed like it had stopped. The air quivered with that same vibration from the night before, just prior to the pronounced shaking I'd felt. Not a single bird or insect dared intrude upon the silence. We halted and listened.

"It's as if they know," Dr. Vickers said. "It's eerie."

Dr. Sykes nodded in agreement, her face darkened by a disconcerted frown. She turned to take a step—only to stumble awkwardly, and with a little "oh!" of surprise, vanish suddenly from view. As quickly as it had appeared, the hole that had opened beneath her feet began to close, filled in by something from below with the very earth it had undercut from the surface.

"Oh my God!" Dr. Vickers cried, his face going ashen. "Alicia! No!"

I dropped to my knees, plunging my hands into the now rising mound of earth, my fingers meeting only solid, unyielding dirt. "Dr. Sykes!" I cried after her. "Please, no!"

I thought for a second I could hear a far-off, agonized scream, but I prayed that it was only my imagination. I felt tears welling in my eyes.

"There's nothing we can do," Dr. Vickers whispered. "She's gone."

My soul cried out to try saving the poor woman, yet I knew it was hopeless. I suspected that even as we looked helplessly at the now repaired piece of ground, Dr. Sykes was already dead.

"Alec," Dr. Vickers said softly, "we must destroy the thing. Now, at this very moment. We can do that much to avenge her. ... Oh no, oh no, her family. I must tell her family."

"What in God's name will you tell them?"

Dr. Vickers' expression chilled me to the bone. "We have prepared for this eventuality since the beginning," he said.

VIII.

It was the most abominable living creature I had ever beheld. Fully five feet in length now, the monster had matured into what was obviously a predatory machine. Its jointed legs had lengthened into prehensile stalks with wicked, barbed ends that looked capable of both grasping and slashing. Above them, its bulbous eyes sprouted from a knobby skull that now bore the beginnings of a bony, ridged crest that spread partially over its back like a shield. The elongated body had broadened grotesquely, its worm-like segments pulsating slowly, as if the thing breathed with lungs. What disturbed me most of all was when its eyes rolled my way, tiny red, slitted pupils gleaming with what was surely *recognition*.

It rested within a cubic casing of transparent material that I thought was Plexiglas, suspended above a six-foot deep pool of water; each surface of the case had been etched with a five-pointed Elder Sign. From the ceiling above, the nozzles of an array of powerful spray guns pointed at the cage as an added measure of defense.

"Beneath the floor is a network of pipes that circulate water constantly, in case any of them try to come up from below," Dr. Vickers said. "You'll note there is a similar, but improved, arrangement in the plans I gave you for the student housing."

We were in a sublevel of the college's gymnasium, which had a swimming pool, thus the apparatus to supply water inconspicuously for the holding pen. From the complexity of the arrangement, I could only assume that the team had hosted any number of similar guests here. Just how much history did Dr. Vickers have with these ancient monsters, I wondered; had he been delving into such dreadful secrets even when I was his student?

"Now," he said, "this horror must be eliminated. Alec, you may feel an assault on your mind at any moment. It may well sing the song of the siren to you, but you must not give in to it."

Even as I nodded to affirm my resolve, I felt that creeping tickle at the back of my skull and realized the thing must have fathomed our intentions. Its feeler-like appendages began whipping at its Plexiglas prison, and I could hear a high-pitched piping from within, a furious challenge to the death sentence we had passed upon it. Inside my head, strange music began to swirl with chaotic rhythms, alternately tranquil and violent, its purpose to draw my attention solely to the sounds, the *sensations* it generated inside me.

"Alec," called Dr. Vickers. "Stand away. I'm going to lower the casing into the water; once it's submerged the compartment will be flooded."

The Dean's words jarred an unexpected, angry response in my brain. Consciously, I knew it had been willed there; the beast was attempting to sway me into interfering with Dr. Vickers' plot. But it would have been so easy to let it overcome me, its power so insidious, so compelling. I could tell from the pained expression on Dr. Vickers' face that he suffered an equally severe attack—but he had the advantage of prior experience and preparation. For a brief moment, I actually made a move to stop him from opening the panel in the wall which housed the controls to the holding pen's mechanisms, and only by the strongest effort of will did I resist.

Dr. Vickers reached for a lever within the control box; giving me a preparatory nod, he grasped it—then turned his eyes to meet those of the beast. For a moment their gazes locked, and I felt the seething rage passing between them: a white hot surge of crackling energy, as tangible as a lightning bolt. Then Dr. Vickers threw the switch, and, with a grinding of gears, the transparent cubicle began to lower into the pool, its tenant now thrashing wildly against the unyielding Plexiglas.

Then the world changed, and I saw one of the panels crack, bulging outward with the pressure from within. A pair of jointed tentacles spurted from the rift, thrashing upward and wrapping themselves around the heavy chains that supported the cage. The sounds of the beast were suddenly amplified as the damaged panel now shattered and fell into the water. As the horror within pulled itself free, it quickly launched itself onto one of the supporting chains, managing to do so with only the tip of its tail making contact with the water in the pool. Even that caused the thing to scream at such a pitch that I thought the very ceiling of the chamber we were in might come crashing down.

Dr. Vickers stood in frozen disbelief, shaking his head helplessly. "It can't do that," he whispered. "Not possible."

It was then I realized that, all along, the sounds that had penetrated my brain had not come solely from our one captive; the weird musical piping surrounded us, wound through the air like an uncoiling knot of serpents. The monster's siblings, I thought; somehow they had found a weakness in Dr. Vickers' defenses.

For long moments both of us remained hypnotized, unable to act or react to the sudden turn of events. Then I saw that Dr. Vickers was trying—and failing—to break eye contact with the thing on top of the casing. I had to intervene somehow, focus all of the beast's attention on me.

The idea of subjecting myself to that thing's entire psychic arsenal nearly melted my resolve. But Dr. Vickers then managed to point to the control box—and I simultaneously saw what he had in mind. By a sudden surge of will, I broke free of my paralysis and leaped for the box to throw the second lever ... and a moment later, there came a thunderous roar as the nozzles in the ceiling opened and four jets of water burst forth with accurate, deadly purpose. Then followed an unearthly, shrill scream as the monster's grip on the chains loosened and the worm-like body plummeted, flailing, into the pool below, sending up a geyser of water that fell over us with a shocking chill.

The sounds of its death throes rose to an ear-shattering pitch, and I saw that, within the pool, the creature's body seemed to be turning *insubstantial*, its rippling flesh turning translucent to expose partially the grotesque, palpitating organs within. Its eyes bulged like inflated balloons, then burst, leaving black, hollow cavities from which purple-colored fluid began to spread and discolor the water. In a moment, the surface had become thick with gray and pink sludge, obscuring the view of whatever remained of the dying monstrosity.

As the thrashing in the water began to subside, the piping sounds around us only increased. I could feel the floor vibrating beneath my feet, gradually intensifying as the sounds closed in, seeming to move nearer.

"It's the others," Dr. Vickers said. "Their combined voices were sufficient to weaken the casing."

A deep, warbling hum that I felt through the soles of my shoes began to rise in volume, and I remembered that what we had destroyed was merely a baby. If these alien things bore any connection with life as we knew it, the assault on us now came not merely from the dead one's siblings, but its vengeful parents. I did not want to guess at how huge they must be, given the depth and volume of the sounds they emitted.

A crunching, crackling sound rose from behind the walls; from Dr. Vickers' expression, I knew that the monsters were breaking through. "Will the water pipes stop them?" I cried.

He shook his head. "I don't know. If there are too many of them—"

"The swimming pool," I said. "We must get upstairs!"

"Too late!" Dr. Vickers cried, as a chunk of tile broke from the wall above him and crashed to the floor, barely missing his head. He pointed to the slime-choked pool behind me. "In there! Go! Quickly!"

Without hesitating, Dr. Vickers leaped into the death-polluted water, just as another portion of wall collapsed and pelted me with dust and debris. From the dark recess now exposed, I saw dual slashes of crimson within a pair of black globes lock upon me and begin to rush forward. With a cry, I followed Dr. Vickers' lead and splashed into the horrible, frothing pool, praying that what we had deposited there was truly dead.

I submerged just as a piercing shriek filled the chamber, and something hit the water next to me that I prayed was mere debris. Now, even under water, I could hear—*feel*—the dirge-like screaming of the invading monsters.

Finally, forced up to breathe, I broke the surface of the water, to find myself facing an unimaginably huge replica of the thing that had expired such a short time previously. A cluster of jointed tentacles, each at least twenty feet long, whipped viciously from the gaping maw in the wall, one of them slicing the air only inches above my head. Having seen its quarry, the creature exulted, raising its head to crash through the remaining portion of wall and ceiling above.

The beast's apparent jubilation proved its undoing. I heard a new screech of agony and a sudden, thunderous crash of water that continued on, and on. The floor beneath the pool had collapsed, I realized, and the water was now pouring down upon the monster—and whatever others accompanied it in its underground burrow. A blast of hot steam billowed from the mouth of the burrow, forcing me to submerge into the reeking water again. I stayed under as long as my lungs dared allow, listening to the rumbling, crashing sounds that completely filled the world outside.

Finally, when lack of oxygen forced me to come up again, the sounds of destruction had begun to fade away, echoing hollowly like the passing of a train in the distance. Most significantly, I could no longer hear the terrible piping sounds, and, to my surprise, I saw several of those long tentacles lying motionless on the floor, already beginning to steam and dissolve. The reek of death began to waft through the chamber, and clouds of greenish mist crept worm-like out of the break in the wall.

Behind me, Dr. Vickers broke surface, gasping and choking. "Good Christ!" he exclaimed. "This is stinking awful!"

I cautiously climbed out of the pool, which even as it had sheltered us had begun to clear of the foul traces of the thing it had destroyed. Dr. Vickers accepted my offered hand and drew himself out of the pool, rather comically straightening his soaking tie. Together, we crept to the opening in the wall and peered into the darkness, unable to see anything beyond the roiling steam.

"They're dead," Dr. Vickers said with a nod of certainty. "I'm guessing that there were two adults and at least two young. They are fiercely devoted to preserving their own kind, especially their offspring; any losses they suffer have a strategic impact on their overall strength."

"Might there be more in the vicinity?" I asked warily.

He shrugged. "Probably not now—but there will be. I think we can assured of that."

"The bad one—Shudde-M'ell—it was not among them?"

"If it were, we would not have survived."

I looked back at the pool, found that the water was now clear enough to see the bottom, with only a thin layer of pinkish-gray discoloration on the top. "Then I'd say there's work to be done, isn't there?"

He nodded. "A lot of work, Alec. And there's no time to lose."

IX.

When we emerged from the wreckage of the gymnasium, I was shocked to find that most of the trees on the campus were toppled or leaning; all the windows of the nearby buildings were shattered, and the neighboring roofs had lost most of their shingles. By all appearances, a very severe but localized earthquake had shaken the college. With no corpses left to corroborate any story I might have to tell, I knew that the difference between what the world at large believed and what had actually happened here would be considerable.

The most anomalous aspect of the event would have to be the deep, snaking trench that wound across the campus, as if something had burrowed its way toward the gymnasium from a point to the west of the college—but moving *around* the new student housing complex, without so much as separating two nailed boards or cracking any of the cement foundations. One would have been hard pressed, however, to make a convincing argument that something other than a natural fault had created the winding underground furrow, the roof of which had subsequently collapsed.

Sadly, the quake had resulted in the disappearance, and presumed death, of Dr. Alicia Sykes, the head of the Biology department.

Since that time, the student housing project has been completed, exactly to Dr. Vickers' specifications; and in a strangely fortuitous twist of timing, the Beckham earth tremor necessitated a major renovation of the entire campus, which was begun, again, with Dr. Vickers' unique designs serving as the blueprint. Given the unsurpassed loyalty and generosity of Beckham's alumni, a substantial building fund was established which allowed the school easily to afford a high-end Pinnacle construction contract.

As for myself, I have set about the campus project with a determination and haste that has not only met but surpassed the difficult deadlines set by the Dean. My dear wife has rather stoically endured my spur-of-the-moment decision to renovate our home, which she complains is aesthetically unnecessary and prohibitively expensive. I think she must wonder if the Beckham earthquake didn't somehow unsettle my sensibilities, but like the devoted and understanding wife she has always been, Maggie has quietly accepted my position that our house has never looked better with its new, pentagram-shaped terraces of granite, and the deep—and I mean *very* deep—moat that flows around the property.

Spaghetti

by Brian Lumley

I

What struck me at once and most forcibly about my friend's proposition, put to me that evening in 1977, in the steak house next door to the Old Horse and Cart in North London, not two hundred yards from the A-1, was that he actually seemed to have some sort of fear of the old house. This is the first insistent thought or memory which returns to me out of the strangeness of it all every time I think back on it: Andrew Carter's *fear* of the place. His fear of entering and working there alone. Of course I understand it well enough now, but at that time ....

Now, I have called Andrew my "friend", but perhaps "acquaintance" were the more accurate description; for in fact we were very different and had only got to know each other over several years and countless tots in the bar of the Old Horse and Cart. Indeed it might be said that the one thing we really had in common was the fact that we both enjoyed a good brandy, and nowhere better than in the comfort and congenial atmosphere of our favourite North London pub. As for the rest of it ... as I have said, we were very different. Or perhaps in the end not so different: You may judge for yourself.

Andrew Carter was tall and saturnine, and (I suppose in retrospect) he had always struck me as being a little shady. His dress, a little too sharp, perhaps; his manner, defensive, even somewhat furtive; his talk from the corner of his mouth, and likewise his glances, always out of the corner of his eye ... yes, I think shady would fit him rather closely. But not unlikeable, if you can understand that. A "bit of a lad", you might say; or a "Jack the Lad", as they are wont to have it in London.

Myself: I was ex-Army, retiring shortly after my majority, and doing nicely, thank you, in property. Not a runaway success, no, but by no means short of the readies, as Andrew might have stated it. So much for me.

And so much for that, except that property could be said to be a second meeting point, of sorts. Andrew Carter owned a house, or would become the owner in just two weeks' time. *The* house, yes—the one I mentioned in my first paragraph.

Nothing odd about that in itself, you might rightly think: Lots of people are householders, millions of them. Except that this piece of property had strings attached, and that night in Greasy Fred's steak house, Andrew told me about them. It was a peculiar story with not a little of mystery, and I don't suppose I would have heard it at all if Carter hadn't had more than his customary two or three doubles.

'It was seven years ago,' he told me. 'I was in a bit of bother at the time—that is, certain people wanted to speak to me who I didn't much care to speak to—and so I'd come up here from the East End to stay at my uncle's place in Muswell Hill. Lying low, sort of. Queer old stick, my Uncle Arthur: His place was full of musty old books and odds and ends; bits of brass and silver, bric-a-brac, you know?'

'Objets d'art,' I helped him out.

'Right. A regular antique shop, it was, and him just as dry and dusty as the stuff he filled his house with. Anyway, my Old Man had used to tell me: "Andy, son, if you're ever in any trouble, just get on over and see your Uncle Arthur; he's a funny old lad but he's my brother and he'll always help you out." That was just before the Old Man died.'

He glanced at me out of the corner of his eye, in that way of his, and ordered two more brandies. And perhaps I'd better explain here that we weren't yet in Greasy Fred's place but still propping up the bar in the Old Horse and Cart where, as I've hinted, we'd both had a few more than our staple diet demanded.

'"And son," the Old Man had used to tell me,' Carter continued while we waited for our drinks, '"you treat your Uncle Arthur right. You and me are the only family he's got, see—not that he's ever been much on family—but that old lad's got more money salted away than you'd ever give him credit for. What? He's worth a bleeding fortune!" And, "Oh?" I'd say to the Old Man: "You mean he has a bob or two in the bank, eh?" "Not in the bank, son," he'd say. "It's all in gold, and he keeps it hidden away in that old place in Muswell Hill."'

This was the most voluble I'd ever seen Andrew Carter, and his story as it unfolded had me interested; but I was hungry, too. 'Andrew,' I said, 'I haven't eaten yet. I was thinking of a pasta, maybe, at La Ristorante di Napoli across the road. Perhaps you'd care to join me and I can hear your story out over a meal?'

His sallow face seemed to grow paler still. 'What? That spaghetti shop on the corner? Not for me, David my old son. Spaghetti? *Ugh!*'

I was a little taken aback. Di Napoli wasn't the Ritz, no, but it wasn't bad either. 'They do a very nice Vecchia Romagna,' I told him.

'Vecky what?' he said, still looking a little queasy.

'Brandy,' I informed. 'Italian brandy. A bit brackish, but very good!'

But I couldn't tempt him. 'No,' he shook his head, 'I don't think so. Spaghetti's not my scene—the very sight of it turns my stomach! Anyway, I always drink a lager with my meals. But I'll treat you to a steak and chips at Fred's next door, if you like?'

'Greasy Fred's?' I was forced to smile. 'You'd turn down thin-sliced Genovese liver and button mushrooms for a dubious bit of old leather at Fred's place?'

'Yes I would!' he answered vehemently. 'Anything, mate, but not those long, pink, pasta worms! No, I won't go near a spaghetti shop. Besides, *he* used to eat the damned stuff ....'

'He?' I repeated him.

'My Uncle Arthur,' he looked at me curiously. 'He had a sort of passion for it. I suppose because it was cheap and easy to prepare. Oh, he had the lolly, all right, but he was a bit tight for all that. He'd eat bleeding spaghetti morning, noon, and night!'

It was no good arguing, so I shrugged. 'So be it,' I said. 'Greasy Fred's it is!' And we paid up and left.

II

Over our meal (which wasn't at all bad, as I remember it), Carter continued his story:

'So there I was at my uncle's place, nearly seven years ago, holed up, as it were, for a couple of weeks. And because of the situation—er, these people wanting to speak to me, I mean, who I wasn't keen to speak to— I was sort of nervous and didn't go out much. I mean, I could have used a drink, see? But Uncle Arthur didn't have a drop in the place. And that was something else the Old Man had told me about him: He couldn't take his booze. Drove him off his head, sort of, and it was bad for his heart.'

'You must have found it all a bit claustrophobic?' I said.

'Eh? Oh, yes, shut in.' He seemed absent-minded. 'Yes, you're right. I never did much care for being shut in. You know, as a lad, I did a bit of time now and then; and I can't really say that it suits me much. And Uncle Arthur being a bit rickety and all. And all that dust, and the old books stinking of damp and going mouldy. Junk and figurines and knick-knacks in every room.' His voice dropped almost to a whisper. 'And the coins, the beautiful golden coins ....'

'Gold coins?' My interest picked up again.

Carter, toying with his knife and fork, looked up sharply. 'Eh, what?' he said. But then his eyes took on a sharper focus and his eyebrows came down in a line of dark suspicion.

'You said gold coins,' I reminded him.

Slowly he nodded. 'Yes, that's right. Five hundred of them!'

'The gold your father had told you about?' I guessed.

Again his nod. 'I suppose so, yes.'

'Oh? Then you didn't actually see it?'

He reached into his pocket and tossed a dull golden piece onto the table. I picked it up.

It was—cold, that coin. Colder than it should be, since it had just come out of his pocket, and the weather still warm in a sort of Indian Summer. But—it certainly had the soft, heavy feel of gold, and there was that in its weight which made it ... attractive, yes. And in that moment I felt rising in me that passion which men have killed for: the love of, the craving for, the lusting after gold.

I examined the—coin? Well, I couldn't be sure about that. Its rim wasn't milled; it bore little of ornamentation; it was too well-rubbed to discern anything other than a soft outline of what might have been a raised picture or pattern of sorts, with a central bulge and eight radiating spokes. Perhaps a kind of rising sun relief, or a wheel, or maybe an octopus? It was somehow reminiscent of designs I had seen in the Mediterranean. This could be Crusader gold: a medallion, perhaps, and not a coin at all.

But it was cold, certainly, with an almost unnatural chill, so that for all its lure I gave it back after only a moment or two. 'Five hundred pieces—like this one?' I asked.

He nodded, answering: 'But I've found only three of them.'

I began to see something of a picture now. Bits of the puzzle began to fall into place. For one thing, Carter's fingernails where he toyed with his food.

Now, I have a thing about fingernails: On a man I like them clean, pink, and long enough that they reach but do not obscure the curve of the finger's end. Andrew Carter's nails were therefore quite loathsome, in my eyes. They were dirty, broken, and badly stained, and several of the cuticles had been pushed right back, exposing raw redness which, in places and at times, wept like wounds. His palms were callused and rough, as from hard work, and over the three or four years I had known him there had been little or no improvement. Indeed, on the night in question his hands were a mess! And these the hands of a man who hardly seemed the sort to even contemplate a hard day's work ....

Another piece of the puzzle: Carter had never once spoken of his uncle in the present tense. Finally he was, or was about to become, the owner of a property other than his small flat. All of this—coupled with his statement about the coins or whatever they were—that he had only found three of them—caused me to jump to a conclusion. And as it happened, I was absolutely right.

'Your Uncle Arthur died some time ago, leaving you the house in Muswell Hill, since when you have searched—in the grounds and cellar, etc.—but with little success, for his hoard!'

Carter sat up straighter and for the first time in his life looked me straight in the eye, looked at me very searchingly indeed. 'Sherlock bleeding Holmes, I presume?'

'Dr. Watson, more like,' I retreated, looking away. 'Sorry if I'm prying.'

After staring at me hard for a few moments longer, slowly he shook his head. 'No, not really. I was going to tell you anyway. No, you're dead right—about most of it, anyway.' He saw me looking again at his hands and gave a sly, knowing grin. 'So *that's* what gave me away, eh?'

I shrugged. 'I put two and two together, and—'

'Yes, I see. Well then, let's cut a long story short and get it told.' He put aside his plate and took up his lager. 'When I was staying with him that time I did manage to get out once or twice, and on one occasion I took a bottle of five-star back with me. When he caught me having a nip on the sly he seemed a bit annoyed at first, sort of agitated, like— but after I'd offered him a tot, and him accepting it, why!—then he loosened up. And my Old Man had been dead right: It was plain that

drink could very easily have done for my Uncle Arthur. He just could-
n't handle the stuff, not even in the smallest doses.

'Anyway, it was then that he kind of warmed to me—the drink, of
course—and produced the piece I've just shown you. Then, too, that he
told me there were five hundred more of 'em hidden away. But he
wouldn't say where. More to the point, after a good stiff belt at my
brandy, he told me that since I was his only surviving kin, when he
passed on he'd be leaving his house and everything in it to me!'

'And I'll bet *that* pinned your ears back!' I commented.

'Yes, it did,' he admitted. 'It really did. Anyway, I watched where he
put the coin when I gave it back to him—in a little tin box he kept on
the mantelpiece in the downstairs front room—and first chance I got I
sort of borrowed it, slipped out and had it valued. Would you believe,
eighty-eight quid?'

'Ouch!' said I, and: 'That being seven years ago ... why, that would
make it closer to a hundred and odd now!'

'One hundred and thirty-seven, right now,' Carter corrected me.

I whistled low through my teeth. 'But if there really are five hundred of them, that makes—er—'

'It makes nearly seventy thousand quid, mate, that's what it
makes!' he cut my calculations short. 'And most of the coins in better
condition than this one. In fact the three I've found so far are near perfect—er, "mint", as they say.'

I nodded. 'But you can't find the rest of them, right?'

'Got it in one,' he said, glumly surveying his fingers.

'How long have you been looking for them?' I asked. 'Certainly
you've been hard at it all of the time I've known you. Say three, three
and a half years?'

'Twice that, David my old son,' he said. 'I've been at it for all of
seven years!'

III

Now it was my turn to stare hard at him. 'You mean your uncle died
while you were staying with him? You know, *while* you were keeping a
low profile, as it were?'

'Ah! No,' he said, 'you've got it just a bit wrong. Maybe I should
have corrected you before. Fact is, we don't know for sure that he *is*
dead. No, not for sure.'

I gave him a blank look. 'Well what then, if not dead?'

Carter shrugged (a little uneasily, I thought) and answered: 'Oh, I dunno. Gone away, like? Hopped it? Disappeared …?' But when I glanced at him suddenly, his eyes were cold and unblinking as those of a fish.

'Disappeared, you say?' I mused. 'While you were there? And of course you reported it to the police?'

'What?' he cried. 'Me? Report it to the filth? Believe me, my old son, I report *nothing* to the filth! God no—not me!'

'But a missing person—' I began to protest, perhaps too loudly.

Carter put a finger to his lips. '*Shhh!* Christ's sake, mate! I mean, let's not tell the whole bleeding world about it. Actually, I did tell 'em—but not until about six months later, when things were a bit cooler for me all round.'

'I should think so,' I nodded. 'He was your uncle, after all!' And I frowned. 'But just *how* did he disappear?'

'Ah!' he said, going on the defensive again. 'Well, perhaps not even that. Maybe it was just that he sort of, well, went into hiding. You know?'

'No, I don't know,' I protested, starting to feel lost. 'I thought it was you that was, er, on the lam? I mean, what on earth did your uncle have to hide from?'

Carter averted his eyes. 'Dunno, rightly,' he mumbled. 'Maybe it was the booze he was scared of—scared he'd say too much, like, when he'd had a nip or two—or again, maybe it was me.'

'Scared of you? But I thought you said he was going to leave you the house and everything?'

'So he was—so he did!' he answered. 'God's truth! But, you know, once I knew the gold was there, well, I sort of kept *prodding* him a bit.'

'Prodding him,' I repeated, and perhaps I made a sour face.

'Hang on, now!' Carter was quick to add, when he saw my expression. 'I mean, no threats or anything like that. God, no! I mean, I'd just leave the bottle lying around, you know? Loosen up his balmy old tongue a bit, see?'

'And you reckon that would make him want to go into hiding, eh?' I asked, maybe a little too suspiciously.

Carter's face hardened. 'Now look here, David my lad. Are we mates or not?'

When a man puts it like that, what can one do? I half-nodded. 'I suppose we are,' I said.

'Then you'll take my word for it that there was no funny business?'
I was a bit reluctant, but: 'If you say so.'
'Good!'
'So?' I said, after a moment's silence. 'What else?'
He looked at me curiously then and seemed to shrink down into
himself a little. 'Do I look like a pushover?' he asked, after a while. 'I
mean, do I look soft or something? You know, the kind of bloke who'd
jump at the sound of a car backfiring, or a squeaky gate swinging in
the wind?'
'Or things that go bump in the night,' I added, on impulse. 'No, I
don't think so. On the contrary. I suppose there are those who'd say
you're probably a bit hard.' And I hastily added: 'I mean, that you can
well look after yourself.'
'And indeed I can!' he growled at once. 'And yet—'
'Yes?'
'It's just that that old house—'
'Yes?'
He got himself together. 'A will was found,' he said, 'and sure
enough old Arthur had left it all to me. But ... there were a couple of
kinky provisos.'
'Such as?'
'In the event he went missing, I wasn't to get the house for seven
years. Oh, I could have access twice a week for inspection—I could even
carry out minor works where they were necessary to preserve the place
or improve it, so long as there was no major building or reconstruction
involved—but I couldn't actually live there. Not for seven years.'
'And?'
'Eh?'
'You said "provisos." Up to now I've heard only one.'
'Oh, yes,' he said, nodding, again absent-minded, or far away. 'The
other one.'
'The other proviso, yes,' I persisted.
He looked at me strangely. 'It's a funny one,' he said after a
moment, seeming to invite comment; but I just waited. Carter shuffled
about a bit. 'Well, it's about a book: one of his musty, crumbling old
books. A thing called the *Dhol Chants*. Seven years to the day after he
disappeared—if he were to disappear, you understand—I was to read
the last paragraph on page one hundred and eleven. I was to read it out
loud and in the presence of a witness ....'
I waited, then shrugged. 'Is that all?'

He nodded.

I had been thinking. 'Metal detector!' I said, changing the subject.

Carter took a deep breath, sat up straighter. 'Tried it,' he said. 'Even a model that discriminates between nails and half-pennies buried thirty-six inches deep, *and* shows you a picture of the object on a small screen. Cost me a small fortune! Nothing.'

'How about the grounds?'

'Big gardens front and rear. I've cleared off the shrubbery, burned it flat, and dug the whole place over down to three or four feet. Two three-penny bits, two old sixpences, and an 1890 half crown. You'd find such in any large garden. Other than that—not a sausage.'

'The cellar?'

He shuddered, gulped.

'Something wrong?'

'Look,' said Carter, 'I'll tell you. Frankly, *I can't stand* the bloody place! It's not right, that old house. And it's getting worse; and time is rapidly running out.'

IV

Ah! Now we appeared to be getting somewhere.

'Explain,' I said. 'What do you mean, "time is running out", and what is it that's not right about the place?' It was like trying to draw blood from a stone.

But: 'Right!' he finally said, determinedly. 'I *will* explain, and then perhaps you can suggest a solution. See, first off, the old house is to come down.'

Well, I was in the business and I knew one or two things about some of the planning in the Muswell Hill area. 'It's under a demolition order?'

'Right. It's to come down, to be demolished, removed. Government planning; a new road is going right through it. Oh, I'll be compensated—and there's a lot of dry rot anyway—but that's hardly the point, is it?'

'I see,' I said.

'Do you?' he asked. 'There's a hundred thousand quid somewhere in that old place, and in just a week or ten days' time it's to disappear just like my old Uncle Arthur!'

I thought about it, and slowly nodded. 'Doesn't look like you've a lot of time left, does it?'

'No, it doesn't. But at least I've managed to get hundred percent access—at last! In fact, for the last fortnight I've been living there. Hah!—and when I haven't been there I've been living here; or rather, right next door, in the Old Horse and Cart.'

'It's getting on your nerves, eh? All this searching, I mean?'

He nodded. 'Damn right! The searching, and the house itself. See, a year ago—er, before things got too funny, which I'll tell you about in a minute—I had a couple of workmen in and made the place liveable. I had a bath put in for one thing, and one of the small rooms painted and a single bed put in—not that I've used *that* much! But see, what with all the digging I was doing, the searching, and pulling up floorboards and what have you, I used to get really dirty. Now, at least, I could have a bath when I wanted one. Before that ... well, it must have looked a bit funny, mustn't it? Me going in there all neat and tidy, so to speak, and coming out covered in dust and muck twice a week! You know, people would begin to notice. They'd think I was giving the old place a right old going over.'

'Which you were.'

'Yes, of course, but I didn't want people to know that, did I? See, there are certain circles where I have a bit of a rep, my old son, and it wouldn't take people long to figure out that if I was looking for something, then that there was something there to look for.'

'I see. So after you'd done a stint of, er, work, you'd take a bath and come out as neat and tidy as when you went in ....'

'Right.'

'But didn't your uncle have a bathroom, then?'

'He had a loo, but no bath. And in his kitchen, if you could call it a kitchen, no hot water. Cold water, straight from the mains, but no hot. No, he bathed at the local public baths—mean old bastard!'

'He did leave you everything,' I reminded him.

'Er, yes—I suppose I have to credit him with that, at least,' Carter returned.

'It was just that he lived rather sparsely,' I said.

'Like a bleeding hermit! I had to have an immersion heater put in, and a tank upstairs in the attic.'

'But at least the place is comfortable now?'

Carter shrugged. 'Bit of a mess, really. But what does it matter if it's to come down, eh? I mean, I've taken up most of the floorboards; been into a lot of the ceilings; the chimneys; ripped out the backs of old fitted cupboards and wardrobes; been down under the floor of the cellar ....'

'Frustrating,' I contributed.

'You're bloody right, mate!'

'But I don't see how I can help, or what I can suggest. And you still haven't told me about the other thing: about the house not being right?'

He looked uncomfortable again, but after a moment: 'Do you believe in ghosts, David?'

I smiled, shook my head. 'No, I'm afraid I don't. When you're gone, you're gone, that's my belief. So you think it's haunted, eh?'

'I didn't say that!' His voice at once took on a sharper edge. 'Do I look soft or something, believing in the bogeyman?'

I tried to nod, shrug, and shake my head all at the same time. 'Well, do you or don't you?'

'I ... dunno,' he sullenly answered. 'I mean, well what the hell *am I* supposed to believe in?'

'There have been ... occurrences?'

'Yes,' he nodded. 'Occurrences.'

The whole thing—but especially his reluctance—was annoying me now. 'Well,' I made as if to go, 'can't sit here all night.'

'You busy then?' He caught at my elbow, not wanting me to leave.

'Not particularly, but—'

'OK, I'll get on with it. Yes, there have been occurrences. Noises smells, things that move by themselves ... and spaghetti!'

'Spaghetti? Carter, what on earth—?'

'Nothing on earth, mate,' he said with a shiver he couldn't disguise. 'Nothing natural at all. Something most unnatural. Ghosts? I'm not sure what they are—but whatever they are—'

'They frighten you.' I made it a statement, not a question. For suddenly I could see the fear writ clear across his face. 'You're frightened of the house, and yet there's nothing for it but to go in there and find those coins!'

'There you have it,' he said with a listless nod. 'There, in a bloody nutshell, you have it.'

'That wasn't so bad, was it?' I asked.

'Eh? What wasn't?' Then he saw what I was getting at. 'Oh!' He managed a grin, however wry. 'It was like going to the dentist!' he declared. 'But there, it's over now.'

'So now we get to the point of all this,' I told him. 'So go on—make me an offer.'

He put his hands on the table, palms down. 'There are others I could go to ....'

'But I'm honest,' I answered, 'and time's running out.' He knew it
was so.

'Ten percent,' he said. '*If* we find it.'

'You're on!' I told him.

V

'This spaghetti thing,' I probed, on the way to the house in Carter's battered old tank of an American car. 'Can you tell me about it?'

'Yes,' he said, and: '—no! Let's say I'd like you to see for yourself.'

'But how will I be able to see anything if you won't tell me what it
is I'm looking for?' I asked. 'And anyway, what's so damned suspicious—or even out of the ordinary—about spaghetti?'

Carter gave a half-shrug, half-shudder. 'Rather depends where you
find it, I'd say,' he said. 'Or in what circumstances.'

'Ah!' I said, trying to lighten the atmosphere a bit. 'A manifestation
of your Uncle Arthur, eh? Dead or missing these seven long years, but
still you find bowls of the stuff lying all over the place.' And I chuckled.
But Carter didn't.

'Funny, is it?' he said, out of the corner of his mouth, his voice a rasp.

I gasped. 'You mean you really *do* find bowls of it lying around?'

'Not bowls, no,' he answered. 'But ... strands—' and I thought he
would continue—but he didn't.

'Strands of spaghetti?' I pressed him, peering at his silhouette in the
car's dim interior where he was hunched over the wheel. 'Cooked? Fresh
made, you mean?'

'Fresh?' he choked. 'God, no!' His hands were like giant spiders
straddling the steering wheel. Passing under a street light, I saw how
tightly clenched they were on the leather. I also noticed how fast we
were moving and remembered how he'd had more than his normal
quota to drink.

'Ease up, Carter!' I said. 'We're not in a race, man!'

He immediately slowed down, but under the next light I saw beads
of sweat gathered on his brow. 'Nerves,' he muttered. 'Me, of all people!'

'But spaghetti, Carter.'

'*Yes, bloody spaghetti!*'

I leaned away from him. Maybe my being here was a mistake. The
story he had told me was, after all, more than a little—

'Sorry,' he said, as if reading my mind. 'Sorry, sorry, sorry! But see, I'm like you. I don't believe in bloody spooks! The only things that frighten me are knives and guns and knuckle-dusters. And maybe the thought of buckets of quick-setting cement—with *my* feet in 'em! But not ghosts. Not me.'

'Squatters!' I said, snapping my fingers.

'Eh?'

'Possible, isn't it, in an old, empty house like that? Squatters making a temporary stay there. Or maybe kids, playing in the place. Even the occasional tramp. And you said it yourself: Spaghetti is a cheap food, easily prepared. Just the sort of stuff your gentleman of the road would be likely to—'

'No.' He shook his head in rejection of my theory. 'I've been living there, remember? Part of the time, anyway. Kids, tramps, squatters? Forget it! Not in the last fortnight, anyway. But spaghetti, yes. And as recently as yesterday ....'

We were almost there. I guessed that once we were inside the place he would clam up again and so pressed what small advantage I still had: 'And what about the noises you mentioned? And the smells? And the things that move by themselves?'

'Smells.' His voice shuddered as he remembered. 'God, yes! Rotten smells. Worse than blocked drains, they are—worse than festering flesh!'

My mind cringed from the picture his words conjured. I didn't like the sound of it at all; not if I was going to be in there with him for any length of time. 'What, all the time?'

'No, just now and then. But it's enough ....'

'And noises?'

'Probably the old house settling,' he tried to shrug it off and failed miserably. 'I dunno. Creaks and groans—timber groans, that is. I think ....'

'And things that move?'

He glanced at me out of the corner of his eye. 'The will,' he said. 'I mean, I searched that place from top to bottom after he ... when he didn't show up. Not for the coins—not right then—but for a will. See, he said he would *will* it all to me. So I looked. Everywhere. But the will didn't come to light until around the time I told the police about him. Then, when I took them to the house—or rather, when they took me there—they found the damn thing sitting there right in the middle of the front room table!'

'So he must have been alive after his disappearance,' I replied. 'So maybe he still Is alive.'

'Yes,' he nodded grimly. 'That thought dawned on me, too—years ago. It also dawned on the filth. God, and didn't they put yours truly through the old third degree? Yes they bloody did! And as the years passed and the old house got funnier and funnier—well, for a long time I thought he was still in there—hiding, you know? Like a crazy man. I thought it was him that was doing it all. Except—'

'Yes?'

'Seven years, mate,' he answered bitterly. 'Seven long years. If he was there, believe me, I would have found him. And if he wasn't dead when I did, he sure as hell would be now! Anyway, it was just about that time—the time they found the will, I mean—that I saw the spaghetti for the first time. It stank bad enough then, but *since*—' And he stopped short.

We turned left around a tight bend, and left again between old gateposts and up a short drive … and whatever Carter had been about to say was left unsaid. There it was, the old house, silhouetted in the night like some darkly gabled, stony ghost, like a gaunt, crumbling mausoleum.

And I felt a little colder for all that the night was a mild one, and I could almost feel Carter sweating as he slowed the car to a halt in the shadow of the dark porch.

VI

We stood for a long time just looking at it, raven black against London's soft night glow. Carter's sweat must be cold on him by now and I was getting no jot warmer, but still we made no move. My heart was no longer in it, and I guessed that Carter must be feeling the same way. But—

—As if he sensed my indecision, now he took the initiative. Keys jangled as he opened up the porch door, put on a dim light, led the way over prised-up flags and between small heaps of rubble to the house door proper, and turned a second key in the rusty lock. Then we were inside and in the next second Carter had the light on. We were in a sort of hall which, like the porch, showed all the ravaged signs of extensive, overt exploration. I looked at Carter where he stood nervously attentive, as if listening for something, and slowly he began to breathe. He had been holding his breath.

Well, the air was musty, yes, but in no way poisonous as he had described it. It was the smell of dust and age (and of debris, naturally, from his digging and delving) but that was all. No blocked drains that my nostrils could discover, and certainly no—

'It's OK!' Carter said, startling me. And more ominously: 'For now, anyway.' He led the way through a door on the right, once again switching on a light, and I followed him. And while he stood there peering about, a little less nervously now, I checked the room out:

It was a huge front room, and it was at least a century out of date, out of style, out of time. The wallpaper (what little of it Carter had not disturbed) was of a yellow-striped and primrose-patterned variety which must have decorated a million front rooms around the turn of the century; the fireplace was of dark marble columns with a marble lintel over a recessed iron grate; the high ceiling was centred by an ornate plaster "rose" from which once, doubtless a great many years ago, some tinkly chandelier had been suspended to lend the room a certain opulence. The skirting-boards were all of twelve inches high and an inch and a half thick, with a fancy moulding along the top edge; likewise the massive cornice where it joined walls to ceiling—and where Carter had not yet torn it down! The great bay window was leaded, with tiny panes of a stained glass above and clear glass at the bottom over a curving window-ledge which looked to be formed of a single solid timber. Except it was no longer solid. No, for *Serpula lacrymans* had a definite hold here; and when I probed, so the tip of my finger sank right in, emerging in a *puff* of powdered wood when I drew it back out. Dry rot: Doubtless the place was riddled.

Carter brushed by me and drew ancient drapes across the grimy windows. 'There,' he said, unnecessarily. 'Front room. I've had the floor-boards up and been down to earth. That's where I found one of the coins. Picked it up with the detector. But I reckon it had simply fallen down there, between the boards. They're all warped, as you can see. Gaps all over the place. And nothing had been disturbed down there before me. So ... I reckon my old Uncle Arthur simply lost the coin, probably while he was counting them or something.'

He moved over to the mantelpiece. 'Here, give us a hand, mate. Heavy, this is.'

The marble lintel was loose; brute force had been used to lever it away from the chimney breast. We lifted it down, Carter on one end and me on the other. Behind was dust and plaster debris. 'Found another there,' he pointed. 'Picked that one up with the detector, too. But see, there was a crack between the mantel shelf and the wall. So I reckon the coin got there by accident, like the first one down a crack in the floor-boards. Old Arthur probably had 'em stacked up there on the shelf at one time or another.'

'He seems to have been remarkably careless with his gold!' I observed.

'Doddering old bugger!' snapped Carter. 'But it was finding them that kept me coming back, else I might have given up long ago.'

I wondered if there might be more in what he had just said than he suspected, but I said nothing. What reason, after all, would his uncle have had in luring him to the place?

We put the mantelpiece back and Carter dropped a flaring match on the makings of a fire he had prepared in advance of our visit. 'What about the third coin?' I asked him. 'Where was that one?'

'Eh?' He turned his eyes from the flickering flames where they burned the edges of crumpled newspapers and caught at the splintered ends of dry sticks. 'Oh, that one was in his mattress. Another job for the old metal detector.'

'His mattress?'

'Yes. He'd sewn pockets into the mouldy old thing. Quite a few pockets, but the coin had found a hole and ended up in the lining. When he shifted his toot, that one must have escaped him.'

'Shifted it?' I repeated.

Carter sighed. 'Well if the coins had been there—in his mattress—and weren't there now, then obviously he'd shifted 'em!'

'Shifted them when you started, er, prodding him, do you mean?' I asked.

Carter slitted his eyes, then looked away. He was silent for a moment, then shrugged. 'Possibly,' he said.

The fire had caught now and its heat was eating into the coals where they shifted on top of their platform of kindling. Smoke blew back from the flue into the room, causing us to back away, coughing. 'That'll clear in a minute,' Carter informed. 'I've been up there, too, you see. Done a bit of damage, not much. A tight squeeze. Didn't much care for it.' He shivered as the chimney began to draw and the smoke was sucked away.

'So where haven't you been?' I asked.

He shrugged again. 'I've not finished with the cellar yet,' he said. 'I keep getting signals on the detector—bits of screws and nails, usually. I'm about half-way done.'

'Then let's get to it,' I suggested.

'Ah, no!' Carter said, holding up a restraining hand. '*I'll* get to it. That's not what you're here for. What, my mate David? Manual labour? Leave it out! No, you'll make coffee for us both—especially for me, 'cos it gets cold down there—and you'll give the old place the once-over, looking for likely hidey-holes I might of missed, and you'll just, you know, sort of be here.'

That suited me fine (even though I suspected he preferred to work alone for a fairly obvious reason: probably to salt away a little of the gold as soon as it came to light, and thereby avoid paying me my ten percent on that portion). 'Very well,' I agreed anyway. 'Show me the kitchen and the way to the cellar, and we'll take it from there. And one other thing: You said that the three coins you've already discovered were very nearly in mint condition. I'd like to see one—if only to get a clearer idea just what we're after, right?'

He raised his eyebrows, looked mildly surprised. But: 'No problem,' he said. 'Why didn't you ask before?' Then he frowned. 'Or maybe you were thinking I didn't really find 'em after all, eh? Like I only used that story as bait—to enlist your help in a doubtful venture, eh?'

He fished about at his neck where he wore a heavy silver chain, drawing into view a little leather pouch. It *chinked* heavily when he gave it a shake. Carter grinned, opened the neck, took out a coin and passed it to me. 'There you go,' he said.

VII

A medallion, as I had expected, the thing was cold and heavy in my hand as the first one had been; but its designs were as clearly visible as those on a fresh-minted ten-pence piece. There it was again, that raised figure with its eight radiating arms. But now I could see that it was in fact an octopus, and such a creature as I would never wish to meet in the flesh, as it were.

Now, I have called it an octopus, but "octopoid" might convey its design more accurately. And yet anthropomorphic—manlike—could equally well be employed. Not that there was anything *really* manlike about the figure on the golden disk, unless it were the sensation of a sort of abyssal *intelligence* which seemed inherent in the staring of those awful eyes. Oh, yes, whoever had designed these medallions, certainly he had worked to great effect on those eyes. The look they seemed physically to throw at me from the surface of the lifeless golden disk was one of utter malignancy—a hatred for the entire human race, for all living things!

As for the rest of the thing:

It had bat-wings, folded back behind the thrusting head. And from that head, face-tentacles radiated outwards in the aforementioned sunburst, mercifully obscuring much of the rest of the body, which seemed bloated as that of some great ocean slug; and central at the roots of those tentacles, there I could see a part-open beak which seemed to me to issue mad laughter or a demented cry. Claws scrabbled at the edge of the stone throne upon which the beast was seated or perched, a throne carved with squids and krakens, crusted with aquatic fungi or corals, and draped with ropes of seaweed. Beneath the figure, at the medallion's rim, were these characters:

ⲨⲅⲎⳎⳐ⳿ⳐⳎ

And on the reverse:

Faint-etched (possibly to create an effect of submersion beneath the sea, for certainly strange fishes swam in the foreground) were the outlines of a city colossal, a place of ziggurats and temples, of columns and turrets and windowless towers, whose architecture seemed conceived or depicted by some crazed cubist. The angles were all wrong; surfaces seemed at once concave *and* convex! I couldn't quite make out how I was supposed to view the scene, or from which aspect. And more of those odd characters, like this:

Ⲕ⳿Ⳑ⳥Ⳙ⳪Ⲏ

I handed the medallion back to Carter. 'I don't like it,' I told him.

'What?' He was astonished. 'Man, that's gold!'

'The currency or sigil of some weird cult, I'd say,' I answered.

He frowned, obviously at a loss to understand my distaste. 'You mean you don't like the designs? So what? Melt 'em down and you've got gold! What does it matter what they look like now?'

'Or what they were used for?' But it was plain that Carter didn't understand that either—and for that matter, I wasn't any too sure myself!

He put the medallion away, glanced at me a trifle wonderingly, said: 'Right, I'm for the cellar. Kitchen's through there,' he pointed toward a door which stood ajar, 'and you'll find the cellar down the steps under the stairs.' And off he went.

I went through into the kitchen—and saw at once what Carter had meant by his sneering. Atop a rickety table, an ancient electrical two-ring cooker stood stained and grimy. Beside the cooker, a fairly new electric kettle seemed to gleam by comparison. I guessed that the kettle was Carter's. There was also a square stone sink and fluted stone drainer, with a single tap for water. Sink and drainer showed the wear and stains of more than a hundred years.

I made a mental note that the tap was the terminal point of a single old lead water pipe that went up the wall and disappeared through the patchy ceiling. And that, when I thought about it, was odd. Carter had told me his uncle had only cold water, direct from the mains—so why did the supply here come from above? Unless ... of course! The WC must be up there, or maybe a hand wash-basin. Whichever, the mains supply would have to serve that first. That must be it. But God!—what an outmoded way of life old Arthur Carter must have led ....

I filled the kettle, plugged it into the kitchen's single socket, decided to take a quick look upstairs while the water boiled. Back I went into the front room, and from there to the hall. Beneath the stairs I found an open door, with stone steps leading down. From below came sounds of shovelling and Carter's grumbling and panting as he exerted himself. He must have donned coveralls, for the clothes he had been wearing were now draped over the back of an old ladder-backed chair where it stood near the head of the steps.

'You OK?' I called down.

And after a moment: 'Yes—where's the coffee?'

'Give me a chance!'

He grunted something unintelligible, following which the sounds of his labours continued.

As I came out from beneath the stairs into the hallway, I spied another small door across the hall. Behind it—the toilet. And this, too, was peculiar. If the loo was down here, why was there a water pipe going upstairs from the kitchen? Then I remembered what Carter had said about having had a bath put in, and so for the moment I put the matter out of my mind ....

Very well, now I would see what the upstairs rooms looked like:

The stairs were something of a hazard in themselves: Loose and rotten, they seemed to sag beneath my very feet. I climbed the treads close to the wall, where there should be a maximum of support. It was dark, too, for the dim light from the hall hardly reached up here at all. But ... on the landing I found a light switch, and a naked dusty bulb on its cobwebbed flex issued sufficient light to show me a passageway with half a dozen doors leading off into as yet unknown rooms beyond.

The large, long room to the far right was Carter's recently converted bathroom; it had small windows which looked out on one side to the suburbs, and on the other gazed down from the hill on a sparkly near-distant London. The room was more or less intact (though I could see that Carter had had the floorboards up) and the old bath he had installed was clean and stood on its four claw feet against the end wall.

Above the bath, the stylish cylinder of a new, fast-action electric immersion heater gleamed in blue enamel and chrome where it was affixed to the wall. The heater was supplied through a small-gauge copper pipe whose other end had been welded or brazed into the old, heavy-gauge lead pipe I had seen in the kitchen, which here came up through the boards at the foot of the bath, climbed the wall and continued up out of sight into the attic—

Now surely this *was* an anomaly! I puzzled over the thing:

If the only water in the house came direct from the mains, why was it routed through the attic? That would normally suggest a tank up there, but Carter's uncle would not have needed a tank, not in his circumstances. On the other hand, the tank could have been a standard fixture when the house was built more than a hundred years ago. So maybe it wasn't so strange after all.

In any case, I wasn't a plumber, far from it. But ... it might be worth asking Carter about it.

Making to leave the room, I glanced into the bath, and—

A greyish-pink strand of what looked like ancient spaghetti lay in the enamel well of the bath, close to the vacant plughole, for all the world like some thin, inert worm of the sewers crawled up into the light to die of its own exertions ....

VIII

Suddenly conscious of a rancid stench, I washed the strand away down the plughole and turned off the tap, then left the bathroom and had a quick peep into the other rooms. What I saw there was sufficient to tell me that it was as well the place was due for demolition. Carter already had the job well in hand; only the exterior brickwork was holding the place together; one tap with a bulldozer and it would come tumbling down! Well, perhaps not so severe, but bad enough. Oh, yes: He desperately wanted that gold!

But I could explore to my heart's content later; right now I must be satisfied that I had at least learned the general layout of the place. I went back downstairs to the kitchen, found instant coffee, sugar, long-life milk, made coffee. The taste was a little off—the water in old houses is always a bit peculiar, I think—but at least my concoction was hot and wet (NATO standard, we used to call it in the Army!), and Carter must be pretty thirsty by now. Then I took up both mugs and ventured to the cellar.

'About bleeding time, mate!' he said as I came into view down the stone steps. 'What have you been doing, then?'

'Oh, nosing about,' I answered.

'See anything interesting?'

I deliberately refrained from mentioning my spaghetti encounter. 'Wasn't really looking; I was just getting the feel of the place, that's all.' And as I talked I looked around.

The cellar was quite spacious, maybe twenty-four by twenty-seven feet, with a high concrete ceiling supported by four concrete columns. The walls (what remained of them) had been of brick, but now at least a quarter of the cellar's floor was covered with broken brick debris and dark earth. The boards of the floor were up and Carter stood waist-deep in an earth hole, his upper body gleaming with sweat and dark with earth streaks. Overhead, a bright, solitary light bulb dangled from its flex; to one side of the hole a sheet of newspaper was covered by a litter of rusty bent nails, old screws and other metallic bits and pieces. And just beside me where I stood at the foot of the steps, there was Carter's metal-detector: a newish-looking "Super-Seeker 7."

Carter climbed out of his hole as I stepped forward. The top of his boiler suit was hanging round his waist. He shrugged into it, buttoned it up and took his coffee from me, drinking it down in a couple of great gulps. Then he said: 'That's it—I've had it down here for tonight.'

'But you've only been working for half an hour!'

'Down here, my son, that's time enough!' he explained. 'Christ! You start craving company after just ten minutes! Anyway, I've a feeling I'm flogging a dead horse—down here, anyway. Not a tinkle on the old detector. And besides, there's still plenty to be done upstairs.'

'I've been up the stairs,' I told him. 'A quick glance, anyway. Queer plumbing.'

'Oh? I don't know much about plumbing.'

'I don't know a lot myself,' I answered. 'But there's something weird about it.'

'Whole place is bloody weird!' he muttered darkly. 'Come on, let's go back up. I could use some more coffee.' He led the way.

Half-way up the steps, Carter paused at the light switch. He looked up and ahead, said: 'You closed the door behind you up there.' It was almost an accusation.

'So?'

He shrugged—but when he switched off the light I knew what he meant. The single bulb in the cellar had thrown its light right up the steps; now that it was out, and with the door closed, it was lightless as the tomb down here. Carter climbed the rest of the steps two at a time, breathing heavily, and I was right behind him. It was only a matter of seconds, but what a relief when the dim light filtered in as he opened the cellar door ....

We went back to the front room and Carter carried straight on through into the kitchen, calling back to me: 'I'll make more coffee. You have a look round the room. It might be as well if you give each room a good going over in its turn.'

That sounded sensible. I gave the room my full attention:

The two walls standing at right angles to the great bay window were deeply recessed. One was an end wall; its recess contained a massive old oak table-cum-desk, half of which stuck out into the room. The opposing recess, in the interior wall, was lined with bookshelves; most of these were empty now but some still contained a fair number of dusty old volumes. I crossed to the bookshelves to have a closer look, calling out to Carter:

'Have you looked behind the bookshelves in the recess?'

'With the detector, yes,' he answered. 'Not a sausage.'

I heard him, but not fully. The title of one of the books had distracted me. No, I'll say stronger than that: It was as if the dull gold lettering on the spine had jumped at me, or seemed suddenly to burn with an inner fire as my bulk threw the books into shadow:

Dhol Chants.

The book was on a shelf level with my eyes. I took it down. The thing was clammy in my hand, and moving it ... it was as if I'd poked about in someone's grave! A rotten stench welled up with the dust which was something very much other than the somehow depressing smell of ancient paper. And dislodged from the shelf, a long strand of spaghetti plopped to the floor ....

It *was* spaghetti, could only be. Carter had said that's what the stuff was, and he had had more experience of it than me. But it had the smell (if that's where the smell originated) of something very, very dead! I nudged it with the toe of my shoe where it lay on the bare floorboards. It broke into two lengths, maybe three or four inches each. It was yellowy-grey turning mouldy blue.

'Ah!' said Carter, coming back into the room. 'The *Dhol Chants*: You've found the bloody thing!' And he paused and sniffed suspiciously at the air.

Now, for the life of me I can't say why I did it, but something prompted me not to mention this second strand of spaghetti, just as it had prompted me to keep mum on the first. Maybe it was greed? If Carter got frightened off, bang would go my ten percent, after all. Anyway, standing with my back to him, I quickly used the toe of my shoe to grind the—whatever—into the dust and the grain of the floorboards.

Carter sniffed again. 'You smell that?' he asked, sharply.

'Eh?' I pretended ignorance; for in fact the smell was quickly disappearing. 'Smell what?'

His frown gradually lifted. 'My imagination,' he finally said. 'God!—I hate this place.'

I crossed to the oak table. Along the sides and back of its recess, a wooden bench, leather covered, had been fitted to the wall. I sat down on one of the short legs of the bench and opened the book. Carter came over, plumped my coffee down, said: 'While you get yourself acquainted down here, I'm going to have a go at the panelling in the room on the far left upstairs. Anything you want to know, come to the foot of the stairs and give me a yell. OK?'

'Fine,' I answered, and as he went about his business so I turned to page one hundred and eleven of the strange old book ....

IX

Before I talk about that page, perhaps I'd best describe something of the book itself. Normally I wouldn't bother, but *this* book was something special. For like Carter's "coins" it literally reeked of age. It was ... hoary! Like the pyramids are hoary, like the menhirs of ancient burial grounds or the megaliths of Stonehenge.

Large, the volume was perhaps eleven inches by eight; and bulky, it was almost four inches thick and weighed like a great brick in my hand.

Whoever "Dhol" was, he must do an awful lot of chanting! The book's covers were of wood—mahogany, I thought—but grotesquely carved and inlaid with ivory and silver. The hinges were also of silver, showing the blue blush of age and filigreed into weird designs which, while not quite pictorial, nevertheless struck chords in my subconscious mind—like scenes conjured in the flames of a hearth fire, or half-remembered from a dream, or visions and pseudo-memories from a previous plane of existence. Anyone who ever experienced *deja-vu* will know what I am trying to convey.

Between the covers: The paper was thick and crude, heavily stained in places and in others crumbling; the edges of the sheets were uncut and uneven, splitting and flaking away; the text and illustrations were hand-wrought, and their subject was ...? Here I was at a loss.

Unlike the characters of the medallions, these were very nearly English letters (early Anglo-Saxon, at least) but strung together in such a way as to make no sense whatsoever. Or ... it was a language previously outside my knowledge. Or ... the thing was in a coded or cryptographic form. And on page one hundred and eleven—

This *was* going to be difficult! How on earth might one read this last paragraph out loud, as in Carter's uncle's proviso, or indeed read it any other way, if one could make neither head nor tail of the rhythm, the pronunciation, or even the message and purpose of the thing? Difficult, yes—and yet now I remember that paragraph character for character, "word" for "word." And knowing as I now do something of its power, I reproduce only this portion below:

> *Gh'ha gn-ka a'hboa um, et-um*
> *T'hn-hla puh-ghtagn bugg-ugg.*
> *Gn-ka um Zg'h nuth-ah'n, et-um,*
> *Elgz-a'hboa puh-atta ull ....*

Rubbish? No stranger, surely, than the gibberish of any coded message before it is deciphered. And if it were *not* in cipher ... then perhaps it represented the English approximation of how the chant would sound in the English (or human?) tongue.

For now indeed I felt that I handled a book in many ways removed from mundane knowledge; nor was this feeling of mine, that it was not entirely of Earth, so far-fetched as the reader might be tempted to believe. Alien?—certainly the language was alien: as unknowable as the Egyptian glyphs in the time before the discovery of the Rosetta Stone.

Ancient?—of course, as I have previously explained; and, by virtue of its remote origin, that much *more* alien. But—

—Evil? Need I add ... yes? At least, I sensed that it treated of evil things. Why else should its meaning be so obscured and deliberately hidden away?

Or was I allowing Carter's prattle to get to me? This was ... a book! Nothing more. Very strange and very old, but just a book. I allowed myself to riffle the stiff, crumbling pages between thumb and forefinger.

The leaves at once fell open at an obviously well-used section, where I noted with renewed interest that someone had crowded a great deal of minute, spidery marginalia around the frame of the pages. The notes were modern, comparatively recent in the scale of years, and they were in English; written, I thought, with a fine ball point. Moreover there was a signature: I was pleased to note that it was that of Arthur Carter.

As for what the notes said: That was almost as hard to understand as the actual text of the book; not the crabbed writing itself, but whatever it signified or *had* signified to the writer:

Against one long paragraph:

"Not as the *Necronomicon* has it, nor to be found in Feery's *Notes*. Possibly a variation on the 8th Agga-ath line. Dangerous to try it without greatest possible precautions. Eliphas Levi's 'lost' liturgy might turn the trick ...."

Or, on another page:

"The Blue Glow (p. 79-3) is a puzzle. I seem to see it, of course, but is it that the spell alters my eyes, or is it that the treasure itself is caused by the spell to emit this temporary radiation? Whichever, it is effective—as are all of these damnable invocations ...."

Or, more baffling still:

"Dhols, according to Prinn, are not to be trusted under any circumstances, and the use of their devices or of those devices accorded to them should be where possible avoided. Their chants may be especially venomous. Prinn notes, however, that while their *beneficial* thaumaturgies are doubtful, their *revenge* sigils are particularly potent though almost invariably posthumous! I have now translated all the harmful chants between 101 and 127, but—God!—who would wish such things on even his worst enemy?"

I shook my head to clear it of all sorts of peculiar images, then returned my eyes to the second such annotation. "The Blue Glow (p. 79-3) is a puzzle ...." Well, I had to agree with Carter's Uncle Arthur there—the whole thing was a puzzle!—but let's at least see what he was getting at.

And so I turned to page 79 and found the third paragraph.

The passage was immediately apparent: Down the left-hand margin, opposite the third paragraph, Arthur Carter had drawn a thin line of biro. But again I was disappointed: The thing was coded, like the rest of the book. In fine script, however, in the narrow margin to the left of his locating line, Carter had also scribbled:

"See Prinn on the dangers of 'The Luring of Dhols', and on 'Occult Discovery of Gold.'"

The occult discovery of gold ....

And now I felt I was really getting somewhere!

Obviously Carter's uncle had been an occultist—a dabbler, anyway—and had employed certain so-called "arts" in seeking out hidden treasures. And maybe he hadn't been such a dabbler after all, for the evidence would seem to have it that he had known no mean measure of success.

"See Prinn on ... The Occult Discovery of Gold."

Prinn ...? Now surely that was a name I had seen on the spine of another book—yes, and one which also stood upon old Uncle Arthur's bookshelves, at that!

I was tempted to go to the shelves again, at once, but instead forced myself to look once more at the third paragraph. It seemed complete and utter gibberish, but something about the juxtaposition of vowels and gutturals kept me staring at it and trying to get my tongue around its oral convolutions. I found myself speaking the thing out loud, straining to force the alien sounds from the back of my throat and off the tip of my tongue—

The ground seemed to lurch beneath my feet!

The entire house trembled!

There came a groaning—of earth shifting, of straining timbers?—and Carter's cry of terror from upstairs ....

X

Carter sounded like a platoon of SAS coming down those rotten stairs. He was white as a sheet under his dust and grime when he burst into the front room. The groanings and the tremors had stopped by then, as if the house had stirred in its sleep and now lay still again. I hadn't moved from where I was seated at the table.

Carter stood there for a moment just inside the door, then seemed almost to fly across the room towards me, his eyes wide in shock and terror. 'What the hell was *that?*' he cried.

The answer seemed fairly obvious to me. 'The old place has started to give up the ghost,' I said.

'Ghost?' his eyes went wider still. It had been a poor choice of words on my part.

But: 'Ghost, yes,' I said. 'You've murdered the bloody place! You've ripped out the cellar walls, been into the support walls, torn up floorboards and what all. Little wonder it's starting to cave in on itself!'

'Subsidence?' He was shaking, but the colour was gradually returning to his face.

I shrugged. 'What else? Of course it was subsidence. Why, the place is already half eaten away with dry rot! So ... that explains away the noises you complained of. "Probably the old house settling," you said, and you were right.'

He came across and gripped my shoulder. 'And the stink?'

How I could have missed it I don't know, but now that Carter mentioned it—

This was a smell different again from the rotten taint of decay which had accompanied my discovery of those vile strands of spaghetti. That had been the smell of—death? I wasn't sure—that *sort* of smell, anyway. But this smell was alive! The acrid smell of a beat, a power, a force; of something waiting with bated breath and bunched muscles; the stench of alien anticipation, the armpit of an ogre ....

It seemed to well up from the gaps in the floorboards, outwards from the tattered walls, out of the very air. It was everywhere, but growing fainter with each passing second.

I stood up—a little shakily, I admit.

We looked at each other.

The house brooded.

Something groaned, but distantly, receding ....

'Out!' said Carter, trembling again. 'Enough—for tonight, anyway. We'll come back in daylight. And from now on we'll *only* come back in daylight. Are you still in?'

Oh, yes, I was. For one thing, there was my ten percent to consider; and for another, I wanted to know more about the Occult Discovery of Gold. Carter—great lout that he was, and for all his digging and delving—hadn't even glanced at his uncle's books, of that I felt certain. But it seemed to me that the answer probably lay right there: on old Arthur Carter's bookshelves. We would see ....

* * *

As Carter took me home in his car, I told him:

'Tomorrow is Saturday. I'm busy in the morning but should be through by midday. I'll meet you at the house between twelve and one.'

'OK,' he said, his backbone beginning to stiffen a little now that we were well away from the place. 'If I work hard at it, I can probably finish off that room upstairs and strike it from my list.'

'And what then?' I asked. 'What about the attic?'

'Eh?' He glanced at me. 'You can take a gander up there if you like, but it's a dead end. A couple of huge old wasps' nests in two corners where the roof comes down to the eaves, but the rest of it is empty as a blind beggar's tin ....'

* * *

In another ten minutes we were close to my place just off the Holloway Road. I lived at the bottom of a blind alley, pedestrians only, and so Carter dropped me off on the main road at a set of traffic lights where they had just turned red. It was close to midnight by now and what few people were about were mostly on their way to their homes. Traffic was very light—almost non-existent—and of course the pubs were long closed.

I walked to the corner of my alley, and as I watched Carter's big rude car pull away up the road and out of sight, so my thoughts went back to that third paragraph or chant on page 79 of the *Dhol Chants*, whose characters in their weird juxtapositions now seemed firmly fixed in my mind's eye. Turning the corner by a jeweller's shop, I found those queer "words" forming themselves on my tongue, so that I muttered—or chanted—in time with my pace as I began to speed my steps home.

It was just then that I noted the very strange display behind the squares of steel shuttering and the plate glass of the jeweller's window: the fact that by the use of some form of lighting under the display shelves, the individual pieces had been caused to emit a bluish radiance. Each piece of gold or silver jewellery seemed bathed in its own pool of blue fire.

The effect was so startling that I would have stopped and gone back, but already I was past the window and into the shadows of the alley; and by then, too, there was something else to attract my attention. It could be, of course, that refuse had been put out for collection—except that I knew it wasn't collected on Saturdays.

Also, it wasn't the smell of refuse.

And I believe it was then that I started to feel something of Carter's fear—I mean *really* feel it—as the ground trembled beneath my feet and there came a groaning as of vast metal plates grinding together deep in the earth. That is what it felt and sounded like, but when I spun in my tracks and stared back toward the lights of the main road ... a huge tractor-trailer was rumbling by, its hydraulic brakes growling as it slowed on its approach to the traffic lights. Exhaust fumes stank, causing me to choke as they billowed into the alley.

With my heart pounding and my skin clammy as clay, I found the doorway of my maisonette and went in out of the night.

And while I couldn't have said why, still I kept my lights burning brightly—all of them—well into the small hours ....

XI

Daylight drives away the fears of the night, and when those fears are hardly understood or ill-founded it works that much faster. By midday I had put aside all fantasies of the dark hours, all weirds and grotesques. Money was something of a spur, too, for by now I had convinced myself that Carter was right, that indeed his uncle's old place was seat to a fabulous hoard.

I was waiting in the grounds when Carter arrived in a crunch of too-wide tires and a blast of a too-loud American horn. It seemed that he was in a good mood, that daylight had turned the trick for him too.

'No messing today!' he said, letting us in. 'I'm straight upstairs and to work; you can do whatever you like. In an hour or so we'll have a mug of coffee. Right?' And without waiting for an answer he left me standing in the front room, his footsteps thudding overhead as he climbed the shuddering stairs.

I waited until I could faintly hear him clattering about somewhere in the upper regions of the house, then went to the bookshelves in the recess and found Prinn's book.

Except it wasn't Prinn's book at all but a translation or treatise on
it. The leather spine—much worn except for the name Ludwig Prinn in
half-inch letters of gold—said:

MYSTERIES
OF THE WORM
by
LUDWIG PRINN
Rediscovered
by:
C. LEGGETT
London
1821

As I took it from its corner position on that same shelf which had
also provided the *Dhol Chants*, its thickish body sprang open and at least
a dozen sheets of fine paper fluttered to the dusty floor. At first I
thought they were actual pages from the book and that the thing was
simply disintegrating in my hand; but upon collecting them up, the
sheets were notes or inserts of sorts in old Arthur Carter's hand, each leaf
numbered to correspond with its position in the book proper. I took
book and notes alike back to the table and sat down with them.

Of the notes: I could make little of them. They were cryptic as the
annotations in the other, older book. There was one sheet, however,
which was headed "Dhols—gold—discovery of—" and this I quickly
scanned—only to be disappointed. The page consisted only of a list of
references to other works (books with such near-fabulous sounding titles
as the *Necronomicon*, du Nord's *Liber Ivonis*, d'Erlette's *Cultes des Ghoules*,
and the *Pnakotic Manuscripts*), none of which were evident in the old
recluse's rather limited library.

Limited, yes, and that was surely another anomaly. For Carter had
told me that the house was full of old books, bric-a-brac, objets d'art,
knickknacks etc. Well, if so, then I had seen very little of it. I determined
to ask him about it.

The sheet was numbered, however (p. 134), and so I turned to that
page in the Leggett volume to see what I might see. And at last I was
to be rewarded, however dubiously.

According to Leggett, Ludwig Prinn had written of Dhol[e]s in his
De Vermis Mysteriis:

"By their *sounds* shall ye know Them, & by Their *stenches*. In ye Vale of Pnoth They rustle & Their touch is as of great snails; but in Pnoth's darkness no man hath seen a Dhole, & that were as well!

"In ye waking world Dholes are singularly rare, though certes They may be called by one so foolhardy. Moreover, They ever attend unto ye Blue Glow, which lures Them irresistibly in its illumination of treasures. Yea, & ye chant of ye glow is of Their device, for by its use in ye Vale of Pnoth They search out ghoul-ravaged corpses; & there They collect up golden rings from skeleton fingers, & nuggets from fleshless jaws, tomb-loot for ye fashioning of Cthulhu's secret treasures.

"Aye, & Their stench is of ye pit, & Their fumblings & rumblings & groanings vast; & They cause ye very earth to tremble & ye stenches of ye pit to rise up out of Pnoth ...."

Now, in retrospect it may seem astonishing that I made no connections—or at best few and indefinite connections—between what was written and what I and Carter had so far experienced in this old house. But consider: I knew and believed nothing of the occult; my past life in the mundane world had been one which kept both of my feet firmly planted on solid ground; and by all accounts old Arthur Carter had been the very queerest of birds, whose obvious interest in such matters could hardly be taken seriously. And could *anyone's* interest in such things be taken seriously?

As for Dhols (or even Dholes), the reason why "no man hath seen a Dhole" seemed very clear and simple to me: There were no such creatures! Yet ... there *was* this mention of treasure, and certainly old man Carter would seem to have had his share of that ....

I put down the book and glanced again through the loose sheets, inserting them in their respective slots as I scanned them through. It was as I was doing this that I came across a sheet which had not fallen from the book but was loosely inserted between pages 88 and 89, and something about the style of the writing upon it—also the fact that unlike the others it was unnumbered—at once arrested my attention. It was Arthur Carter's handwriting, most definitely, and crabbed as ever; but there was a hastiness, or furtiveness, to the strokes hinting of an unaccustomed speed and stealth employed in their writing.

Let me explain:

The handwriting of another has this peculiar effect with me: that I almost invariably picture the writer at work, pen in hand, in whichever attitude or mood the piece would seem to dictate. Thus in perusing the other notes, I had imagined Carter hunched over this very table, muttering to himself as he pursued whichever eldritch studies or copied from whichever "august" works as interested him, slowly but surely working toward his unguessable goal.

But with this sheet in my hand the feeling was entirely different. For here was the old man in a hurry, breathless, excited or afraid, and almost before I had read what was written I had guessed at the source of his excitement, his fear:

"It has come to this," [he wrote], "and I am at a loss. Greg's lad is a bad lot. Well, so was his father—though he at least had honour! But this one .... He has found my weakness and constantly tempts me, and like a fool I have partaken and have said too much. He would get what there is anyway, all of it, but can't seem to wait; and I fear that in his greed and eagerness he might go too far. And after all these years I only now realise how alone I am here and how isolated. Of friends, I have none. A metropolis close by, and I am alone ....

"At the moment he is out, however, and so I can get a little more done. This morning, while yet Andrew slept on, I was up and busy with the *Cthaat Aquadingen*. I have difficulty reconciling Dhols to any allegiance with Cthulhu (even though I know that He is a master of dreams) and am given to wonder if they could be man's subconscious shoggoth-memory or -awareness? Dreams are after all only a sub-level of man's entire sphere of existence as a whole. We 'exist' in dreams as surely as we dream them: 'I dream, therefore I am—in my dreams,' one might say. And Gerhard Schract ponders much the same question. It is, though, a fearsome thought that our blackest nightmares may exist in reality, just around the corner, as it were, in the parallel lands of dream ....

"But ... really, I cannot concentrate. Andrew has frightened me (his demands, while sly and as yet not overtly hostile, may soon develop into full-fledged threats) and I am defenceless. I have come to realise how old I am—and how fragile. And Greg's boy little better than a common thug. ... If only he were not my brother's son; I would order him out of the house in a moment ....

"Yesterday I searched Feery's *Notes* for his interpretation of Alhazred's meaning (in respect of a connection between the *Dhol Chants* and the Sathlattae), but found nothing. It would seem to me that the following: 'the soul of the devil-bought hastes not from his charnel clay, but fats and instructs the very worm that gnaws; till out of corruption horrid life springs', has a certain degree of bearing on the invocation bottom p. 111.

"... Enough for now; Andrew will be back soon. And he is company, at least. Possibly I have grown too reclusive and so misjudge him ...."

And the rest of the sheet was empty.

XII

I decided, for better or for worse, not to make any accusations. Not for now, anyway. And in any case, what I had read had only served to confirm all that Carter had so far confided. So far ....

I made coffee and went upstairs to where he had fairly reduced the room to the far left of the stair-well to so much rubble. Panting from his exertions, he was seated on a pile of debris when I entered the room. 'Has it been an hour?' he asked. 'Already?'

I shook my head. 'No—but I have some questions for you.'

'More questions?' He tilted his head onto one side and squinted at me through his grime. 'About the house?'

'Yes, and about—'

Carter waited, his squint growing more pronounced.

'—other things.'

He nodded and, after a moment: 'Ask away.'

'About the plumbing: If the water supply is direct from the mains, and if your uncle had no hot water, why does the pipe come from the attic?'

He shrugged. 'Dunno. I'll tell you what I know of it. When I first started to come here, after the old miser went, there was water. But it tasted foul and pretty soon dried up to a trickle. I got in the plumbers and had 'em take a look. The old mains pipe went up a brick conduit in the end wall and so into the attic. There was water in the pipe, all right, and under mains pressure, too, but it wasn't getting through. The pipe was old and must be blocked or limed up where it climbed the wall. So they bypassed the blockage for me by sloping a pipe up the wall from the base of the mains pipe, and in through the bricks to a new tank which they installed centrally in the attic, close to the hatch.'

'There was no old tank?'

Carter looked puzzled, shook his head. 'Is it important?'

'It's queer, that's all. I mean, if your uncle only ever intended to run a tap in the kitchen, why take the mains pipe up into the attic in the first place?'

He shrugged. 'Maybe it was like that when he bought the place.' Which, since it had also been my solution, had to satisfy me.

'But … if you were getting foul water through the blockage before, how do you know you're not still getting some of it now?'

'Look, is this *really* important?'

I wasn't sure if it was or wasn't. 'It might be.'

"Well, like I said, the water dried up completely. So—no foul water! In fact, no water at all until they put in the bypass. Anyway, I wanted them to drop a pipe to the bathroom heater, but there was no need. They were past the blockage now, so they simply re-routed the water from my tank back into the old mains pipe, which drops right through my bathroom. That's as much as I know. Oh, it's a rough job, I know, but hell—it's only temporary!'

'Done on the cheap,' I nodded.

'Of course. I mean, the place is coming down, you know!'

I considered it. Then: 'Where does the waste from the bath go?'

'To the WC. The old pipe was rotten so they put in another from the bath waste to the WC cistern.'

'But doesn't it overflow?'

Carter grinned smugly. 'Into the toilet basin,' he said. 'Self-flushing, so to speak.'

I shook my head, half in amazement, half in disgust. 'This house probably has the weirdest plumbing ever!' I finally said. 'And I would-n't be at all surprised if it's not the most unsanitary!'

'Temporary,' he repeated, shrugging in that couldn't-care-less way of his. 'So what?'

Something else was prodding away at the back of my mind, trying to break out; but for the moment it eluded me. I changed the subject.

'Where are all the knick-knacks you told me about? The bric-a-brac? The books, brass, objets d'art, etc?'

Carter surveyed the room's rubble, picked up his metal detector, led me out into the corridor and back to the landing. He took a swig at his coffee, swallowed, said: 'Gone, most of it. Flogged. I mean, it was going to be mine anyway, wasn't it?'

'But—'

'And once I'd given up my, er, regular gainful employment, so to speak, in order to give over more of my time to this place—'

'But—'

'But nothing, mate! A bloke has to eat! And some of that old junk was bloody good stuff!'

'Valuable?' I asked, following him downstairs.

'God! You wouldn't believe. I mean, the British Museum took half of it—through a go-between, you understand—especially the books! Amazing! Bloody mouldy old things!'

'So you've had a bit of money out of the place already,' I pressed.

'I'm not skint,' he answered, '—but I'll say no more than that.'

At the bottom of the stairs we heard the rattle of the letter-box flap in the front door. Rates bills and ... a letter from Haringey Council. I had had dealings with them and recognised the envelope, the franking, the lettering of the printed return address. Carter ignored the bills but ripped this envelope open. He read the contents of the letter, then waved letter and envelope angrily in the air. 'That's torn it!' he snarled.

We went through into the front room.

'What has?' I asked.

'They've brought the demolition date forward,' he said.

'Oh?'

'Bloody Tuesday!' Carter groaned. 'Tuesday! Why, that's just—'

'Three more days,' I finished it for him. 'We have what's left of today, Sunday, and Monday, and that's your lot ....'

He slumped down onto a leg of the bench in the recess with the table, slammed his hand down hard and flat on the old oak surface. '*Shit!*' he snarled.

Dust jumped up in little clouds from cracks in the tabletop; something squelched; there came a stench.

Carter jerked to his feet, gazed in purest horror and loathing at the palm of his hand. A smear of something vile adhered to his hand and a blob of the same nameless stuff dangled from his twitching fingers. Twin strands of spaghetti, their ends splattered, lay in the dust atop the table, previously unnoticed. But old Arthur Carter's book, the *Mysteries of the Worm*, was no longer there. I was sure I had left it there, lying open on the table, but now it was—

I glanced across the room.

—Back on its bookshelf!

And the *Dhol Chants*! Come to think of it, I had left that book on the table last night, when we left in such a funk of a hurry. Yet now ... it too was back on its shelf.

And dangling from that shelf, a third strand of spaghetti.

Well, that answered another question I had intended to try on Carter: the one about things that move by themselves ....

XIII

After that there would have been no keeping Carter in the place—not even in broad daylight, of that I am quite sure—if not for the fact that the house was to be demolished in the very near future. But because his chances of discovering his uncle's loot seemed now much narrowed down, he at least swallowed sufficient of his revulsion to accompany me as I went about the place, until at last I had fixed a broad picture of it in my mind.

Briefly, in addition to what I have already told of its dilapidated and much ravaged condition, this is my description of the property as it was then:

It had a rectangular base some thirty feet wide by sixty feet long, stood two stories high under a low, grey, slate-tiled roof. Twin stacks stuck up in grimy, worn yellow brick above the fairly shallow gable ends; upper windows were small, those on the ground floor were large, mainly bays; a small door to the rear of the property (facing away from the city) had been boarded up. Not in the least picturesque or "pretty", architecturally dull, the place looked gaunt and seemed to form an angular blot of a silhouette even in daylight.

Internally:

On the ground floor there were, as previously described, a porch, hall, stairs to the upper reaches, steps to the cellar, a WC, large front room, and kitchen. But on the side of the stairs and hall opposite the front room was an even larger (or longer) room whose access was from the boarded-up rear door, and also through a locked door in the kitchen. Carter showed me this room—at one time a study-cum-conservatory, I guessed—but such was the mass of rubble he had accumulated there that it was literally impossible to enter. It had been, Carter told me, the major repository for those aforementioned, now "flogged" items whose collection must have occupied a major part of old Arthur Carter's lifetime.

So much for downstairs. Above:

There was a passageway which split the house lengthways, terminating at both ends in two large rooms which took up the width of the house. Between these end rooms: On each side of the passageway were two doors entering into smaller rooms, making six upstairs rooms in all. The large end room to the right was Carter's converted bathroom; its completely demolished counterpart to the left had been his temporary bedroom (little used, as he had explained). What the other rooms had been used for I could not rightly say; storerooms, I suspected, but now in such an abused state of damage and disarray that their actual use must remain forever hidden; though one of them did contain an old, rusty iron bed and an ancient mattress which, upon inspection, I discovered to have hidden pockets just as Carter had described them.

And finally the attic, and another anomaly ....

Now, during the above tour of inspection (the first proper look I had taken at the place, for my previous visit had been at night), Carter's not unnatural revulsion had quietened down somewhat and he had regained something of control over himself; so that when I suggested we look into the attic he agreed, however reluctant he might actually have been. It seemed to me as good a time as any, however, while there was still plenty of light, for I sensed there would be little more of work that day. Not on Carter's part, that is. Indeed, I am certain that if I had so much as mentioned the matter of the books—their restlessness, so to speak—he would have left the house there and then and that would have been that.

As it was I did not mention it (it could be that I was mistaken, that in fact I myself had replaced them on their shelves and had simply forgotten doing so) and after a while and another mug of strong coffee, he led the way back upstairs to the landing. There, producing stepladders from one of the small rooms, Carter climbed to the ceiling and lowered a trapdoor, disappearing through the gap and into the attic. I followed him.

The first thing that struck me was purely academic: I was after all "in the trade." The attic was not insulated. There was no lagging between the joists, nor had floorboards been laid upon them. Moreover, the slate tiles were visible through the rafters; there was no internal covering to prevent the escape of warmth. Worse still, there were many small chinks which possibly let in the rain, and Carter's "plumbers"— what a gang of odd-jobbers *they* must have been!—had left a gaping, drafty hole in the wall where they had breached it to obtain access for the bypass pipe. And there was Carter's tank: a small, galvanised iron affair, bolted none too securely to two of the joists; and there to the far left, the wasps' nests he had mentioned in the very corners of the gables over the eaves.

The ridge was low, causing us to stoop a little; the light was feeble, coming as it did through gaps in the tiles; the entire place was dusty, where between the joists masses of ancient cobwebs were layered inches thick; the going precarious, since one might not step in the spaces between the joists for fear of crashing through the ceiling. And nowhere (or at least nowhere visible) that a man might hope to conceal a hoard of gold.

But I have mentioned an anomaly, and it was this:

From the grounds I had seen two identical chimneys, one atop each gable. Here inside, there was only one chimney breast: a brick structure situated centrally in the gap between the wasps' nests and going up to the ridge where it disappeared from view. To the far right, however—

Just a plain, blank brick wall.

I said nothing, but silently calculated the length of this triangular-sectioned gallery beneath the roof, which I judged to be a little less than fifty feet. And that was very odd indeed, for the house itself was all of sixty!

In the dusky silence, with only a thin moan of wind where it came in under the tiles, Carter and I stood spread-legged upon two of the joists and faced each other. 'Well?' he said, after a moment.

'You've had the metal detector up here?' I asked, because it seemed that at least this much was expected of me.

'Saw no point,' he answered. 'There are no floorboards, and nothing but thin air on the other side of the tiles.'

'Hmm! Well, that appears to be that.'

We climbed down again to the landing, Carter leading, but when I stepped down beside him I found him backed up against and clutching at the wall. Beneath the stepladder, where certainly they had not been before, were now haphazardly strewn five or six strands of that same sticky substance which Carter insisted was spaghetti. And that, as might well be expected, formed for him the last straw; it finished the day for him.

On our way out of the house I collected the two books, Prinn's *Mysteries of the Worm* and the *Dhol Chants*, then waited in front of the porch in the suddenly chilly air of the afternoon while he locked up. Still white-faced, finally he turned to face me. 'And now perhaps you'll still insist there's nothing wrong with the place?' he challenged.

And like a petulant fool I was needled into the provision of a solution, however dubious:

'The timbers are ... are so rotten,' I stumbled over the words, 'so full of moisture and rot, that they exude strands of this foul fungoid paste. It's a fungus excretion, nothing more. The pressure of our feet on the boards—our very weight—squeezes it out of the cracks like pus from a boil!'

He looked at me a moment longer, then turned back to stare at the brooding house. 'A boil, yes!' he said then, nodding. 'A bloody great malignant growth! The place is poisoned!'

As we went to our cars I said: 'Will you give me the keys?'

'What?'

'The keys,' I repeated. 'I may come back for some more books.'

'Today, you mean?' His voice was incredulous.

'Today, perhaps. Perhaps tonight.'

Now his jaw dropped. 'You'd come back here, alone, tonight?'

'I might, if I think it's necessary. We have only two more days, remember?'

For a moment he was suspicious, but then he simply growled and shrugged and gave me the keys ....

XIV

I got very little from the books.

According to Charles Leggett, Prinn had been a Flemish sorcerer, alchemist, and necromancer, whose travels in strange lands and studies of dark, forbidden matters had made him brilliantly, dangerously learned in all the occult sciences. So dangerous in fact that in the end he had been burned at the stake!

In Prinn's cosmology, there were three clear states or spheres of reality/existence. These were: the waking world, in which Man rules, however ineffectually; the lands of Man's dreams, which have been shaped by him since first he had strength and intelligence to dream; and finally a dimension parallel to both of these realities, neither recognising Man nor even considering him as remotely important in the cosmic cycle.

But while the cosmos itself was blind and impersonal, there existed in that universe parallel to Man's domains Beings who would use Man, if only as a means to an end. Here Prinn had drawn on the works of wizards immemorial and texts of incredible antiquity—shards and fragments which pre-dated Man himself—to compound a pantheon which might only be described as fabulous. This was the Cycle of the Mythology of Cthulhu, encompassing such awesome-sounding entities or "gods" (demons?) as Arzoroth, Shub-Niggurax, Yibb-Sartle, Zathoggua, Yott-Sottot, and others. In pre-dawn times these Beings had been found wanting. Themselves black magicians (indeed, the very foundation of *all* EVIL), they had warred against the forces of DIVINITY. Crushed, cursed, chained, and thrown "outside", they now occupied various adjuncts of that dimension parallel to the twin states of Man, the merest newcomer in the vast cosmic cycle. Even now, in their imprisonment, still these Beings strove to influence Man—primarily through his darkest dreams, into which Cthulhu had access—in the hope that one day through his own evil Man would bring about their release, their return from extra-dimensional exile.

This was all very interesting stuff, but it wasn't really what I was looking for. There was, however, a detailed description of the Loathly Lord Cthulhu (⊢⊢⊣⊐ ᴸ⊣⊐) locked in his submarine city of R'lyeh (⊾⁻⊾⊐ ⊾⊣), who could only be that same monstrous cephalopod whose representation I had already had contact with in the shape of Carter's "coins." Which would seem to place those pieces firmly in that category "Cthulhu's secret treasures …."

I went on through the book as quickly as I could, simultaneously attempting to tie in the text with Arthur Carter's marginalia. Prinn had seemed to take an inordinate interest in the "inhabitants of the Dreamlands"—specifically of such places as the Abyss of Numh, the Peaks of Throk, the Vale of Pnoth, the Caverns of Tuth-Ahn, Kadath in the Cold Waste, Leng, etc.—giving them such names as Zoogs, Gugs, Ghouls, Ghasts, and Night-gaunts (not to mention Dholes) and stating that ghouls in particular are wont to impinge, on occasion, upon the waking world, whose "debris" of mortality forms for them the uttermost *delicia*. Of the precious metals they take from corpses, and transform, and tally to Cthulhu's coffers, he said very little other than to reiterate his statements regarding the Blue Glow; also to repeat, over and over again, his warnings in connection with Dholes, their chants, spells, conjurations, etc. ….

So much for *De Vermis Mysteriis*.

As to why I had taken the other book home with me, the *Dhol Chants*: perhaps I had hoped to find some clue to its deciphering in Prinn. If so, then I was once more disappointed; I could make nothing at all of it. Indeed, all I knew of it was that it consisted of "spells" ascribed to Dhols, and that the passages between pages 101 and 127 (which included the chant at the bottom of p. 111) were harmful. But that was all.

By 6:30 it was dark outside and my eyes were rapidly growing tired in the electric glare of my maisonette's lights. Since by that time it seemed that I would get no more out of the books, I put them down, made myself a light meal, sat thinking the thing over while I sipped hot coffee. After a little while, this was how I finally had the puzzle fixed in my mind:

Arthur Carter had long interested himself in the occult. His studies in the main had been in vain: pointless metaphysical exercises, doomed to failure as all such must be: There is no supernatural. But he had come across a "device" (though doubtless one with a perfectly sound and completely scientific explanation) by use of which the discovery of certain sorts of treasure trove was made practical. Using this "device" or method, he had accumulated an amount of gold. Naturally so remarkable a success had strengthened and added substance to his occult resolve, his belief in the "magic" to which his studies were dedicated.

As for the "device" or method he employed: That as yet remained a mystery (even though, again in retrospect, the answer lay right there under my very nose), but it was possible that further clues existed in the remaining books still in the old house, and in certain volumes now missing or "flogged", for which unforgivable stupidity I thoroughly cursed Arthur Carter's loutish nephew. Overwhelmingly curious now, and restless to the point of obsession, I further cursed myself that I had not thought to bring home all of the books with me; and then, because I knew I would not sleep, I determined to go back there and then and fetch them at once.

Minutes after that I was seated at the wheel of my car, headed north for Muswell Hill ....

As I drove carefully through light evening traffic, my mind dwelled almost of its own accord upon that pair of cryptic and possibly coded passages from the *Dhol Chants*; the one beginning: "*Gh'ha gn-ka a'hboa um, et-um*", and the other in respect of the Blue Glow, whose queer arrangement of sounds had so fascinated me that I had retained an almost perfect picture of them in my mind's eye.

Oddly, the more I toyed with the memory of those weird paragraphs (chants, yes) the more familiar they seemed to be, like meaningless but fascinating jingles from some child's book of nursery rhymes; moreover, I began to feel that I was getting the pronunciation very nearly right. The thought disturbed me a little—that I should now be proficient in these queerly alien lines, whose meanings and purposes were utterly conjectural—so that I frowned as I drove my car into the grounds of the old Carter house and parked it before the porch. But then I uttered a forced laugh. Ridiculous!: that I should even consider the discovery of anything of substance in so much sheer gibberish.

Climbing from my car into the sharp darkness of evening, which seemed almost to have a taste of its own, I allowed something of that sing-song of unearthly sounds—that dark liturgy—to flute and gurgle

once more from my lips, its discordant echoes swelling and vibrating in
the shadowy niches of cold brickwork.

But—

I approached the house no further.

The ground had commenced to tremble beneath my feet and there
came a smell as of sulphur ... or of something else. Dark cracks
appeared in the cold, hard earth, from which puffs of rank vapour sprang
out like vented steam; and a rumbling, deep in the earth—a rumbling
and a distant groaning, as of tortured metal plates—instantly clove my
careless tongue to the roof of my mouth.

As the rumbling and groaning subsided I stared at the house, stared
harder still at its high, bleak silhouette against the starry skies. Then I
got back into my car and drove away. Tomorrow would be time enough.

In my rear-view as I turned the car back down the drive, I could still
see the brick column of the chimney poking up into the night—where
within, no chimney breast was visible—and all about it the tiles, end gable
and eaves were aflame with a cold blue St. Elmo's fire of their own ....

XV

The next morning I was at the house a little after first light, at least two
hours in advance of Carter, valuable time which I spent in the front room
studying the few remaining books. Despite the presence of several like-
ly-sounding titles, however—books such as the archaic *Liber Miraculorem*
and de Metz's *Image du Monde*—I was unable to find anything else in
connection with the "occult discovery of gold", and nothing at all concerning dhols, ghouls, Cthulhu, and the like. Thanks to Carter's avarice,
all of the more important works were now doubtless firmly ensconced in
the musty archives of the British Museum.

As to why I searched: It was not so much that further information
was imperative, but if I were now to admit the feasibility of certain
occult or paranormal devices, then I must also accept their attendant
dangers. The discoverers of mordant acids have seldom burned iron
without first burning their fingers ....

What, *exactly*, the Blue Glow was and how a simple "spell" might
draw it forth were still mysteries; but for a fact the thing itself was
demonstrably real, and I no longer doubted but that it served its alleged
purpose. And thinking on this I wondered: Had there then been a
"philosopher's stone" after all? But more to the point ... were dhols, too,

real? And if they were, hadn't Prinn (and old man Carter) warned against any sort of truck with them?

But in any case the chant *had* served its purpose, and I was relieved to note that its position did not fall between pages 101 and 127 of the *Chants*, which must mean that it was not intrinsically harmful. And by now ... but by God!—how easy it was to fall in with all of this stuff, to become involved, to begin to believe ...!

... I did not go up into the attic.

Now, I would like to believe that this was because (a) I didn't quite fancy going up there on my own, or (b) that I believed in any case that Carter should accompany me, since the gold was rightly his, or (c) that I would have enjoyed explaining step by step the work of detection I had performed on Carter's behalf. But now (once again in retrospect) I find myself confessing a degree of shame in respect of my real motives. Quite simply: Men are greedy, and I was no exception.

(a) I did not want Carter to find me up there when he arrived, which might have been to give the show away; and (b) I no longer cared to share with him either gold or the device by which I had re-discovered it; and (c) I considered him a brutish untutored lout who doubtless deserved whatever misfortunes had been arranged for him. Which was why, when he arrived, I was waiting for him in the front room, fore-armed with certain very pointed questions.

Whether I really would have broached what was on my mind, or held back in the face of his suspect humour, his hard bulk, and possibly violent reaction, was a question which did not arise. For from the moment he joined me it was plain that he had been up most of the night, and equally obvious was the fact that he was drunk or very nearly so. And this at only 9:30 in the morning. What's more, he had brought a bottle with him, pouring liberal splashes into two glasses before grinning and stating:

'If we're to be here all the live long day, and we are, and if I'm to work like a bloody nigger to get done, which is what I intend, then it strikes me that the best way to go about it—'

'Is to anaesthetise yourself?' I snorted.

'I have been up,' he suddenly stated, waving his arms expansively, 'most of the night. Some of it with a lady—tart, if you prefer—the rest with a bloody bottle.'

'The one to soothe away your aches and draw off your excess physical energy,' I answered, 'and the other to deaden your nerves, eh? Dutch courage!' But Carter failed to notice, or perhaps chose to ignore, the sneer in my voice.

'Correct!' he slurred, clapping me on the back. 'And now—to the final wrecking!'

'One moment!' I felt emboldened by his condition. 'Sit down. Here's coffee fresh made. I have more questions—just two, I promise— before you begin.'

He peered at me baggy-eyed and for a second seemed inclined to argue, then perched himself swaying on top of his uncle's table. 'Shoot!' he said, carelessly slurping coffee.

'What was it you said to him—what was it that you finally did— to make your uncle so fear you that he ran off and left this old place? What threat, Carter, so unmanned him that he took to his heels and left it all to you?'

And still he failed to notice, or perhaps continued to ignore, the edge of contempt, the malice in my voice. 'I told him,' he answered at once, only pausing to belch brandy in my face, 'that if he didn't tell me where it was, I'd creep upstairs when he was asleep and put a pillow over his face!'

I was unable to stop myself from drawing a sharp breath. 'You ... threatened his life?' (This was exactly what the old man had feared would happen—or had he feared the act as opposed to the mere threat?)

But now Carter dazedly shook his head and gulped more purpose-fully at his coffee. 'What?' he blurted, beginning to frown, his features darkening over as his mouth grew tight. '*What?*'

'You said you'd kill him?' I repeated, drawing back a fraction.

But Carter only looked puzzled, relaxed a little, and then finally grinned like an ass. 'Eh? Did I say that? No, no—that's not what I meant. What I *meant* was this: that at any time he could be burgled, that a couple of young buggers could break in here and do him in without even trying! Not *me*, no—I meant anybody! I was warning him, do you see?' He broke into drunken laughter.

Oh, yes, I saw.

I shrugged, laughed with him, said: 'Finally, one last question. When exactly, by your reckoning, anyway, do we take care of the second proviso: that is to say, your reading aloud of the passage at the bottom of page one hundred and eleven of the *Dhol Chants?*'

'What?' He was sobering by the moment. 'You think I really will?'

I was cautious: 'But what's to stop you?'

'Nothing at all! But why should I? It's rubbish!'

'But surely you must. It's a provision of the will, and—'

'And you are my witness!'

'You'd have me perjure myself? Remember, even if we don't find the gold—'

'But we will, we must!'

'But if we don't, still the compensation will be yours. After the demolition, I mean. If the conditions of the will have been met, that is.'

'You want me to read it? I'm not even sure I can pronounce the damn thing! Oh, I looked at it once, certainly—but once was enough. Double-Dutch! Gibberish! I don't know if I could do it.'

'And I am not sure that I could swear it on oath if you hadn't at least tried. You took me on for my honesty, remember?'

'Bloody honesty!' he said, looking surly again. But then he put aside his coffee, grinned, once more took up the bottle. 'It's today!' he said. 'Seven years today, as I judge it, since the scurrying, frightened little bag of bones ran off and hid himself away. And a good job he did, for by God I would have done it!'

I nodded, watching him drink. 'Then you shall read the prescribed paragraph tonight, and I shall be your witness. What's more, I'll help you with it.'

'OK, if that's what it takes to satisfy you.' He stood up, however unsteadily.

'I'm not the one to satisfy,' I told him. 'You satisfy the will, that's all.'

He gazed at me murkily, the corners of his bloodshot eyes twitching. 'Queer bastard!' he said, swaying a little. 'You know that? You're a *queer bastard*!'

'It takes all sorts,' I said, and shrugged again. 'Here, have another drink ....'

XVI

By noon he had wrecked beyond recognition all the upstairs rooms, with the exception of the bathroom, with which he had long since satisfied himself. The ceilings were down, the floors up, the walls out; but throughout, his metal detector had showed never a blip, and Carter was very grimy and almost sober. But by then, too, I had nipped out to purchase salty fish and chip lunches, plus plenty of lager to wash them down, and as a special favour to Carter another bottle of the best—and headiest—five-star brandy.

An hour later he was reeling, from fatigue as much as from his replenished alcoholic content, but could not be stayed from venturing down into the cellar one last time to make a final assault upon the remaining walls; not that I tried too hard to dissuade him. And all the while, as time slipped by, I wandered through the house and tried not to look too often at the ceiling, and forced myself to put from my mind and tongue the insistent chant I felt sprouting there with every slightest relaxation of my will. And I admit that I was excited.

But it was also important that I kept Carter topped up, which I did until the combination of drink and sheer hard work had just about finished him; and when at last he finally staggered up from the cellar I could see that he was done for. Caked with sweat and soil and dust, he was a sorry sight indeed: his hands bleeding and his eyes hollow as doughnuts in a pasty, dirt-streaked face. And so he collapsed into a rickety chair and said: '*Shit!*'

I'm not much for curse words, but: 'I agree,' I told him where he sprawled; for I had had my share of the brandy and beer, and it had made me frivolous. 'Let's call it a day.'

'Damn right!' he said. 'I can definitely call it a day for I have worked my balls off! But you—'

'I've done as you wished!' I protested. 'I've been company for you; I've fetched, and paid for, our lunch; I've even treated you to an ample supply of drink. And all, it would appear, a dead loss. All you've come up with is—what was it? Shit?—and there's not much in ten percent of that!'

My logic seemed to surprise him. 'Huh!' he grunted. 'There's still tomorrow.'

I passed him the last of the liquor and glanced out of the bay windows. 4:30, and already the sky was darkening, with huge black clouds scudding low.

'And what will you do now?' I asked. 'For the rest of today, I mean?'

'Today's finished. I'm for a long, hot soak.'

'I'll switch on the immersion heater,' I said, heading for the hall and the stairs to the bathroom. 'You finish your brandy while the water gets hot.'

Going upstairs I counted seven strands of spaghetti, and on the landing there was more of the Stuff. I quickly scuffed it all away, ignoring the stench; but in the bath was a little more, which I despatched to the loo with a jet of cold water.

On my way back down to Carter I could feel it building—*something*. But ... no reason why it should feel ill-disposed toward me ....

'Weird, you are!' he told me as I entered the front room. He sprawled there in his chair where I had left him, glowering at me. 'You'd think I was your bloody wife, the way you've run about after me today.'

'You've been working against time,' I told him. 'You needed encouragement. There's a can of lager left; would you like some?' I poured half for him, half for myself. Carter gulped his down.

'Bath!' he said, starting to rise.

'Not hot yet,' I said. 'Anyway, there's still that passage to be read.' I handed him the *Dhol Chants*.

He lurched to his feet. 'What the hell is it with you and this bloody book?' He tossed it down on the table and it fell open at page one hundred and eleven.

'The will,' I said.

He grimaced, took up the book, slowly began. 'Gb'ha ... gn-ka ... a'hboa—*shit!*'

'You're doing fine,' I said, willing him to continue. And oddly enough—or perhaps not so oddly—as he read so he seemed to grow more fluent!

'... Um ... et-um, T'hn-hla—bloody *thing*!—puh-ghtagn bugg-ugg. Gn-ka um zg'h—why, it's easy!'

'Fine, fine!' I said.

'Nuth-ah'n, et-um,' and so on to the end. And then he once more tossed the book down, staggered from the front room and tramped wearily upstairs. 'Now are you satisfied?' he called back down to me.

I made no answer but quietly followed him, waiting until he'd locked the bathroom door and was running his water, then getting out the stepladders and climbing into the attic. Maybe it was the brandy, or maybe it was just impatience. Whichever, it was certainly greed. But even with that *feeling* growing all around me, even sensing that Carter had started—well, *something*—still I had to know for sure about his uncle's gold, had to test just one more time the efficacy of the Blue Glow. I had kept it back all day, but now it could wait no longer.

And there in the attic, stepping as carefully as I could between the joists, I approached the blank end wall which should have but did not have a chimney breast, and under my breath I mumbled that other chant which was now so familiar to me.

From beneath the central section of the wall, directly under the ridge beam, a neon-like blue light at once shone out. Accompanying it came the low, distant rumble of unearthly engines and the merest whiff of that nameless dhol stench. Ignoring these side-effects I shoved at the glowing section of bricks, three brick-lengths wide and eight thicknesses high—and the wall moved!

It pivoted, jammed for a moment, finally stood open.

I got down on my hands and knees, crawled through. In my pocket was a torch, but I didn't need it. I could see all I wanted to see in the light of the Blue Glow.

Behind the false wall was old Arthur Carter's hiding place, his priest's hole, his wizard's den. Oh, yes, for that much at least I knew about occultists: that they all have their secret places, their retreats, the inner sanctums where they pore over their runebooks and practice their magicks! And this was Arthur Carter's.

The hitherto secret section of the attic which now lay before me was entirely different from the empty space behind. Old Carter had put down floorboards here, and there was even a light switch with a naked bulb dangling from a cobwebbed flex. I tried the switch but the bulb was dead. Over my head, the rafters were lined with tar-paper to keep out drafts; central stood a small table with a chair; books deep in dust and cobwebs were heaped on the floor and under the table; and upon the table itself—

The entire "room" was bathed in the Blue Glow, but the table, and what lay upon it, was the true source. Quite simply, it was Arthur Carter's gold, and no amount of dust and cobwebs and desiccated spider debris could disguise it! So much for the "young" Carter's metal detector: the table was nearly thirty inches high, the boards a good inch, the joists about a foot, and under all of that the good old fashioned lath and plaster ceiling. It might have been different if the old boy had stacked his money on the floor, but he hadn't.

In my excitement the alcohol was rapidly burning itself out of my system, and as the process continued so my senses became more acute. The Blue Glow was fading now and I wasn't inclined to use the chant again, not just yet. God alone could say what things had been stirred already that night, and I questioned the wisdom of further experimentation.

It was then that I fancied the dhol odour grew suddenly that much stronger, and then too that the eerie occult illumination faded entirely and I was left in the dark. Which was when—as the last nimbus of phosphorescence shimmered away into pitch darkness—at last I recognised or remembered the recent upsurge of fetor for what it really was:

Not, in fact, dhol-smell at all but more properly the vile stink of rot which invariably accompanied manifestations of Carter's "spaghetti!" And I knew that this—whatever manifestation this was—was not in response to my utterance of the Chant of the Blue Glow, but rather in response to Carter's recent reading of the malignant spell at the foot of page 111 of the *Dhol Chants*.

Whatever that spell had put in motion, it was even now abroad and full of intent in the body of this old and ill-omened house....

XVII

Petrified for a second or two, I simply stood trembling, my hair on end. Then I fumbled out the pencil torch from my pocket to send its bright but narrow beam all about me in that secret attic room. And by its light, suddenly I saw or became aware of several mundane items gone unnoticed in the *extra*mundane radiance of the Blue Glow.

There by the chimney breast was a metal-framed folding bed and a tumble of mouldering blankets; and on a crude wooden shelf affixed between the rafters several cans of beans, empty now, their labels peeling from rusty cans. To one side but raised high from the floor on a frame of stout timbers was a bulky old-fashioned tank or cistern—the one I had suspected should be here—with the old mains pipe entering its body high on one side, and the now familiar lead pipe leaving it low down on the other. Each pipe had a stopcock close to the tank, but the one which controlled access from tank to house had been turned to the "off" position, which explained away the blockage. But as I began to regain control of my nerves—

—Oh, God!—something *moved* in the body of the tank!

Something *heaved* itself in there, and with the movement came such an overpowering stench that I actually reeled, almost dropping my torch. I steadied the beam as best I might and aimed it again at the tank, at the pipes. And then I began to understand, and in my mind's eye I saw it all:

Old Carter, fleeing up here to this secret place, trembling in terror here and waiting for his brute of a nephew to go away. And the other Carter *not* leaving but ransacking the house in his greed for gold. And days passing with the old man hardly daring to move a limb lest Carter hear him; growing weaker on his meagre diet of beans, until they ran out; until all there was left for him was water in the tank to drink, a miserable cot to sleep on, and black hatred growing in his heart.

Perhaps that was when the idea had occurred to him and he had put the thing in motion. Oh, he had once questioned how any man might wish or visit this sort of thing upon even his worst enemy, but now in his extremity he had seen that all things are possible. His nephew had threatened him and might yet carry out that threat. Very well; but if he did, there would be a price to pay. Posthumous revenge, indeed!

Perhaps those "coins" the young Carter had found had lodged themselves accidentally in their places on concealment, and perhaps not. What if the old man had put them there deliberately, bait for the trap he intended to spring on the ingrate son of his brother? I could see it clearly: old Arthur waiting patiently until Carter left the house, perhaps to purchase food or drink, then creeping down from here to slip a piece of gold down the crack behind the mantelpiece, and another through the floorboards, and a third into the lining of his old mattress; then sneaking back to his attic den weaker than ever. For of course, even if there had been food, old Carter dare not touch it; for that would be to let his nephew know that he was still here.

And desperate, finally he had turned off the stopcock, denying water to his nephew while retaining his own supply; and still Carter had held him in siege, while his age and infirmities and weakness all seemed conspiring to kill him.

Then it was, I supposed, that the old man had set the seal on his occult scheme—his revenge—and then too that the accident must have occurred. If it was an accident. It might well have been suicide, there was no way I could know for sure. But certainly the old man had drowned—and in this very tank which my torch beam now illumined for me!

I pictured him climbing up there to drink, balanced on the platform of timbers, then slipping, falling headfirst into the tank, struggling and becoming fixed between rim and rafters and so expiring. Perhaps the final straw had been the sudden shock of immersion, the bitter cold of the water, I don't know. But as a direct result of his nephew's greed and threats, die there he did, definitely—*for he was there even now!*

As I have said: In the tank something seethed and bubbled, more energetically now, giving off wave after wave of poisonous fumes. And over the rim and down the pipe to the stopcock crept a loathsome revenant of what had once been a hand and wrist, a thing of bones and rotted tissue now, leaving a hideous trail of gelatinous ooze behind it; and under those disintegrating fingers the stopcock turned with a squeal, and turned again; and even as I fell to my knees, lowered my head and thrust myself screaming through the gap in the false wall, so there came a thick, glutinous gurgling which told of movement in the old pipe.

Then—

Tripping and tumbling over the naked joists I aimed myself at the rectangle of light from the trapdoor, and with the ceiling sagging and threatening to give way under my feet I made it to that blessed opening, somehow managing to get back down the stepladder without breaking a leg. And it was then that I heard Carter's first screams.

In my mind—even above his shrieking—I could still hear the squeal of the stopcock turning beneath that awful corpse-hand and wrist. Once the old man had denied Carter water, and now?

"The soul of the devil-bought hastes not from his charnel clay ... *till out of corruption horrid life springs!*"

Few men, knowing what I knew, would have done what I did then. But while by nature I am a cautious man, I was never a coward. And so—if only to know, to be *sure*—I ran or stumbled to the converted bathroom and jerked at the doorknob, then threw my shoulder against the door again and again until it finally gave as the lock was wrenched from the rotten frame. And as the door sprang open so I saw—

Carter—or a screaming, nightmare-transformed caricature of Carter!

He sat there in the bath, beneath the shower, clawing at himself and screaming that shrill animal scream. The scream of a trapped rabbit— or stricken rat. The sight of him and of what *afflicted* him rooted me to the spot, a paralysis I was unable to break until at last his cries were choked off and he jerked spastically to his feet, then collapsed naked— or not naked—out of the bath and face down upon the floor.

Impelled by the horror and the stench both, I turned, staggered, and finally fled full tilt; nor did I pause until I was out in the grounds, when a sudden sharp wrenching of the earth knocked my feet from under me and threw me down.

From deep down below I heard that awful, subterranean groaning, and when it stopped turned my head to look back. As in that fabled scene from Poe's masterpiece, the Carter house was crumbling into itself, saving those who would demolish it the effort. Down it went in dust and rubble and ruin, and Carter with it, and all that was left of his uncle; and I would be a liar if I said that I was anything less than glad ....

XVII

But ... that was almost seven years ago, and since then much has happened. For one thing I've grown rich, and for another I've explored a good many occult possibilities. But what was there, really, to explore? Whoever heard of a wizard or occult dabbler coming to any good end? No, for there is always a price to pay.

Nor can I complain. There were warnings enough along the way, and it seems these things even themselves out in seven-year cycles. So be it—as long as I don't go like Carter. But ... dare I take that chance?

At any rate I have my pistol, which I carry loaded at all times, and that alone should ensure that I do not share his fate, or any other of a like sort.

As to that fate itself: I think that already I have said enough, but if you are still curious then let us return once more to the scene as I burst open that door and entered Carter's makeshift bathroom:

Carter: shrieking there under the shower—which did not issue water alone but a writhing, coiling, continuous stream of rotten, stinking ribbons of flesh or what had once been flesh. A monstrous flood of corruption which, imbued with a life of its own, covered him and clung to him and filled his eyes, his ears, his nose, and his mouth with its seething mass, until at last it shut off his screams and his air both and pitched him dead on the floor at my feet!

And so much for Carter's "spaghetti" ....

My gold I leave to whomever may find it. In the end it belongs to Cthulhu, anyway ....

THE NYARLATHOTEP CYCLE

The Mighty Messenger of the Outer Gods, Nyarlathotep has also been known to deliver tidings from the Great Old Ones. He is the only Outer God who chooses to personify his presence on our planet. A god of a thousand forms, he comes to Earth to mock, to wreak havoc, and to spur on humanity's self-destructive urges. This volume of stories and poems illustrates the ubiquitous presence of Nyarlathotep and shows him in several different guises. Among them, his presence as Nephren-Ka, the dread Black Pharaoh of dynastic Egypt, dominates. The thirteen stories include a Lin Carter novella. Selected and introduced by Robert M. Price.

5 3/8" x 8 3/8", 256 pages, $10.95. Stock #6019; ISBN 1-56882-092-5.

THE HASTUR CYCLE
Second Revised Edition

The stories in this book represent the evolving trajectory of such notions as Hastur, the King in Yellow, Carcosa, the Yellow Sign, Yuggoth, and the Lake of Hali. A succession of writers from Ambrose Bierce to Ramsey Campbell and Karl Edward Wagner have explored and embellished these concepts so that the sum of the tales has become an evocative tapestry of hypnotic dread and terror, a mythology distinct from yet overlapping the Cthulhu Mythos. Here for the first time is a comprehensive collection of all the relevant tales. Selected and introduced by Robert M. Price.

5 3/8" x 8 3/8", 320 pages, $10.95. Stock #6020; ISBN 1-56882-094-1.

THE XOTHIC LEGEND CYCLE

The late Lin Carter was a prolific writer and anthologist of horror and fantasy with over eighty titles to his credit. His tales of Mythos horror are loving tributes to H. P. Lovecraft's "revision" tales and to August Derleth's stories of Hastur and the *R'lyeh Text*. This is the first collection of Carter's Mythos tales; it includes his intended novel, *The Terror Out of Time*. Most of the stories in this collection have been unavailable for some time. Selected and introduced by Robert M. Price.

5 3/8" x 8 3/8", 288 pages, $10.95. Stock #6013; ISBN 1-56882-078-X.

THE NECRONOMICON

Although skeptics claim that the *Necronomicon* is a fantastic tome created by H. P. Lovecraft, true seekers into the esoteric mysteries of the world know the truth: The *Necronomicon* is a blasphemous tome of forbidden knowledge written by the mad Arab, Abdul Alhazred. Even today, after attempts over the centuries to destroy any and all copies in any language, some few copies still exist, secreted away. Within this book you will find stories about the *Necronomicon*, different versions of the *Necronomicon*, and two essays on the blasphemous tome. Now you too may learn the true lore of Abdul Alhazred. Selected and introduced by Robert M. Price.

5 3/8" x 8 3/8", 320 pages, $10.95. Stock #6012; ISBN 1-56882-070-4.

THE CTHULHU CYCLE

Millions of years ago, when the stars were right, Cthulhu ruled from his black house in R'lyeh. When the stars changed, R'lyeh sank beneath the waves, and Cthulhu was cast into a deathless sleep, eternally dreaming. He has used his dreams to communicate with his believers, from prehistoric times through to the present day. Cthulhu has been, is, and always will be. Now the stars may once more be right, and Cthulhu may rise from his millennial sleep and reassert his rightful rulership of the Earth. The thirteen stories in this book trace Cthulhu and his influence through the centuries. General introduction and individual story prefaces by Robert M. Price. Winner of 1996 Academy of Adventure Gaming Arts & Design Best Game-related Fiction Award.

5 3/8" x 8 3/8", 288 pages, $10.95. Stock #6005; ISBN 1-56882-038-0.

THE DISCIPLES OF CTHULHU
Second Revised Edition

The disciples of Cthulhu are a varied lot. In Mythos stories they are obsessive, loners, dangerous, seeking not to convert others so much as to use them. But writers of the stories are also Cthulhu's disciples, and they are the proselytizers, bringing new members to the fold. Published in 1976, the first edition of *The Disciples of Cthulhu* was the first professional, all-original Cthulhu Mythos anthology. One of the stories, "The Tugging" by Ramsey Campbell, was nominated for a Science Fiction Writers of America Nebula Award, perhaps the only Cthulhu Mythos story that has received such recognition. This second edition of *Disciples* presents nine stories of Mythos horror, seven from the original edition and two new stories. Selected by Edward P. Berglund.

5 3/8" x 8 3/8", 272 pages, $10.95. Stock #6011; ISBN 1-56882-054-2.

THE DUNWICH CYCLE

In the Dunwiches of the world the old ways linger. Safely distant from bustling cities, ignorant of science, ignored by civilization, dull enough never to excite others, poor enough never to provoke envy, these are safe harbors for superstition and seemingly meaningless custom. Sometimes they shelter truths that have seeped invisibly across the centuries. The people are unlearned but not unknowing of things once great and horrible, of times when the rivers ran red and dark shudderings ruled the air. Here are nine stories set where horror begins, each story prefaced and with a general introduction by Robert M. Price.

5 3/8" x 8 3/8", 288 pages, $10.95. Stock #6010; ISBN 1-56882-047-7.

MADE IN GOATSWOOD

Ramsey Campbell is acknowledged by many to be the greatest living writer of the horror tale in the English language. He is known to Mythos fans for the ancient and fearful portion of England's Severn Valley he evoked in narratives such as "The Moon Lens." This book contains eighteen all-new stories set in that part of the Valley, including a new story by Campbell himself, his first Severn Valley tale in decades. This volume was published in conjunction with a trip by Campbell to the United States. Stories selected by Scott David Aniolowski.

5 3/8" x 8 3/8", 288 pages, $10.95. Stock #6009; ISBN 1-56882-046-1.

THE BOOK OF IOD

Henry Kuttner (1914-1958) was a friend of young Robert Bloch and a promising writer in his own right. He also became one of the Lovecraft Circle, submitting plot ideas and draft manuscripts to Lovecraft. He had an important impact on the development of the Cthulhu Mythos, especially with his contribution of a mystical tome, the *Book of Iod*. This collection of stories comprises all of Kuttner's Mythos tales (including one cowritten with Bloch) and a story by Lin Carter about the infamous *Book of Iod*. Introduction and commentary by Robert M. Price.

5 1/2" x 8 1/2", 224 pages, $10.95. Stock #6008; ISBN 1-56882-045-3.

ENCYCLOPEDIA CTHULHIANA

The Cthulhu Mythos was first created by H. P. Lovecraft (1890-1937), a Providence author considered by many to be the finest horror story writer of the twentieth century. His tales are a blend of fantasy, science fiction, and horror, with the latter being especially prominent. He described a pantheon of powerful beings known as the Great Old Ones. Other writers, among them Robert E. Howard, Ramsey Campbell, August Derleth, Robert Bloch, Brian Lumley, and Stephen King read his works, tried their hand at writing similar stories, and added to Lovecraft's pantheon. This book is the first attempt in many years to provide a guide to the "Cthulhu Mythos." Written by Daniel Harms. Winner of 1995 Academy of Adventure Gaming Arts & Design Special Achievement Award.

5 3/8" x 8 3/8", 288 pages, $10.95. Stock #6007; ISBN 1-56882-039-9.

THE AZATHOTH CYCLE

At the heart of the universe the mad god Azathoth pulses like a cancer. As with the physical universe it created, no purely reasoned argument, no subtle scientific proof, no brilliant artistry, no human love affects the unyielding will of Azathoth. As an entity it is of transcendent power and unthinking immortal sway. It can sometimes be avoided but never challenged. Here are fourteen tales concerning Azathoth by authors as diverse as Ramsey Campbell, Lin Carter, John Glasby, and Thomas Ligotti. The macabre poet Edward Pickman Derby contributes his immortal "Azathoth", the title piece of his single printed volume. Introduction, exegesical essay, and notes by Robert M. Price.

5 1/2" x 8 1/2", 256 pages, $10.95. Stock #6006; ISBN 1-56882-040-2.

THE SHUB-NIGGURATH CYCLE

Although she is among the most familiar names in the Lovecraftian litany, Shub Niggurath, the Black Goat of the Wood, the Goat with a Thousand Young, is never met personally in Lovecraft's stories, but is often referred to in rituals and spells. This deity mutated and was adapted as Lovecraft crafted and revised tales spawned by other authors. Here for the first time is a comprehensive collection of all the relevant tales concerning Shub-Niggurath. Selected and introduced by Robert M. Price.

5 1/2" x 8 1/2", 256 pages, $10.95. Stock #6004; ISBN 1-56882-017-8.

CTHULHU'S HEIRS

"Cthulhu's Heirs" are the literary heirs to H. P. Lovecraft's creative legacy. This book is a window: Throw back the curtains and find more than twenty writers' visions into the landscape of Lovecraft country and beyond. Some of the landmarks are familiar, while others are entirely new. Witness hidden truths and places best left unamagined. Stories selected by Thomas M. K. Stratman. Winner of 1994 Academy of Adventure Gaming Arts & Design Best Game-related Fiction Award.

5 1/2" x 8 1/2", 256 pages, $10.95. Stock #6003; ISBN 1-56882-013-5.

MYSTERIES OF THE WORM

New Second Edition, Revised and Expanded. At the end of H. P. Lovecraft's life, the young Robert Bloch was an enthusiastic member of Lovecraft's literary circle. This is a new edition of the long out-of-print volume that collected most of Bloch's early work concerning the Cthulhu Mythos. The new edition includes three additional tales from the period—"The Brood of Bubastis", "The Sorcerer's Jewel", and "The Creeper in the Crypt." Bloch also slightly revised the texts of three other stories. Seventeen tales, introduction by Robert M. Price, the original afterword by Bloch, and a supplementary essay by Lin Carter.

5 1/2" x 8 1/2", 272 pages, $10.95. Stock #6002; ISBN 1-56882-012-7.

All titles are available from bookstores and game stores, or by mail from Chaosium, Inc., 950 56th St., Oakland, CA 94608-3136; (510) 547-7681.